D1253089

Scent of Cloves

BY NORAH LOFTS

Norah Lofts

SCENT
OF
CLOVES

Doubleday & Company, Inc., Garden City, New York

*This book is fiction,
and all the characters and incidents in it are entirely imaginary.*

PART ONE

Ireland
1649-1657

When the dream reached its horrifying climax she began to scream, and woke herself and lay for a moment with the sound of her own voice and the screaming which had shrilled through the dream mingling in her ears. Then she was fully conscious, in her own bed and the night all quiet about her. Just another dreadful dream.

She hoped she had not awakened the child in the next room, or poor old Maire, already so frightened, and Edward, who usually woke at her first whimper. She moved her hand in search of the comforting solidity of his body and found his place beside her empty and cold. For a moment fear clamped down again; dead, dead, everybody dead. No, only a dream; nothing has happened *yet*.

And there was the difference between this waking and all the other times when she had come out of dreams of terror to find herself safe and unthreatened. This time it was not enough to be awake, for the dream had merely been the extension, seemingly logical and inevitable, of the situation which had overtaken them all. By this time tomorrow the dream might very well be accomplished fact.

Only an archway, hung with a curtain, separated the two rooms and now from the inner one came the sound of a voice, tremulous with terror.

"Lady, what is it? Have they come?"

One must not show fear before servants.

"No. I was dreaming, Maire. Go back to sleep."

A mumbling grunt answered her, and then there came the sound of steel scratching flint, a faint glow of light that outlined the curtain and that presently pushed aside to show the old woman, fully dressed as she had lain down, her headcloth all awry and the newly lit candle wobbling in her unsteady hand.

"Lady. Indeed and you sounded as if the Devil had hold of you. Or Cromwell's own self."

As the light wavered nearer Lucy Ashley wiped her sweating face with her sleeve, a quick, furtive movement.

"I told you to go back to sleep, Maire." The evil flavour of the dream still lingered; she longed to be comforted, not to be obliged to pretend to be calm in order to comfort an hysterical old woman whom it had been difficult to persuade to go to bed at all.

"The sleep has gone from me," Maire said. She shuffled forward shielding the candle with one brown, wrinkled hand, reached the bed-table by Lucy's side and carefully transferred the flame to the other candle there, saying, as she always did,

"God be thanked, we have light. Lady, lying there, wakeful in the dark, a thought has come to me. A good thought. I remembered my young years when I was a girl, gathering cockles on Cloonmagh beach, and my hair to my waist. And I thought of the caves at Cloonmagh." She set her candle beside the other and dropped on her knees by the bed, clutching the clothes with her hands.

"Lady, I could lead you and the little one to the caves at Cloonmagh and we should be safe there till the trouble is past."

"We are safe here," Lucy said steadily. "Where could we be safer than in a castle, with strong walls, and a moat, held by the best soldier in Ireland and provisioned for twelve months?"

(All that was true, yet it was taken, jeered the memory of the dream.)

"They took Drogheda," Maire said.

Lucy had said the same to Edward, and he had laughed, not

with forced false laughter but with genuine amusement. "And who held Drogheda? A mob of Irish, without loyalty or conviction, and a few politicians whose tongues were sharper than their swords. An old woman with a donkey stick could have taken Drogheda. Master Cromwell will find Arghama a very different proposition. I can hold Arghama for a year and he hasn't that much time to spend battering my walls. By that time England will have turned against him, the Scots will be in arms and even his own army will be giving trouble."

"Drogheda was different," Lucy now said. "Here we are all of one mind, and under one command. Sir Edward will never let Cromwell take Arghama."

"Sir Edward is a bold gentleman, a bold, pretty gentleman, so he is indeed . . . but Lady dear, in the night I was thinking. This Cromwell is going from Drogheda to Wexford, they say; he's not likely to leave this strong castle and a bold gentleman in it, standing behind his back. And him with a great army. Lady, in times of trouble it's safer to be in a secret place. And I'm thinking of the caves at Cloonmagh." The light from the candles had gathered strength and shone on her face, deepening every wrinkle and showing the urgent fear in her eyes. "God be good to you, Lady, as you have been to me, but I'm Irish; I have no part in this quarrel. Your King that they chopped the head off, poor man, God rest his soul, was never King of mine. Into Arghama I came six years ago to earn my bread; Bridget in the kitchen and Patrick with the horses, the same way. It is a hard thing if we must die in the English quarrel."

The bitter words opened a gulf. It was hard to believe that Maire, always so devoted, so humble, so grateful for kindness, could have spoken them.

"Cromwell," Lucy said, "looks on everyone inside the English Pale as his enemy. Irish or English, he takes no count of that; the English Pale is Royalist, and loyal, and that is enough for him. The Puritan soldiers are killing Irish peasants everywhere."

"So they are, God help us. But not in Cloonmagh! In the

ancient times when the Horned Men came in the long ships and burned and robbed and killed, the people in Cloonmagh took to the caves and were safe. And in the days of the pirates too. They say, 'Safe as the caves at Cloonmagh.' Sir Edward did me a wrong, taking up the bridge so sudden. . . . Lady dear," her hands scrabbled for Lucy's through the bed-clothes, "do you suppose, if you begged him, he'd let it down for just so long as I could run across? I'd be blessing you and praying for you all the rest of my days. . . . Though you'd do well to come with me, you and Little Miss."

"I don't think anything would persuade Sir Edward to lower the bridge again," Lucy said. "And you wouldn't be safe outside, Maire. You might meet the soldiers."

"Not the way I would take. I know a safe, secret way. Lady dear, for the love of God will you *ask* him?"

"I could ask," Lucy said, unwillingly. "But I know I should waste my breath. . . ." She could imagine Edward saying, If she has a mind to commit suicide let her jump in the moat, the silly old crone!

"Most times the master is anxious to pleasure you," Maire said, "and rightly too, for a sweeter lady never lived. . . ." Suddenly, disconcertingly, she burst into tears, letting loose the pent up fears and conflictions of feeling of the last forty-eight hours. Through the sobs and snuffles and the harsh intakes of breath a word or two here and there emerged, every one of them dovetailing into Lucy's dream. The gist of it all was the asseveration of what all the Irish, and quite a few English believed —that Cromwell had made a bargain with Satan: Cromwell was to desecrate all sacred things, smash down the images of the saints, destroy every cross and relic, defile altars, stable his horses in churches . . . and in return the Devil promised him complete and unchallenged power. Who, no matter how brave, well-prepared and determined, could stand against that?

". . . in blood and flames," sobbed Maire, "this place will go down, the way of the others. . . . The Lord's anointed—

and he was that, King of England if not of Ireland—could not stand before him, how then can we?"

Following so hard upon the dream, this was unbearable, and presently Lucy said, "Maire, be quiet. I will ask about the bridge in the morning if you will be quiet now. Be quiet and go away."

The relationship between them, upset by circumstance, fell back into balance.

"Would you be wanting anything before I go to my bed?" Maire asked.

"No. Just go and lie down and try to sleep," Lucy said.

She lay awake after Maire had gone, thinking of many things, but chiefly of her own fears, her shameful lack of courage. She thought of all the stories she had heard lately of women who, in the civil war just brought to its sorry conclusion in England, had acquitted themselves with astounding valour and competence, holding castles and manor houses for weeks on end during the absence of their husbands. No such demand had been made upon her. Edward was down there, in the courtyard or the guard-room, or on the walls, all she had to do was to trust him and maintain a calm demeanour. And she was so cowardly that she woke, screaming from a dream, and thus precipitated a scene with old Maire and gave a promise the keeping of which in anticipation alone filled her with dread.

Over and over again, before the first light of the summer morning turned the narrow window grey, she imagined herself going to Edward and saying, "I promised Maire . . ." She doubted if she could do it. I haven't even courage enough for that, she thought dismally. She realised that courage could not be suddenly acquired; you were born with it, or perhaps you attained it by constant practice. She had always been afraid of everything, of the dark, of a bad dream, of making someone angry, of being laughed at, of being afraid. . . .

The window lightened at last, and down in the courtyard the first cock cried. She rose gladly, and, moving quietly about the room, dressed and did her hair carefully. No sound came from

the inner room and when she was ready she pulled the curtain
aside and went in. Maire was sound asleep and the baby was
sleeping too, snug in the heavy oak cradle which had already
rocked four generations of Ashleys. Lucy stood looking down
on her daughter with love, with the inevitable, fleeting regret
for another child who had died, and with a fresh upspringing
of fear. She remembered the dream, the child's body, limp and
bloody on the end of a pike. Almost she turned then to Maire,
to shake her awake and say—If I can persuade Sir Edward to
let you go, promise to take the child and keep her safe. . . .
But that was foolish, superstitious and disloyal. She turned abruptly, crossed her own room and began to descend the spiral
staircase whose steps were worn hollow and the curves of its
walls smooth and shiny from the passage of all those who had
gone up and down it throughout the years.

She was forming and re-forming the request she must make
as she entered the courtyard, where the castle's state of preparation for a siege was evident. Cattle were closely penned along
one side, and piles of fodder for them were stacked nearby.
Arghama would have fresh meat as long as the fodder lasted;
then the remaining animals would be slaughtered and their
flesh salted down. In a separate pen a newly calved cow was
blaring her misery at separation from her calf, and another, due
to calve later in the year, stood placidly by. Edward had thought
of everything.

The soldiers who had stood guard during the night had begun their breakfast. Edward was not with them and before she
could ask his whereabouts she saw him coming briskly down
the ramp which led to the outer wall.

He kissed her heartily, and said, "A quiet night and a bright
morning. I hope you slept well. Broken your fast yet? Let's go
in then. I'm hungry."

It was never expedient to make a request of a hungry man.
She fell into step beside him. As they passed the soldiers one
of the men had just fitted a piece of cold fat bacon onto a
slice of bread and was about to lift it to his mouth.

"Spare a crust for a starving man, your honour," said Edward, in tolerable imitation of a beggar's whine, and took the piece from the soldier's hand. They all laughed. He walked on, cramming the food into his mouth.

"It'll be today," he said cheerfully. "There's smoke to the north of us. I'd send out a scout for news, but if I lower the bridge now there'll be trouble."

"Oh," she said. "Why?"

"There's a crowd of country-folk there, begging admission. They've been arriving all through the night, babies and old grannies, and donkeys and all. I could use the men too. . . ."

She could imagine how safe the castle looked to those who were locked out of it.

"It seems hard, doesn't it," she said falteringly. "They aren't on either side, and yet . . ."

"War always hurts somebody," he said curtly. "Don't look at me like that, Lucy. I'm not to blame. And I can't take in a lot of hungry mouths. I've been up there, shouting to them to turn about and go inland. Cromwell's going straight through to Wexford—his men may fan out a bit in search of food, but they won't go far. The fools out there'd be safe enough if they got well out of his road. But they won't listen. The donkeys have more sense."

He had begun to eat, quickly but without haste and giving the food his full attention; a hungry man whose next meal might not be quite on time.

"Maire says she knows a safe place not far from here, some caves, at Cloonmagh."

"Cloonmagh. That'd be no help to them. You can only get there by boat, I believe." He laid down his knife for a moment and put his hand over hers. "Sweetheart, don't look so miserable. There's nothing you can do for them now. I'll go up and shout at them again; threaten to shoot if they don't move away. Squatting there like that they're as good as dead already." He put the last bit of food into his mouth, took a long draught of ale and stood up.

"I'll come with you," she said.

"You'll only begin to cry and say 'poor things' and beg me to have them in. And I tell you frankly, Lucy, I shan't, because I can't. If the twelve Apostles stood there asking to come in I'd be bound to say No."

Something in his voice hinted to her that he was distressed by the plight of the refugees.

"I won't cry," she said, and after that, saying and doing nothing to call attention to herself, she followed him out, across the courtyard, up the ramp and onto the wall. The ramp ended in a kind of shelf, wide enough for two men to pass one another with ease; and above the shelf the wall was head high, except for the places where it dropped to waist height. At each of these places cannon were in position, heaps of balls ready and men standing by.

Edward went to the cannon station nearest the drawbridge, and she went and stood beside him. It was a perfect August morning, the sky the colour of a harebell and cloudless. The moat at the foot of the wall lay smooth and glassy, mirroring the sky's blue. Across it four swans moved with stately grace.

"Yes," Edward said. "It's smoke right enough. That'll be Shallyran. We're next." He looked down at the huddle of people on the other side of the moat, pressed together at the spot where the drawbridge, if lowered, would touch.

"You must get away," he shouted. "Shallyran's burning. They'll be here within an hour. Go inland and keep off the roads."

They turned their helpless-looking faces upwards and some held out their hands; but they made no move to go away.

"Do you think they can hear you? Do they understand?"

"Listen," he said.

It came up with dreadful clarity, "Let us in. Sir, sir, in the name of God, let us in. . . ." An old woman went down on her knees and held up prayerful hands; a younger one showed her baby, just about Julia's size. Helpless, stupid as sheep, and as pathetic.

"Tell them about the caves."

"There are caves at Cloonmagh," Edward shouted. "Go there. You can't stay here. You'll all be killed. I can't take you in. Go to the caves."

A man came forward, tugging at the head of his donkey.

"There's no getting to Cloonmagh without a boat, sir. Take us in. You can't leave us here to perish."

She saw the sweat break out on Edward's forehead; a drop gathered and rolled down his cheek and fell, with a little plopping sound, onto his breast-plate. She knew what he was going to say and she knew what it was costing him.

"I won't have you stay there to be slaughtered," he bellowed. "If you don't scatter I shall fire on you."

They moaned and pressed closer together.

"Edward, Maire said she knew a way through the woods to Cloonmagh." He looked at her for a second, his lips pressed together; then he looked to the north where the smoke was now a grey column, distinct against the sky, and then down at the huddle of people with their bundles and their babies and their cooking pots, their deadly, hopeless obstinacy.

"Fetch her," he said.

As she lifted her skirts and ran down the ramp she heard him shout that he was sending somebody to guide them all to safety.

Maire was like all the rest of them, like peasants the world over; she owned very little but that little was precious and must go where she went, even in the face of inconvenience and danger. She began, with hardly a word, to gather her poor possessions.

"And Lady, I'll need food too. If I go in the kitchen they'll not believe . . ."

"I'll fetch you food," Lucy said, her voice gritty with impatience. "I'll take it straight to the bridge. Maire, you must hurry. Men who should be busy at other things are waiting on you."

Maire had hurried; by the time that Lucy reached the inner

end of the drawbridge, carrying some hastily gathered food tied up in a cloth, the old woman was there, clutching a great bundle under the shadow of her shawl.

Above their heads, out of sight, Edward was shouting again.

"All you down there, pick up your gear and walk back twenty paces. Now stay there. Anybody who moves a step when the bridge comes down will be shot. Shot dead, d'you understand. Follow the one who comes out and she'll lead you to safety. All right! Lower awaaay!"

Gently, with the muted screech of well-oiled wheels and chains, the great bridge came down and spanned the water.

"Run, Maire. And God go with you," Lucy said.

"And have you in His keeping, and all you love," said Maire. Looking very small, looking like an ant carrying away its egg to safety, she scuttled across. She landed on the farther side and cried, "After me, all of you!" and without waiting to see whether they followed or not, set off, skirting the moat and then making for the woods.

"Bring her up!" Edward shouted. The chains wound in, link after link, and the bridge rose, slanted across the water, was upright. . . . Edward turned and began to descend the ramp. As he did so there was a sharp crack, louder and more reverberating than a musket shot. It was followed by the rippling rattle of an out-running chain. The bridge remained poised for an instant and then fell with a crash which had a desperately final sound.

Despite all their agonised efforts to raise it, to hack it through, to blow it up, enough remained to afford a passage across the moat for the Puritan soldiers an hour later.

In one respect reality differed from the dream; Lucy was spared the sight of Julia at the end of a pike, for Maire's confidence in the caves of Cloonmagh as a hiding place had given her courage enough to carry Little Miss away with her.

CHAPTER II

     Johannes Belderdik, owner and master of the "Sea Maid," had, in the years before Cromwell's Navigation Act, made regular voyages between Amsterdam and the Irish ports and knew the west coast well. He had never called at Cloonmagh, which was not a port, just a tiny fishing village, set close under the cliff and remarkable only for its church. The tiny, ancient grey stone building was surmounted by a cross, disproportionately tall, and gilded. It constituted a landmark, and Captain Belderdik was on the look-out for it on this bleak February morning in the year 1657. On this voyage he would put in at Cloonmagh, because that was what he had been hired to do.

  A mystery, which he was content to allow to remain so, surrounded his errand. A gentleman, giving the name of Mr. Bull, and telling some specious story about wishing to inspect an Irish horse for another gentleman, had approached Johannes and asked whether he would take the risk of carrying him to a small place on the Irish coast, land him, wait for an hour and bring him back again. Mr. Bull said that he realised that it would be an expensive trip, since no incidental trading could be involved; but that did not matter; he was willing and able to pay the price demanded.

  That in itself deepened the mystery. Holland was full of fine English gentlemen who had followed their young King into exile, and hardly any of them had any money at all; even their card debts had to be settled by I O Us drawn against property now in Puritan hands and only to be recovered when the Restoration came. That Mr. Bull had money enough to hire a whole ship and its crew in order to make a visit lasting one hour indicated that something very secret and important must be brewing. But that was no affair of Johannes'. He had only to find Cloonmagh.

It was more difficult than he had anticipated. The weather was bad, visibility frequently obscured by squalls of sleet, and careful study, through his glass, of one little huddle of houses after another, failed to find for him the unmistakable landmark of the tall gilded cross. Finally he knew that he had overshot his mark and must turn back.

"It may well be that the Cross has been removed," Mr. Bull said. "Cromwell passed this way, and we know his attitude towards the holy emblem—the same as the Devil's to holy water, and for the same reason! If all else fails we must put in at one place after another."

So they turned about and at the next little village, of which Johannes said dubiously, "It could be Cloonmagh—if it had the Cross," made a careful approach and, when the sounding revealed that the ship could go no nearer, lowered a boat.

"Sir," Johannes asked, as his passenger prepared to embark, "do you speak Gaelic? Then you will have difficulty in ascertaining whether this is Cloonmagh or not. I will come with you."

They landed, in the middle of another squall, on the desolate beach and walked over the wet sand towards the cluster of poor clod hovels. The place gave no sign of human occupation; there was no sound, and not a thread of smoke rising from any roof. But as the sleet-storm cleared they could see, beyond the hovels, set a little higher and slightly apart, the squat stone church, and protruding from its roof a broken stump, gilded.

"This is Cloonmagh," Johannes said. "And it's a dead village."

"It suits me well," said Mr. Bull forgetting caution for a moment. "If this is Cloonmagh I have only to follow my directions. I shall be back in an hour." It was a speech of dismissal. He began to walk, at a spanking pace, towards the church, was lost to sight for some moments and then appeared again scrambling up the cliff and finally vanished behind a screen of gorse bushes and wind-twisted fir trees.

It was not a pleasant day, or a pleasant place for a walk, but after the confinement of shipboard it was good to stretch one's legs. Mr. Bull had skirted the houses and made straight for the church, and in order to avoid the slightest appearance of following and spying, Johannes turned in the other direction and walked between the houses. They were a sorry sight, their mossy roofs falling in, the wet walls sagging, gently sinking back into the earth from whose sods they had been built. What had once been little gardens was now a green tangle of winter-defying weeds.

He walked until he had reached the church, stood for a moment regarding the white mass of bird droppings in its little porch, looked up at the stump of the Cross and remembered how often, sailing down to Wexford, he had seen it gleam in the morning sun or shine wetly through the rain; and then, depressed by the brooding desolation of the place, he turned back. Facing the houses again he heard, and then saw, something which indicated that the place was not so entirely deserted as it seemed. He heard the food-demanding squeal and grunt of a pig, and saw emerge from behind one little house and go to stand by the doorway of another a great, gaunt sow, heavily in pig. In prompt answer to the demand the low door opened and a very old woman crept out, dragging a wooden bucket. She pushed and heaved it a little way from the door, the pig rushed to it, and she crept back into her house.

Then something happened which brought Johannes to a standstill. Out from some hiding place, crouching low and moving with animal stealth and swiftness, came another figure, a bit of fluttering rag, a tousled mass of hair, arms and legs as thin and angular as twigs. An animated scarecrow. It darted to the other side of the bucket, crouched down, thrust its arms in beside the sow's guzzling snout and brought up handfuls of food and shovelled them into its mouth. The sow moved, pivoting round, swinging its bulk, trying to shoulder the intruder away; the child simply moved around and went on feeding. The sow stopped eating just long enough to let out a cry, disconcertingly human, a complaint, a call for aid. A human child eating like a pig, a pig crying out like a child, Johannes thought.

The door opened again, and out crept the old woman, this time carrying a stout stick. For all her seeming frailty the blow she struck would have hurt had it fallen where the old woman intended, but the child was too quick. It was upright and on its feet and running when the stick thudded down on the edge of the bucket and the sow squealed again, this time in angry reproach. Running, the child betrayed its sex—it was a girl. She had filled her hands with the dripping, revolting looking pieces and as she ran she carried them, one after the other, to her mouth, and was so intent upon running and eating at the same time that she was close enough to Johannes for him to smell her before she noticed him. When she did she stopped short, dropping her hands and staring at him with enormous eyes set in a filthy, blue-white face.

He said quickly, "Don't be frightened. I shan't hurt you!" but he spoke, without thought, in his own tongue. He repeated the assurance in halting, painstaking Gaelic, unpractised these many years; but even before the words were out he realised that there was no need to tell her not to be frightened of him. She looked over her shoulder at the old woman, now hobbling towards them using the stick as a prop, then she looked at him with an expression of confidence as well as appeal and moved to his side, slightly behind him, sheltering.

"Help me," she said.

The old woman, now close to them, seemed to sense his partisanship; in a spate of Gaelic, too swift for his understanding, she made a speech of self-justification and complaint. The gist of it—so far as he could make out—was that the girl always robbed the pig and the pig must eat or die.

"The child also," he said.

The old woman shrugged, a gesture of helpless indifference.

She spoke again. The girl was nothing to do with her. Maire had brought her and now Maire was dead; everybody was dead.

The child beside him said, "Yes. Maire is dead and I am hungry."

"Have you food in the house?" he asked the old woman. "I could pay," he added. An intent, greedy gleam in her eyes raised hope for a moment, but it vanished and a dull indifference took its place again.

Of what use was money, she asked, when there was nothing to buy. What food she had would hardly last for herself until her son came back; everybody was dead, and she would have been dead too except that she had a son who worked at Shallyran.

Rummaging in his mind for the Gaelic words, halting, improvising, he asked her if anyone else lived in the village.

No; they were all dead or gone away.

"And the child has no parents?"

No; she never had any; Maire had brought her; Maire was dead, and soon the child would die too, only by robbing the pig had she kept alive so long.

He looked at the girl. He thought of the good food at that moment being prepared in the ship's galley and made an instant decision, with no more thought, at that moment, of its results than a man would have when he put down a saucer of milk for a starving cat.

"You come along with me," he said, "I'll find you something to eat."

Her dirty little face took on a look of pure bliss. Then it was grave again and assumed a "remembering" look. To his enormous surprise, she stepped in front of him and made him an elegant, competent curtsey and said, "Sir, I should be very grateful."

"Come on then," he said, smiling.

"God be thanked now," said the old woman, "the pig can eat in peace."

The sailor who had been left with the boat was walking

briskly up and down, stamping his feet and beating his arms across his chest. He stared to see his captain appear accompanied by a filthy scarecrow child. Johannes lifted her into the boat, thinking how piteously small and light she was.

"Put your back into it, Daan," he said, "this child is starving." Of Julia he asked, "How long have you lived like this?"

"Since Maire died."

"How long ago?"

"It was Christmas. . . ." Tears filled her eyes and slowly spilled over, making tracks down her dirty face.

"All right," he said hastily, "we won't talk about that. You're all right now. I'll look after you." He took off his jacket and covered her rags. Washed and fed and properly dressed, he thought, she would be a very pretty little girl. And Geertruida would love her—surely. Geertruida's childlessness had been a great grief to her in the early days of their marriage. . . .

"What is your name?" he asked.

"Julia. Maire said remember always . . . Shall I say it?"

"Yes," he said, intent and curious, "tell me what Maire said you were to remember."

It surprised him again. He had once heard a grey parrot with a bright pink tail recite in a prim Amsterdam parlour some of the choicest obscenities of the forecastle, and in exactly that same accurate, uncomprehending way his waif now said, in English:

"My name is Julia Ashley. I am English. Cromwell killed my father and my mother and Maire saved me." She breathed hard with the effort and went on. "My mother was a good lady and my father was a brave man. I must be good and brave."

He must now summon up his smattering of English, the legacy of visits to London and Hull and Grimsby in the old days when the two Protestant sea-faring nations had been good friends.

"Say . . . that . . . again," he told her, in English.

She looked at him blankly. Apparently the little recitation

was all the English she knew. Asked in Gaelic to repeat it she did so instantly.

"Do you know how old you are?"

She looked down at her fingers, moving them against one another, and finally held up her hands, both thumbs tucked down.

"Eight. You are eight years old?"

"In summer. Maire told me."

They had reached the "Sea Maid."

"Well, here we are. We'll soon have some good hot food inside you," he said.

Eight, he thought, was a good age, young enough to have something left of entrancing childishness, old enough not to be too heavy a responsibility. Geertruida would love her. . . .

PART TWO

Holland
1657-1664

CHAPTER I

For the third evening in succession, Geertruida Belderdik, having made sure that everything was in readiness for Johannes' return, sat down to await his arrival. She took up her knitting—a pair of long warm stockings for Johannes—but her fingers were clumsy with excitement and impatience and after she had dropped several stitches and missed a line of the pattern she abandoned the attempt, rose to her feet and began to move about the room.

Twenty-two years of marriage to a sea-faring man had not trained her to accept with calm the inevitable rhythm of such a life. Still, when he went away she felt the wrench of bereavement; then, when all her tears were shed there was the waiting time, during which she could hardly be said to live at all. The lonely empty days dragged themselves over her, she did nothing, saw nobody, seldom left the house. Finally there was the rebirth, with its own pain, a time when she must count the days, the hours, the very minutes, with so much to be done making ready her feverish welcome, and the exact time was never certain, she must bear the impotent dependence upon wind and weather, she must listen, day and night for the sound of his coming.

Tonight the weather was as bad as it could be. The wind came screaming down from the frozen North and flung handfuls of rattling sleet on the closely curtained windows. Moving about the cosy room she could see, with her inward eye, the

"Sea Maid" so small upon the waste of waters, and her very heart shuddered.

She went to the table, where, on a white cloth, glossy with starch, all Johannes' favourite cold dishes, in ridiculous abundance, were set out. Cold ham, smoked sausage, spiced beef, pickled red cabbage, honey, her home-made cherry pie, her apricot jam, a rich plum cake. In the kitchen various hot dishes were being slowly brought to perfection, or kept warm. It had been the same yesterday, and the day before; it would be the same tomorrow, and every day, until he came.

She thought—as she touched everything on the table, moving one thing and then the other, until it was all rearranged—that this was exactly how she had *not* intended to live her life. She had planned that as soon as they were married, he should give up the sea.

There was plenty of money: her father was an East India merchant, not one of the princely ones, but wealthy enough, and she was his only child. Johannes was, at the time of their marriage, one of his hired captains, and in marrying him she had mated below her station. Secretly she had felt confident that that would help her to have her way with him. Secretly she had relied upon her father's wealth to make up for what she thought she lacked in looks and charm.

Towards the money Johannes' attitude had been disappointing, arbitrary, not to say cursed and awkward from the very first. Geertruida was not alone in being conscious of the difference in their stations and Johannes was—also secretly—so suspicious that people might think that he had married for money that he had refused to have anything to do with it at all. It took some persuasion on her part to make him consent to live in the big Hoogenstrasse house. He had his eye on a small place near the water-front; he had some pieces of furniture made, and left to him, by his grandfather. Humble hired captain he might be, but he was in a position to provide a home for his wife, and he rather wanted everyone to know it.

Over the house he capitulated; Geertruida pleaded that it

would be cruel to leave her aging father there alone; it was her home, and she loved it; there was ample room there for his cherished furniture; the little house he had in mind could only be a temporary home anyway, there was no room there for children. All sound sensible arguments, such as would appeal to a sensible man.

Over the money he was adamant.

"It's your father's now; and when he dies it will be yours, Geertruida. I want nothing to do with it. I shan't always be sailing other men's ships. When my father dies I shall have my share of the farm, and I shall buy a ship of my own."

It was then that she had said that she had hoped he would leave the sea. She had been angry, hysterical, tearful, all without effect. Johannes Belderdik married intended to continue—with only the slightest modifications—the life which he had led as a bachelor. He pointed out that he loved the sea, had left his father's farm in Zeeland and served a long hard apprenticeship on account of that love. He demanded to be told what in the world would he, a healthy sea-faring man, find to do with himself ashore. Her father, she said, would find him some kind of a job.

"I have a job, Geertruida," he said gravely, "and I intend to continue in it until I'm beached by old age."

Beaten down at last, humble as a dog, she had said, "At least buy a ship now. Let me do that for you." She imagined that when he was his own master he could at least order his comings and goings, or allow her to do so. In the end the "Sea Maid" had been bought with her money; but when, in the following year, his father died, he had paid her back, and she had taken the money, resentful and respectful at the same time.

She had tried, in the early days, to do what many captains' wives did—go with him on his voyages; but she proved to be a hopelessly bad sailor, constantly, irremediably sea-sick, not just for a day or two but all the time. She was sensible enough to realise that a sea-sick woman, in the close confines of a ship, was

not an attractive companion. In the end she had stayed at home
and begun the pattern of parting and waiting and reunion that
simply led to another parting. And never once did she suspect
that the irksome pattern contributed to keeping their love alive
and fresh. She had never, in fact, brought herself to believe that
Johannes loved her at all.

She considered herself very ugly. She had decided that in
early childhood, noticing the differences between herself and all
the other little girls she knew. She had always been small and
thin; her skin was dark, her eyes very black and her hair—also
black—quite straight and far too heavy and stubborn to be affected by curling-irons or rags, however tightly wound. All the
other little girls were plump and fair-skinned and had light-
coloured eyes and hair that was either curly or capable of being
made to seem so. To be so different, to be, at the age of twelve,
out-topped by blonde beauties of nine—that was bad enough,
but when she was fifteen something worse happened. Her father, who doted on her, brought home from his warehouse a
length of superb silk, the colour of flame with stripes of a
darker shade, almost tawny. It would, he told her, make her a
fine new dress.

She had unrolled the shining length of it and draped it over
her shoulders and gone to look in the glass. It changed her;
against the strong vivid colour her skin looked creamy, her hair
and eyes blacker than ever, her mouth a dusky red. She studied
her reflection, first with surprise and then with growing dis-
pleasure. Then, throwing the silk to the floor she cried,

"I can't wear it. It makes me look like an Indian."

Perhaps she had expected contradiction; when he said nothing she looked at him with growing consternation and suspicion. She seized his arm and shook it, demanding in a loud
voice,

"Is that it? Am I an Indian? Am I? Am I?"

He said slowly, "Your grandmother was Javanese—a princess.
And your mother was the most beautiful woman I ever saw."

"A beautiful *black* woman!" she screamed in derision.

"She was not black," he said, speaking with a sternness he used seldom. "She was beautiful, I tell you." He paused as though searching for words which would convey that remembered loveliness and found them, fatally. "Just for a minute," he said, "with that silk about you, you looked just like her."

She gave him a look of pure hatred, spurned the silk with her foot and rushed out of the room.

By the time she was eighteen—and fell in love with handsome young Johannes Belderdik—the consciousness of being ugly, different, somehow inferior, had imposed upon a nature fundamentally passionate and arrogant, a deceptive meekness and an apparent desire to please. That, and her smallness and the piquancy of her tiny features and unusual colouring, made a strong appeal to Johannes. With some diffidence—because of the difference between their stations—he began to pay her attentions which, to his surprise, were well received, not only by Geertruida but by her father, who had been troubled by her surly withdrawal from social contacts, her moods of bitter misery and attitude of self-denigration. Johannes had been, and remained, astounded by his luck; his faithfulness to her had been effortless, he knew he had the sweetest, prettiest wife in the world.

Tonight, when she had fidgeted with everything on the table, she moved restlessly about the room, went to the window and pulled back the curtain and saw the sleet sliding over the glass. Not to be borne, this endless dread and uncertainty. No man who loved a woman would subject her to such torment unless he had to. . . .

As she let the curtain fall and turned back to the room with the intention of snuffing a guttering candle she heard . . . and it was more a matter of heart than of ear . . . the sound of a footstep in the street. In a moment she was out of the room, across the hall and opening the heavy front door. The wind helped her, pressing the door inwards and flinging the sleet against her.

The Hoogenstrasse was inhabited by good citizens and well

lighted in compliance with the rule, a lantern at every door, but the sleet was so thick that each lantern was just a yellow blur and for a moment she could see nothing. But she could hear. It was Johannes' step, though slower, less springy than usual. He'd had a trying voyage, she thought. Leaving the door open she ran back to the head of the kitchen stairs and shouted,

"The master is back, Anna." Then, just as she was, she went into the street. The half-melted sleet between the cobbles soaked her frail indoor shoes, the wind buffeted her and tore at her carefully arranged hair, but what did she care?

She flung herself at him, saying his name over and over. Ordinarily at such a moment he took her in his arms, and because she was so tiny, swung her off her feet and held her high. Tonight, under his heavy, sodden cloak his arms were occupied, clutching something immensely bulky. He never came home without bringing her a present, and as she put her arms about him as far as they would go, she had time to think . . . a roll of the woollen cloth the Irish made . . . a wolfskin . . .

"Dear Truida! Dear Truida!" he said as her lips travelled over his wet face. "Run in! You shouldn't be out in this."

"You run too," she said, and felt under the cloak to take his hand. He quickened his pace a little, thrusting her along with the pressure of his body, but he did not free a hand to take hers. At their own door she ran up the steps ahead of him, let him enter, and then, with a great effort, closed the door against the wind. And that was always the loveliest moment of all, the moment when he was safely back and the door shut on the weather and all the outer world.

"Safe home once more!" she said in a voice tremulous with joy. She loosened the clasp of his cloak and gave it a little tug so that it fell with a sodden thump on to the spotless floor.

"What have you . . ." then she saw. The child's head stuck out from the muffling folds, a pale sleeping profile, a tangle of bright hair, tucked between his upper arm and his breast.

She was to think, a thousand times, a thousand thousand times afterwards that that moment was symbolic of it all—

herself running to meet him and throw herself into his arms, and his arms not free to take her any more.

"It's a little girl," he said.

"So I see. Who is she? Why have you . . . brought her here?" She heard the sharpness of her voice.

"I'll tell you all about it," he said, and looked about for some place to lay his burden, selected a settle on the far side of the hall and gently laid the child down.

Then, too late by an unreckonable age, he took Geertruida in his arms.

When he set her down they both turned to the settle.

"I found her, starving in a deserted Irish village. . . ." He had started his story when Anna, carrying a covered dish, came into the hall. She made a stiff bob and said, in a voice of genuine pleasure, "Welcome home, Master."

"Hullo, Anna. Something smells very good . . ." By that time Anna's gaze, following Geertruida's, had lighted upon the child. She gave an exclamation of surprise and the lid of the dish rattled.

Geertruida, who often eased her suppressed irritation with Johannes by snapping at the servants, swung round and said, "Be careful, Anna. And take that stupid look off your face. It's only a child. By the way you're gaping one would think it was a monkey."

"You might have thought so if you'd seen her as I did. I have cleaned her up a bit, and she's put on . . ."

"Dearest," Geertruida said, "the food will get cold. You haven't even taken your hat off. And your feet must be . . . Anna, fetch the master's slippers. Johannes, come to the fire."

He removed and flung down his hat and then went to the settle. "We'd better take her in. She might wake and wonder where she was. Not that she's timid, she's as friendly as a pup. And if there's food about . . ." He laughed. "You never saw such an appetite!" He lifted the child and shook her gently. "I wanted to keep her awake, so that you could see her with

her eyes open. She has beautiful eyes." As he spoke Julia's eyes
opened and he spoke to her gently in some foreign tongue.

"Can't she walk?" Geertruida asked in that same sharp way.

"Of course she can. And run. But she hasn't any shoes, you
see. We rigged her up as well as we could but the shoes beat
us."

He carried Julia into the parlour and Geertruida drew up a
third chair. Johannes set the child down and pulled away the
coat in which she was muffled. Geertruida saw that she was
wearing Johannes' best shirt, with the sleeves rolled up, and a
pair of drawers securely tied about her small waist with a length
of tarry string. She was now wide awake, looking from one to
the other and then about the room. Johannes smiled at her
and spoke in that same strange tongue and after a moment
she slipped from her chair and curtseyed to Geertruida.

"You see, somebody has taught her manners. I don't think
she'd run wild long," Johannes said in a silly doting voice, as
though he had been responsible for training the brat.

Geertruida served the food. The table had been set for two,
and she deliberately refrained from ringing the bell and asking
Anna to set another place. She sat with her hands clenched together in her lap, ostentatiously not sharing the meal. Johannes
did not notice. He ate heartily himself, praised the food and
kept pressing the child to eat. Once he drew Geertruida's attention to her pretty manners. Then he began naming the
things on the table, the food in the dishes, making her say the
names after him. She joined in the game eagerly, laughing at
her failure to imitate him perfectly. Her laugh was delightful,
gay and musical. And her eyes, as Johannes had said, were
beautiful, the soft dark, almost purple-grey of a thunder cloud
and set between long lashes that were dark at the roots and
just brushed with gold at the tips.

The meal lasted a long time. When it was done Johannes
eased his chair back and said, as he always did, "That was
good! God, I am glad to be home."

And he had not noticed that she had not shared this, their

reunion supper. Tears of self-pity dripped—not down her cheeks where they would have done no harm—inwardly, corrosively onto her heart.

The child ate, lingeringly, gloatingly, slice after slice of bread and honey while Johannes told how and where he had found her, speaking of the pig, the old woman, the desolation of Cloonmagh.

Then Geertruida said, "And what are you going to do with her now?"

For the first time he wondered whether he had taken too much for granted.

"Well," he said, "I thought you'd like to keep her, Truida. She's a very nice little girl. I thought, when I'm away, she'd be good company for you. A bit of life about the house. But of course," he looked her straight in the face and spoke with honest directness, "if you don't take to the idea you're under no obligation. I could make some other arrangement for her."

"What? The Klopstock Home?"

"Good God no! That'd be the very last place. No, I'd find somebody who did want a nice little girl. Or failing that, keep her aboard. She was no trouble and the men all loved her."

"She'd be better here. Would you like her to stay?"

"Of course I should. That's why I brought her home."

Julia had been following this conversation, turning her eyes from one to another as though she sensed that the talk concerned her. Johannes now spoke to her in the strange tongue, and she smiled and nodded and then broke into that ripple of laughter.

"I told her she was to stay here and be our little girl," he explained. "And I told her that she must be quick and learn Dutch because I find the Gaelic very difficult."

"I'll have a bed made up," Geertruida said. But she did not ring the bell to summon Anna or Wilhelmina. She went out of the room and stood for some moments in the cold hall, doing battle with herself.

It was true that in time past she had regretted her childlessness but the children for whom she hungered had been great sturdy boys exactly like Johannes, each one a link in the chain binding him to her more closely.

This strange girl-child, appearing out of nowhere, would never be a link; she was a wedge. Already she had come between them, spoiled this happy evening.

In the end the long years of hiding her true feelings, hiding even her real nature, came to her aid. Once again it was a matter of pretend, submit. Opposition at this stage would be unwise; give way but be watchful and when the slightest excuse offers itself, edge her out.

She was able to give her orders about the preparation of a room for Julia in a manner which gave no indication that the child's arrival was other than a pleasure to her.

CHAPTER II

The thought came to her in the night. Johannes was already asleep and she was lying, drowsy and sated with love-making, under the weight of his arm, just slipping into sleep, when the obscene thought came into her mind as though an enemy had spoken it in a loud clear voice.

She tried, on this first occasion, to refute it, but feebly and with little conviction. It followed so naturally on her secret fears that within a few minutes she had accepted it as truth and told herself that she had always known it to be true. Always, wherever he was bound, even Alexandria or Tripoli, she had visualised the place full of tall, full-bosomed hussies with pink-and-white skins, light eyes and fair hair. That had been part of her misery, that she, who could never bear to have about the house a servant-girl who was not old or positively ill-favoured, must bear the dread that at each landfall Johannes betrayed her.

Every time he came back she questioned him closely. "Tell me what you did, where you went, whom you saw. I want to share it all with you." His answers, apparently frank and certainly meticulously detailed, could, all too easily, have been lies. People could hide anything from one another; she knew that, for she had hidden from him her conviction that he had married her without loving her. She had never, in all the years, had the slightest confirmation of her suspicions; he was a loving, even uxorious husband, tender, indulgent, passionate, but her wounded self-esteem had been past healing long before she met him, and it had gone on festering despite the balm of a seemingly happy marriage.

And now she knew.

That was a bad night. And from that night on always she woke. Always suddenly, as though someone had roused her, and always just before the clock struck two from the church tower. And always she thought, flinching—I'm not going through all that again! And except that every day added to the weight of evidence, the night's ordeal was always the same.

Always the same . . .

The child's hair, now that it is properly washed, is just the colour his was as I first remember him, a colour hard to describe, unusual because it is made up of so many; brown, a brown made up of copper, and dead beech leaves and honey, always changing. And her eyes are beautiful; he mentioned her eyes almost before he was inside the house, beautiful, because they remind him of other eyes, set in a pink and white face.

She's eight years old. Nine years ago he went twice to Ireland. I remember every voyage he has made in twenty-two years: the log of the "Sea Maid" is not more accurate than my memory. And this year, with every port closed to the Dutch, at the risk of his life he must go to Ireland again on an errand

I always suspected. There was no horse. I asked what colour and did it travel well and he said that there was no horse.

And what a careful plan to fool me! She has not, he said, run wild long; see what pretty manners she has! She had not run wild at all. A week of fasting would strip the flesh from the bones of a child that size. . . .

Who was she? God damn her, damn her, damn her wherever she is; may she rot in Hell forever and ever. . . . May he . . . Oh no. I love him; he is mine; he belongs to me. Not true. If he loved me, if he belonged to me he would have given up the sea. . . .

He did not give up the sea because this woman, this child's mother, lived on the other side of it.

Presently the clock would strike three.

Sometimes there were fresh things to consider. There was the day when Johannes had told Julia to say her piece for Aunt Geertruida. She had said it and Johannes had translated it into Dutch and added, "Isn't it exactly like Mevrouw Beets' parrot?" Of course it was exactly like the parrot—it had been learned parrot-wise. It meant nothing—at least it meant a great deal. "I am English. . . ." that was just meant to hide that she was Irish. All part of the plot.

And look how he loves her. "Where's my girl?" before he has the door open. "How's my girl?" "That's my girl." I was his girl once. O God! Those happy days when I was happy and didn't know it. But she is, in very truth, his girl. No man could dote so on another man's child.

Turn over, gently so as not to disturb him; weep, but softly, so that he does not hear. Think of something else, because this one thought, going round and round, will wear your wits away.

Once or twice he woke and found her crying. Why, Truida? Why, my dearest? She had her reason ready. Time was running short, soon he would be gone again; she would be alone and he in danger from the sea.

The "Sea Maid" was a good ship, he said, and, even if he said it himself, he was a good sailor. Nothing to fret about.

"And this time, when I go, you will not be lonely. You'll have Julia."

Yes, indeed; she would have Julia!

CHAPTER III

Outwardly life in the Hoogenstrasse house went on in orderly serenity, and whenever, in later life, Julia looked back upon this time, she saw it golden with sunshine. Even in winter, when the canals froze and she went skating with a crowd of little boys and girls, the sky seemed to be blue and the snow, when it fell, fell through sunshine.

Her memories of Maire and of the dreadful time after Maire's death, dimmed every day, despite Aunt Geertruida's efforts to revive them with questions.

Aunt Geertruida spared no pains to teach her to speak Dutch, and since, as soon as Uncle Johannes had gone back to sea, nobody about her spoke a word of any other tongue, she acquired it quickly and easily. Then the probing began.

"With whom did you live before Uncle Johannes brought you here?"

"With Maire, but she died."

"What was Maire like?" That was a question hard to answer; she had never noticed Maire much, she had been accepted, missed and mourned but not observed in a way that furnished a description.

"She was kind."

"Was she young or old?"

"Oh, very old." But what did that mean? To a child of eight any person fully adult would seem old.

"As old as I am?"

Julia would ponder this, bringing her delicate, clearly marked brows together in a frown of puzzled concentration.

"I don't know, Aunt Geertruida. I don't know how old you are."

"Did she look old? Was her hair grey?"

"Yes. Maire was old. Her hair didn't show. She had a shawl." Julia brought that proof of memory forward with an air of triumph.

Then possibly Maire was not the mother; the grandmother; bastards often ended up in their grandmother's care.

"Was Maire married?"

"I don't know."

"Who else lived in the house?"

"Only Maire and me."

"And Maire taught you manners?"

"Yes. Because she said one day they would come back and she must say that I knew my manners."

"Who would come back? Julia, try to remember."

"I don't know, Aunt Geertruida." She knew that this answer, so often the only possible one, was unwelcome. She tried hard to remember, to catch at the fleeting memories of those days and have something more to offer. "There was a place. Maire went there to wash, but they were different people. Not the ones who would come back to see if I knew my manners. Maire cried."

"Why? What about?"

"She said—Now they will never know how hard I tried. And she said I must remember."

"What?"

"What Maire told me. I do remember that, Aunt Geertruida. Shall I say it for you?"

"No thank you. I know that part."

Conscious of another failure to please, Julia would sigh. She had known, almost from the first day, that it was necessary to please Aunt Geertruida, who did not feel towards her as Uncle

Johannes, or even as Anna and Wilhelmina did. Aunt Geertruida never looked at her as though the sight gave her pleasure,
and this, Julia thought, was because Aunt Geertruida did not
like her hair. She often mentioned how untidy it was. Nothing,
no amount of combing and brushing, could bring Julia's hair
to the state of perfection of Aunt Geertruida's, which looked
as though it had been painted on her head, but finally Anna
and Wilhelmina between them devised a coiffure which resulted in a cessation of complaint, though it evoked no spoken
approval. They brushed it flat with a wet brush, plaited the
ends back hard and turned the plait back on itself and tied it
with a narrow ribbon.

It was the first thing Uncle Johannes noticed when next he
came home. "What have you done to your hair, my pretty? You
look like a skinned rabbit."

That day Aunt Geertruida took Julia's side; she knew she had
done her best. She said,

"That is the only way to keep such a mop of hair tidy."

"Well, I don't like it. It makes me think of orphans."

"I *am* an orphan," said Julia brightly, "and I'm very lucky
not to be in the Klopstock Home."

Uncle Johannes looked displeased. He untied the ribbon and
loosened the plait, ruffling her hair with his hand.

"You're not that sort of orphan," he said. "You'll never be
an orphan so long as I'm alive."

"I know," she said happily.

She knew about the orphans. They lived in a big house on
the Herrencanal and when they went for a walk they went two
by two and never spoke above a whisper. They had very dull
grey clothes that looked scratchy, and their hair was dragged
back and their faces were sad. They never joined the other children at the skating; Anna had explained that kind gentlemen
gave them food and clothes but couldn't afford to provide them
with skates. It was however, not Anna but Aunt Geertruida
who had pointed out that Julia was lucky not to be in the Klop-

stock Home, and Julia, in hearty agreement with the remark, had sensed no unkindness in it.

She never thought Aunt Geertruida unkind. Strict, certainly, and rather sad and gloomy, especially when Uncle Johannes was at sea. Everything cheered up when he was at home and as the seasons wheeled round Julia came to share, though naturally with less violence, Geertruida's pattern of life, the sad parting, the long waiting, the glad reunion.

Time passed quickly because there was so much to learn; needlework and knitting and embroidery, spinning and bleaching and laundry work; how to cook and how to clean house.

Very soon, it seemed, they were celebrating Julia's twelfth birthday.

Johannes had decided that Midsummer Day should be her birthday. She had said that it was in summer and, "Nothing," he said, "could be more summery than Midsummer Day. Also," he added teasingly, "it will help us to remember."

He was home for that birthday, and gave her a string of coral. Aunt Geertruida had made her a blue dress which laced down the front with a coral-coloured ribbon. Anna had contributed a handkerchief edged with lace she had pegged herself and Wilhelmina had given her a tame green finch in a cage. It was a wonderfully happy day—until supper-time.

The parlour faced north and for just a few evenings in the height of summer was granted a brief share of the setting sun's light, not quite direct, but diffused and other-worldly. On this evening, as they sat down to the special birthday supper, the light came in and cast its enchantment upon Julia. It touched the edges of her brown hair so that her head had a nimbus of gold, it shone on the youthful moistness of eyelid and lip, it transformed the unfinished prettiness of her face into something of momentary, dazzling beauty.

Geertruida saw it as she handed the girl her plate and sat for a moment staring as though she had never seen her before. Then her gaze went to Johannes, and she saw that he was staring too, doting, entranced.

All at once she knew that she could bear it no longer. She let the serving spoon drop into the dish with a clatter, put her hands to her face and burst into a fury of weeping.

They jumped up and went, one on either side, to pat and clasp her, to ask, over and over again, what was the matter. The real reason could never be told. Presently she gasped out that she did not feel well, had not felt well all day.

Johannes held one of her hands in his, and laid his other on her forehead. "You have a fever," he said. "Come, up to bed with you. Julia, run and tell Anna to make some hot lemon tea." He lifted Geertruida and carried her upstairs.

His concern and the concentrated attention soothed her. She drank the lemon, said that she felt better, lay for a while feeling rather ashamed of her outburst, and presently fell asleep.

At some hour in the short darkness of the midsummer night she woke, and now she felt genuinely ill; very ill indeed. All her limbs ached, her head was spinning, her ears buzzed and she felt extremely sick. Soon, miserable and apologetic as in her sea-going days, she was sick; and, as in those days, Johannes tended her with matter-of-fact kindness. During the rest of the night the fever mounted steadily and in the morning Johannes sent for Doctor Beets.

The doctor, as soon as he saw her, said he knew what it was; it was the summer fever which had been raging through the poorer part of the town for three weeks or more; now it was appearing in the better class districts. It was nothing to worry about, he said; even without medical attention most people recovered in a few days. He bled the patient, prescribed a nauseous draught, and advised that she should drink as little as possible, despite her raging thirst.

"It is the fever which demands water," he explained gravely. "Deny it and it will depart the sooner." He then departed himself, having added unassuaged thirst to the misery Geertruida was already bearing.

It was the season for voyages to the Baltic ports and Johannes was due to sail for Riga in three days' time. The "Sea Maid" was refitting and taking on cargo and there was a good deal that demanded his attention but Geertruida clung to him and he stayed at home all day, until, at about six o'clock, the medicine seemed to take effect. She stopped asking for water and complaining of pain, and became drowsy.

He left Julia sitting by the bedside, said he would not be long and hurried away to the docks. Julia was very pleased to take his place; for a long time now one of her private day-dreams had been concerned with *doing* something for Aunt Geertruida which would convert tolerance into positive affection; this seemed to be her chance.

Johannes returned in the last, long-lingering twilight. As he hurried along he hoped that Anna or Wilhelmina would have had the sense to relieve Julia of her watch—for he had been delayed far longer than he had expected; but as he passed the kitchen window on his way into the house he saw two white caps just visible behind the potted geraniums which he had brought back, years ago, from the Cape and which Geertruida had relegated to the kitchen because she did not like their colour.

He entered the house and ran upstairs two at a time. Before he reached the landing he could hear Geertruida's voice, louder than usual, hoarse and scolding.

She lay high in the bed, her face dark and dusky against the white pillows, and she seemed not to notice his entry; she did not cease talking. Julia had left the chair and was standing against the wall, as far from the bed as possible; she turned as he entered but did not move.

"Oh," she said, "I am glad you've come. . . ."

". . . away, right away," Geertruida said. "This is my house. You have no right here, it was a plot. . . ."

He stood, poised for a moment between the raving woman and the frightened girl.

"Run along, Julia. Go and get your supper."

He went to the bed and tried to take one of Geertruida's wildly flailing hands. She tore it away with a loud cry.

"Don't touch me! I've had enough of this pretence. I know how you've plotted and lied and . . ."

"Julia," he said, "I told you to go. Send Wilhelmina to fetch Doctor Beets."

That set her in motion—and once she had gone, with her frightened white face, he felt that he did not mind what Geertruida said. It was only the fever talking.

Only the fever talking . . . He tried to remember that as it all came pouring out, unstanchable, sometimes incoherent, sometimes obscure: leaping from complaints about looking like an Indian to complaints about there never having been a horse at all. Only the fever talking . . . but it was Geertruida, telling the truth at last; the truth as she saw it.

By the time Doctor Beets arrived with a soothing opium draught, Johannes knew what had lain concealed behind the façade of his marriage. It was as though, undressing one night for bed, he had discovered his clean flesh rotted with leprosy.

CHAPTER IV

As soon as Geertruida was quietened he left Anna by the bed and went in search of Julia.

He found her sitting by the untouched supper-table in the parlour. She had lighted the candles and drawn the curtains and she looked calm, which was a relief to him. He was also calm, outwardly, but there was a tremor in his stomach, and before he sat down to the table he took a bottle of schnapps from the cupboard.

"You shouldn't have waited for me, my dear," he said.

"Oh, I wanted to. Shall I cut the bread?"

While she did so he took a drink and felt the spirit run, warm

and steadying, through his stomach. His mood lightened. He
told himself that what Geertruida had said to him hardly mattered, so long as what she had said to Julia had been harmless
or not understood. That he must discover, so that if damage
was done he could mend it.

"Your aunt," he began, setting down his glass and taking up
his knife, "is out of her mind with fever. You do understand
that, don't you?"

"Did she say terrible things to you, too?"

"Terrible!" He pretended, not to amusement exactly, but to
something akin, something which would invite confidences
without seeming to do so. "I never guessed there were so many
things to be accused of. And that just shows you what fever will
do—because in her right mind your aunt doesn't think I have a
fault at all."

"She called me a bastard. Once I heard a boy say to another,
'You bastard.' He was angry so I knew it wasn't a nice word.
She said it over and over."

"What happened, exactly? Tell me from the beginning."

"She woke up and asked me to lift her in the bed. Then she
asked me for water and I told her what you told me—about
Doctor Beets. And then she was angry. It was all muddled, but
it was about you and me and Maire and not wanting me here
and my being a bastard. She said I was *your* bastard. I stayed
up, not for my supper, I'm not very hungry tonight, but to ask
you what it meant. And Uncle Johannes, you can tell me the
truth because even if it's not a nice thing to *be*, if it makes me
belong to you it would please me very much."

He said, "Nothing could make you belong to me more than
you do. We belong to one another for the best of reasons, because I'm fond of you and you're fond of me." It occurred to
him that, up to a very short time ago, that was the kind of be-
longing which had been between him and Geertruida. He
poured and hastily swallowed some more schnapps.

"I'm not your father," he said. "I only wish I was. But your
father, I reckon, ranked high. Do you recollect that piece you

were taught to say? I do. Your mother was a lady and your father was a brave man. You must hold on to that. And being brave . . ." he hesitated, knowing exactly what he wanted to say but finding the words elusive . . . "being brave isn't only about not minding being hurt or in danger—all that sort of thing. There's another way of being brave. For instance, now. Just forgetting all those things that were said, and not meant; not minding a bit about what is said. Do you see what I mean?"

"I do if you mean not *crying* about it. But you must *mind* what people say, mustn't you? Aunt Geertruida is ill. But it did sound as though she didn't like me and never wanted me to live here. It is her house, isn't it?"

"Yes. And we live here because she wouldn't move. It was her father's house and when he died I wanted . . ."

I'm as bad as she is, he thought with a sense of shock; have I been brooding over *that* all these years and now go bursting out with it, without even the excuse of fever?

"Nothing she said this evening meant anything," he said firmly. "The only thing, the only kind thing to do, is for us to forget it all. And it's time you went to bed."

When she had gone he emptied the bottle and finally fell asleep where he sat.

CHAPTER V

In the morning Geertruida, though weakened and still slightly drugged, was herself again. She had missed a day and seemed to think that this was the day after the birthday.

"I must get well quickly," she said. "You have only three

more days. Oh dear, this was such a short time and I spoiled it, being ill. I spoiled the birthday, too. Really I didn't feel well all day yesterday but I kept about not to spoil the day."

"Yesterday," he told her, "was not the birthday. That was the day before. Yesterday you . . . you slept most of the time. Doctor Beets gave you some medicine and you . . ."

"Then you leave the day after tomorrow. Oh Johannes! Oh, why couldn't I sleep and lose a whole day when you're away and time seems so long? I've wasted two precious days then. I must get up at once."

In the end he promised her that if she would stay in bed and not fret he would defer his sailing for two days. She was delighted.

"Johannes, that is the first time, the very first time you've ever done that for me. I am honoured. Thank you, my dearest. I shall be quite well tomorrow."

"I hope so," he said. He knew what she was thinking and felt sick. At the moment he felt that he could never, never as long as he lived, share her bed again. "It isn't just to humour you, Truida. Things are all behindhand with the ship. I shall have to sleep aboard tonight—probably every night until we *do* sail."

Twice before he sailed he made indirect reference to what Geertruida had said in delirium.

"Julia is twelve now. It's time we began to think about her future."

Geertruida, touchingly convalescent, had insisted on going on with her knitting and was counting stitches.

"Twenty-five," she said. "What do you mean, dearest, by her future? She'll be married one day."

"Not before she's seventeen if I have any say. That leaves five years. I've been thinking she should go to school."

"To school? Girls don't go to school." Geertruida's voice was calm, but she had taken her finger off that twenty-fifth stitch and was looking at him intently.

"Call it what you like. Mevrouw den Hage has four girls of her own and accommodates five or six others and hires a teacher for them. What's that but a school?"

"A private arrangement to spare Mevrouw's purse, I should say. Do you think she would take Julia?"

"I could ask. Den Hage does business with me. Would you like me to find out?"

Sudden, almost unbelievable happiness welled in her heart.

"It would be a very pleasant and advantageous arrangement for Julia. I have taught her what I know, but that is little and she does sometimes mention a desire to learn to read. Also, now that she is twelve I don't like her to walk in the streets alone; I prefer to stay at home and a servant can't always be spared. . . ."

"You don't think that you would miss her company?"

"I should miss her, certainly; but we must consider her first."

Then it was true; she had resented the child's presence. And if that were true, so might the rest be; that she believed he had been consistently unfaithful to her.

"I'll go and ask about it now," he said, and fled from the stifling room.

The other reference concerned the house. Geertruida said something about his retirement from the sea and he said,

"When I do, I shall build a house, somewhere on the other side of the Zee, looking south over the water."

"You mean leave this house?" she asked incredulously.

"Yes. I never liked it, you know. It gets no sun."

"You've never said so before."

"While I'm at sea it doesn't matter. You chose to live in it and you do. But when I retire I shall have a house of my own—that's every man's right; and I shall have an apple orchard and keep bees. Still, that's far ahead. There's ten years' sail in me yet."

"I hope you will change your mind about that, Johannes. I should like us to have some life together before we are too old."

And suddenly the idea of retirement was more than ever detestable to him, and he wondered whether, poor woman, she had been right in doubting that he loved her.

In this unaccustomed uncertainty of mind and mood he made his final arrangements; said his farewells and gladly made his escape.

CHAPTER VI

They expected him back on the last day of September, and on the twenty-seventh day of that month preparations for his welcome were already in full swing.

Geertruida, wearing a huge mob-cap to protect her hair, was washing the inside of the window in a back bedroom which Johannes had never entered and probably never would; and under her stern eye Anna and Wilhelmina were beating all the rugs in the garden. The servant at the next-door house was standing on a stool gathering pears from an espaliered tree and every now and then she would rear up her head and say something to the Belderdik servants, who would stop their thumping to reply. Then Geertruida would rap on the window. So much noise was being made that the door-bell rang twice before Geertruida heard it and sent Anna in to answer.

After a few minutes she lumbered into the room.

"It's a Captain Wilhelmsteen, of the 'Dolphin,' Mevrouw. He asks to speak with you."

"Did he say . . . It isn't bad news is it?"

"He didn't say. Just asked for you," Anna said. But after Geertruida had pushed past her and gone down the stairs, Anna stood, clasping her hands to her stomach. She said afterwards that her inside knew before anyone in the house did.

And it had known rightly. Captain Johannes Belderdik would not be coming home from this voyage. He was dead and already buried in far-away Riga. And he'd been the victim, not of the storm Geertruida had always dreaded but of a simple accident, a silly little accident.

Captain Wilhelmsteen had seen it happen; his ship and the "Sea Maid" lay side by side, "Dolphin" already laden and waiting for the tide, "Sea Maid" taking on casks of tar and turpentine. A hoisting rope, insecurely lashed, had slipped and a cask had fallen, and rolled overboard, carrying a seaman with it. It smashed his leg, too. Johannes, who was watching the loading, dived over to his aid and the frantic man had grabbed him by the head as he came out of the dive. They'd both gone down to death together.

"It should never have happened," said Captain Wilhelmsteen. "That sort of accident doesn't happen once in a hundred years. But happen it did, and to one of the best men that ever sailed. That's all I can say, Mevrouw, except that we gave him a proper funeral and Dick Marsman is bringing 'Sea Maid' home."

Geertruida said nothing. Her sallow face had turned waxy yellow and that was, for a moment, the only sign that she had heard and understood. She remained sitting stiffly upright in her chair and then, quite slowly, she heeled over and lay on the floor, looking so curiously unsubstantial and crumpled that Captain Wilhelmsteen thought the news had killed her. He'd told her clumsily and too suddenly. But how could you break such news? However much you beat about, it had to be said in the end.

As he blundered out to call the servant, he thought of his own wife and the possibility of someone coming to deal her such a blow; and he was ashamed to find himself thinking about that at such a moment.

Geertruida lay for several days in a darkened room, refusing all food and comfort. In the past she had—she believed—often

faced the prospect of Johannes' death and had always found a
dismal consolation in the thought that she would die too. Now
she lay and longed and prayed for death, but did not die. And
though death would be the end of her misery she lacked the
physical courage needed for self-destruction; lacked, in the final
issue, the obstinacy to carry her fast to its logical end. Anna
tipped the scales, in the early, death-inviting hours of the morning of the fifth day, by spooning a little brandy into her
mistress' flaccid mouth. The spirit, rapidly permeating her de-
pleted body, had a curious effect. It made her very angry with
Johannes.

If he'd done what I asked him to, she thought, this would
never have happened and I would be spared this misery. He
never did love me or he'd have wanted to stay at home with me.
The sea and his other women, that was all he ever cared about.
He dared to bring his bastard home and expect me to take care
of her. Even that I did. Why should I grieve for the death of a
man who used me so badly?

Oh, the relief of that anger! The joy of not grieving.

Anna came along with her routine, hitherto fruitless, persuasions—a little milk, Mevrouw, a sup of broth, just to please
me, Mevrouw. This time she was successful, and presently,
nourished and slightly tipsy, Geertruida slept.

She woke, of course, to misery again; to gazing down the long
grey avenue of the future, cold, hopeless. He'll never, never,
never come home again. How can I bear it?

Only with the help of brandy could it be borne.

She swung now between moods of sober anguish and
drunken anger. In neither mood could she bear the thought or
sight of Julia. When she was sad and mourning for Johannes,
Julia was the creature who had filched away some of his love
and much of his attention, the creature who had spoiled their
last days together. When she was angry and reviling Johannes,
Julia was the living proof of his heartless infidelity.

There was the real Julia, swollen-faced, red-eyed with weeping, trying to share the grief.

"Poor Aunt Truida . . ."

"That was his name for me."

"I know, that was why I used it. . . ."

"Leave me alone. Go to the kitchen."

("You'd think now of all times she'd like the child's company," said Wilhelmina.

"Sorrow takes people in queer ways," said Anna, who had noticed the brandy-drinking.)

Misery and anger agreed on one thing—Julia must be got rid of.

"The Klopstock Home?" "Good God no, that'd be the last place." "You're not that sort of orphan. You'll never be an orphan while I'm alive."

Klopstock Home. Orphanage. Refuge for bastards and unwanted brats. The proper place! And Geertruida knew Mynheer Kinker, one of the Governors, slightly. One day, in her widow's clothes, well-fortified with brandy, Geertruida was going to walk out and call on Mynheer Kinker. She knew exactly what to say.

CHAPTER VII

Mynheer Kinker was sympathetic, but a little puzzled. In June, when Johannes was ashore, he had met him with Julia and had thought what a pretty, pleasant-mannered little girl she was. Mynheer Kinker was very partial to pretty, pleasant-mannered little girls; he'd had two of his own, now grown up and married, alas, and he hoped to live to see his grand-daughters. In the meantime he devoted a few minutes here and there—and a whole hour each January when the accounts came in—to helping to run the Christian Benevo-

lent Orphanage for Girls, more familiarly known as the Klopstock Home. He fully believed it to be a well-run and kindly
place but . . .

He said now, "Could it be, Mevrouw, that this disobedience
and naughtiness of which you speak are the result of her grief?
I can well remember when Elsa—my eldest, you know—lost a
puppy to which she was devoted. She uprooted and stamped
upon all my best tulips!" And could naughtiness go farther?
his voice and expression demanded.

"It's not that. Not that at all," said Geertruida. "Julia was
becoming unmanageable long before my poor . . . One of the
last things he did in June was to try to make arrangements to
get her out of the house. He asked Mevrouw den Hage to have
her but . . ." She left it there without saying that Mevrouw
den Hage had said she would try to make room for Julia at
Christmas. Let him find a reason for himself. "It is a great
worry to me, Mynheer. You see I feel so responsible, and if
I can't control her I can't be responsible, can I? At the Orphanage the girls always look so very well controlled."

"I sometimes think," said Mynheer, pulling at his lower lip,
"that they are a little too well-behaved. But of course when
one is dealing with large numbers one must have more discipline than would be desirable in a private home." He was quot-
ing word for word the retort which the Superintendent of the
Orphanage had made to one of his mild remarks about the orphans' unnatural orderliness.

"Control is just what she needs. I do realise she will be an
expense to you. I would gladly make a donation of, shall we
say a thousand guilders? Would that cover her keep and everything for four years?"

"Good gracious! That would be enough to . . ." he was
about to say—keep *four* of them for four years, but thought
better of it and ended, "send her to Mevrouw den Hage's."

"Exactly," said Geertruida. "If Mevrouw den Hage would
have taken her I should have paid, so it makes no difference."

His mind's eye presented him with two little pictures, one

of Julia so happy with Johannes on that summer day, the other of the orphans quietly and listlessly taking their daily walk, with a big, surly-looking girl at one end of the line and the Superintendent's assistant, a sour-visaged woman, at the other. It seemed a pity, but if Mevrouw Belderdik couldn't manage— and really, poor thing, she did look frail and helpless; and she certainly wasn't trying to evade her financial responsibilities.

"Well," he said. "In such a case, of course . . . Let me take the particulars. Now, her name?"

"Julia." He wrote that and held his pen poised. *Not* Belderdik, Geertruida thought fiercely. There'd been some other name tacked on to Julia in that parrot recital, but she couldn't think of it. "Maire" she could remember. And it was near enough. Bastards took their mother's name.

"Maire," she said, and spelled it. "It's an Irish name I suppose. I explained that my husband brought her . . ."

"And she is—how old?"

"Twelve last Midsummer's Day." The effects of the brandy which she had gulped down before leaving the house had been gradually wearing off for some time now, the mood of anger was dying, leaving her vulnerable to the memories of that day. My last happy day, she thought. Then I was ill, and somehow . . . he never slept with me again. And now he's dead. I can't bear it, I can't bear it.

"Mynheer Kinker," she said, as the quill ceased squeaking, "all this . . . so upsetting . . . I feel a little faint. Do you think . . . a little brandy, *please*."

CHAPTER VIII

For Juffrouw Klopstock, Superintend-
ent of the Orphanage, and for Juffrouw Hoorne, her assistant,
each day ended with a pleasant little ceremony—chocolate-
drinking. In winter they drank it by the fire in Juffrouw Klopstock's sitting-room, in summer on the balcony overlooking the
garden. Their position entitled them to certain privileges, more
numerous of course in Juffrouw Klopstock's case, but perhaps
of them all the chocolate-drinking was the most cherished.
Chocolate, imported via Spain from the new lands in the West,
was a very great luxury indeed; even the very wealthiest people did not drink it regularly. The Juffrouws managed to do
so because Juffrouw Klopstock, under her plump pink lethargy,
concealed a genius for financial shift and contrivance. For her
the chocolate-drinking was a symbol of triumph over adverse
circumstance; for Juffrouw Hoorne it stood for social achievement.

All day, every day, Juffrouw Hoorne did Juffrouw Klopstock's bidding, shouldered the whole burden of the Orphanage routine, accepted meekly the orders, the complaints, the
reprimands. All day long she went about in a state of smoul-
dering revolt, carrying on a silent, angry monologue—There
she goes again, lazy cow, lazy pig! Complaining, complaining,
harrying me to death, making me do all the work and taking
all the credit. Just because she was born a Klopstock and this
was her aunt's house! I won't stay. I won't be treated like this.
I'm nothing but a slave.

Then it would be nine o'clock; even the small amount of
noise made by the orphans would be hushed and Juffrouw
Klopstock's musical voice would call, "Klara! Come along!"

And that was the signal for the luxurious moment, the cosy
little chat, the easing of weary feet, the salving of the bruised
self-esteem. By bedtime the furrows were smoothed from Juffrouw Hoorne's brow, the harrow marks from her soul, and
she would retire asking herself where in the world could she
find another job where her only work was to see that work was
done by other hands, where else could she be sure of a fire in
her bedroom in cold weather, drink chocolate each evening and
be admitted to the company of a lady like Juffrouw Klopstock?

On the evening when Julia was admitted to the Home the
October gales had set in. Outside, the leaves were being whirled
from the alder trees and dashed onto the ruffled waters of the
canal. Juffrouw Klopstock's sitting-room seemed more than ordinarily cosy as the two ladies settled down by the fire, the
silver chocolate pot and two delicate china cups on the table
between them.

Earlier in the evening the Superintendent had received
Geertruida and Julia. Idle as she was, she never missed that
kind of contact with the outer world. Juffrouw Hoorne, in her
rebellious moments, always thought of this as "keeping me in
the background," and "making a show of herself."

"I thought," said Juffrouw Klopstock, lifting the silver pot,
"that she seemed a very quiet little girl, not at all what Mynheer Kinker had led me to expect."

"She cried when Louisa gave her her clothes," said Juffrouw
Hoorne.

"Quite understandable. Her own dress was very pretty."

"I don't like new girls of that age. They don't settle. And
if they're rough their language is shocking and their manners
appalling; and the few from decent homes, pine."

"Twelve is rather old," Juffrouw Klopstock admitted. "But
I couldn't go against Mynheer Kinker." She answered, as she
always did, the complaint which her assistant had not quite
dared to voice. "However, I don't think Julia will give you any
trouble. Her origin is very obscure—even Mevrouw Belderdik

seemed to know nothing of it—but I'll wager that she is well-bred. She has the *look*. Did you notice her hands?"

If there was one word which Juffrouw Hoorne really hated it was "well-bred." Juffrouw Klopstock used it very often, sometimes innocently, sometimes with malicious intent. This evening it was an impersonal observation and had no connection with Juffrouw Hoorne's lowly birth, nor with her large, red, coarse-skinned hands, which had been irretrievably ruined, before she was sixteen, by scalding hot water, icy cold water, sour cheese-whey and salt. Anybody set to work in a dairy at the age of ten would have hands like that, irrespective of breeding, she told herself, as she tucked them under the shawl she had donned before making her rounds of the draughty dormitories.

"I didn't look at her hands. I go by faces, their expressions. I thought she looked surly and too much head-in-air. I should say she'd been spoilt to the point of becoming unmanageable, and then pushed off on us."

"Well, I know of no one better qualified to manage the unmanageable than you, my dear Klara," said Juffrouw Klopstock, perhaps a trifle too sweetly.

Juffrouw Hoorne considered the remark. Something, somewhere had gone slightly wrong this evening. Ordinarily, whatever the day had brought, the chocolate-drinking hour found them in full, if precarious, accord; tonight, in the space of three minutes, Juffrouw Klopstock had been—she thought deliberately—twice offensive. Well, if that was the way she felt . . .

"If you mean that as a criticism," she said, "I would like to point out that I am responsible for keeping forty noisy girls of all ages so quiet and unobtrusive that you can pretend that they aren't in the house at all."

That was the first time, in almost nine years, that she had allowed a piece of her private monologue to slip out. She was astonished to hear herself saying such a thing; but, she thought stubbornly, it is the truth.

It was.

The big grand house on the Herrencanal had been built by

Juffrouw Klopstock's grandfather, who had made a fortune in the slave trade, a fact of which he was so little ashamed that when the house was built he had two full-sized Negroes, carved in wood, to flank the wide doorway. Juffrouw Klopstock, the orphaned daughter of the old man's younger son, had been brought up there by her aunt and uncle. There had been some thought of her marrying their only son, a delicate boy two years her junior, but he had died of the lung rot in his teens. The uncle had died soon after and the two women had lived on alone, the older dwelling in the past, the younger in the glorious future, for the aunt was always saying, "You'll be well provided for, Ellen." The years crawled by. When the aunt died she left the big house and the bulk of her fortune to the Christian Benevolent Refuge for Orphans. She expressed a wish that her niece should be appointed as Superintendent.

It had been a calamitous blow, but after a period of bitter rage at the injustice, of furious soul-searching as to *what* she could have said or done to deserve such treatment, Juffrouw Klopstock had settled down to make the best of things. It was still possible to be *comfortable*, and when she had completed a number of what she called "arrangements," she was pleased to realise that her position had, after all, improved. She now had authority; she had Juffrouw Hoorne and anything from thirty to forty downtrodden little girls to wait upon her and do her lightest bidding, and the Governors gave her no trouble at all. By adopting a high-handed manner towards them from the first she had bamboozled them into regarding her as patron, not as employee. The place became known as the Klopstock Home and quite a number of people believed that Juffrouw Klopstock's charity was largely responsible for its maintenance.

Oh yes, what Klara, bristling like a hedgehog, had jerked out, was quite true.

"My dear Klara," Juffrouw Klopstock said, "why in the world should I criticise your methods when they are so effective and fit so well with my design? You might as well criticise some of *my* financial arrangements—which benefit us both. Let me refill your cup."

The smooth devil! thought Juffrouw Hoorne with a mingling of hatred and reluctant admiration; she has an answer for everything.

But this evening the chocolate-drinking had not had its usually emollient effect, and for that the new girl, Julia Maire, was to blame. That idea took its place in Klara Hoorne's hard, narrow mind and nothing could ever dislodge it.

CHAPTER IX

Julia woke to the clanging of the rising bell. She had cried herself to sleep and her eyes were gummy, her head thick-feeling and heavy. There were five other girls in the small room and as they rose, yawning and stretching, she was conscious of their eyes on her. Their stares were almost impersonal, their curiosity dull—as though they were cows in a field and I was another, just let in through the gate, she thought.

For quite a while nobody spoke to her. Indeed there was very little talking at all, and what there was was whispered. They dressed quickly and Julia, following their example, began to put on the ugly clothes, the sight of which had, on the previous evening, broken down her fortitude. But it was not, as Juffrouw Klopstock had suggested, the contrast between her own dress and *this* which had made her cry. It was the memory of the time when, from the security of Uncle Johannes' home, she had pitied the orphans in their sad garb. Now she was one of them!

There was an iron tripod in the corner of the room. It held

a brown basin, and below, where the legs crossed, a little wooden dish with a piece of rough soap in it. On one side of the tripod stood a jug, and on the other a wooden bucket. Two girls took their turns at washing, and then Julia went forward.

"You're last," a girl said.

She said, "I'm sorry," and waited her turn. When it came there was not a drop of water in the jug. Holding it in her hand she turned with the intention of asking where she could fill it. They stood in a group, watchful, inimical; a ripple of smothered laughter, derisive rather than amused, ran amongst them. Occasions for amusement were rare in the Klopstock Home. . . .

Hateful, she thought, setting the jug down. This is a hateful place; and you'd think it was bad enough to be in it, without playing tricks like that and making it worse! She looked at the towel, thin and grey and sopping wet. She couldn't bring herself to put it to her face, but she wiped her hands on it.

The door opened; the giggling stopped. The girl called Louisa, who had handed out the clothes last evening, was standing in the doorway, running a calculating glance over everything and everybody.

Last night her flat face with its reddened snub nose and thick eyebrows drawn together in a perpetual scowl had been just one more disquieting, disheartening thing. This morning, because she had quelled the giggling by merely looking in, she had the face of a friend.

"Please," Julia said, "could *you* tell me . . ."

"You mustn't speak to me till I speak to you. I'm the chief orderly."

All the five faces took on exaggerated expressions of shocked disapproval.

"Good morning," said Louisa, formally.

"Good morning, Louisa," said five sycophantic voices in unison.

"You may go down." She passed on, and Julia, lining up

behind the others, could hear, from the next room, her formal greeting and the chanted response.

They moved, in line, with exaggerated care not to make a noise, along the passage and down some stairs, turned a corner, descended some more stairs and came at last to a door which led out into a yard. There, behind a trellis, netted with the bare stems and withered leaves of some creeping plant, six doorless privies stood in a row. They were occupied; they were vacated; occupied again under the eyes of those waiting. Horrible, horrible.

After that, still in line, they went into a large, half-underground room in which there were three tables, two long ones running lengthways and, between them, at one end, a square one. One place at the square table was served by a red cushioned chair, like a throne; everywhere else were narrow backless benches. Girls were moving, quietly and busily, between the tables and the kitchen next door. They set wooden bowls on the tables, took their own places behind the benches and waited. Juffrouw Hoorne entered, walked through the hush to the red chair, and said, "Good morning, girls." Everybody said, "Good morning, Juffrouw." Juffrouw Hoorne said,

"God bless this food and make us thankful Amen."

There was porridge in the bowls, well-made, pleasantly salted and hot. To eat with it, or afterwards, according to your taste (and that was, Julia discovered, about the only thing which was left to your choice), there were thick slices of bread, one for each girl. To drink there was milk, not the fresh creamy liquid which the Governors visualised when they read "Milk" on the accounts, but a pale, bluish fluid, twice skimmed, supplied by a cheese-maker with whom Juffrouw Klopstock had made one of her "arrangements."

The day was to come when Julia was to eat all her portion and long for more, but on this first morning she was too wretched to be hungry. She sat staring round, loathing all she saw.

At the small square table Juffrouw Hoorne was carving a

large joint of pink and white salt pork, and the bread at that table was cut, not in hunks but in slices, so that the meat could be laid on it and eaten so. Nobody else in the room had meat; and perhaps, Julia thought to herself, the extra food was provided at that table to make up to the girls there for their afflictions. They were all disfigured in some way; one had an ugly birth mark, one a hare-lip, one a squint. There was a girl with one hunched shoulder, and two scarred by scrofula and two wore expressions of mild idiocy. And there was Louisa, whose fearful scowl was in itself a disfigurement. Julia wondered how it was possible for Juffrouw Hoorne to sit at that table and eat as heartily as she was doing.

Julia was looking, although she did not know it, at one of the outward manifestations of Juffrouw Klopstock's genius. As soon as breakfast was over all these afflicted girls would go off to the saltings, to split and clean fish, and throw it into the barrels.

When Juffrouw Klopstock took over the Superintendency of the Home, girls had stayed there until they were thirteen or fourteen according to their size, and had then been placed out in domestic service; their ties with the Orphanage were severed and whoever, thereafter, profited by their labours it was not Juffrouw Klopstock.

The two simple-minded creatures had helped her to remedy this state of affairs. When they reached an age to go out into the world Juffrouw Klopstock told the Governors that she was gravely worried about them; they were not capable of holding their own in a workaday world and they would be certain to come to grief. Suppose she tried—with permission, of course—a little idea of her own. The poor girls could be found some easy mechanical work, well within their capacity, and they could remain in her care. Their wages would cover the cost of their keep.

The idea was original and that year the Governors took the trouble to look at the girls, who were, all too obviously, exactly as the Superintendent had described them. So they went to

work in the fish saltings, and from time to time they had been
joined there by other girls whom Juffrouw Klopstock deemed
unfit to face the world. Their earnings were the matter for some
very complicated "arrangements"; in her accounts, which she
kept meticulously in a legible hand, for she had had the advantage of sharing her boy cousin's lessons, Juffrouw Klopstock
always proved that this variation of the Home's original purpose was self-supporting, in fact a trifle more than that; but
the real profit of the enterprise did not appear in the accounts
or anywhere else, it was concerned with the supply of fish, both
fresh and salted, to the Home, at a cut-rate price. The orphans
were appreciated at the saltings, never absent, never late, never
seeking other employment.

Nobody lingered over breakfast; Juffrouw Hoorne rose and
said grace again and the labour force marched out, each girl
taking with her a packet of food to eat at midday, something
which would compare very favourably with any other meal carried to the saltings, all evidence that Juffrouw Klopstock did
not stint on food.

The other girls remained standing, and somebody whispered.
Louisa spoke quietly to Juffrouw Hoorne who nodded and said,

"I understand that you did not wash this morning, Julia
Maire."

Blushing hotly, Julia said, "I couldn't, because . . ."

"I did not ask you a question. One rule of the house which
you must learn is that girls speak when addressed or when given
permission to speak, not otherwise. Another is to be clean, in
your person, in your clothing and in your work." There, at any
other time, Juffrouw Hoorne would have left it, but she remembered last evening. She looked at the new girl with disfavour.
Julia's neck was very long and slim, and this morning, between
the collarless neck of the uniform dress and the scraped-up hair,
it looked longer than ever and gave her, despite the burning
humiliation in her face, a proud look, easily confused with defiance to a spiteful eye.

"Whatever you may have been accustomed to in the past," said Juffrouw Hoorne, "*here* you will be clean."

"There wasn't any water——"

"Be silent!"

"——and I didn't know where——" said Julia, now as angry as the Juffrouw.

"You will have no supper this evening."

"——to get any."

"Louisa, show Julia where to find water, and see that she washes, thoroughly. Has any other rule been broken?" Had there been, nobody would have been so extravagant as to report it *now*. This was excitement enough for one morning. What an exciting morning, indeed.

"Very well, you may disperse," said Juffrouw Hoorne.

"You'll soon be in trouble if you go on like that," said Louisa happily.

"But it was *true*. The other girls had used all the water and when I asked you, you said——"

"That you shouldn't speak without you were spoke to first. I'm saying it now. It's the rule."

"Then it's a very unfair rule."

"Now you're finding fault with the rules. Your very first day too!"

"But it is unfair," Julia said stubbornly, "if you've done something you couldn't help and then mustn't even explain."

"You keep on," said Louisa, "and you won't get supper tomorrow either."

Provoked past caution, Julia used a word she had heard Uncle Johannes use, but which she would never have let him hear her say.

"Damn the supper! And you too!"

There had not been such a day in the Klopstock Home for a long time. What the new girl had said to Louisa was whispered round and round. The memory of the morning's scene was still bright; and then in the evening when the coarse salt

fish—the orphans' favourite food—was served and Juffrouw
Hoorne said,

"Julia Maire, stand out," and pointed to the place by the
wall where she was to stand, near enough to see and smell what
the others were eating, that was interesting, too. The new girl
stood by the wall and although she didn't say anything—and
even she wouldn't dare to—she stuck her nose in the air and
had a look on her face which said very plainly that she didn't
in the least mind having no supper, and what a very nasty supper it was.

"Well," said Juffrouw Hoorne, quite happily, "I've had trouble with the new girl already." She ran off the list of offences:
failure to wash (so much for your breeding!), insolence, criticism of the rules, swearing at Louisa. "And then, when I stood
her out at supper, she stood there looking down her nose as if
she despised the good food—and us for eating it."

"Dear me," said Juffrouw Klopstock, "we can't have *that*,
can we?"

The words had the wrong sound; not sufficiently shocked,
almost . . . almost amused. Once more for some strange reason Juffrouw Hoorne found her inward monologue going on,
here, in this hitherto sacrosanct room. That's right, she thought
angrily, find something funny in a girl answering me back and
making trouble; I don't have enough trouble, I suppose, running this place single-handed.

Aloud she said firmly, "I don't *intend* to have it. She'll have
to learn to knuckle under, like the rest." The two red spots of
colour which might have been painted on her high cheek-bones,
so even and symmetrical they were, suddenly melted and ran
outwards, until her nose and forehead were red too. Juffrouw
Klopstock looked at her with mild surprise and said, with a
genuine intent to soothe,

"She's new, and I expect she had been spoiled. But she
looked intelligent. She'll soon settle down."

CHAPTER X

The settling down was very hard. There was nothing, so far as Julia could see, to mitigate the bleak dreariness of the place. The one seemingly obvious advantage, plenty of company, proved to be illusive; you were lonelier here than you would be in the middle of a desert. In the Klopstock Home everybody was the enemy of everybody else. For this Juffrouw Hoorne's system was partly to blame. It was her task in life to keep the girls busy, quiet and unobtrusive. She was aided by Juffrouw Klopstock's housekeeping, an almost entirely farinaceous diet not being conducive to uproarious high spirits; but even underfed and lethargic girls were capable of chattering in the passages and on the stairs and of scamping their assigned tasks, and she could not be everywhere at once. So everybody was a spy, a willing spy, since it is a rule of human nature that some of your own misery can be lightened by seeing somebody else in worse case. Julia quickly learned that every word she spoke was reported and that every gesture of friendship was regarded with distrust as being likely to lead to some incautious word, which she, in turn, would eagerly betray.

You didn't have a friend; you didn't have a moment's privacy; you had very little leisure. Juffrouw Klopstock, in addition to her arrangement with the fish-salter, ran several subsidiary employment schemes with private households. The Home took in washing and plain sewing and embroidery; it was common enough for a lady in Juffrouw Klopstock's social circle—which was wide and growing—to say that she had a superfluity of pickling cabbage, or plums or apples or lavender or fat pork, and that if all those willing little hands at the Orphanage

would do the pickling or the preserving, the making into bags
or the drying down, and let her have back just what she needed,
the rest could go into the store-room at the Home. Charity was
a virtue, after all.

It was by way of one of these arrangements that Julia made
her bid for escape.

A lady of Juffrouw Klopstock's acquaintance, come down in
the world and able to retain only one, rather elderly maid, had
in her garden in the summer after Julia's admittance to the
Home a heavy crop of black-currants, a troublesome fruit, tiresome to pick, tedious to free from the stalks, in fact precisely
the job for the Klopstock girls. Ten of them, under Louisa's
stern eye, did the picking and struggled home with the heavy
baskets of fruit, and practically everyone, during the next few
days, had a hand in the preparation, the boiling, the straining,
the bottling and the tying down of the preserved fruit with
tightly stretched pig-bladder. About two thirds of the finished
product was to go back to the old lady, and one afternoon two
orphans set off, pushing the little low wooden cart often used
for such errands.

Juffrouw Hoorne saw them off, and turning back into the
house remembered that a piece of plain sewing, just completed,
could be delivered along their route. It was ready to hand and
she took it up, thrust it at the first orphan to come in sight—
who happened to be Julia—and told her to run after the pair
with the cart and give it to them to leave on their way.

Julia ran out of the house and then stopped. The two orphans, pushing the cart with their behinds stuck out ungrace-
fully, were now at a little distance along the path which edged
the canal. She began to follow them, her feet going slowly, her
thoughts very fast.

The idea of running away was not a new one; she had entertained it from the very first day and had been watchful for a
chance; there had been none, there might never be another.
She was now alone, and out in the street, but there were the
clothes, instantly recognisable by anybody. Then she realised

that she held, folded in her arms, somebody's winter cloak, prudently sent, in high summer, to be relined by the orphans.

The cart-pushers were now much farther away. With her heart beating so violently that it seemed it might shake her to pieces, she turned down the next side street, shook out the cloak and put it on. Then, still walking, quickly now, she pulled at her hair and shook it loose. The long, heavy cloak was eccentric wear for a hot summer's day, but at least it covered her completely.

Now, where to go? What to do? She realised that she had never carried her plans for escape thus far in her mind. Getting away had always been the problem.

Life in the Klopstock Home had taught her one thing—there was plenty of work in the world; four of the girls with whom she had shared a room had gone into service at the New Year and she had watched them go with great envy. The thing to do, she told herself firmly, was to find a house which looked as though servants were employed there, go to the door and ask if they wanted one.

She was now in a poor street of small, shabby houses and unprosperous-looking shops—the sort of street which Anna, in the old happy days, would avoid, or walk quickly along, talking of "catching something." Some children, ragged and dirty —but happy and lively-looking compared with the orphans— were playing marbles in the gutter. As she drew level with them, one of them looked up, pulled a rude face and said jeeringly,

"Got her mother's cloak on!"

She tried to take no notice. With sad lack of originality the others took up the chant and the words,

"Got her mother's cloak on," followed her to the end of the little street.

The thought—Do I look so funny? undermined her small self-confidence.

The shabby street led into another of much the same kind, but that, at its farther end, opened out into a square of good, solid-looking houses, nine of them.

Now she must do it; and the jolt and beat of her heart told her how much she dreaded the ordeal. No good lingering. She walked straight to the first house along one side and knocked on the door.

It was opened by a pleasant-looking, middle-aged woman in a voluminous apron.

"Good afternoon," Julia said. Her voice sounded strange, very high and shaky.

"Good afternoon," the woman said, pleasantly.

"I wondered if you wanted a servant."

"What did you say?" It was not meant deterrently, it was a request to repeat something not quite clearly heard. Julia said it again.

"Why, no. We don't. And if we did we know where to go. I've a niece of my own waiting for a place."

"I see," Julia said.

The woman's attitude changed; she laid her hand on the door, which had been wide open, and pulled it half closed. Suspicion wiped the pleasantness from her face.

"Are you a gypsy?"

"Oh no. No."

"Or in with thieves or anything?" Her eyes sought the square, all quiet in the sunshine. "I know that old trick, sending somebody to look for a job and spying about. We've got a savage dog in this house, let me tell you."

She slammed the door.

Well, that was horrid, but it was only one house. There were eight more, here in this very square.

"No, we do not. We have more than we need at this moment, idle rogues that they are."

"No thank you. And we never take chance comers."

"No. Our mistress always has girls from the country."

"No."

"No. The family is away. I'm the caretaker."

"No."

"No. We always get our new girls from the Klopstock Home."

And all the time the curious, speculative, assessing eyes, noticing the too-long cloak. Better get away from here, quickly.

Down another street, across a canal—not so nice as the Herrencanal, dirtier, with a dead thing floating.

Now another pleasant street. Try again.

The strange thing was that as her need and urgency increased, her opening sentence, no matter how much she tried to word it differently, sounded more and more false and like something a gypsy or a thief would say. In the end she sounded like, she almost *was*, somebody trying to get in, to spy, to betray.

Twice more she heard reference to the Klopstock Home.

The sun began to sink, gilding the trees.

Presently she was convinced that it was not, after all, possible to get a servant's place in that way. But there were other things. Saltings. The one which employed the orphans couldn't be the only one in Amsterdam . . . but that one must be, at all costs, avoided. The thing to do was to get down near the harbour, find a place to sleep and tomorrow morning keep a sharp look-out, see into which shed the orphans marched to work and pick the one farthest away.

Now the streets became familiar, full of sad memories. Here, and here and here, she had walked, swinging on Uncle Johannes' hand, coming down with him to visit "Sea Maid." Right here on this corner was the place, half tavern, half eating house, where only last June, on the day before her birthday, returning from the docks, he had said, "Are you thirsty, sweetheart? I am." And they'd gone in and sat in a kind of box place, with high sides and a table all scored with names and initials and dates, and he had drunk schnapps from a small glass and water from a big one and she had had a long cool drink that tasted of lemons.

The window was lighted, and except that now it was evening instead of mid-morning, and a whole year and a month had passed, it looked exactly the same; there was the ham on the dish, the pies and the pastries, the little three-cornered cakes.

I'll have no supper tonight, she thought; but without much feeling. In the Klopstock Home she had often been punished, sometimes with reason, more often without, by forfeiting supper. It was Juffrouw Hoorne's favourite punishment. She kept canes of varying thicknesses in her room, and sometimes used them, but she believed that having no supper for a week was more effective. The cane's impact was a thing of the moment, the other meant seven separate reminders that rules were not to be broken. Having no supper was a thing Julia had trained herself to bear, and although a voice in her mind added—And no breakfast tomorrow, it was not hunger which made her stare into the little window. She was looking at the enclosure, made by two facing settles, where she and Johannes had sat, and taken their drinks, and laughed. . . . He had teased her by pretending that he had forgotten about her birthday tomorrow. . . .

The voice said, "Feeling peckish, eh?"

She turned; it was a sailor . . . the same clothes, the same face almost as she remembered, the general sort of sailory look, calling to mind Daan and Pieter and all the others who had made such a fuss of her every time she visited "Sea Maid."

"No. I wasn't looking at the cakes. I was just looking in."

You couldn't share memories with sailors, nice as they were.

"Well, come in then, and take a good look. I'm going in myself. Home from home I call this place. Come in and keep me company, eh?"

"I haven't got any money. You'd have to pay for me."

"What'd you want with money? Pretty little girl like you. Come right in and ask for what you want."

He was the first really kind person she had met for a long time. But then sailors were kind.

"That *is* kind," she said.

"Come right in," he said again, and flung open the door.

Only one of the little boxes was unoccupied, the one immediately on the left of the door.

"Sit you down," he said, giving her a little push. "Now, what d'you fancy, eh?"

"A meat pie," she said eagerly.

"And what'll you drink?"

"Last time I was here I had a nice lemon drink."

He said something that she didn't understand at all. Something foreign perhaps. He left her sitting there and went to the counter and a fat man in an apron put four meat pies on a pewter plate and then gave the sailor two mugs which he carried carefully to the little table and set down. He then seated himself beside her, and she smelt the old, familiar smell of tar and salt water, and sweat.

"There you are," he said, "lay to!"

Now that the food was before her and she was heartened by his kindness, she was hungry. The pies were delicious, the best food she had tasted for a year. She ate three of the four; the sailor ate one, rising now and again to have his mug refilled. She found the drink he had brought her less agreeable; it didn't taste of anything much, just vaguely musty, and every time she sipped it she choked. He drank it as though it were water.

"You like it, don't you?" she said, and smiled at him.

"Why not?" he said, genially, "it's the best schnapps."

"Oh, is that what it is! My . . . somebody I once knew used to drink it sometimes. I'll try again." She sipped and coughed.

"I think it's for men," she said; and smiled again.

He asked her her name, and she told him "Julia," with which he seemed content.

"And what's yours?"

"Hans."

"I shall remember that," she said.

"Maybe you will," he said in a rather peculiar way. "You live around here?"

"Well . . ." she hesitated. "Not exactly. Just now I don't live anywhere. I'm looking for work."

"You've found it," he said; and as he spoke something happened to his leathery, sunburnt face. It smiled, but in a way that made her feel uncomfortable. And what did he mean?

"Get that down of you," he said, jerking his head at her mug. "Perk you up a bit. What'd you like now? One of them cakes?"

"Yes, I would, please. That is . . . if you think you can afford it."

He laughed, and the sound shared the something that had been in the smile.

"I got money and I don't mind what I spend. That's a sailor's life, that is—hard-tack and maggoty meat and water that foul you have to hold your nose to drink it, and then good schnapps, and your belly full and a right pretty girl."

He lumbered away and came back with a refilled mug and one of the little cakes held between his finger and thumb.

"Get *that* down," he said, "time I drink this. Then we'll go."

"Where?"

"I know a place," he said, exactly as he had said that he had money.

"You mean you know a place for me? A place where I can work?"

He had to take the mug away from his mouth in order to laugh.

"Now then," he said, quite good-naturedly, "don't give me too much of the bloody innocence. Little of that goes a long way. Work, eh?" He laughed and again said something which had no meaning.

She was now liking him less; and she knew why. He was getting drunk. That was the prime failing of all sailor-men—except of course, Uncle Johannes; they were the nicest, kindest people in the world, but they did get drunk.

The cake lost its flavour suddenly.

He emptied his mug again and sat for a moment looking at her.

"You don't want *that,*" he said suddenly. "What you want . . ." He put his arm, hard and heavy, around her shoulders, pulled her round and kissed her full on the mouth. It was very unpleasant; his lips were wet and his breath smelt of schnapps and something else even more horrid; and that wasn't the way people should kiss other people—more like trying to eat them. She pushed him away with all her might and would have got to her feet but that his arm pinned her down. But she wasn't angry with him, just confused and rather sorry, because he had been nice to begin with, and now was drunk.

Still pushing at him she said, "You mustn't do that. I think you're a little drunk."

And he wasn't angry either.

"Drunk, am I? Maybe I am but I ain't so drunk . . ." and once again he said something she didn't understand. He lurched to his feet, still holding her, and said, "Come on, let's go."

She said, "But you are drunk and I don't think anybody'd give me a job if you went like that to ask for me. Thank you all the same; I don't think it'd be any good."

Then all at once he *was* angry; and that was the thing she had been afraid of ever since she suspected that he was getting drunk. Drunk men did get angry all over nothing at all. Once she'd been with Uncle Johannes and they'd seen Daan and Pieter, the best of friends aboard "Sea Maid," fighting on the quay, trying to kill one another. Uncle Johannes had separated them and knocked them both flat.

It was the same with this sailor; he'd invited her to go in and eat with him; he'd said he didn't mind what he spent, and now he was angry about it, and grudging, shouting about how much he had bought her, and saying many other things which, although she did not understand them, were certainly unfriendly and rude.

He was trying to force her round the end of the settle and towards the near-by door, but she had her hands clenched on the settle's side and her body partly braced against it. They contested silently—except for his accusations and curses—for several minutes, and she looked around the room, searching for one friendly face.

There was none. Four sailors at one table stopped the game they were playing and stared with delighted interest, beginning to laugh and call jeeringly. They were probably drunk, too. A man sitting alone at a table looked up and then down again, indifferent, disgusted. Two gaily dressed women, sitting with another sailor at a further table, were watching her with exactly the same expression as her roommates had worn when she lifted the empty jug.

Even the fat man behind the counter, though he was watching, had a dull look, as though he had seen similar scenes too often to be much interested.

Suddenly the man abandoned the attempt to push her away from the settle. He lifted his hand and dealt her a stinging blow on the side of the face. It jarred her to her heels, so that her hands dropped from the settle and she staggered.

The sailors let out some hilarious cries.

Now, in no time at all, he would have her through the door; he was reaching for her again. He clutched a handful of the cloak; she twisted out of it, leaving it in his hand, and darted across the room, ducked under the counter flap and came up beside the fat man.

"Help me, please," she gasped. "He's drunk."

The sailor came, lurching and cursing, up to the counter, and the fat man proved to be more of a champion than she had dared to hope. Leaning forward he said,

"Leave her be, Jack. She's nothing but a kid! You go get yourself——"

The sailor broke in, violently. Of all he said Julia only understood, "You mind your own bloody business, Fatty," "cheating little bitch" and "wreck the place."

The last words were taken up by the four sailors at the table. The fat man looked frightened.

It was one of the hard-eyed women who saved the situation.

She got up and walked down the room, swinging her hips and holding her head high. She slipped her hand under the sailor's arm and said,

"You can do better'n *that*, Jack. What good's a green girl to you? You come along with me."

Astoundingly he stopped cursing, blinked and grinned and let himself be led away.

"Now you . . ." said the fat man, with a look of annoyance, and then a disbelieving stare. . . . "For Christ's sake," he said, "it's a Klopstock girl!"

CHAPTER XI

She stayed in the Klopstock Home for almost two years more but she never lived down the escapade. Juffrouw Hoorne, who had always disliked her, had been made to look silly and careless. As long as Juffrouw Hoorne remembered, Julia would have good cause to remember also—and regret.

After that all the most repulsive tasks, the heaviest punishments, were hers. She spent a good deal of time locked in the cellar—popularly supposed to be haunted by the ghost of a girl who, it was whispered, had been locked in there and forgotten until she starved to death. She was almost invariably prevented, on some excuse or another, from going on the daily walk, which was the one break in the long day's monotony, and the days on which she went supperless to bed far outnumbered the others.

It was a life which must either harden or break any nature, and something in Julia refused to be broken. In the cellar it was cold and damp and dark, but if there was a ghost Julia never saw it, and it was peaceful there. And who wanted to go on those stupid, deadly dull walks? Not she! The loss of supper, by this time, did matter rather more, but you could always pretend that it didn't. And when Juffrouw Hoorne, in desperation, took to caning you could always remember that blow from the drunken sailor's fist and take this pain—less because it had no emotional accompaniment—with an unflinching grimness which, quite plainly, made the Juffrouw more angry than ever.

She remembered how the sailor had hit her, how the fat man had half-heartedly befriended and then betrayed her, and how she had been turned away from all those doors, how the very children had jeered, and her cynicism reached out and embraced all the outer world. The process had begun when Geertruida had ignored her pleadings not to be sent here; it had been delayed by her certainty that if only she could get out of this hateful place things would be better; it had been completed by that brief excursion into the world.

Everybody, everywhere, was an enemy. You walked warily, outwitted the enemy when you could and when you could not bore the penalties as though they meant nothing. You hoped for nothing and cared for nobody.

It took a little girl named Katje to change all that.

Katje was brought in by a kind-hearted old market woman who had seen her begging amongst the stalls by day and sleeping in an upturned barrel at night.

Katje knew her name and that she had once had shoes, which some other children had taken away—and that was about all. Juffrouw Hoorne, experienced in such matters, said that she thought she was about five years old and had been homeless for a long time.

She was as pretty as a doll, with a china-white face and black eyes and a mop of black curls which could not be dragged back into the regulation hair-dress because they were so short.

She was not, however, at all pretty when she came in; she was caked with filth and smelt so horrible that the task of cleaning her was naturally one for Julia Maire.

By the time she had cleaned her, Julia, without knowing it, had fallen in love with Katje, who had, most marvellously, fallen in love with the Klopstock Home.

"Got shoes again!" she said, with wondering delight, as Julia helped her into a pair of tiny shoes, clumped and re-clumped on the soles, patched and repatched on the uppers. (Shoes were a problem. Juffrouw Klopstock realised that clogs cost less and wore better, but they made such a noise!)

For the first time Julia saw the purpose of the Orphanage, and realised that although to her it had always been a hateful place, to such as Katje it was indeed what its proper name implied, a refuge. How horrible the poor little thing's life must have been.

She was on her knees, helping on the shoes, and she looked up, her eyes level with the child's.

"You must be very *good*," she said seriously. "If you're very good and do just what you're told, you'll be all right here."

Katje was, for several days, not merely all right but blissfully happy. Three times a day she encountered, with positive enjoyment, food which, whatever its deficiencies by ordinary stand-ards, was wonderful when compared with what could be begged or picked up in the market after the stalls had been cleared away. She rapidly put on flesh, as many poor children did im-mediately after admission. It was a fact noted and reported upon by Juffrouw Klopstock every year.

For a week, at the risk of breaking rules and incurring wrath, Julia watched over Katje, told her what to do and what not to do, forestalled the tricks always played on any newcomer, and eased her into the life of the place. On the morning when boredom overtook Katje, Julia was in the laundry where she spent most of her time, and her protégée was in the kitchen.

Juffrouw Hoorne had found a simple little job for Katje. She had to grate some salt from a block and then pound it until it was fine enough for use.

There were several other girls there, working away in the near-Trappist silence that the rules demanded. Katje, bored with her job, tried to talk, and was hushed, frowned upon, ignored; later on she would be reported as well, but that she did not know. She was determined to make the others notice her, so she proceeded to show off the simple tricks which had often gained her an apple, a cake or even a small coin in the market place. She turned some expert somersaults, walked on her hands, clapping her feet, and with her hands round her ankles and her head tucked between her knees rolled over and over like a ball. The other girls gave way to temptation and watched, and Katje worked harder. Juffrouw Hoorne, entering the kitchen, found the pudding saucepan boiled dry, and the bread which had been set to rise on the hearth brimming, forgotten, over the edge of the wooden trough. The girls were watching, wide-eyed, while Katje stood on one leg, the other stuck out at right-angles, arms at full length and shoulder level, as she spun round on one toe. The mortar in which she should have been pounding salt was balanced on her head.

Juffrouw Hoorne cried "Stop" in a terrible voice, and Katje did stop, so suddenly that the mortar lost balance and fell, and smashed a dish full of sliced apples for Juffrouw Klopstock's pie. The apples were smothered with salt.

"You naughty, naughty, *naughty* little girl," said Juffrouw Hoorne, seizing Katje by the arm and administering, with each "naughty" a sound smack on the ear. Katje had often suffered similar attacks during her short life and she defended herself as she had learned to do. She ducked her head and set her sharp little teeth into Juffrouw Hoorne's thumb—that loosened the clasp, and kicked her in the shins—that delayed pursuit, and then she ran behind the table and stood poised to dodge when pursued.

"It was just like dealing with a wild animal," said Juffrouw Hoorne to Juffrouw Klopstock over the chocolate cups that evening. She wore a conspicuous bandage on the injured thumb and would have been prepared to show, at the slightest hint of sympathy, the bruise on her shin.

"How unpleasant. Where is she now?"

"In the cellar. And not quelled yet; she screamed and banged on the door for hours. A most truculent girl!"

A slight look of uneasiness crossed the Superintendent's placid pink face.

"Neighbours," she reminded Juffrouw Hoorne, "always expect places like this to have a torture chamber. If they hear screaming . . . We don't want any scandal, do we, Klara?"

No sympathy, no support. Criticism, direct or implied, all the time.

"I shouldn't think even old Kinker would expect me to be bitten and the little ferret to go unpunished. I said she should stay there until tomorrow evening, but of course if you'd prefer to deal with her yourself. . . ."

"Good gracious. I shouldn't have the faintest idea what to do. Anyway, she's quiet now, isn't she?"

No sound reached this cosy room, but in the passage at the other end of the house as she went to her bed Juffrouw Hoorne could hear noise coming from the cellar. It was muted by distance and indistinct, but she knew that in the street it would be much more audible. Despite her bold, scornful words about Mynheer Kinker, she did not want a neighbour or passer-by running to him and saying that shocking things must go on in the Klopstock Home, for she knew who would be left to bear the blame. She went to her room, selected her stoutest cane, and carrying it, the cellar key and candlestick, descended the stairs again.

The cellar door lay at the far end of the laundry passage. The yelling and the banging, which had grown louder as she approached, had died down before she reached the passage; when she turned into it she could hear another voice, speaking in a firm, soothing tone.

". . . I can't. I haven't the key. But I'll stay and keep you company. I'm here, right outside the door, as close as I can get."

It was being locked in that Katje minded; company and being talked to did little to lessen the wild panic that possessed

her. She began again to scream, "Let me out, let me out," and
beat on the door.

"Katje! you *mustn't* make that noise. You'll be punished
more. Katje, please . . . Oh."

Julia had seen the light, and behind it Juffrouw Hoorne. She
was startled, but almost immediately calm again. She had
broken Heaven knew how many rules, and she would be punished, but none of that mattered now. She broke another rule
by addressing Juffrouw Hoorne without permission.

"Oh, please, Juffrouw, let her out. She can't bear it. She's
going mad."

"Be silent," said Juffrouw Hoorne. She set the candlestick
on a stone slab near the door and beat on the door with the
cane.

"Be quiet, in there!" she shouted. "If you keep making that
noise you will *never* come out! You'll stay there until you are
quiet. Do you hear me?"

Katje gave several staccato screams and then fell to whimpering.

"When you have been quiet for a whole day I shall let you
out. If you make a sound, I shan't."

The whimpering, now and again rising to a hysterical scream,
went on.

"I can still hear you!" said Juffrouw Hoorne.

"She can't help it," Julia said. "She'll go mad. Please, please,
Juffrouw, punish her some other way."

Juffrouw Hoorne had come down with the half-intention of
letting Katje out, caning her thoroughly, and sending her to
bed; now a fatal obstinacy rose and overmastered her. That
Julia Maire, of all people should be telling her what to do!

"You'd do better to begin thinking about your own punishment!" she said with venomous relish.

"I don't mind what you do to me, Juffrouw, if you'll just let
Katje out. She can't bear to be locked up. She'll go mad."

"She will stay there until she is quiet. I've said so and I mean
it."

"Then I shall fetch Juffrouw Klopstock."

In the whole history of the Klopstock Home no one had ever dreamed of approaching the Superintendent except by order or invitation at any time; and it was now ten o'clock at night. The foundations of Juffrouw Hoorne's solid little world rocked, quite literally; for half a second everything went black and moved sharply sideways. She thought again about the possibility of a stroke.

She opened her mouth to say: You wouldn't dare! But Julia had already turned and was walking away along the passage, a ridiculous, yet purposeful figure in her too-short, skimpy nightgown and bare feet. Juffrouw Hoorne took two swift steps and caught hold of the looped-up plait which offered itself as a convenient handle at the back of her head. She jerked at it savagely, turning Julia about and at the same time giving her two cuts with the cane. Pulling at the soft, firmly braided hair gave her a feeling of mastery, a vicious pleasure.

"You insolent little bastard," she said between her teeth.

Julia bent and bucked and writhed, trying to free her head. Juffrouw Hoorne, held on and raised the cane again. The key of the cellar door jerked from her hand and fell with a clatter to the stone floor.

Then Julia went mad; she wrestled with the Juffrouw, she pushed her; she hit her with clenched fists. She stepped by accident on the key, and kept her bare foot on it. Then she gave Juffrouw Hoorne one last mighty shove which carried her some distance along the passage, and stooping, picked up the key.

"Give me that! Give me that key!"

"I'm going to let Katje out and take her straight to Juffrouw Klopstock," Julia gasped.

Juffrouw Hoorne made as though she would come to grips again, and then thought better of it. The girl was mad, dangerous; nothing but madness could have given that frail-looking body such strength.

"Very well," she said. "I shouldn't like to be you, in the morning. That's all."

Julia put the key in the door and turned it. The door opened outwards, and was heavy. The strength which had enabled her to grapple with Juffrouw Hoorne had gone; she had to exert all that was left to open the door at all.

Katje lay crouched on the top step, silent now, and as the door opened she sprang towards it, almost unbalancing Julia. At the same moment Juffrouw Hoorne pushed the door from the outside. Its swing caught both Julia and Katje, thrust them inwards and downwards. They rolled to the bottom of the cellar stairs together, and above them the key turned again.

CHAPTER XII

". . . so there they are, both locked in the cellar. And what I want to know now is what are we going to do with them."

It was the first time that "we" had been used in such a context and Juffrouw Klopstock lost no time in countering the suggestion it conveyed.

"I should suggest that you give the small one a thorough whipping and find some humiliating punishment for the other."

"Do you realise that she was coming to disturb you? Past ten o'clock at night."

"I should have tried to settle things without—I trust—indulging in a bout of fisticuffs."

The red colour ran over Juffrouw Hoorne's face. Really, it was maddening; the effort to keep her temper in the face of such provocation made her quite dizzy.

"What I want to know is--how am I going to get them *out* of the cellar. Both those girls attacked me yesterday. I'm not going alone to release them and I can't take another girl to witness what may well be a scene."

"No," said Juffrouw Klopstock, sensibly. "I see that. I will come with you myself, as soon as I am dressed. Dear me, how very tiresome! And I always thought your discipline was so good!"

The release was an anti-climax; they emerged meekly enough. Katje, who had spent the night curled up against Julia, and who was fully dressed, had suffered little damage except that she had beaten her hands raw by hammering on the door. Julia, thrust into the cellar in her night-gown, was in a palsied rigor from cold and quite speechless from the chattering of her teeth. One of the blows from the cane had broken the skin just above her eyebrow.

"You take the little one, Klara. I'll deal with this," said Juffrouw Klopstock, and moving more quickly than she had done for many a year, she took Julia to the laundry and made her get into one of the tubs of warm water and kept her there, with a girl bringing fresh hot water to add to the bath, until the rigors grew less violent. She then told her to go and get into bed, and a few minutes afterwards came to the bedroom herself, followed by an orphan carrying a bowl of steaming hot porridge.

"Don't imagine," she said coldly, "that I'm overlooking your behaviour. You acted like a wild savage and I am completely disgusted with you. You haven't heard the last of this, by far."

It was a pity that Juffrouw Hoorne was not present when that speech was made; she was, actully, enjoying the sight of two big girls forcing Katje's raw hands into a bowl of hot salt water. She did not know what Juffrouw Klopstock had said, only what she had done—which was to treat Julia as though she were sick. She brooded over that for the rest of the morning and all through the midday meal, and immediately afterwards climbed the stairs and for the second time that day intruded upon the Superintendent's privacy.

Juffrouw Klopstock sat in a cushioned chair with her small

neat feet on a stool; she was stitching at the embroidery which occupied so many of her idle hours.

"Well, Klara," she said and raised her eyebrows.

"About Julia Maire . . ."

A glimmer of concern showed in Juffrouw Klopstock's pink face.

"Is she . . ."

"Oh, she'll be all right. She's very well. Bathed and put to bed and coddled! What I want to know——"

"You saw the state she was in. I only took sensible precautions. We didn't want her ill, did we?"

"I don't want her, well or ill. That's what I've come about. She's fourteen. Two years ago she was unmanageable, but I have tried. I've tried very hard. You don't know what trouble I've had. But I don't intend to have any more. She struck me. . . . Now there she lies, lolling in bed, and when the others go to bed, *think* what a tale she'll have to tell! Before we know where we are every girl in the place will be hitting me to get a plate of porridge!"

Juffrouw Klopstock saw the funny side of that, and laughed.

Something, stretched tighter and tighter inside Juffrouw Hoorne, tighter every day over all these years, snapped.

"That's right. Laugh. All these years I've played your silly game so you could pretend to be a lady. I've done all the work and taken all the blame while you had the money and the praise. I'm sick of it, do you hear me, sick to my bones. Every way I turn you get the better of me. Because that little bitch hit me, you take her side. Let me tell you this—unless she's out of this house this very day, I shall be. And then you'll know!"

Yes, she would. Juffrouw Klopstock, successfully deceiving so many people, seldom deceived herself. She knew Klara's value exactly. She used her hard, goaded her . . . but that meant nothing. It was like whipping a donkey: that didn't mean that the donkey had no value.

And out of the whole tirade she picked the single item about which something could be done.

"She shall go this very day," she said firmly. "My dear Klara, if I had known you felt so strongly . . . that she'd given you such trouble, I'd have got rid of her long ago."

Juffrouw Hoorne was conscious of an odd feeling of deflation.

"What will you do with her?"

"That I don't know . . . yet. But I shall think of something."

"Get up," Juffrouw Klopstock said, quite pleasantly. "Dress as far as your petticoat and then come to my room. And be quick."

The short November day was dying. A sad grey light lay in the bedroom, and in the passages; but Juffrouw Klopstock's room was warm and light.

"Now, let me look at you. That cut on your face . . . something will have to be done about *that*. Loosen your hair."

When she turned back to Julia she held a pair of scissors in her hand.

"Stand still," she said, and snipped, pulling the clipped ends forward. "That hides it well. Now, let us see." She turned to two dresses which hung over a chair. One was blue sprigged with little flowers; the other was grey with bands of purple. Juffrouw Klopstock held them up, measuring them against Julia.

"Fortunately you're tall. How old are you, I forget."

"Fourteen last Midsummer Day."

"You forget too. It was fifteen. The blue suits you better but the other makes you look ol—your age. Put it on. Now, listen carefully to what I have to say. . . .

"You've been a very wicked, ungrateful girl. You know that, don't you? And you deserve to be punished, severely. But in this world people don't always get what they deserve. If you are careful, and clever . . . we may arrange something for you which will be much better than you deserve. When you're spoken to, speak up. And smile. Try to look as lively and attractive as possible. We're going out and I wish to be *proud* of you."

She stepped back and regarded Julia critically. She looks very delicate, she thought with some dissatisfaction, far too slender —but girls often are at that age, you can't grow both ways, and she *is* tall. And she's graceful too, and hasn't, thank God, that cowed look. I may manage it.

"You're really very pretty," she said, bracingly. "You may look at yourself in my glass if you like. Now, smile—you see what an improvement that is."

"Juffrouw, may I speak?"

"Of course. Oh, forget that ridiculous rule. I want you to be *natural*."

"Where am I going?"

"Out. I am making a great effort to arrange something for you. For your future. You realise, I suppose, that you can't remain here after last night's . . . performance."

"Oh," Julia said and her pallor warmed a little. "Juffrouw, is it a job?"

"You could call it that. But you must have some training first and you must seem suitable for it. Here is a cloak. When we arrive, push back the hood, but keep that short curl well forward—if that mark is seen you'll be asked how you came by it and that would be quite fatal."

Juffrouw Klopstock put on her own cloak, a fine one lined and edged with fur.

Along the Herrencanal the lanterns by the doorways were being lighted and a thin rime of frost glittered on the roadway and on the leafless trees. Juffrouw Klopstock set a brisk pace. They took the turning down which Julia had stolen on that ill-fated afternoon, and, avoiding the street where the children had jeered, emerged, from a different side, into the square where she had tried in vain to find work. After that their road was different, though in the same general direction, but they stopped short of the harbour and finally turned into a well-

lighted street of tall houses, of which every ground floor was
occupied by an office. Through many lighted windows Julia
could see the long desks and high stools occupied by frantically
scribbling clerks.

They turned in at a doorway. Twelve heads were raised,
twelve pairs of eyes stared. The clerk on the nearest stool slid
to the ground and came forward and said,

"Yes, Mevrouw?"

"I'm Juffrouw Klopstock, of the Klopstock Home. I should
like to speak to Mynheer Dekker." Her manner, here in this
strange place, was as easy and authoritative as in the Orphanage; Julia noticed that with admiration, for she was herself embarrassed by all the staring eyes.

The clerk hurried away and came back.

"You wait here, Julia. Possibly someone could find you a
seat."

The clerk offered his own stool, and Julia, blushing, sat down
on it, folding her hands in her lap while Juffrouw Klopstock
followed up the long room and through a door.

She was gone a long time; then at last the door opened again
and there she was in the doorway, smiling and beckoning.

They all looked again as Julia walked the length of the room,
so she arrived in Mynheer Dekker's presence pink-cheeked and
with that air of shyness which, on a young girl, is like the bloom
on a grape.

"Ah yes," said Mynheer, "I see what you mean."

"Julia, this is Mynheer Dekker."

She made him the curtsey which Maire had taught her so
long ago, and remembering Juffrouw Klopstock's admonition,
smiled at him.

"Good afternoon, my dear," he said, smiling at her. "I trust
you are well. Do you enjoy good health?"

"Oh, yes, Mynheer. I'm never ill."

"Splendid. And you are fifteen years of age?"

"Yes, Mynheer."

He studied her attentively. He had small, very bright brown

eyes in a clean-shaven, rather yellowish face. He looked kind and she thought that she would like to work for him. So she smiled again with innocent seductiveness.

He made a little noise of assent, "Um-m-m."

"It seemed to me such a pity, such a waste," said Juffrouw Klopstock.

"I must say she does you great credit. And so does your concern. I hope she realises . . ."

"Oh, I told her nothing. It would have been unkind to risk the disappointment."

"We can consider the matter settled," he said.

"You have done me a great favour, Mynheer."

"No, no. On the contrary, Juffrouw. There are plenty of girls, but so few suitable. Things have changed very much lately; the demand has increased and the type of demand has changed too."

"That is largely due to you, Mynheer," said Juffrouw Klopstock sweetly.

Mynheer pooh-poohed that but he was obviously pleased.

"And I may leave her now? There would be so much envy . . ."

"I'll take her round to Mevrouw Helmers myself."

Juffrouw Klopstock rose.

"Julia," she said, taking one of the girl's hands, "you are a very very lucky girl. You are going to be a Company's Daughter —the most fortunate thing that could happen to a girl in your position. I hope you'll be very happy, and very good," she gave the hand a little conspiratorial squeeze as she spoke the last word.

Julia was confused, she knew nothing about the Company's Daughters or the nature of the good fortune which had overtaken her; but that, for the moment hardly mattered at all. She was out of the Klopstock Home; and it was the Juffrouw's doing. She raised the hand which held hers and kissed it and said,

"Oh thank you, Juffrouw. Thank you." And Juffrouw Klopstock took her into an embrace which was surprisingly soft and

warm, and said with an emotion that seemed entirely sincere,
"Goodbye, my dear. I know you'll be happy. Bless you!"

Their parting made quite an impression upon Mynheer
Dekker, who, like most people, had heard several contradictory
stories about Juffrouw Klopstock's management.

That evening Juffrouw Klopstock was very pleased with herself and with the day's arrangements. Julia had done her great
credit and for a long time the faintest hint of criticism could
be met by the incontrovertible remark that it wasn't everybody
who could turn a Klopstock orphan into a fit candidate for the
Company's Daughters' Home.

She also looked forward to telling Juffrouw Hoorne the news.
She had not forgotten the extremely rude and rebellious things
Klara had said. She had ignored them at the time, but she remembered. Now Klara would be annoyed to hear that Julia,
her enemy, was so well placed, and Juffrouw Klopstock would
be able to say in a soft, innocent voice, "But you told me she
must go—what else could I do with her?" That would teach
Klara to issue ultimatums.

The soft, innocent remark was never to be made.

Juffrouw Klopstock said, as she poured the chocolate, that
she had got rid of Julia Maire, and Juffrouw Hoorne asked
where she had gone and Juffrouw Klopstock told her.

"Y . . ." said Juffrouw Hoorne, and her mouth seemed to
slip sideways. "Y . . . y . . . y . . ." she said. Her head shook;
the chocolate cup danced in its saucer and then fell to the floor.
"Y . . . y . . . y," she cried accusingly as the red mist closed
down.

The stroke she had so often expected smote her to the floor.

Juffrouw Klopstock had given her donkey one whack too
many.

CHAPTER XIII

Her time in the Home for Company's Daughters was very brief, only a year and a few days long, and, in the sense that it was extremely happy, with every day's passing a thing of regret, it seemed very short; in the sense of experience and education, it seemed very long.

There was a great deal to learn.

"You *must* learn to read and write and reckon," Mevrouw Helmers would say. "A wife who can do so is a help to her husband, and improves her own status. Look around and ask yourselves what women count for most in this world—the wives of small shopkeepers who understand and help with their husbands' businesses. They are indispensable and the men know it. I want *you* to be indispensable to your husbands!"

"You *must* learn about illnesses and how to deal with accidents. Where you are going there won't be a doctor on the nearest corner and a midwife in the next street. And if your husband is a nutmeg planter you may find yourself responsible for slaves as well as for your family."

"You *must* learn deportment. Girls of very good family go out to the Islands now and when you are married you must be prepared to meet them on their own ground. We can't have your husbands making unfavourable comparisons."

"You *must* learn to occupy your free time. Life in the Islands can be idle for white women, and it can be lonely. Your husbands will have their work and their interests."

She never for a moment allowed the girls to lose sight of their destiny. They were Company's Daughters, being trained to make good, acceptable wives for the Dutchmen who lived in the Molucca Islands and grew nutmegs and cloves for the Company's trade.

The system was an old one. It had begun in the days when few girls would voluntarily face the long sea-voyage—seven months of it, at least—and spend the rest of their lives in exile; the white men then had been glad of wives of any kind. Then there had been a middle period, when the nutmeg growers had made great fortunes and—as Mevrouw Helmers said—quite important families had been willing to spare a daughter to be the wife of a nutmeg "prince." Then there was a slight social slur in being a Company's Daughter, or the husband of one. But the private arrangements, generally made by ships' captains acting as go-betweens between distant husbands and greedy families in Holland, had not always worked out well; several plain girls, disagreeable girls, sickly girls, had been shipped out. Mynheer Dekker, who in his young days had spent many years in the Islands, had known several small tragedies, and when he came home and was elected to the management of the Company's Home he had put into practice a scheme of his own. The Daughters were now all picked girls, and properly trained; and they were not sent out, as in the earlier days, just anyhow and to anybody. Negotiations must be conducted, credentials produced, and in most cases the formal marriage by proxy—known as a Glove Marriage—was performed with as much ceremony for an orphan girl as for one of good family.

Mynheer Dekker fully deserved the little compliment Juffrouw Klopstock had paid him.

He had chosen well in making Mevrouw Helmers head of the establishment; she had also lived in the Islands, where her husband had been a low-grade clerk. That she had then been, and still was, Mynheer Dekker's mistress, though it had affected his choice to some degree did not make it less a wise one. She was shrewd and practical, knowledgeable and kind.

In all ways, except one—and that vital—she did prepare the girls for their futures; she spoke of "your husband" in a sensible and realistic fashion; but she shared the prevailing view that "innocence" in a bride was no drawback. She had been a very innocent bride herself, believing that babies were got by kissing. Learning otherwise had done her no harm at all; in fact the lesson had pleased her so much that in the end she had practised it "out of school" as it were. She believed that it was a lesson which nobody but a husband *could* teach a girl. It wasn't a thing that could be talked about, there were no words, except rude ones.

The girls, of course, were not innocent at all and the words in which enlightenment was spread would have shocked Mevrouw Helmers very much indeed, as much almost as the discovery that her relationship with Mynheer Dekker was common, though secret, knowledge.

A very pretty, jolly, friendly girl named Frieda was Julia's mentor in this matter, and a promising friendship died untimely. From the evening when Frieda "told" until she sailed in January for the Moluccas, Julia had to avoid her because she couldn't bear to look at, or touch her.

She thought it was all intensely horrible. As Frieda ripped away the veil she saw again the face of the sailor who had pretended to be kind, the face of the woman who had led him away. "So that was it!" she thought with sick disgust. *Now*, because Frieda's pretty lips were shaping to them, she understood some of the words he had used when he had abused her.

So that was it. Jolly Mevrouw Helmers and kind Mynheer Dekker, too. Aunt Geertruida and Uncle Johannes. *Quite* unbelievable; and horrible, horrible!

Curiously enough, side by side with this deep revulsion against the physical side of the man-and-woman business, she developed an interest in, a yearning for, something called "love."

Mevrouw Helmers thought girls should be able to read, should take delight in reading, and she read to them, and gave them to read, the kind of story most likely to provoke avid perusal. In these, pairs of lovers figured prominently: two French ones, oh and a very sad story, Heloise and Abelard; two

Italians, and what a tragedy, Romeo and Juliet; two English, long ago but still achingly sad, Tristram and Iseult.

Julia saw them, clean, brightly yet delicately coloured, made of china, moving stiffly against a background of trees and flowers; the young men carried papers upon which they had written poems, the young women walked along with fawns pushing their noses into their hands. They spoke, they said, "I love you. I love you," but their words had nothing to do with *that!* Sometimes they touched hands. In such an interchange Julia would gladly have taken part, with a young man, tall and slim, with yellow hair and blue eyes, a younger Uncle Johannes.

That was "love." But Mevrouw Helmers never spoke of that. She said, "your husband," and every time she said it—once Frieda had explained things—Julia saw the drunken sailor, felt his slushy kiss and the weight of his arm.

Being a Company's Daughter was pleasant indeed, but it was a short-lived business, a mere prelude to something else— and very often, when she looked into the future Julia wished that Juffrouw Klopstock had sent her to the fish saltings.

Mevrouw Helmers had a very clear-cut idea of what the prospective brides should know about their duties, but in many other matters concerning the Moluccas and the life there, she was curiously vague. Listening to her might make one believe that the Islands, except for the nutmegs and the slaves—and, of course, the husbands—were not so much unlike the Dutch countryside. Her brisk, practical nature was not one equipped to absorb atmosphere and then, years later, to convey it by spoken words.

The girls currently under the Home's tuition had therefore a choice of two pictures when it came to throwing their thoughts forward to their future home. There was Mevrouw's—rather ordinary and unexciting, a Dutch landscape with nutmeg trees, some dark-skinned slaves and "your husband" superimposed upon it; and there was the one composed of rumour, truthful reports, products of overstrained imaginations, of old sailors' tales, ancient letters, things overheard—and that was a picture of a nightmare paradise. This was the one which the girls held up to one another, with shudders, with delight, with yearning, with dread foreboding. They whispered of slave revolts, of nutmeg planters and their families wiped out in one night of fire and rapine and slaughter; they told of a mountain which spouted fire and sent streams of red-hot molten metal pouring through groves and houses; there were bats as large as rats which drank your blood as you slept; there were frogs in your shoes and snakes in your bed, sharks in the sea and crocodiles in the rivers. Even cannibalism was not overlooked. But there were also the flowers—twelve inches across, some of them, and of such fragrance that if you smelled them too close you swooned; there were fruits of a flavour unimaginable; there was unending leisure, if you had a baby you did not even have to carry it in your arms, a brown slave did that; there were parties every evening, picnics every day; just to be white in the Islands conferred such status that the humblest Dutch woman lived like, and was treated like, a Queen.

Against this colourful and contradictory background were set the individual stories of things that had happened to other Daughters of the Company. There was the girl who sailed in a ship that was attacked by the Moorish pirates and who was sent as a present to the Grand Turk, in whose harem she ended her days; the girl who went to Java and whose husband hated her on sight, made her get into some kind of bath which dyed her brown, and sent her out to work amongst his slaves; the girl who was married to a clerk in the Company's office, but was so beautiful that a rich planter persuaded the clerk to exchange her for the best plantation in Macassar.

Nothing too unlikely; nothing too fantastic. Yet some healthy scepticism, some optimistic selection, must have been at work, even as, with an accompaniment of shudders and little screams, the tales went round; for most of the girls looked forward with impatience to the time when they should embark into the unknown. The horror stories had the thrill, the fascination, of stories of ghosts or bloody murder, but you could never seriously imagine that you, yourself, would play a part in such a drama. Other people saw ghosts, other people were murdered; not you. Stories of the delights of the Islands had, on the whole, a rather more personal application; most of the girls did look forward to a life of leisure, of wealth, of happy marriage and motherhood. Shivering on a cold winter's day they would speak of the delights of living in perpetual summer; doing the household tasks that they shared they would say how wonderful never to wash a dish, scrub a floor, scour a saucepan, again. Brown hands to labour for them were a certainty. So, also, were new dresses; the least self-assured girl was positive that, given a husband, she could find ways of making him give her pretty clothes.

Julia never really saw either picture of the Islands, was never much affected by the threats or the promises of the future; when she looked forward she saw one thing only—"your husband."

And so the weeks sped on; and the months; inescapable, relentless as death, the future advanced.

One day in November, a mild, mist-moisted day, she and a girl named Marie with whom she had made a pleasant but carefully-not-intimate friendship were in the garden, cutting the very last roses of an unusually protracted season.

"And I hope," said Marie, snipping the last bud, "that next time I gather roses it will be in my own garden."

"Do roses grow there—in the Islands?"

"Yes, all the year round," said Marie happily. "Think of it, no winter. . . ."

Mevrouw Helmers opened a window and called them. They went in, their hands full of the damp flowers, drops of moisture clinging to their hair and their eyelashes. They made a pretty pair, Marie all ebony and ivory and rose, Julia leaf-brown and cream and grey. Mynheer Dekker, who was in the room with Mevrouw Helmers, looked at them with a kind of wistful lechery. He put out one of his brown-speckled hands and touched both their heads, remarking upon the dampness of their hair, to cover the gesture. Then he remarked upon the flowers,

"And you look just as sweet and fresh," he said.

Mevrouw Helmers watched, without jealousy. They came and went, an endless line of them, pretty young things with all their troubles still to come. Hers—and she had known trouble—were over, she rested easily in a relationship which was as worn and easy as an old shoe.

On the table stood a package which had been opened and then just folded together again, and a bottle of Rhenish wine and four glasses.

"Well, shall I tell them, or will you?" asked Mevrouw Helmers.

"I can guess!" Marie cried, clutching the roses to her breast. "*It's our turn!*"

"They just live for the day," said Mevrouw Helmers. "Yes, it's your turn, Marie, and yours, Julia. And I may as well say at once that you are both very lucky girls."

"Both Glove Marriages," said Mynheer Dekker with an air of personal achievement.

"When?" demanded Marie.

"At the end of this month."

"There you are, Julia. I said I hoped the next rose I cut would be from my own garden. And it will! Oh, Mevrouw, who is he?"

"I must be off," said Mynheer Dekker. "I'll just drink to your happiness and then you can know all the details."

Mevrouw Helmers began to pour out the wine. Marie turned to Mynheer Dekker and said, prettily,

"Mynheer, will *you* be our proxy?"

"I shall give myself that melancholy pleasure," he said, and took the proffered glass and swung his beaming smile around. The dark girl, bless her, was all right, flushed and sparkling, her ordinary youthful prettiness transformed into beauty by the glow of excitement . . . but the other looked as though she had received a mortal blow. And, of course, it *was* a step in the dark, disguise it how you would. He caught Mevrouw Helmers' eye, flicked a significant glance at Julia and was reassured by a nod. All that sort of thing could be left in her capable hands. He raised his glass,

"To your future, my dears, may it be happy and prosperous!"

They drank and he left, and before he was well out of the room Marie said,

"May we look?"

"Certainly not. How would you know which was which? Since you are so impatient I'll deal with you first. Here you are. . . ." She handed Marie a buff-coloured glove, made for the left hand, its cuff embroidered with scarlet silk, "You are to marry Hendrik Oltman, who is twenty-six years of age, and a clerk in the Agent's office in Banda Neira. He has good prospects and his disposition is said to be amiable. I congratulate you." She added quickly, "Oh no! You mustn't try it on, that brings bad luck; glove on, wedding off, did you never hear that?"

"I think it will fit me," said Marie, measuring the glove against her hand. "And smell it! Doesn't it smell lovely? Hendrik Oltman. I like that name. Marie Oltman . . ."

"I'm glad that you are pleased. And now for Julia."

It was a glove of yellow silk with pearls sewn in a pattern on its gauntlet. "Isn't that pretty? Well, take it, dear. It's for you. Your husband is named Pieter Vosmar and he is twenty-two. His father has a nutmeg plantation on a little island called Rua. You are to be congratulated, too."

"Isn't it wonderful?" said Marie, and Mevrouw sensibly allowed her to speak for them both.

"Run along," she said, "show off your gloves and make the others envious. This is your day; theirs will come."

Julia carried her glove straight to her bedroom and there, with a shudder of distaste, pushed her hand into it, grimacing at her own credulity as she did so. Once, she supposed, somebody had tried on her glove and then not been married after all; that was how such superstitions began. Nevertheless she was missing no chance!

The next few days were very trying. Everything centred upon the wedding, everybody shared in the preparations. You were never allowed for one moment to forget that you were a bride-to-be. If it were forgotten for a moment Marie would say or do something to bring it back into focus and somebody was sure to add, "And Julia too!" Behind Marie's gaiety her own glumness passed, she thought, unnoticed, but Mevrouw Helmers had seen it and was not surprised—or worried—when, one evening, a mere five days before the wedding, Julia came to her room and asked if she might speak with her.

The thing she had come to say, and which seemed so easy, and sensible, and simple, when she tried it over in her mind, wasn't easy at all. Mevrouw was sewing—on the wedding clothes—and she looked up with a bright kind smile which seemed the very epitome of the general mood, a mood in which she alone could not share.

"Mevrouw, I don't want to be married."

Mevrouw Helmers hesitated, while she decided between several possible replies and then laughed,

"Oh," she said, "the *times* I've heard that, here in this very room!"

It was clever. It removed Julia's sense of being different, of being unsuited for marriage.

"Oh. I didn't know anybody else ever felt that way."

"Bless you child; everybody's felt the way we do about everything. The world is pretty old, you know. I've prepared dozens of girls for marriage and they took it in one of two ways; either, like Marie, they couldn't wait for the day, or they insisted that they'd rather be dead. And do you know, so far as I can make out, they were as happy, or happier than the others. Sit down, Julia and tell me what's in your mind. You'd rather be dead, is that it?"

"I wondered whether Betta couldn't go instead of me. She's longing to be married."

"Now that, at least, is an original idea. Nobody ever suggested that before. Betta cannot, she must wait her turn. She's only fifteen."

"So am I."

A single question and answer elucidated that little mystery. Mevrouw Helmers thought that Juffrouw Klopstock had done rather well.

"It's too late to do anything about that, now," she said. She put out her hand and tapped Julia's knee. "You forget all about that year, Julia, save it up until you're thirty-nine. Every woman hates her fortieth birthday and on the eve of yours you can give yourself a whole year for a present."

It was all so cosy, so feminine, so almost irresistible.

"I wish I were forty now. Then I'd be too old to go. Mevrouw, please, couldn't I stay here? I'd do a servant's work. Or go out and get a job." It was an echo of her pleadings with Aunt Geertruida.

"Now Julia, don't be tiresome," said Mevrouw Helmers, using the term which, in this easy-going little world, was extremely derogatory. "The arrangements have all been made. Even if I wanted to I couldn't send Betta in your place, she wouldn't be at all suitable. The Vosmar family is old and important; you don't realise how very fortunate you are. There are girls with good homes who would change places with you, gladly. *Naturally* you have doubts and fears. I've always found that a very good cure is to take the thing that is worrying you and look it straight in the face, and if possible talk it over with somebody of greater experience. Come along now, tell me exactly what is the trouble?"

The very thought of putting it into words made her face burn.

Mevrouw Helmers took up her sewing and made several stitches. Without looking up she said, "It's the . . . physical aspect, isn't it?" She took silence for assent. "I do *wish* you girls wouldn't pry and chatter, the blind leading the blind! When it comes you'll find it as natural as eating. That is true,

Julia. After all, men and women were made and put together in this world by the good God, and He never makes a mistake. Even this reluctance of yours isn't going to be wasted—you'll be all the more delighted when you find how wrong you were."

She spoke with sincerity and conviction, and Julia recognised the good sense of what she said. But . . .

"As for staying here and remaining unmarried," Mevrouw Helmers went on, "that's a fate I wouldn't wish on anybody. An unmarried woman, whoever she is, becomes in time a pitiable object. And you're so pretty; that young man will *adore* you. Look, you sew on this, it's for Marie, and I'll sew on yours. I want you both to look beautiful." She planted some sewing in Julia's lap and went on, "I know Mynheer Dekker isn't a very exciting proxy—I expect you girls think he's old and too fat; but he is so kind and so interested in you all, and so proud when it's a Glove Marriage, so I do want you both to look pretty . . . and happy. Try to look happy, to be happy, Julia. The years go by so quickly. . . ."

In her voice there was something of the wistfulness which had been in the old man's eyes when he looked at the girls with the flowers in their arms.

They sewed for the rest of the evening and Mevrouw Helmers chatted on, making it all sound safe and ordinary and quite, quite inevitable. As they put away their work she said, "Are you sleeping well? I thought not. Go and warm a cup of milk and bring it back here." When Julia returned Mevrouw had a little box in her hand; she opened it and took out a pinch of grey powder which, placed in the milk, instantly dissolved.

That night she slept heavily, and all the next day moved in a placid daze; nothing, not even her own hands and feet, seemed quite real. Mevrouw Helmers repeated the dose each evening until the wedding, and on that day not even Mynheer Dekker, very sprucely dressed and gallant in manner, helping them on with the gloves, kissing them and calling them by their new names, seemed quite real. But she was now Julia Vosmar, properly married, in the sight of God and man, to Pieter Vosmar whom she had never seen.

PART THREE

The Moluccas
1664-

CHAPTER I

They had seen the island of Banda and its little satellite islands come up out of the water, blue blurs which took on, as they watched, the shape and substance of reality. The smaller islands were out of sight now; the ship lay in Banda harbour with the town of Banda Neira, Marie's future home, directly ahead of them. There was the circle of houses and warehouses along the water-front, white and cream and yellow, and blue and pink and ochre-coloured, and behind it the massed roofs of many houses, and behind them a climbing sweep of green, rising up to a sharp conical peak, which, the captain had told them, was the Fire Mountain.

He had stood with them by the rail, pointing out things of interest. Then the "Trade's Advance" had stopped moving, coming to rest like a tired swan upon the clear, hyacinth blue water. And the boats had come shooting out from the shore, and he had gone away to meet the men who must see that there was no case of plague aboard, the men who had come for the mail, the Company's agent, Mynheer Aaden.

The two girls stood alone together, and Marie, who had looked forward so joyously and confidently to this moment, suddenly turned pale.

"I do hope he will like me . . . that I shall like him. I hadn't realised . . . You did, didn't you?" she asked, almost accusingly. "All along you knew how dreadful it would be."

"We shall soon know the worst," Julia said.

The Agent came aboard. He had brought two assistants with him, the good penman to make the cargo lists and the strong fellow to take charge of various boxes addressed to the Agent's wife.

To the latter he said, "Yes, I know you've got a wife aboard, and sorry you'll be, my boy. Don't let that take your mind off your duties; I've got a wife at home and she's waiting for what the Captain has brought—or God help him!"

"May I just take a moment to look at her, Mynheer?"

"You may," said the Agent, "but only a minute. You've got the rest of your life to look at her, God help *you*."

The girls saw him coming, shouldering his way along with unmistakable intensity of purpose.

"We should have worn our gloves," Marie said.

He saw them. One small and plump and dark; the other taller and fairer. His heart rose. He didn't give a damn which was which; he'd be happy with either, happy with both, given the chance.

Marie looked at him and hoped; Julia looked at him and feared. His thigh muscles bulged against the thin material of his tan-coloured breeches, black hair fuzzed at the opening of his shirt and along his bare forearms; beads of sweat stood on his broad sunburnt face. He was rather horribly like "your husband."

Just short of them he stopped and made a bow, clumsy to begin with and ruined by someone behind him brushing against his hindquarters. To keep his balance he had to take two steps forward, but as he straightened he smiled and said good-naturedly and somehow endearingly, "That *would* happen to me! May I bid you both welcome to Banda and ask which is Mevrouw Oltman?"

Marie said, "I am," and then he knew that she was the one he had favoured all along. He threw his great arms round her and hugged her. "Oh, I'm lucky," he said. "You're so pretty. I never thought you'd be so pretty."

"And you're handsome," Marie said.

Julia had taken a step away and stood looking at them. It was just right; exactly what Marie had expected and exactly what Mevrouw Helmers had foretold. The good God had made men and women and put them together. He'd made Marie and Hendrik and had—with a little help from the East India Company—brought them together and for them all was well. But for me . . . the man isn't born to whom I could take so instant a fancy . . . and somewhere here, somewhere very near now, a man is coming who will . . .

She felt sick and turned away and looked over the rail.

Coming in towards the ship's side, very noticeable amongst the other boats was one painted white with a yellow canopy. It was rowed by two brown men who wore short drawers of the same yellow and had metal collars around their necks. They brought the boat alongside, and one took hold of the ship's ladder. As he steadied the boat by his hold on the ladder and the other rower steadied it with his oar, a small man, dressed entirely in pale grey, came out from under the awning and began to climb.

"That must be somebody very important. What a fine boat!"

Julia was surprised to find Marie beside her.

"Hendrik has some work to do, so I have to wait. Julia, don't you think he's *nice?* I do hope yours is too."

The small man in grey had gained the deck, looked sharply this way and that and now came towards them, and whereas Hendrik had had to push his way through, everybody stepped back to allow this man free passage. A few people greeted him, and he nodded or lifted a negligent hand in recognition.

"It must be the Governor himself," said Marie, "and he's . . . yes, he is . . . coming to welcome us."

And it seemed so. He came straight towards them. He was, despite his short stature, an impressive figure, very upright and taut. His hair, worn long and elaborately curled, was as near as could be the colour of his clothes; fine lace frothed whitely at his wrist and breast. He halted, looked at them both in a way only just saved from insolence by its seriousness, and then asked,

"Mevrouw Vosmar?"

"I am, Mynheer."

As she made her curtsey Julia heard him say, "Ah," just an outletting of the breath, but it held relief, as though he had said, "Thank God."

He bowed.

"I am Simon Vosmar. My son was unable to meet you himself. I trust you had a pleasant voyage. And now, if you are ready . . ."

He turned, pivoting like a dancing master and offered her his arm.

Julia said, "Please, Mynheer . . ." and turned to Marie who was still staring, wide-eyed. They embraced, with a warmth hitherto unknown in their relationship. Mynheer Vosmar watched them with impatient tolerance and, as they exchanged some muddled promises about meeting soon, soon, he said,

"Doubtless you will—unless this young lady is proceeding to Java."

They both spoke together—I am—she is—Banda Neira.

"Then you will certainly meet—often," he said, but there was in his manner a contemptuous dismissal of Marie which Julia resented.

"And there is my baggage, Mynheer," she said. He dismissed that even more contemptuously.

"That will be seen to."

The bone of his arm under her hand was sharp and frail, but his hand, as he helped her onto the ladder, had an astonishing strength and steadiness.

They took their places, side by side on yellow silk cushions under the yellow awning; the boat's head swung round and they shot away over the silken water, leaving the curve of the harbour upon their right.

"Well," said Mynheer Vosmar, and the single word had a

note of accomplishment, of finality. Something else was over and done with. After a moment's pause he began afresh.

"I'm very glad to see you. I hope you'll be happy in Rua. My son—as I told you—was unable to meet you."

"I hope he is not ill." How perfunctorily polite it sounded.

"Thank you, no. His health is uniformly excellent. He had an accident—a long time ago, and he is recovering, but slowly. He is . . . disabled. That is Rua," he said, pointing to what, at this distance, was no more than a flat dish, filled with feathery green.

As though the mere sight of his home filled him with impatience to be there, he picked up the silver-knobbed cane which lay at his side and rattled it against the boat, exactly as Julia had seen carters rattle their sticks against the front of their wagons. Just like horses the boatmen increased their efforts for a moment or two and then fell back to the more comfortable pace.

"Rua," said Mynheer Vosmar, "is a small *island*, but a large plantation; and it is one of the oldest. My grandfather was producing nutmegs there when Banda was still in a state of chaos. And several times, when catastrophes of various kinds have befallen the Banda groves, they have been replenished by young stock from Rua. My grandfather had his own ships; but now that the Company is so . . . so active, I have given up the ships. Otherwise we remain a self-contained community. We even have *cows* in Rua."

"Is that very unusual?"

"Most. In fact it is singular. Cows need pasture, you see. On Banda, Lonthoir and Api even gardens are rare and regarded as an extravagance. Why grow a rose where one could grow a nutmeg? My gardens are very beautiful."

He chatted on and seemed content with her brief responses. As he talked she had an opportunity to study his face and attempt to guess from it something of his nature. It was not a genial face; his pale lips were thin and closely folded, his nose delicate, sharply hooked, an arrogant nose; but it was his eyes which drew and held her attention. They were very large and set far forward between fleshy lids; the prominent eyeballs were yellowish and veined with red, the pupils a light, glassy grey. She thought suddenly that with his thin legs, his spare figure and huge eyes he was like an insect.

Perhaps she regarded him a trifle too openly, a second too long, for presently he broke off his talk and shifted a little in his seat and looked at her, so searchingly that she found it difficult to maintain composure.

"You *look* to be a sensible girl," he said at last. "I must confess that just now I had a moment . . . The girl who was with you, to whom is she married?"

"Hendrik Oltman."

"Oh yes. A stupid young man, breaking his back with a view to being Agent one day. He never will!" In three words he banished the young man to perpetual obscurity. "Look, you can see the house now."

She had seen a white building, enormously long, single-storied, some moments before he drew her attention to it, and thought that it was a row of sheds or warehouses; it was like no house that she had ever seen before.

"That also is singular," said Mynheer with great complacency. "It was my grandfather's most original idea. You will find, when you visit in Banda, that the stupid stubborn Dutchmen build, in this climate, houses exactly like the ones they lived in—or admired from a distance—in Holland. They have bedrooms just under the roof, where it is hottest, and then complain that they cannot sleep! My grandfather had travelled a great deal and, when he built, combined most sensibly the principles of a native hut and a Spanish-Moorish house. Above us, between roof and ceiling, we have ten feet of cool space, and nowhere is the house more than one room deep, so what air there is can blow through. Actually we suffer less from the heat in Rua than they do in Banda. I think you will soon become accustomed to the climate. This is the hottest season.

Soon we shall have the rains." He lifted the cane again and rattled it threateningly.

The island seemed to rush forward, and soon she could see the house in detail. It was thatched and the thatch jutted out far beyond the walls and was supported by pillars covered with creeping, flowering plants. Urns, set between the pillars, brimmed with flowers.

"It's very beautiful," Julia said.

He gave her a glance of approval. "I'm glad you think so. I do," he said.

The boat ran in alongside a little stone jetty. And now, in just a minute . . .

"Welcome to Rua," said Mynheer as he helped her from the boat. "You are shivering. I do assure you, you have no cause for nervousness. None at all."

He took her elbow in his firm grasp and led her along the stone path, flanked with smooth greensward, and up the steps of the verandah.

"It faces west," he said, "and it is very pleasant to sit here and watch the sun set over the water."

The entrance to the house was through an archway, and there was no door in the ordinary sense; two gates of fine wrought-iron work which, when closed, would fill the archway were flung back against the walls. Within was a large, stone-paved hall, unfurnished save for a few silky rugs, some statues on pedestals and several small flowering trees growing in huge pots of gaily painted pottery. Later on she was to appreciate the beauty of it all, but at the moment apprehension filled her.

Mynheer Vosmar guided her across the hall and out into a kind of stone cloister overlooking a garden brilliant with colour. They turned right and passed at least a dozen doors before he halted and opened one.

"These," he said, "will be your own apartments and, of course, they must be furnished to your taste. I have merely provided what I thought you would need, and a few things that I hoped would please you. But you must ask for anything you want, anything you fancy. . . ."

She looked, without seeing anything, about the two rooms. Mynheer Vosmar said, peevishly, "Where is that . . . Oh, *there* you are. This is Juno, whose sole duty will be to look after you." A handsome woman with a skin like brown silk, had entered silently. She carried a tray in her hands. Mynheer Vosmar inspected it critically and nodded.

"At midday we eat very sparingly and take our main meal in the cool of the day. You will find it advisable to rest afterwards—I invariably do myself. I will see you again at four o'clock." He turned away, swung round again with his dancing-master grace, "Juno understands Dutch," he said, "and she knows her duties, but she is incorrigibly idle. You must keep her up to the mark." He went away.

"Is hot now, Mevrouw, please," Juno said in a soft, sibilant voice, indicating a tea-pot that stood on the tray. "Why I am not here . . . see you come, go make tea hot."

"I should like some tea." She went towards the table and Juno pulled a chair a little way out, and pushed it a little way in, took up the pot and poured the tea. The tray was laden; there was meat, sliced very thin, a green salad, some strange but delicious-looking fruit, tiny bread rolls, fresh butter. But she could eat nothing; even the tea, delicious and fragrant, went down with difficulty. Twice she had braced herself, once on the ship, and once when entering the house, and each time the ordeal had been postponed. Except for the single remark about his being disabled, Pieter, her husband, had not been mentioned; in his talk Mynheer had never said "we" in a way which implied "my son and I"; even when he spoke of preparing these rooms for her he had said "I provided." He had also said, "your own apartments."

It was impossible to sit still. She put down the cup and stood up.

"You do not like?" Juno asked humbly. "Other things. Much other. I fetch?"

"Oh no, thank you. It's all very nice. I'm not hungry now."

"Mevrouw wish to sleep?"

"I couldn't." Even the sense of being watched irked her and she walked restlessly from the sitting-room to the bedroom beyond. The rooms communicated by an arch hung with silk curtains, yellow, with white dragons. Each room looked out upon one side to the verandah, upon the other to the cloister and the garden beyond; the windows had no glass, only screens of that same fine iron-work. Even at this, the hottest part of the day in the hottest part of the year, the air flow and the white walls, the pale silver-grey of all the woodwork, contributed to an impression of coolness.

Suddenly she noticed, standing alone and looking oddly out of place in the luxurious bedroom, her own small trunk.

There was a job for Juno. She called her.

"You could unpack for me, and spread out my other dress to get rid of the creases."

"Mevrouw has many dresses."

"This and one other." And the other was her wedding dress. . . .

"Many. Please, many dresses." Juno opened a door and showed a cupboard which might have held a rainbow, five or six dresses in different shades of colour, all delicate, hung there.

"Not finished," Juno explained. "I make fit. Wear today."

Just for a moment her mood lightened. The provision of the dresses showed a kindly forethought—and her welcome, though strange, had been kindly too. The ordeal was still ahead of her, but what better support could any woman have in any ordeal than a brand-new dress? She hadn't had a new dress since her twelfth birthday, except for the wedding dress, and that was now seven months old.

"Which one shall I try first?"

Juno put out a diffident finger and just touched a yellow dress.

"Is Vosmar colour. Mynheer has fondness that colour."

It was a chance to slip in a question.

"And the young Mynheer, Mynheer Pieter. What colour does he like?"

"Mynheer Pieter very sick."

"I know. How sick?"

Juno rolled her fine black eyes, moved her brown hands, alongside but not touching her own head, down, down.

"Sick, all sick," she said.

"But he might like one colour more than another."

Juno found the perfect answer and offered it with relief.

"Mynheer Pieter like what Mynheer like."

"Then I'll try that one," Julia said.

She always remembered that instance of her father-in-law's passion for detail. He had prepared a wardrobe for an unknown woman; how tall, how plump or slender she was and what her colouring would be, he could not know; so there they were, in many colourings, with the lace ruffles stitched in, the eyelet holes worked for the lacings, the embroidery bright on the skirts, but the hems were not turned up and the side seams not stitched. An hour's work would have made any one of those dresses fit any one of the Company's Daughters.

When the dress was fitted, Juno said,

"Mevrouw sleep now?" But it would be impossible to lie down and be still, and think, and wonder, and surmise.

"Mevrouw like bath?" Answering the questioning look Juno laid the dress aside and opened another door. It opened onto a small square room lined entirely with marble, with an oblong bath sunk into its floor. Some tall white jars with double handles stood on its edge.

"Mevrouw go there. I fetch water and pour," Juno explained.

"When the dress is ready," Julia said. "Now I'm going in the garden."

"Much hot. In shade please, Mevrouw."

Mynheer's pride in his garden was justified; it had been carefully planned so as to seem larger than it was; bright, tough-foliaged native flowers, whose names Julia did not know, grew

in open beds that looked like strips of embroidery; roses and
lilies were cunningly placed so that they were tree-shaded at
noon. In one corner a little artificial mound had been made;
on its summit was a seat, shaded by a tree whose branches had
been trained over it; and when you sat there and looked straight
ahead you saw nothing but a mass of shrubs with dark, shiny
spear-shaped leaves and great clusters of blossoms in many
shades of pink and purple and beyond them the sea, intensely
blue.

Julia sat on the seat and looked at the vista, and the sense
that she had come to a very pleasant place and that once the
worst was over she might be happy there grew. She pondered
the "disabled" of Mynheer, the "very sick" of Juno, and began
to visualise a gentle invalid, confined to a chair, a man who
might, perhaps, make no demand upon his wife except that she
be a companion to him. She thought of Mevrouw Helmers'
insistence that every girl who had the slightest capacity for it
should learn to play chess and backgammon, and she thought
how strange it would be if, after all her fears, she should find
that there was nothing to fear at all. She knew, from the inti-
mate talks which the long weeks aboard ship had forced upon
them, that Marie, indeed perhaps most girls, would little relish
the idea of an invalid husband. But it would just suit me, she
thought.

The faint hope reawakened her apprehension and she could
no longer sit still. She walked to the bounds of the garden on
that side. At one point it ended in a wall which curved round
and made a kind of enclosure against the side of the house.
Flowering trees lifted their heads above the wall, so there was
evidently another garden within, but it was not to be reached
from without. She turned back, anxious about time, and went
into the house.

At four o'clock she was ready, bathed and dressed, her hair
smoothly curled by Juno's expert hands. She looked, she knew,
her very best; and Mynheer Vosmar, coming for her punctually
at the hour, surveyed her with grave approval.

"I am glad you chose that dress," he said. "It is my favourite colour. It is supposed to symbolise *Hope*. Did you know that?"

With a faint smile she shook her head.

"Well it is. And hope is something we must cling to. Now, if you are ready . . ." He offered her his arm again.

For the last time she braced herself. In a few minutes now she would meet the man with whose her life would be linked until death severed the bond; she would know the worst—or the best, of all she had feared, and hoped for so many months.

But, once again, the critical moment was to be deferred. Instead of taking her directly to her husband, Mynheer Vosmar embarked upon a leisurely tour of the house, explaining its peculiarities and virtues as they moved from room to room, and every now and then lingering, gloatingly, before some special treasure. It was difficult at first to give him her attention, apprehensive as she felt about the coming ordeal, and impatient, now that it was so near, to get it over and done with; but gradually Mynheer's calm, yet insistent, claim for her attention succeeded, and her interest woke.

The house covered a good deal of ground, being, as he had said, only one room thick anywhere; every room looked out onto the verandah at the front and onto the cloister-like passage at the rear. Most of them could be entered only by doors from the cloister, but some were connected, like her own sitting-room and bedroom, by open archways. Coolness and airiness had been the aim; all the walls were white, the floors of stone, or tiles or bare polished wood.

"The folly of some settlers is quite unbelievable," Mynheer said. "You'll see houses made stifling with rugs and curtains and glass windows. And young women still arrive with feather-beds and pillows as part of their dower. The resultant heat rash they blame upon the climate, poor fools!" He paused by a cushioned chair and thumped it. "Stuffed with raw cotton," he said, complacently.

He threw open another door and said, "This is the salon. A

beautiful room, I think. Too little used, of late; but now that we have a lady in the house again, things will be different."

Julia stared around, momentarily forgetful of everything save what she saw. The salon was beautiful—and it was magnificent, too. The walls and the high arched ceiling were white, the floor black and highly polished and everything in the room was black and scarlet and gold. Facing one another from opposite sides were two identical pieces of furniture, the like of which she had never seen before, huge scarlet cupboards standing upon golden pillars, and topped by golden domes, and decorated, all over, with entrancing pictures in black and gold, pictures of birds and butterflies and flowers and twisted trees.

"You are admiring the cabinets," Mynheer Vosmar said in a satisfied voice. "They came from China. China is supposed to be the closed land, they boast that nothing goes in and nothing comes out—but my father obtained these, many years ago. He furnished the room around them, so to speak." He opened one of the doors and showed the arrangement of little drawers, all painted, and the arched recesses. "Do you play chess?" he asked, with seeming irrelevance.

"A little. Mevrouw Helmers taught us . . . just the rudiments. I'm not very good at it."

"You and I must play," he said. "I'm not very good either. I've had no one with whom to play . . . for many years."

Her latest mental image of Pieter quivered and vanished.

They came at last to a door at the end of the cloister. Ahead of them, just beyond the door, a wall ran out at right-angles, ten or twelve feet high and thickly covered by masses of climbing flowers, pink and purple, rose-coloured and white.

"Joshua's Trumpet," said Mynheer, seeing her admiring stare. "Well named, left to run riot it could have brought down the walls of Jericho." He opened the door. "This is my library," he said. One side of it was lined with shelves, filled with books. She had never imagined that there were so many books in the world, leave alone in one man's possession. Under the window at the verandah end was a big desk, and a chair. There were other chairs, more comfortable, and several low tables, upon one of which was a tray bearing a bottle and two tall fluted glasses.

Mynheer Vosmar pulled forward a chair.

"At this time of the day I find a glass of wine agreeable," he said. "Well-cooled that is. I hope you like wine."

It was associated with Mynheer Dekker's announcement, and the gloves, and a feeling of nausea.

"I don't think I do, Mynheer."

"Then you must learn to," he said, but quite pleasantly. "I should hardly imagine that your experience of *good* wine is wide enough to justify an opinion. I chose this for you and had it hung down the well, to cool, before I came to meet you."

All at once the thought struck her that he was deliberately postponing the moment when she should meet Pieter; the lengthy tour around the house, and now this. . . . Was he nervous too? Was the truth something that even he hesitated to reveal? Without knowing it she linked her fingers and kneaded them.

"You are nervous," he said. "I assure you, you have no need to be. Nothing is demanded of you except that you should be happy!" He handed her one of the glasses, and raising his own said, "To your happiness in Rua." He took a little formal sip.

She said, "Thank you, Mynheer."

"One thing will be lacking," he said. "How much, or how little that will matter to you I do not know." His bulging, glassy grey eyes looked over her speculatively, and to cover her embarrassment she lifted her glass. The wine was light and cool and fragrant, almost flowery.

"I told you," he said, "that my son had an accident. It happened eighteen years ago, when he was four years old. He had a careless nurse, and she left him alone. He fell." A change took place in his face as he spoke; his eyes bulged even more and reddened, and she was suddenly conscious of his teeth behind his thin lips. "He bruised his brain, and it has never healed. You must understand that anything resembling normal married life is quite out of the question." He looked at her with a faintly challenging air and waited for her to speak. For a moment she could not do so; she was so much relieved, and at the same time obscurely ashamed of her relief. Finally she said in a stiff, prim little voice,

"You have my sympathy, Mynheer. And he . . . I am sorry for him, too."

He looked at her sharply, and with some surprise.

"You may well, in course of time, become sorry for yourself. You may think that I have brought you here under false pretences. In that case, of course, you have no redress. But if you choose to be helpful and amenable you will find me—not ungrateful. I shall, in any case, do my utmost to enable you to lead a full, and interesting, and I trust happy life. That being understood we may as well go in."

He rose and, to Julia's astonishment, took a bunch of keys from his pocket and, choosing the one he wanted, went across to the door which stood in the centre of the book-lined wall. Opening it he gestured to her to pass ahead of him into the room beyond.

CHAPTER II

It was a large, well-lighted, sparsely-furnished room; and at a long solid table in the centre two men were sitting, one with his back to the door, the other in profile. The one who had his back to her, and who did not turn round, was, she judged, young, he had light-brown, very dry-looking hair, and wore a bright blue jacket; the other man, who rose as they entered, was older, heavily built, and wore dark clothes with plain white linen bands at his throat. His face was pallid, much lined, and jowly.

Mynheer Vosmar, having closed the door, stepped forward and took Julia by the elbow. He then said, "Pieter" in a voice of peculiar clarity, as though addressing someone slightly deaf, who, at the same time must not be shouted at. Very slowly and clumsily, moving his whole body in order to turn his head, Pieter Vosmar looked round.

She had seen that face, or rather that kind of face before. Once on a little girl who lived in the Hoogenstrasse, a beautifully dressed little girl who never played with other children and never went out alone. ("Fourteen years old, the poor creature, and her mind like a baby's," Anna had said.) Once on a poor boy who roamed the streets with a little cart, sweeping up horse-dung and selling it to people for their gardens. He was known as "Mucky Karl" and some children regarded him with a half-pleasurable dread, and would call him by that ugly name until he was angry and shambled after them, brandishing his broom. ("He shouldn't be loose; he'll do somebody an injury one of these days," said Anna.)

She remembered this as she looked at the red, puffy face, with its blunt nose and small raw-rimmed eyes and loose damp mouth. She tried not to show, in her face, anything of what she felt.

"Stand up," Mynheer Vosmar said, "I've brought someone to see you."

Clumsily, laboriously, Pieter rose, turned himself about and with the air of one who makes a tremendous effort, held out his hand.

"Good morning," he said. He spoke indistinctly, in a thick, flannelly voice. But his face creased into the caricature of a smile, and taking his hand Julia felt her first revulsion melt into pity. She said,

"Good morning, Pieter. My name is Julia."

"Julie," he said; and again, trying it over, "Julie."

His hand seemed to have no bones, it lay in hers like a stuffed glove; yet it clung, and there was power in it. He pulled her to the table and pointed to a curious tangle of cane and dried grass with which he had been engaged when interrupted.

"Nice," he said, "nice basket."

"A very nice basket," she said. "Very nice indeed." A piteous expression of pleasure dawned on his face. He pulled at her hand again.

"He won't hurt you," Mynheer Vosmar said.

"Oh no, I know that," she said and allowed herself to be led across the room to where a clavichord stood open on a smaller table under a window.

"Music," Pieter said.

"I'm sorry. I can't play."

"Perhaps some day you can learn a simple tune," said Mynheer. "He is very fond of music."

"I'll try," she promised. She looked out of the window and noticed that it opened neither onto the verandah nor the cloister, but directly into a small walled garden, a patch of trampled-looking grass, surrounded by flowering bushes. She had just time to see that before Pieter tugged her away again; this time towards an archway opposite the door by which they had entered.

Again Mynheer, watchful, reassuring, said, "It's all right. I think he wants to show you his garden."

"It's all right. I'm not afraid of him," she said.

Beyond the archway was a bedroom of monastic austerity; from it an open doorway led into the little garden. Once there Pieter dropped her hand, and moving very purposefully, went to a bush which bore large clusters of pink flowers.

"Pretty," he said.

She said, "Very pretty." And her throat ached with sadness because he, so grotesque and ugly, yet recognised beauty when he saw it.

He began to tear at the bush, grunting, and breathing hard as he bent and broke the tough, leathery stems from which the pink flower sprang. She was aware that Mynheer Vosmar and the man—keeper, tutor, what did he call himself?—had followed and were standing in the doorway, watching and now and again exchanging a few words.

At last Pieter succeeded in ripping away a bunch of the flowers and, turning, held it out to her.

"Pretty," he said. "Pretty for . . ." he breathed hard, "Julie."

"Thank you, Pieter. Thank you very much."

It was the first time in all her life that anyone had given her a flower, but instinctively she first held it away and looked at it admiringly, then sniffed at it, and then tucked it into the lacing of her bodice. Pieter gave a kind of caper and then lumbered over to the bush again and tore off another cluster.

Again she accepted it, saying, "Thank you," but holding it in her hand.

"Pretty," he insisted, "pretty for Julie," and looked at her anxiously. She realised that he wanted her to wear this offering too. She tried to push the second cluster into place beside the first, and Pieter gave his dreadful, pathetic smile and capered and lurched off again towards the flowering bush. . . . How many more?

Mynheer came to her rescue.

"I think that will do for today," he said. "Daan, if you were to play, that would distract him and we could slip away."

The man disappeared and within a few seconds the music rang out, masterfully and beautifully played. Pieter ceased his mangling of the bush, turned, and without a glance at his father or his wife, blundered towards the clavichord.

"Come," said Mynheer.

As soon as they were back in the library Mynheer turned from her and walked to the window. She saw him put his hand over his mouth and grip his lower jaw. He was fighting for self-control and all at once the pity which, half an hour earlier, had been merely a matter of words, sprang up in her, real, vital, overruling all the other mingled emotions of the moment. She said nothing, but walking over to the book-shelves, studied the serried titles attentively.

After a moment he said, in a far more warm and friendly tone than any he had so far used,

"You will excuse me, my dear. God knows I have had time to accustom myself. It was the occasion which made it seem less than usually tolerable. My only son . . . meeting his wife . . . for the first time. It should have been very different."

She did not know, at that moment, the reach and vastness of his pride in his family, in his name, which was the motive power of his life; the dynastic aspect of the tragedy was hidden from her. She saw a rather frail-seeming, elderly man grieving over his son's affliction.

"I'm very sorry," she said, "more for you than for Pieter. He seems quite happy."

Mynheer said, a trifle harshly, "He has no reason to be otherwise. You did very well. It must have been a considerable shock for you. I thought it wise to hide nothing from you. But you need never again enter that room, unless you wish. He is not, I realise, a pleasant sight."

"Sad, but not unpleasant," she said, with a degree of firmness. "Unless my presence upsets him in any way I should like to help to amuse him. He is gentle, and means well. I found him rather—touching."

Mynheer looked at her with an expression which she did not recognise as distaste. This product of an Amsterdam orphanage, this virtually nameless nobody, had looked upon the heir to Rua and found him "touching." Now, surely, he had drained the last dreg of his degradation.

He said, "I'm sure that if you care to devote a little time to the poor boy Doctor Hootman will be very grateful. But that must be as you wish. Don't look upon it as a duty. You were not brought here for Doctor Hootman's benefit."

That enabled her to ask the question which, from the moment when Pieter turned his head, had been nagging at her.

"Why was I brought here? I mean, Mynheer, you must have known . . . all along . . . that Pieter did not need a wife."

He did not immediately answer. He had turned from the

window, and she from the book-shelves, and now they were
facing one another across the room.

"That is a thing that you must understand," he said. "I have
managed to conceal from the world, even from other branches
of my own family, the extent and the nature of the damage
sustained by Pieter when he had his accident. It has not always
been easy. I have let it be known that he was disabled and disfigured and has become, of his own choice, a recluse. I believe
that rumour—always so kind—has it that he is so grossly ugly
that he cannot bear to be looked upon. That I do not mind.
My business has been to hide the fact that he is mentally in-
firm. Obviously my only son, whatever his appearance, would
be expected to marry, one day. You are a pretty girl, and, which
matters more, a presentable one. I shall be very proud to say,
'This is my daughter-in-law.' That will confound the gossip-
ing fools. And if you prop up my story and play your part well,
you will find me very grateful."

"I understand, Mynheer." She was on the point of adding
that she already had cause to be grateful to him. The dark
threatening figure of "your husband" had been laid low, never
to rise again; she was grateful for that. But something checked
her tongue. Partly it was the selfish caution inculcated by the
years in the Klopstock Home. Let him feel himself indebted,
let him *be* grateful. Partly it was a flash of unselfish insight.
After all, it was only by the merest accident of chance that she,
who did not wish to be married at all, had come here to be
part of a marriage that was no marriage. Suppose it had been
Marie, or any one of any other dozen girls who really wanted a
husband and a normal married life. . . . Mynheer had, quite
obviously, given no thought to how the girl would feel. Let him
be grateful!

She said, "I shall always do my best to try to please you."

"Yes. I think you will. I think we shall get on very well together. The situation is unusual, I admit, but I hope you will
find that it is not without compensations."

She remembered suddenly, and with great clarity, her inter-

view with Mevrouw Helmers, and the kind easy voice saying
that God never made mistakes. Could it be, dare one for a moment believe it to be, true?

CHAPTER III

Doctor Hootman dined with Julia and
Mynheer, and by the end of the meal she had formed the opinion that he was a sulky and unfriendly person. Mynheer sat at
the head of the table in a high-backed chair which did not
match the others; Julia sat on his right hand, Doctor Hootman
on his left, so they were face to face across the table. Inevitably,
now and again she would look up and meet his eyes—dull
brown eyes, heavily pouched, and always he looked away
hastily. He did not speak a word to her, nor did he once smile,
and when addressed by Mynheer, answered in a brusque way
which dismissed her first impression, which was that he was in
great awe of his employer.

Mynheer seemed unaware of any discordant note. He talked
easily and well, and encouraged her to talk, and tried, repeat-
edly, to draw Doctor Hootman into the conversation. He was
—she was to learn—always at his best at table; for him meals
had a certain ceremonial value, and even when he was suffering
some emotional stress, he would set it aside and preside at his
table with a detached and punctilious courtesy.

He told her the name of the main dish—ritzplatzen.

"We have it very often, but it has so many variations that I
never tire of it. If, after a time, you do, my dear, you must say
so."

She thought she would never tire of it; not only was it delicious, it was so nice to look at. It was served in a great number

of very delicate china bowls of varying sizes, all beautifully painted, both inside and out, with flowers and reeds and blossoming twigs. The largest bowl was full of rice, the smaller ones held eggs, meat, fish, vegetables and spicy preserves in a bewildering number, prepared in unusual ways. You helped yourself, Mynheer explained, to a mound of rice and then added whatever you fancied.

"Some of the side dishes will taste strange to you, but you will become accustomed to them in time. At least I hope so. I deplore the attitude of some in the Islands who insist upon oversmoked ham and salted herrings. Their leathery Dutch cheese I must forgive—they have no choice."

He gave one of his complacent glances at the side-table, where, on a silver dish, in a nest of crisp green leaves, a large freshly made cream cheese lay.

They were waited upon by a brown man, who looked, to Julia's unaccustomed eye, exactly like Juno, but male. His name was Pluto.

"My grandfather," Mynheer explained, "instituted the custom of naming all his house-slaves after characters in mythology, and I adhered to it."

"With some strange results," said Doctor Hootman; "Cupid for example."

Mynheer gave him a sharp look, but said, agreeably,

"That is so; but they are named as babies and who can tell what their looks will be later on. As with dogs; an aunt of mine named a puppy 'Tiny' and it was the size of a donkey when full grown."

Pluto removed the last plates and then the glistening white table-cloth, not folding it carefully for use again, but gathering it into a bundle. Mevrouw Helmers, discoursing upon behaviour, had spoken of gentlemen sitting over their wine, and of ladies retiring with promptitude. But Mynheer was speaking as the cloth was withdrawn, and he went on, composedly. And then Pluto set the table again, with plates of the same flowered pattern, and with huge bowls, piled with fruit, and with small bowls with water in them. Flower-petals floated on the water.

Mynheer finished speaking, and Julia, following Mevrouw Helmer's instructions, said, "Mynheer, I will leave you."

"Oh no," he said. "No formality when we are alone. I want to introduce you to some of our Rua fruits." He leaned forward and studied the bowls. "Pears, of course, you know. These are not good. They are Chinese stock but even so the climate is too moist for them; edible and that is all one can say. These are mangoes—I think myself the most delicious of all fruit, the peach, the nectarine and the apricot, all in one, with something in addition. And these, in Malabar, are called *pala*, but the African name is banana—they, I contend, are an acquired taste, I have never, myself, acquired it. This curious-looking thing is a pine-apple—aptly named, don't you think? May I prepare you a piece? At least an inch of its outside must be cut away. . . ."

She tried everything, and everything was delicious. Copying Mynheer she dipped her fingers now and then into the flower-strewn water, which was delicately scented. Her sense of having come to a beautiful, comfortable, wonderful place grew, and grew. She thought of her own room, the wide, silk-covered bed where she would sleep, alone, untroubled—for the first time in many months—by the thought of another bed, to be shared by "your husband." Oh, how soundly she would sleep tonight! Suddenly, and, she felt, with an appalling lack of manners, she yawned.

"How inconsiderate I am," Mynheer said instantly. "You must be very tired after such a day. Allow me to take you to your room."

"I can find it myself, Mynheer."

"Very well. Juno will be there. Good night—Julia."

"Good night, Mynheer." She hesitated, looking towards Doctor Hootman, but he was rather ostentatiously giving his attention to the peeling of his fourth banana. And Mynheer was waiting, holding the door for her. As she passed him she smiled and he said, almost fondly, "Good night, my dear. Sleep well."

He closed the door, and turning back into the room, looked at Doctor Hootman's back with a scowl. It was gone, however, by the time he had reached his own place at the table, and his tone was genial as he refilled his glass and said,

"You're in peculiar mood this evening, Daan. What's the matter?"

Doctor Hootman raised his heavy eyes, and, speaking deliberately, said, "In the comparatively humble station in which I was reared it was thought desirable that a man should be introduced to a woman before he engaged her in conversation."

"Good God!" Mynheer said. "Did I omit to do that? I apologise. I must confess I was very much preoccupied. I fully expected a scene, you know."

"All the same, I think that the owner of the menagerie, bringing a visitor into the cage, would have said, 'This is Doctor Hootman, who has charge of the wild beast.'"

"I find that a very offensive comparison."

"I found your behaviour this afternoon very offensive."

"Daan, don't be silly. It was remiss of me, I admit; but think of the situation. I should never have thought you were so touchy."

Doctor Hootman hunched a heavy shoulder.

"No. Dealing, as you do, exclusively with slaves and sycophants you are bound to become insensitive to other people's feelings. I am not your slave, or your sycophant; merely a hireling. Hired to attend, control, and as far as possible train, your idiot son."

Mynheer Vosmar was not a man given to impulsive words or gestures, but now he brought his hand down on the table with a smack which slopped the wine from the glasses and made several pieces of fruit hop from their dish and go rolling about the table.

"I will not have him called that! Idiots are born, not made.

Pieter was like anybody else until that pig of a woman let him fall."

Doctor Hootman swallowed the last piece of banana, dipped his fingers and wiped them.

"It pleases you to think so. But it isn't true. He was a born idiot; but since, in the first few years of a child's life no great demand is made upon the intelligence, that fact escaped your notice. When you could no longer ignore it you siezed upon the nearest excuse—a timely, trivial bump on the head. But that isn't true and nothing you can say or do can make it so."

It was one of those speeches, stating a truth too unpalatable to be accepted, which, aimed at a wider target, have often taken the speaker a long step towards martyrdom. Had Mynheer Vosmar been at that moment a mob, with many mouths, every one of them would have been open, yelling, "To the Stake," "To the Gallows," "To the Cross." His eyes did bulge and redden, but although he was angry his anger was not pure; it had an alloy of curiosity.

"What makes you say this now? Is it just a retaliation for my lapse of manners this afternoon, or something more?"

Before answering Doctor Hootman lifted his glass and with finnicky care wiped first the foot of it, and then the place where the wine had slopped over when Mynheer had hit the table. He sipped, swallowed, and sipped again.

"I was," he said, "annoyed this afternoon. Taken for granted, treated like a piece of furniture. Still . . ." he shrugged again, "let that go. I had another reason for frank speaking. I agree with you that providing Pieter with a wife was a very pleasing little touch to the façade. And you were fortunate . . . she seems sensible. But it is my duty, at this point to warn you."

"To warn me?" Mynheer said. "What do you mean?"

"Shove them into bed together," Doctor Hootman said brutally, "And you'll have an idiot grandchild on your hands."

Mynheer lifted his glass and with a fastidiousness matching his companion's, wiped it, and the wet ring from the table top.

"You've been with me for eight years," he said solemnly,

"it doesn't seem possible that you can so entirely misjudge and misunderstand me. I never dreamed . . . I should no more think of shoving them into bed together, as you term it, than I should think of . . . of . . . well, taking Juno into my own bed. I don't believe, and you will never make me believe, that Pieter was a born idiot, but he is an idiot now. The very idea is obscene. And the result might very well be, as you say, another idiot. No, what I have in mind is something quite different. Shall I tell you?"

Doctor Hootman's expression, which had relaxed into relief, tightened again, became wary. As though he knew this, he looked down at his plate, and then up again, with a carefully blank face which matched his careless, "If you like."

"You've been in my confidence from the first," Mynheer said, "and you've done marvels for Pieter. Perhaps you should know what I propose; it may make you feel a little less like a piece of furniture." His eyes twinkled. "Listen," he said.

CHAPTER IV

Around her, day by day, the new life fell into pattern. It was a life of unimaginable ease and luxury, and of leisure which, as Mevrouw Helmers had warned, might become tedious to anyone incapable of finding occupation for herself.

The day began early. At dawn the great brass tong-tong in the compound sounded the call to begin work. Mynheer always rose then and went to the plantation. Julia, who often slipped out of bed and looked out of the window to enjoy the sight of the dew-drenched garden, striped with sunshine and long shadows, would see the spare, trim figure, stepping daintily across the lawn towards a pergola, thickly hung with roses, which marked the boundary of the garden upon that side.

Almost immediately Juno would come, with a beaker of cool sweet fruit juice and a pot of the peculiarly fragrant tea. In her soft velvet voice she would wish Julia good morning and inquire if she had slept well, and what she would like for breakfast. Then she would vanish again, to return with an armful of freshly laundered linen, a smoothly ironed dress, clean shoes.

On most mornings, by the time she was dressed and had had breakfast Mynheer was back, and had had his. During her first week on Rua he devoted what remained of the cool morning hours to showing her over the island.

The nutmeg trees, evergreen, feathery and sweet-scented, grew in orderly groves all over the island, and paths ran this way and that through the green gloom.

"It's hardly likely that you would ever lose yourself," said Mynheer, "but if you should, don't keep taking side turnings; keep straight on. Eventually all the main paths run out at the shore."

He enjoyed showing her things and explaining how the "nuts" were gathered, and dried in racks over slow fires, turned at regular intervals until the outer shells could be broken and stripped away; how every nutmeg must be plunged into a lime bath to be made sterile: the whole wealth and importance of the Islands depended upon the monopoly, so no fertile nut must ever be shipped out. Julia watched and listened and tried to remember, hoping in time to know enough to be an acceptable companion to him.

Everywhere they went the slaves were working and there was never any flurry when Mynheer appeared. Rua was a well-run plantation, with just a hint of running by clock-work, she thought. The slaves all looked well-fed and were far better clothed than many she was to see later in the streets of Banda; Mynheer's passion for uniformity extended to his slaves' wearing apparel; even the lowest grade, those who gathered the nuts, even the children, wore neat, taut loincloths of the

Vosmar yellow, in a coarse cotton material. Overseers wore drawers, like the boatmen.

The slaves were of all colours, from dark blackish brown to pale coffee-colour. There were, Mynheer explained, no Banda-nese amongst them. The natives of this island group, having put up a fierce and bloody resistance to the white men, had then taken flight; what remained of them now lived on two small islands, keeping to their old tongue, plying their old crafts. "They were very fine people, the aristocrats of the Islands," said Mynheer; "they would not have made good slaves."

In one of the drying-sheds Julia was surprised to see a white man wearing the overseers' yellow drawers and armed with the overseers' cane. He was out of earshot, so she mentioned him, and her surprise to Mynheer.

"If you were nearer to him you would see that he is not quite white, my dear. Very nearly, yes. His mother, I should say, had some white blood, and his father, I know, was a Dutchman. These things happen, you know." He gave her a little sideways glance. "Most regrettable, I agree. Such a thing has never happened in Rua."

"Why is he a slave? If his father was Dutch?"

"The child of a slave is a slave, my dear, whatever his colour. This one, his name is Mercury, was one of a batch I bought some years ago. I tried him as a house-slave—that is why he has a house-slave's name—but it didn't do at all. His manners were bad, and he . . . well, he was above himself. He actually used to try on my clothes. I caught him at it, preening in front of my looking-glass."

"What did you do?"

"Burnt the clothes, of course, and degraded him to planta-tion work. It was kinder really. When he'd learned his lesson I made him overseer, and he is excellent. He hates everybody —which is a splendid thing for one in his position."

Despite the heat in the drying-shed she was conscious of a little chill. In a few words, neither callous nor sentimental,

Mynheer had told a tragic story. She cast another discreet glance at the subject of it; he had turned and was now in profile to her. He had a fine profile, with a nose as arrogant as Mynheer's.

"What a sad story," she said.

"Yes. The least his father could have done—in my opinion —was to free him and have him taught a trade. But he shuffled off his responsibility and we can't alter that, can we? Come along, it is very warm here."

On another morning Mynheer said, "Now I will show you the compound. That is one place which I should wish you to avoid. Oh, not that there's any danger; they're all tame enough, but they are primitive and one has to allow them a certain freedom there. You might see some unedifying sights. . . ."

The compound lay, as nearly as she could judge, in the very centre of the island. It consisted of a circle of small, low huts ringing a space of bare stamped earth in the middle of which was a well. A few immensely old, or extremely pregnant, women were cooking on little fires outside the doors of the huts; a number of children, too small yet for work, were playing, rather listlessly, in the dust. Here, unlike other places which they had visited, their arrival did cause some disturbance. The women left their fires and stood up; the children ceased playing and huddled together.

"I don't often come here," Mynheer explained. "Three generations of us, at the very least, to my certain knowledge have tried to enforce some rules of cleanliness. Fifteen years ago I had every hut burnt, the whole compound dug over, tons of sand from the beach spread, two feet thick and stamped down, and these huts erected. But look at it now. Smell it!"

It reeked of too many people, too closely pressed together; wood-smoke, the stink of the pan of rice that had boiled dry, the fat that had flamed, the dough that had gone sour, the meat that had scorched, the sick baby, the burnt rag . . . it was all there, intermingled with the overwhelming, main odour of human excreta. It was the smell of defeat, too.

She looked at the children. All but one of them looked healthy enough and some were quite beautiful. The one was a little boy, three, four years old, with sore eyes.

She said to Mynheer, who, having said "Smell it!" was looking this way and that with evident disgust,

"Mynheer, that little boy . . . Mevrouw Helmers, at the Company's Daughters' Home, told us how to make an ointment which she said would cure all sores. I have the recipe for it written in my book. May I try it on him?"

"Just a minute, my dear," he said. "Now that I am here, I must look in on Toeg. He was once one of my boatmen, and when we capsized in a sudden storm, he saved my life. If he knew that I had been in the compound and not visited him I think his heart would break." He moved purposefully towards a hut, almost immediately opposite the well, and she went with him. "I think perhaps you had better stay outside," he said. "I don't know how far you are capable . . . Toeg suffers, you see, from a very rare, and—if you are capable of detachment— a very interesting disease; but it isn't pretty."

They had reached the door of the hut, which, even from the outside, looked better kept than the others.

"What is the disease?"

"Nobody knows. It is called, for obvious reasons, elephantiasis. Of course, if you could face it, a visit from you would be . . . I can hardly explain what it would mean to Toeg."

"Then I can face it," she said.

Ducking his head at the low doorway Mynheer entered the hut and she followed him. Inside the hut, seated on a solid wooden bench was a tiny, shrivelled brown man with a monkey's face and grey speckled hair. Laid out on a kind of low table in front of him was a leg, one enormous leg, larger, thicker, bigger round, than the whole of his body.

As though from a great way off she heard Mynheer say,

"Toeg, I've brought the young Mevrouw, Mynheer Pieter's Mevrouw, to see you."

A voice, so small, so thready, as to be almost inaudible, said, "Greetings, Mevrouw. God is kind to let me see this day."

A small brown monkey's hand came out, and she put her own to it—just touching her finger-tips. Toeg lifted them to his brow.

"They're looking after you properly?" Mynheer asked.

"In every way, Mynheer, your orders are obeyed."

"You get your meat?"

"Three times in every week."

"Splendid," said Mynheer, briskly, sweeping a critical glance about the hut, and seeming satisfied with what he saw. "Keep that daughter-in-law of yours up to the mark, Toeg; and if you want anything, let me know." He smiled at the old man affectionately and they took their leave.

Outside Mynheer said, "Now what were you saying? Oh, I remember. Sore eyes and ointment. The suggestion does you credit, my dear, but I'm afraid there's nothing you can do, in that way. That the boy? Ah yes, I see what you mean; nasty sight. But your ointment would do more harm than good."

"Mevrouw Helmers had great faith in it. . . ." she said.

"Mevrouw Helmers probably knew more about ointment than about slaves. All these people are very mixed, races, religions, nonsensical observances," his voice hardened and his glassy eyes reddened. "I'll give you an example—that child may be Hindu, we have a few here; you put something greasy on his eyes; fat from a cow, sacred animal; his eyes may get better, they probably would, but his grandmother would fall and break both legs; his mother would miscarry and his father go blind; and who would be to blame? You and your ointment. Or he may be a Moslem; then your ointment would be suspected of being made from lard, untouchable pig. Again, his eyes might get better, but he would be unclean for the rest of his life, his aunts would all go crazy and his children be born dumb!" He paused. "You think I exaggerate? I do not, I assure you. The amount of superstition in this one compound is unbelievable. Within my lifetime a Hindu family here, in this place, were all hell-bent to shove a widow into the fire where her husband's body was burning. I had to go down and rescue her myself, nobody else could stop them. They're best left entirely alone."

"With their sore eyes?"

"Now you're not to fret about that," he said in a kinder voice. "When the moon is right and all the other auguries auspicious, they'll daub on some cure of their own—some holy man's spit and cow-dung, or something like that. And it'll work; they'll have faith in it, which they wouldn't in your ointment, you see. And faith will move mountains."

"Even superstitious faith?"

"Any sort of faith. Even—no, not even, most of all—faith in oneself."

After the morning walks, and again after her rest in the afternoon, she would go along to Pieter's room and help to amuse him. He always greeted her with every sign of affection and pleasure, smiling his wide, pitiable smile, and rubbing his head against her. Very soon she was hardly aware of his appearance, conscious only of his gentleness, his pathetic anxiety to please and his fondness for her. She had known so little affection, since Johannes' death, that even that of an idiot boy was not to be despised. She developed a corresponding fondness for him, as for an ugly but good-natured dog.

Now, as he completed each piece of fumbled handiwork he would present it to her, "Pretty for Julie." He knitted her a scarf of bright purple wool, wide at one end, narrow at the other and full of holes where he had dropped stitches, and, little as a scarf was needed in Rua at that season, she wore it often when she visited him, remembering the hours of frowning, hard-breathing labour that had gone into its making.

Sometimes they went into his little garden, and there she would play ball with him. His movements were too clumsy and unpredictable to allow him to catch a thrown ball, but he loved to retrieve it when it was thrown and bring it back to her to throw again. When she tired he would scrawl on the ground with a stick, or gather flowers—"Pretty for Julie"—until her lap was full.

These visits brought her into frequent contact with Doctor Hootman. His original surly manner, which she now attributed to shyness, had changed into one of formal civility, and there it rested. He seemed neither to encourage nor to resent her visits. As soon as she arrived he would turn away and busy himself, tidying cupboards and drawers, preparing something for Pieter's next employment, or simply reading his book. Sometimes he would say, "Don't let him tire you, Mevrouw"; and occasionally, "I think that will do, it does him no good to get excited." His manner towards his charge was unvarying, kindly, authoritative, oddly impersonal. He had two words of rebuke, "dirty" and "naughty"; he used them sparingly, but when he did Pieter would hang his head and seem to wilt, to grow smaller, like a scolded dog.

The late afternoons usually found her with Mynheer on the verandah to watch the swift, dramatic going down of the sun over the sea; and often, while the sky flowered and faded, and the earth poured out its many-flavoured scents, and the sea whispered on the beach and slapped against the little jetty, from the compound there would come the sound of music, played on the gamelins; strange, monotonous, rather mournful, muted by distance and sweet, it would come to them and weave a kind of spell, so that to speak, or move, demanded a definite effort. Sometimes Mynheer would touch her hand, or her shoulder,

"It's pleasant here, is it not? I hope you are happy?"

"Very happy, Mynheer."

"Not lonely? Not bored? Not sorry you came?"

She could truthfully say no to such questions.

"All the same," he would say, "I must not be selfish. We must entertain; go visiting; you must make a call on your little friend."

She grew fond of him, too; there was nothing intimidating about him when you came to know him; the formal stateliness of his manner made his occasional unbending the more to be valued; he was an easy, undemanding companion, and if, now and then, his conversation had a cynical flavour she reminded herself that he was old, ripe in experience, and that she was young.

And so the golden, sun-drenched, scented days went by.

The weather grew warmer, or, if not warmer, more oppressive. The days were not invariably fine; it rained—she thought —quite often, sudden showers falling from what was virtually a clear sky, sometimes even through the sunshine. The rain would cease as abruptly as it had begun, and all the wet leaves and flowers would sparkle for a moment, and the ground would steam. But Mynheer and Doctor Hootman and Juno were all beginning to talk of the rainy season which was coming. The real rain, upon which the crop and everything else depended; the rain which would soak in and cool the earth. They held it out to her—the newcomer—as a kind of promise: "Soon the rain will come." "It will be cool." Mynheer produced, from some hidden treasure chest, a shawl of fine lace, silky, not quite white, white which had lost its purity from being laid away, for a long time, in darkness.

"When the rains come, my dear, you may be glad of this in the evenings. Tell Juno to hang it out in the sun."

There came an afternoon when, rising from her rest, she was aware of a change, something missing. The light had altered. It was just as hot—even hotter—but there was no sunshine, and the slight movement of the air, too slight to be called a breeze, which, in Rua, had tempered the heat hitherto and made it tolerable, had ceased to flow between the verandah and the cloister. Pushing her damp hair from her forehead she went to the window and looked out at the garden. Every leaf, every flower, even the hardy cannas, the native orchids, looked limp, their vitality drained away. Something threatened and they cowered under the threat.

Inside the room it was gloomy and stifling. It would be better, she thought, out of doors. She went, moving listlessly to her favourite place in the garden, the seat on the little mound by the bank of flowers—azaleas, as she now knew. The mention of impending rain suggested clouds, but there were none, just a sullen, dark purple-grey pall drawn over the sun and the blueness; under it the sea lay flat, leaden-coloured, and the pink and rose-colour and scarlet of the bank of flowers had not so much faded as been drowned in the general gloom.

It was very depressing and, after a few minutes during which her spirits sank lower and lower and she began, for the first time, to feel homesick and lonely, she jumped up and decided to go for a walk. In the groves, between the tall trees, it was always shady, and there, she imagined, the change in the light would be less noticeable. She would not, she decided, go far, in case the rain began.

The main path, the one Mynheer took each morning on his way through the compound, began at the edge of the garden, behind a pergola of carefully trained roses. It ran straight, but branching off from it were many paths, well used by the slaves who gathered the nutmegs. Julia knew them all by this time, and knew that by taking any left-hand turn she came through the groves and out at the shore. Ordinarily, in order to take as long a walk as possible she pursued the main path until she was almost at the forbidden compound and then turned off. Today, on account of the threatening rain she took the first turning.

She had been wrong, she realised, to imagine that in the groves the change in the weather would be less noticeable; the purplish gloom, with the strange sense of foreboding which it conveyed, was thick in the narrow path, and the heat was stifling. It was stupid to have come for a walk, the house would have been much cooler. She came to a standstill and stood hesitant; would it be quicker to walk on, reach the place where

the path came out on the shore, or turn back and retrace her
steps? The gloom seemed to deepen as she stood there. And
then she heard the sound, a low, miserable moaning, the sound
of someone in pain. She listened, trying to determine from what
direction the sound came, never an easy thing to do, and less
easy here amongst these closely growing trees. Listening, she
realised that she could no longer hear the doves. She imagined
that the sound came from ahead of her along the path, but not
directly, slightly to the left, she thought. She moved forward,
and the noise seemed to come more clearly, but she could see
nothing that would account for it. Then she saw, on her left,
the opening of a path much more narrow than any of the others which intersected the groves. They were all wide enough to
allow the passage of two men with a load of nutmegs slung
between them, this was a mere track and not, by the look of
it, much used.

In the purple, ominous gloom it had an uninviting, almost
a sinister look and she hesitated before entering it. But she was
certain now that the moaning came from somewhere along it.
A few steps brought her to a length of fencing, made of roughly
hewn tree trunks placed close together. The fence ran parallel
with the path, was about ten feet high, and had no opening;
but it was a mere façade, one had only to step into the grove
to get behind it. The agonised sound came from its other side,
and now, mingling with it she could hear a clink, a rattle, as
though someone were shaking a chain.

Again she stood hesitant. She had a very clear feeling that
behind the fence might be something that she would not wish
to see, perhaps should not see; much the easiest thing would
be to turn and hurry away. But someone, or something—for
the moaning noise sounded sometimes human and sometimes
not—was behind that fence and in trouble. Also she herself
was curious. She stepped into the grove and rounded the fence.
At the back of it some trees had been hacked down and in
the space stood a square cage. The bars were five or six inches
apart and behind them she could see something which moved

and moaned and rattled a chain. Unwillingly, touched already by dread, she went near and put her face to the opening between two of the wooden bars. A stout post stood in the centre of the cage and attached to it by a length of chain linked about its waist was . . . what? For a moment Julia thought it was some kind of monkey; it was bent over, very brown, shrivelled, and had its back to her as it strained against the chain and towards the bars on the farther side of the cage. And all the time it moaned and whimpered.

As she watched it turned, ran back and then lunged forward again, rattling the chain. With a slow, draining sense of horror Julia realised that it was a woman, skeleton thin and stark naked.

Moving almost unwillingly she went around the cage to the side where the woman was scrabbling at the bars. Then she understood. Just outside, just out of reach, stood a bucket with some water in and two little wooden bowls, one empty and one containing a handful of rice. She looked from them to the face of the woman behind the bars and was so shocked that she turned dizzy and found herself suddenly addressing God— Don't let me faint, keep me up so I can do something.

She kept up, and she did something. She took the empty bowl, dipped it in the bucket and pushed it between the bars. The woman seized it, drained it, thrust it out again. There was just enough water in the bucket to fill the little bowl three times; the last time Julia set the bowl down and tipped the bucket to pour out the very last drop. When the bowl was returned she said,

"I'm sorry, there isn't any more," and her voice sounded as though she had been crying for a long time.

She handed in the rice bowl. She noticed the rice as she did so; it had been cooked some time before and in the day's heat had begun to dry and curl again. Even if the three little doles of water had quenched the woman's thirst for the moment such arid fare would quicken it again.

The woman took the bowl and held it under her chin with

one hand while with the other she scooped and shovelled the rice into her mouth. She did not chew, she swallowed, just as a dog, watched by another, would swallow food. Four dips, four gulps and the bowl was empty. She handed it back and retreated towards the post in the centre of the cage, squatted down on the heap of filth which lay there, put her elbows on her knees and her head between her hands and from under the curtain of matted black hair regarded Julia with a dull, incurious, animal stare.

People did go mad, of course; there were people so mad they tore off their clothes; so mad that for their own safety and the safety of others they had to be very strictly confined. It was possible that this was a mad woman, and that today whoever had the duty of looking after her had forgotten. . . . One mustn't go jumping to hasty conclusions, imagining the worst. There might be some explanation.

She gathered her skirt, a handful on each side, and began to run, but running meant drawing quick breaths and today there seemed to be nothing to breathe. No air, and though it was still half an hour before sunset, no light; the heavy purple pall pressed down, closer and closer, stifling, blinding. It was like the end of the world. It was like one of those dreams when you run and run, from some undefined but dreadful thing, and run and run, and make no progress.

Breathless and quite distraught, she came to the rose pergola; that too was changed, no longer a pleasant, shaded place through which to walk idly, a dark tunnel now, littered with shrivelled petals, going brown at the edges.

It was with the utmost relief that she saw, coming towards her, wiping his neck with his handkerchief, Mynheer. He moved with his ordinary, nimble, dancing master's grace.

"My dear Julia," he said, as soon as he was within speaking distance, "I have been worried about you. I should have warned you not to go far today. The rains are about to begin." A low, long-drawn-out rumble of thunder shook the dark pall that hid the sky. "You might have been caught and drenched," he said. "Or frightened by the early darkness. Take my arm; you're out of breath."

She could not speak. She took his arm gratefully and he hurried her across the lawn towards the house. Another clap of thunder shook the very air and a few, very large, very deliberate-seeming drops of water showered down.

"I should have prepared you. I do blame myself," Mynheer said, as they reached the steps of the cloister. "It came very suddenly. My dear, it is only thunder, there is no reason to be alarmed. You are trembling. Come and sit down." He led her to the salon and up to one of the red-and-gold-covered chairs. She sat down, mastered her breath, and said,

"It isn't the thunder. I've just seen something *horrible!*"

"In the compound?" he asked sharply.

"No. In a cage. A woman . . . on a chain . . . in a cage . . . starving."

"Oh." The single word rang out as it might have done had she hit him in the face. "She isn't starving. She is keeping Ramadan—a Moslem fast."

Horror receded. If the torment were self-inflicted, part of some strange creed . . . then it was different. Sick pity gave way to a puzzled, unwilling admiration. She steadied herself, brushed back her damp hair and wiped her hands on her handkerchief.

"She looked so awful. I thought she might be mad."

"She may be, now. She was sane enough once," said Mynheer, and his voice was cold, cruel. Julia, looking at him, startled, curious, saw the exact expression which had been on his face when, on her first day, he had mentioned Pieter's fall.

"Is she . . . Oh no!" she said, putting her hand to her mouth.

"She is Psyche. She was Pieter's nurse. She was a Moslem so she must keep the Fast of Ramadan; that means that for a full lunar month nothing, no food or water, may pass the lips between the moment in the morning when a white thread can be distinguished from a black one and the same moment in the evening. One evening, at the end of a parching day, she left him, to fetch herself a cup of water, and he fell. So, since Ramadan meant so much to her, more than her duty or my child's well-being, I decreed that she should keep it for the rest of her life." The disturbance in his face had not invaded his voice, he spoke calmly and with great simplicity.

"How cruel!" she said.

"That I can hardly deny. What I can deny is that her suffering has matched mine, or could, if she stayed there for a thousand years."

There was something frightening about his absolute calm, his imperviousness. It denied the friendly, almost fond relationship which had built up from day to day between them; her opinion, anything she might say, meant nothing to him. Knowing this, sensing the futility, even the unwisdom, of saying anything more, she yet felt compelled to attack.

"You can't even be sure that she *was* to blame. I knew two people who looked exactly like Pieter, in Amsterdam. They hadn't both had falls!"

"How can you be sure of that? In any case that is quite irrelevant. Pieter fell and is as he is, and Psyche is where she is. And think," his voice lightened, became sardonic, "of the merit she is acquiring. In the next life she will doubtless be Mahomet's plumpest houri—or better still, his favourite camel."

She thought of the cage, of the woman squatting on the heaped filth . . . of the cold-hearted spite which could take so protracted a vengeance for a moment's carelessness . . . and her soul sickened.

"You see, you must be careful never to provoke me," Mynheer said. "I had no idea that you would penetrate so far, or I should have warned you. I'm warning you now. Don't walk that way again. You have no need to go in search of objects of pity, you know. Pity yourself. A married woman without a husband, and with no hope of children."

The silence that followed his words was broken by the sudden roar and hiss of the rain.

CHAPTER V

The finding of Psyche had ruined Julia's sense of being perfectly happy in a perfectly beautiful place. She was like a person who, having bitten into an apple, lowers it and sees the fat maggots crawling; the impulse is to spit out the bitten piece and throw the apple away. But life, circumstances, relationships with other people, are not to be so lightly abandoned.

The emotional disturbance, coinciding as it did with the season of heavy, almost persistent rain, when exercise out of doors was impossible, resulted in wakeful nights, haunted by the thought of the woman in the cage, and also by worrying thoughts about herself and Mynheer. He had dismissed the matter entirely, and although for some days her manner to him had been stilted and unfriendly, his to her remained exactly the same, indulgent, paternal.

Lying awake, listening to the drip and patter of the rain, she tried to think, coolly, reasonably, and finally came to the conclusion that merely feeling sickened, sorry, disgusted was not enough. She must *do* something. She decided that as soon as the rain stopped she would visit the cage every day and take some food and some water. She could do it in the afternoon when Mynheer invariably slept.

Once that was decided she felt better about Psyche, less haunted; it wasn't, she realised, much to do, but it involved disobeying Mynheer, risking discovery and his wrath and was thus shifted out of the class of easy charity.

That decided she turned her thoughts to Mynheer. She had always hitherto identified herself with Psyche, put herself in the woman's place; now she tried to think of the whole affair

from his point of view. He believed—she thought sincerely—
that the woman had ruined the whole life of his son and heir;
he was angry, and he was, in Rua, completely powerful. In his
place mightn't she, mightn't anyone, act with similar ferocity?
She remembered how willingly she would have killed Juffrouw
Hoorne that night in the Klopstock Home. . . .

So, carefully, deliberately, as one might mend a precious,
broken piece of china, she endeavoured to repair her mental
image of Mynheer. The mended thing served, seemed much the
same, would last, maybe for years; but it had lost something.
The fondness that she had begun to feel for him, roughly
plucked up that afternoon, never rooted again.

He attributed her mood to the season; spoke often of the
delightful weather which would follow the rain, and of the
entertaining and outings that he planned. Several times he
mentioned Marie, and Julia, while looking forward to that visit,
at the same time shrank from it. In the circumstances some
comparison of their experiences seemed inevitable, and what
could she say?

There came a day when the rain fell less heavily and less
persistently and another when the fair periods outnumbered
the showers; and then it was sunny again, the world washed
clean and everything springing into lush new life.

"Now," said Mynheer, "we must set about some entertaining. We've led a quiet life far too long. Not, I must in all fair-
ness, warn you, that the company will be very lively. The men
have one subject of conversation—the nutmeg; and the women
discourse, I think exclusively, upon the peccadillos of their
house-slaves, sometimes so gruesomely that one has a slight
hesitation in accepting their invitations! It takes a certain in-
sensitiveness, you know, to do, as one lady did to me, first to
relate how she caught her cook straining jelly through one of
her husband's dirty stockings, and in the same breath ask me to
dinner! However, it will divert you to see the dresses and coif-
fures, and the gentlemen will pay you compliments. And as you

listen to the stories you may reflect—as I do—how much better
we do in Rua."

Their first guests were to be the Governor, his wife and a
visiting niece, and Captain Kraemer, who was in command of
the soldiers at the Fort.

"That," said Mynheer, "will make six, with us, which I think
the perfect number for dinner. It will also come to the notice
of the Agent, and he will feel rebuffed. Nowadays the com-
mercial element has become so overrated that many people
rank the Agent with the Governor. I do not."

He asked her which dress she proposed to wear, and when
she said she had not yet decided, he asked,

"Is there not one, a rather dull, slaty blue?"

"Yes. I've never yet worn it. I thought it the least attractive
of them all."

"I consider it suitable for this occasion .Will you allow me
to be judge, or do you resent my interference?"

"I'll wear it," she said.

That evening, when the dress was on, and fastened, she regretted having been so weak-willed; the dress, of beautiful,
heavy silk, was so plain as to be unbecoming. Unlike the others
it had no decoration at all; no lace, no frills, no embroidered
posies. It made her look old, and staring at her reflection she
wondered whether that might be the reason why Mynheer had
suggested it; she could think of no other.

"I don't like it," she said, turning her head to Juno. "Do you
think we could pin in a lace collar or—or something to brighten
it up a little."

"Is dress for old woman," Juno said unhelpfully. "Much
other dress, pretty dress, Mevrouw."

As she spoke a gentle tapping sounded on the sitting-room
door—the entry from the cloister. Juno padded away and in a
second or two Julia heard Mynheer's voice inquiring whether
Mevrouw was dressed. She rose, and with a rustling of silk
skirts, went into the sitting-room.

Mynheer had not chosen himself a dull and unbecoming outfit; of a paler grey than usual, his jacket and breeches had the smoothness and gloss of polished silver and the lace at his breast and wrists was particularly fine. He carried a flat square box, covered in leather.

He looked her over with critical attention.

"It is ugly, isn't it?" she asked. "Shall I change?"

"Not immediately. Try this first. . . ." He opened the box and held it out towards her. Lying on a bed of faded blue velvet was a necklace, diamonds and sapphires set in very pale gold. The chain was formed by the stones, set alternately, every one as large as a pea, and hanging from it were seven pendants each made of one large sapphire surrounded by a ring of diamonds. As she stared at it, he tilted the box slightly so that the light of a near-by candle shone in the perfect, unfathomable blue and struck sparks of scarlet, green, purple and yellow from the whiteness.

"It's pretty, isn't it?" She knew that his choice of the slight, the faintly derogatory word was deliberate.

"It's beautiful."

He put the box on the table and lifted the necklace from it, shimmering and glittering.

"Permit me," he said, and laid it around her neck and fastened it under her hair. The stones fell into place, icily, against her skin.

Stepping back he regarded her gravely.

"Yes," he said. "Yes—but see what you think, my dear."

She ran to the glass. The dress, she herself, utterly transformed; the blue and the sparkle seemed to have invaded her eyes.

"I am sometimes right," said Mynheer modestly. "When I ordered that dress I bore in mind that my daughter-in-law might be someone whom I could bear to see wearing that necklace. It suits you very well. I hope you will wear it on many pleasant occasions."

"I don't know what to say, Mynheer."

"There is no need to say anything. What there is need of . . ." he lowered his voice a little. "Julia, this evening I'm afraid you must be prepared for a mild form of inquisition. The ladies will hardly miss such an opportunity of satisfying their curiosity. They will ask you all the questions that the people of Banda have been asking themselves for so long—and never quite dared ask *me*. So imagine that Mevrouw Van de Lijn has you in a corner and asks you about Pieter's disfigurement. What will you say?"

She thought for a moment, and then looking straight at him said,

"Mynheer, I shall tell her that Pieter's disfigurement is grossly exaggerated by everybody, including himself."

Behind the bulging, clear glassy grey eyes something popped up and looked out for a moment; something surprised, uneasy, vaguely respectful. It gave her the look which an expert might give a novice who had proved astonishingly adept at some game. It was not altogether pleased.

Then he smiled. "A beautifully ambiguous answer, my dear; and nobody else will be conscious of its ambiguity. I couldn't have thought of a better myself. Stick to that and you will do well."

She experienced, that evening, something she had never known before—a feeling of pride, pride in the place which she now called home, pride in the family of which she was now a member. It was so plain that these people—the most important members of Banda's society—regarded Mynheer with a respect that was little short of awe; even the Governor deferred to him, saying, "With your long experience . . .", saying, "Now on this I should value your opinion. . . ." And Mynheer, presiding with geniality, with easy dignity, at his own table, was at his very best. It was impossible not to admire him, difficult not to like him. Here at this table, bright with flowers and the best service of silver-gilt, watching the skill with which he directed the conversation, everyone included, everyone provoked to animation, feeling about her throat the cold clasp of the necklace, being praised, displayed, smiled upon, was it narrow-minded, she wondered, to withhold something, to resist the appeal of his personality, to remember Psyche in her prison?

Half-way through the meal something happened for which Julia was not prepared.

Every evening, just before the candles were lighted, screens of the finest gauze, stretched tight over wooden battens, were placed inside the iron grill-work of the windows to keep out the night-flying things which might be attracted by the light. The verandah outside was ordinarily left in darkness, but this evening—she had imagined for the convenience of the guests arriving and departing—lanterns had been placed at intervals between the flower-brimming urns; the windows were pale golden transparencies, traced with black, curving patterns.

Suddenly Mynheer broke off in mid-sentence and looked fixedly at one window, thus drawing everyone's attention to it. Blocked darkly against the lantern light, filling the window, was the whole of one human figure and half another, a jutting hat brim, one shoulder. The one seen fully Julia recognised as Doctor Hootman; the other? Pieter? Even she could not be *quite* certain. Doctor Hootman turned his head and seemed to address his companion, and lifted his hand and laid it on the other's shoulder, and they moved away in such a direction that the man who was half-glimpsed was never fully seen.

"Pieter and his friend have resumed their walks now that the rain is ended. That is something to be thankful for," said Mynheer.

There was a moment of slightly embarrassed silence; then the Governor said,

"Such a pity—to take it so hard." He turned to Julia and said, "I suppose, Mevrouw, you hardly notice anything amiss, now. I am sure that, given the same opportunity, we should all become equally accustomed."

"Only today . . ." she said, and tried out the neat little speech.

Captain Kraemer, with the best intentions, broke in with an account of a fellow officer, a handsome man, who had been shot through the jaw. "Never could close his mouth properly afterwards, poor fellow. But we soon got used to the sight of his teeth."

"Ah, but he was of reasonable age," said Mynheer. "One cannot reason with a child. Before we realised what was happening Pieter's habit of seclusion was fixed and nothing will alter it now. Still," his voice brightened, "he is very fortunate. He has his Doctor Hootman, and he now has Julia, who shares all his pursuits, except music." He smiled at her, indulgently, mock-reprovingly. Captain Kraemer, who was musical, tactfully took that as a cue and the conversation drifted away from Pieter.

Even the inquisition for which Mynheer had prepared Julia, did not take place. Mevrouw Van de Lijn was engrossed with anxiety about her own child, a daughter, married and living in Holland, and due about now, so nearly as the mother could reckon, to have a baby.

"And whether things go well with her or not, whether I have a grandson or a grand-daughter, I can't possibly know for another seven months. That is what I find so hard. I don't mind the climate, I'm not afraid of a slave revolt, or of the Fire Mountain erupting, or of finding a snake in my bed, but I do mind, I mind very much, these separations and the feeling of being at the world's end, so entirely cut off."

Using slightly different words she said the same thing several times.

The niece, a plump, pretty but very dull girl, had no thought to spare for Pieter Vosmar either, being intent upon Captain Kraemer, whom she hoped to marry.

At the evening's end, however, attention was drawn to Pieter again. As the guests were leaving, about to make their way from the house to the little jetty where the Governor's prahau with a lighted lantern at its prow bobbed and looked like a dancing fire-fly, the sound of the clavichord, played in a mas-

terly manner, came from the end of the house where Pieter's
apartments lay. It was far from being the pleasant, tinkling
tune produced by the average performer. In the wild, stormy
music there seemed to sound the cry of a soul unsatisfied, lonely
and searching, racked by a measureless yearning. Exactly so
might the legendary Pieter have played.

"Ah," said Captain Kraemer in a voice of awed appreciation.

"Poor boy! So gifted too," said the Governor.

His wife gave a little shiver. The music spoke to her of the
miles of tossing, perpetually discontented sea which lay between her and Holland where her heart was this night.

Turning back into the house Mynheer laid his hand on
Julia's arm.

"My dear, you did splendidly. I was very proud of you. Your
manner to that tiresome old mother-hen could not have been
bettered. People really *should* learn to leave their private concerns at home."

It was an unsympathetic speech, and that part of her mind
which was now alert for such things duly took note of it. The
other part remarked that he, of all men, was justified in making
it.

After that there were other dinner parties, and several times
Mynheer and Julia went to dine in one or another of the big
houses in Banda. There was never time on these occasions to
visit Marie, he said; and Julia was glad, she had no wish to
appear before Marie finely gowned and bejewelled.

One day Mynheer returned from a visit to Banda and said
that he had made an appointment there for the morning, two
days ahead; his business would take about two hours and he
thought it would be a convenient time for Julia to make her
visit.

"I took the liberty of sending word so that she may expect
you. You must take her some flowers, they have no garden I
believe."

Marie lived in a narrow house squeezed between two taller, larger buildings. It was faded pink in colour and except that it had shutters might have been any house in any humble street in Holland.

She opened the door herself and Julia had difficulty in suppressing an exclamation of surprise. Marie had greatly changed, grown so fat that she almost filled the doorway; lost all her trimness, all her good looks. Behind her, in the narrow passage stood another woman with two children peering from behind her skirts.

The population of Banda Neira had grown rapidly and since the town could not spread outwards without filching land from the precious nutmeg groves there was a shortage of houses and the Oltman menage was typical of many. Marie and Hendrik shared a house with his brother, his wife and two children and an unmarried clerk from the Agent's office.

". . . and now he wants to get married too," said Marie, explaining the situation, "and we haven't the heart to say he can't; so where we shall be then, I don't know."

She had lost none of her cheerfulness, of her vivacity, Julia was glad to find. Chattering gaily she led the way into a hot, cluttered sitting-room, called her sister-in-law and introduced her and asked her to put the flowers in water, and shooed away the children.

"Now," she said, "let me look at you! And tell me quickly, while we're alone, which we shan't be for long, are you all right, Julia?" She asked the question with a peculiar urgency.

"I'm very well. Are you?" But surely it was wrong to have grown so very stout, so pale and puffy of face in so short . . . how long? Good Heavens, six whole months.

"I'm as you see," said Marie, looking down at her bulging figure with some pride. She giggled, "Almost at *once!* Hendrik is so pleased. He wants a girl to look like me; and I want a boy to look like him. And it *could* be twins, couldn't it, the size I am."

So that was it!

"I'm so glad for you."

"I'm glad too. Mind, I shall be more glad when it, or they, have arrived. I look so awful. It's no use being polite and trying to contradict me. I look as ugly as sin. And the odd thing is, Hendrik doesn't think so. He says honestly that I'm prettier now than ever. Do you think something comes over men who are going to be fathers, a sort of blindness?"

Deep in Julia's mind something stirred. Men and women were made and put together by the good God . . . no mistake . . . even such a veiling of a man's sight. That, she thought, must be real love. . . .

"I wanted to come and see you," Marie ran on. "But the Vosmars are so rich and important, and we aren't yet—though Hendrik is so clever and hard-working, he's bound to get on—it didn't seem quite right for me to come to you first. And then this happened. And you didn't come and didn't come. I have been a bit worried about you."

"Why?"

Marie looked away and a little, unbecoming, colour crept into her pasty cheeks.

"Well . . . such tales go round," she said. "Don't mind me asking. Is it true that your husband had a terrible accident and is dreadful to look at?"

Once again the neat little sentence served.

"And then there's that frightening old man. Oh, when I saw you go off with him Julia . . . I did pity you."

"But he's very kind—to me. I'm not frightened of him." But that is a lie, every afternoon when I steal out of the house to visit Psyche I can hardly breathe for fear.

"If he's kind, his looks belie him. But I'm glad he is. And what about your husband, apart from his looks? Did you get a nice one? Oh, I like Hendrik so much, I couldn't help wondering about you."

"Pieter and I get on very well. He's very fond of me. He'd do anything he could to please me." That at least was true.

"Well, that just shows. They say he's surly, never sees anybody, never speaks. They even say he's a bit . . ." she tapped her head with her finger and laughed, then, leaning forward took Julia by the hand. "I suppose you'll think I am crack-brained too, but truly, when somebody told me that, I was upset. All I could think of was Mucky Karl . . . being married to him! Ughhh!" She gave an exaggerated shudder and was about to laugh again. "What's the matter? You have turned white," she said.

Julia made the effort.

"The thought of being married to Mucky Karl is enough to turn anyone white, isn't it?" And he isn't like Mucky Karl; he's very clean. (Because he is so well-looked after, Doctor Hootman. . . .) Not dangerous either. (Because he is sheltered, not sent out in the street to be jeered at. . . .)

"It turned me more than white," Marie was saying, "it made me really sick; but of course that might have been . . ." She looked down at herself again; then at Julia and said brightly,

"You'll have to have a baby, won't you? A boy for you. Look what he'll inherit!"

Another effort. "Give me time! Slow starters often go farthest."

But Marie had succeeded in diverting her own attention.

"They're vastly rich, aren't they?" She looked at the simple dress Julia had chosen to wear for this visit; and wondered if—like so many rich people, they were mean. She didn't quite dare to ask the question directly, so she said. "I expected you to walk in all silks and satins and covered with diamonds."

"But I had to come in a prahau. I have a silk dress. . . ."

She could see that Marie was so happy, so contented with her lot that she was safe from envy, so she described one or two of her dresses.

"Have you one of those native things? You know, a sarong and little jacket? Oh, well, Hendrik and I were asked to the Agent's once—I don't like *her*, nose-in-the-air, but that's by the way—and she was wearing one, pink and purple, very thin stuff the jacket, it looked so cool and pretty. I meant to make myself one—you only have to do straight hemming on the sarong, easy—but then this happened and it didn't seem worth it for a while. But I shall after, if I ever get back to my right size that is. It seems unlikely doesn't it?"

In such girlish chatter the time passed swiftly. The sister-in-law came in, carrying Mynheer's offering of lilies and roses and orchids which she had crammed into an ugly brass bowl; she went out again and returned bringing strong black coffee and some rather stale little cakes. The children stole into the room, soon forgot their shyness and began squabbling and had to be sent out; the lack of garden was deplored. Soon it was time to go.

At the moment of parting, Marie had a resurgence of anxiety.

"You really are all right, Julia? Happy?"

"Of course. You must come and see for yourself."

"I can't take a boat trip just now. I will afterwards—if you invite me."

"I am inviting you," Julia said. How would Mynheer take that?

The prahau swung out of the harbour and headed for Rua.

"Well, and how did you enjoy your visit?" Mynheer asked.

"Very much, thank you. We had such a lot to talk about."

"Your little friend is enjoying her new life?"

"Oh, very much."

"Not feeling the heat too greatly?" Such interest in Marie was rather surprising; it struck, for some reason, a slightly false note.

"She didn't complain. Of course in that small house it is hot; and they have no garden. She was delighted with the flowers and sent you messages of gratitude." That was not true. Marie had handed the flowers to Rita and hardly looked at them when they were brought in. Save for a flash or two in Julia's direction Marie's eyes were turned inward, self-absorbed.

"I expect she told you all the gossip of the town."

"No. I don't think we gossiped at all." Or was Marie's mention of the Agent's wife being nose-in-the-air gossip? "We talked mainly about ourselves, I'm afraid."

She could feel, without turning her head, that he was looking at her closely. He was wanting, waiting for her to tell him something more. What? Oh, of course . . .

"She did ask me a few questions about Pieter, which was only natural. My answers satisfied her, and, I think, would have satisfied you."

"I'm sure of that. I rely upon your discretion absolutely."

He seemed to wait again. Then he said,

"Well, perhaps it is true—as some ladies aver—that men are the real gossips. It seems that my business talk has provided me with a tit-bit that you missed. Unless you saw fit not to mention it to me."

"You mean about Marie . . . that she is going to have a baby?"

"Yes. Is it true? Then was it modesty that kept you silent on the subject. Or envy?"

She had a sudden, strange, utterly unwarranted suspicion that he had known all along; that he had deliberately postponed taking her to visit Marie until he had, somehow, on his previous trip, heard that she was pregnant. But that was stupid, why should he? And why this sudden probing?

"Neither. I just felt that, in the circumstances, it was a matter better not mentioned between us. That was all."

"Now why?" he asked. "Between us there should be complete understanding. We two are alone as few people are; if we cannot confide in one another in whom can we confide? My dear you do, despite the poor little house, the lack of prospects and everything, envy her, do you not?"

What did he want her to say?

"I suppose every woman, if she could, would like to have a child of her own, but . . ."

"Exactly," he broke in with something less than his usual courtesy. "And every woman *should*. It is her *right!*"

In the circumstances an astonishing, a challenging thing to
say. But I can't, she thought, go into it with him, now; once
I might have. But I must answer. . . . She said, "Many women
remain unmarried, Mynheer. What about them?"

"This is an imperfect world, my dear. The rules are made,
hit or miss; often by knaves to exploit fools, or by fools to control knaves. I never pay heed to the rules, I never have. I still
say that any woman, married or single, should have a child if
she wants one."

It all seemed to be leading somewhere, but where?

"That is a very original idea," she said.

He laughed. "I'm sure somebody said just those words to the
man who first thought of harnessing a horse, or setting the
wind to work a mill or sail a ship. Today's innovation is tomorrow's commonplace. Where would the world be if no one
had ever had an original idea? I feel very strongly . . ."

She waited, feeling that the next words would reveal his purpose, make everything plain.

"I talk too much," he said. "And for that you are partly to
blame. You're very easy to talk to, very sympathetic in the real
sense of the word. I often forget that you are so young, and a
female. Never mind. One day . . ."

He left that sentence unfinished too, and reached out and
patted her hand. Then he took up his cane and rapped it
threateningly.

CHAPTER VI

One day during the next week Myn-
heer made another visit to Banda Neira, this time alone.

"I will not ask you to come with me today, my dear, because my business will take longer. Also I may bring two guests back for dinner and I want you, if you will be so kind, to do a job for me." He took out his keys and removed one from the chain and handed it to her. "That is the key of the plate cupboard. Pluto knows what to get out, but I would like you to be there. He will overload a tray and then things fall and are dented. Make him bring out one piece at a time." He smiled at her as she stood with the key in her hand. "It is very pleasant for me to have someone to whom I can entrust these little domestic details," he said genially. "And of course you must begin to take charge. One day you will rule this house; rule all Rua in fact."

She said, with sincerity, "I hope that day will be long in coming, Mynheer."

"Thank you, my dear. But it will come. That is a fact to be faced. However, I have made every possible provision . . ."

The vision of the future, thus conjured up, cast a slight gloom over the bright morning. Day-to-day living in Rua was— apart from the ever-nagging memory of the woman in the cage —very pleasant and carefree, but to look ahead was to see a time and a situation curiously shapeless, empty of the landmarks which ordinary people saw along the years.

She tried to throw off her bewildering and foreboding thoughts by being busy, but Pluto suggested, in the most humble fawning manner, that the removal of the silver should take place in the afternoon. Speaking so servilely, not even looking sulky, he managed to convey to her that her supervision was hurtful to his feelings, so she agreed to the postponement without demur or question. When afternoon came he was so exaggeratedly careful in the handling of the many pieces of the silver-gilt dinner service which was to be used that evening that the afternoon was well advanced before Julia could relock the cupboard and go away.

On any ordinary afternoon this would have worried her, but today, with Mynheer safe in Banda, it did not matter. She went calmly to her room, picked up a rather large bag of pale pink brocade with a piece of embroidery sticking out of it, and set off to pay her daily visit to Psyche. Concealed under the embroidery was some food saved from her own midday meal and an old wine bottle full of water.

Ordinarily she made this furtive little journey during the hottest hour of the day, when she could be almost certain that Mynheer was asleep. *Almost,* never *quite* certain, and it was always with a feeling of trepidation, an increase of the heartbeat, that she went into the garden, sat on a seat and stitched for a few minutes and then with a purposeless, wandering air, strolled into the nutmeg grove and broke into a brisk walk.

Psyche now knew her, and watched for her coming; every afternoon she was at the bars of the cage on the side from which Julia appeared. Apart from this recognition of identity and purpose their relationship had remained static and Julia was not even sure whether the woman was fully sane or not. On the first few occasions when she had brought the extra food and water, she had been appalled by the way in which she, herself a woman, fully dressed and at liberty, had handed food and water through bars, to another woman, naked and caged as though she were an animal, and to mitigate the situation she had tried to talk to her, calling her by name. There was no response; eighteen years of slow torture and solitary confinement had reduced Psyche to something less than human, and eventually Julia could see that this was merciful. It would be unkind, wrong, to make any attempt to recall the mind, the soul, the personality, whatever it was which did distinguish people from animals. Julia contented herself with handing in what she had brought and hurrying away. Sometimes, on her way back she cried a little; and sometimes she felt a renewed upsurge of dislike for Mynheer.

This afternoon Psyche was waiting as usual at the corner nearest the point where Julia entered the little clearing. An extra meal every day for some weeks had done nothing to change her dreadful appearance; under the filthy scaly skin every bone, every ligament showed plainly. Her eyes, under the shadow of the mat of hair, flickered with recognition and avidity, and Julia was glad to think that today there was meat in the bag. She could remember, from her own hungry days in the Klopstock Home, how meat-hungry one could become, even when otherwise sufficiently fed, and how wonderful the sailor's meat pies had tasted.

Ordinarily, as soon as Julia arrived, Psyche, after that single, human-seeming glance, would run, with a clanking of the chain, to the other side of the cage where the water and rice were displayed in their Tantalus inaccessibility. Today, however, she stayed where she was, pushing her claw-like hands through the bars and whimpering. She was more thirsty than usual, Julia thought, because of the delay.

"I'm sorry I'm late," she said, forgetting her resolve not to attempt any communication, "come along." She walked around to the side where the bowls and the bucket stood. Psyche, legs bowed, shoulders bent, ran across with a clanking of the chain. Julia put the bag on the ground by the bars, removed the piece of embroidery and the packet of food and revealed the bottle, standing upright with the pink folds of the brocade bag collapsed around its base. She reached out for the bowl into which she always poured the water. As she did so Psyche's hand shot through the bars and snatched at the bottle, drawing it into the cage. Poor thing, she is thirsty, Julia thought; and, despite all evidence to the contrary, she can still reason. It is quicker to drink from the bottle than to have a bowl filled, handed in, handed out and refilled. No animal could have worked that out. Yet Psyche, bottle in hand, was retreating towards the centre of the cage with exactly the look of a cat that has made off with a piece of fish.

"It's all right," Julia said. "Drink out of the bottle if you like. But you must give it back to me. I must have it back, Psyche. I must have it back." She heard a certain shrillness in her voice, and thought, I mustn't frighten her, I must keep calm.

"Drink it and give me back the bottle, for tomorrow."

Psyche made no attempt to take out the cork. Perhaps she

had forgotten. . . . She wasn't even handling the bottle as though she intended to drink out of it. She held it by its neck.

She is mad, after all, Julia thought.

Holding the bottle by the neck and swinging it as though it were a club, Psyche hit it against the post. It broke, the water splashed out and pieces of glass fell down onto the heap of filth. The neck of the bottle, with the cork still in it, remained in her hand until she dropped it amongst the other fragments. Then she bent down, looked at the pieces of glass and quite deliberately chose one. With it in her hand she stood up, and then, with that same deliberation, drew the edge of it across her stringy throat.

It made, to begin with, a cut, like a little mouth with red lips; then, in a flash, the wound, Psyche's hand, the piece of glass which it held were all lost in a gush of blood. Nobody could have believed that that dried-out, emaciated body could have contained the fountain of blood which shot out until it reached the bars of the cage, hit them with such force that it ricochetted and spattered Julia and her dress and the brocade bag.

It all happened so suddenly that there wasn't time even to close one's eyes, or look away.

Psyche did not fall down immediately; the arching fountain of blood had slackened before she fell to her knees and then forward from the waist until her face touched the ground. In this prayerful attitude her body gave one or two convulsive twitches which jerked it slightly sideways; then it was still.

It had all happened so suddenly, and been so unexpected, that it was difficult to believe that it had happened at all. But it had happened. There lay Psyche, dead, with the bits of broken glass around her, and there was Julia, sick and dizzy, clinging to the bars of the cage for support. Despite the heaving of her stomach and the unsteadiness of the ground under her feet and of everything around her, she could think, quite clearly.

Psyche was dead; she was glad of that; her troubles were

over. Mynheer would come, at feeding time, see the corpse and
the bits of glass. He would instantly suspect Julia, because she
had once shown interest in the dead woman. He would be
furiously angry. Baulked of the rest of his vengeance what
would his vengeance be? There was only one answer to that.
He would put her in the cage. She would spend the rest of her
life there, naked, chained to a post by a heap of filth. There
was no escape. She was on an island, she couldn't get away,
there was nowhere to hide; except for Marie, inaccessible in
Banda, she hadn't a friend in the world.

She began to tremble, so violently that her hands could no
longer clasp the bars, so violently that her head jerked and
shook like that of an old person with palsy. I must get away,
she thought, away from this place of horror. The idea of drowning herself slipped into her mind. Yes, death in the cool, crystal-
clear blue water would be better than facing Mynheer in his
rage. He had warned her, said she must be careful not to provoke him.

She staggered out of the clearing and onto the path, turning
away from the house and towards the shore. She had taken
only a few jerky, shuffling steps when she stopped to listen,
thinking that she heard other steps coming towards her around
the curve of the path. It was so. Mynheer, back from Banda
rather earlier than he had expected and coming from that direction towards the cage.

She would have turned and run the other way, or darted off
and hidden in the nutmeg grove, but she now could not move
at all except to shudder and tremble. She could only stand in
the middle of the narrow path and wait.

It was not Mynheer. It was nobody she had ever seen before.
A man, giving, at that slight distance, an impression of youth
unconfirmed, she was to learn, by a closer view. The same clarity of mind which had enabled her to realise at once what she
had done, what the result might be, and the hopelessness of
her situation, came into play again now as she stood paralysed
and palsied and watched him approach. She even noticed that

he looked surprised, a little startled at the sight of her, and that as he drew nearer his expression changed to astonishment, and concern.

He came close enough to touch her, looking at the path behind her and into the grove on either side.

"Have you had a fright? What's the matter?" he asked.

She tried to speak, but she had no more control of her jaw and tongue than of her legs; her teeth chattered and that was the only sound.

"I didn't frighten you, did I? I'm harmless."

He saw the splashes of fresh blood on the front of her dress, the state of her hands where she had clutched the blood-splashed bars. He tried again.

"Have you had an accident?"

Almost unwillingly then he touched her, put his hand under her arm and turned her slightly.

"Sit down," he said, and helped her down and propped her back against the trunk of a tree. Her head was still jerking so uncontrollably that her hair rubbed against and was caught in the rough bark.

The man carried a brown jacket over his left arm. He now turned it about, searched for and found the pocket and brought out a small, dented silver flask. He removed its top and bending down held it towards her.

"Take a sip of that. It'll pull you together."

She tried to lift a shaking hand, then tried to shake her jerking head to indicate inability.

"Poor girl," he said, "you are in a state." He threw down the jacket, knelt beside her, put an arm round her shoulders and with his other hand held the flask to her lips, exactly as though she were a baby. Even with his firm hand on the flask it was difficult for her to hold its top between her chattering teeth and some of the liquid jerked out, ran over her chin and onto her dress.

"You got some," he said. "Try again." He tightened his clasp on her shoulders, steadying her, and that time she did better.

"Once more; that's right." He set the flask down, reached for his jacket and put it between her and the tree as he withdrew his arm. "Just sit back and wait for a bit," he said. He capped the flask and put it this time into the pocket of his worn, faded blue breeches. And again he looked this way, that way along the path, and into the trees on both sides.

Whatever it was he had given her ran warmly down from her throat to the pit of her stomach and after a minute or two from there it began to spread out. Every rigor that shook her was now a little weaker than the one before. Presently she tried to move her hand again, and this time it came up at her bidding, she took her lower jaw between her finger and thumb, held it for a few seconds and then managed to say,

"Thank you."

"Now," he said, with an air of getting down to business. "Are you hurt?" She shook her head. "Then where does all this blood come from?"

"Psyche . . . she killed herself." The radiating warmth which had run about, loosening the grip of the shaking paralysis, had now reached the very core of her mind; she burst into tears. "It was awful," she gulped out between two sobs. "I was glad for her, but it was . . . an awful way to die." She drew two, harsh snuffling breaths, felt in her sleeve, found her handkerchief and used it, and gasped out, "Unless I drown myself I think he'll put me in the cage instead. Oh, I know it all sounds crazy, but this is a crazy place. You don't know!"

Now the extreme, painful clarity of mind which had enabled her to observe everything so minutely—even to the fact that his shirt had once been fine, and that now its frill was in tatters—had given way to emotional confusion. She hardly noticed that he had slipped his arm around her again and was holding her close to his shoulder and urging her to have her cry out because then she would be able to tell him what was the matter and he would see if there were anything he could do.

With her mind she was hardly aware of all this; but her body remembered that in just this way Uncle Johannes had held

her and comforted her when something had gone wrong with
her childish world. Since his death her life had been singularly
devoid of physical contacts; the drunken sailor had kissed her,
she had hugged Katje in the cellar, amongst the Company's
Daughters light fleeting kisses had been current, and Mynheer
sometimes touched her arm or patted her hand, but nobody,
for years, had held her with intent to comfort or sustain. Despite everything, she was comforted.

At last, in the encroaching calm, she was able to say,
"Are you a friend of Mynheer Vosmar's?"

"Let's say an acquaintance. I'll tell you this. If it's trouble
between you and him, I'm on your side."

"Why?" she asked, lifting her head from his shoulder and
mopping her eyes.

"Because I'm always on the side of ladies in distress. No,
seriously, you're safe with me. What *is* the matter?"

While she had been crying he had been trying to decide her
status. She was white, and the soiled dress was pretty and expensive; but amongst the wealthy planters white concubines
were not unknown. An agency in Java specialised in the supply of girls for the purpose, mainly Greek or Georgian. . . .

"If there's anything I can do to help, tell me," he said. "I
haven't much time."

"I don't see that anyone could help me. Mynheer kept a poor
woman in a cage and slowly starved her—kept her short of
water too, so every day I took her some and just now she
snatched the bottle and cut her throat. He'll know it was me.
She's been there for eighteen years and nobody else ever bothered. He'll put me in the cage instead—unless I drown myself."

"Or I said I gave her the bottle. . . ."

She moved her head a little so that she could look into his
face, and instantly he slackened his clasp on her and shifted
his position so that they were no longer in contact.

"Could you do that? Would you?" she asked in an awed
voice.

"I don't see why not. He can't do anything to me."

His eyes, she noticed, with some part of her mind which had disengaged itself from the main problem, were blue; not the soft periwinkle blue of her dream porcelain-figure lover, a brighter, harder blue, and they were narrow, wrinkled at the outer corners as though he were always screwing them against the glare of the sun.

"I don't know," she said doubtfully. "He'll be *very* angry, and he's a ruthless man."

"The most ruthless man I know, and I have known a few. But his anger wouldn't hurt *me*. Don't you fret about that. Let's work it out; I'm coming along this path, carrying a bottle of wine, nothing extraordinary about that. What draws my attention? I've walked this path before and never noticed anything . . . where is this cage? How did you find it?"

"Behind that fence," she said, looking in that direction and then quickly away again. "I heard her moaning."

"All right. *I* heard her moaning. I gave her the bottle of wine. That is, I might say, and will seem so to Mynheer, quite out of keeping with my character, but then the circumstances are somewhat unusual. Will that do?"

She said slowly, "I don't know what to say. I should be so deeply, so everlastingly gr . . ." She began to cry again.

"Ah, don't!" he said. "It's over now. You'll just puff up your face and that will look suspicious. And we haven't much time. He'll soon be back. You've got a lot of cleaning up to do. So that shall be our story, eh?"

"If you're *sure* you don't mind the risk."

"All I risk is that he should burst with fury, and I don't think he will. Tell me," he said in a different voice, "what hold has he on you that you should be frightened of him?"

"He's my father-in-law."

"Your *what?*"

"My father-in-law."

"Great God in Heaven! You don't tell me you're married to that idiot boy!"

For the first time she felt something shameful about her situation. Hitherto it had been unusual, false, bewildering, but nothing more, in no way a reflection upon herself. Her face grew hot and she looked down as she said,

"I didn't know; it was a Glove Marriage. And of course it is in name only."

He said nothing for a moment.

"Are they kind to you?"

"Oh yes, very kind. Today, of course was different. I did disobey him. . . ." That was a reminder. "Mynheer, if you do take the blame for what I did, when can you tell him? I think he comes to feed . . . her, at sunset every day. If he came before he heard your story he would think of me and if he spoke of it, or questioned or accused me I'm afraid I should give myself away."

"He shall know that I am waiting to see him, on most urgent business the moment he sets foot on the jetty. Make your mind easy. All you have to do is to clean up; and forget all about it. Especially forget that you ever saw me."

"Oh, I couldn't do that. I shall remember you and what you've done for me every day of my life."

"No, just forget it." His voice changed again. "Do you see much of Daan Hootman?"

"Every day, several times."

"He's a good chap. If ever you need a friend he'd stand by."

"I'll remember that. But I shall be all right. I've learned my lesson. I shall never interfere with anything again."

"That's right," he said. He rose lightly to his feet and reached down a hand to help her to hers. "How do you feel?"

"A little shaky, but all right, thank you."

"I'll walk a little way with you. Then I'll look behind that fence, so that my story hangs together."

"It's a dreadful sight," she said with a shudder.

"Don't think about it. It's over. She's in Heaven, Paradise, whatever you call it, the place where everything is made up to us."

"You believe that?"

"Sometimes. Anyway, you think that, and remember you helped her on her way. I think you've been extremely brave."

"I'm not. I'm a coward to my bones. Every time I've come I've been so frightened that I felt sick."

"But that is the very essence of bravery. Well, I mustn't come any farther; I have an appointment. Just forget all about it and be careful in future. I hope everything will work out all right for you."

He had stopped in the path and she realised that now she must go one way and he another; that she would never see him again, and must even try to forget that she had ever seen him.

"I haven't thanked you properly . . . but then I never could. And now we have to say goodbye. . . ." Tears rushed to her eyes again. She held out her hand and he took it. Then, suddenly, acting on impulse he gave it a little pull, drawing her nearer, and bending his head, kissed her on the forehead, just where the brown hair grew in a little peak.

"That's for luck," he said lightly. "You're the sweetest thing I've seen for many a long day."

She threw her arms round his neck and kissed him on the mouth, for luck, for gratitude, for goodbye, with a kind of innocent passion. He stood rigid and unresponsive for a second; then, under hers, his lips moved, once. Instantly he reached up his hands and caught hers.

"You really must go, it's getting late," he said stiffly.

She knew that if she tried to speak again she would cry, her throat ached and her eyes were swimming. She began to walk quickly away; but at the path's end she turned and looked back. He was standing where she had left him, his shabby old jacket slung over his arm. He raised a hand and she waved back, taking a last look at him with her heart in her eyes.

As she hurried along the rose pergola she saw Doctor Hootman on the other side of the garden, but he entered the grove from that side by a less frequented path, and she was able to reach the house unobserved.

CHAPTER VII

       Beneath his stolid appearance, phlegmatic manner and slow-moving calm, Doctor Hootman concealed a lively and sensitive perception and an imagination more than averagely facile. The instant the man he had come to meet was within sight, before a word or glance had been exchanged, he sensed that something had happened and that this meeting was in some way different from their former ones. Circumstances being what they were anything different held the threat of disaster and within his big slack body his spirit braced itself for the reception of bad news.

Philosophically he reminded himself that those who play with fire must expect sooner or later to burn their fingers: he congratulated himself that his connection with the dangerous element had been more or less a vicarious one.

They met, shook hands; and in the doing of it Doctor Hootman asked,

"What's the matter Charles? You look perturbed."

"Do I?" Charles rubbed his hand over his face as though to right his expression. "And well I may," he said, a faint grin coming and going and leaving his look unchanged.

"Is something wrong?"

"Oh, with the job? No. All safe in Madagascar by now, or should be, and the money lodged. I wasn't thinking about that. It's what has been happening *here*, that's what I want to know, my boy."

"Here? Everything here is as usual."

"You're an old oyster. You've got an addition to the family, I understand."

"Oh, that," said Doctor Hootman with an air of relief, dismissing Julia as of no importance. "The jungle drums don't miss much, do they? Yes, in addition to all the other trappings of normality, Pieter has now been provided with a wife."

"I've just seen her."

"Good God! Did she see you?"

"We had a long conversation."

"Most unwise. Suppose she mentions you."

"She won't. She can keep a secret." Charles flung himself down on the crisp, aromatic leaves that had drifted beside the path. "She's had one of her own which I bet even *you* never ferreted out."

Lowering himself more awkwardly Doctor Hootman also sat down.

"I must confess it had never occurred to me to look into her activities."

"Well, listen to this." Doctor Hootman did listen, intently, while Charles told him, briefly, the story of Julia's visits to Psyche and how the last one had ended.

"Next thing I know I shall have a case of apoplexy on my hands," Doctor Hootman said, speaking as though he relished the prospect. "He'll be so mad with anger, and the conflict between his fury and the paternal attitude he must preserve will be enough to make him burst a blood vessel." He hugged his knees and looked pleased.

"He won't be angry with *her*. Me. I'm the scapegoat. We worked it all out. I was walking along, found the poor wretch and gave her the bottle of wine which I was bringing up as a present for himself. That'll burst all his blood vessels, eh?"

Charles laughed outright, and Doctor Hootman's pleased look warmed for a moment into a smile. They were men of entirely dissimilar character, breeding and experience, with nothing in common except the furtive bit of business they carried on behind Mynheer's back, but that was in itself a strong link. They were a little like two schoolboys in league against a master.

Doctor Hootman's smile soon vanished.

"I don't call that a good move at all. You're not supposed to be here today."

"I've got a story to explain that, too. Don't you worry."

"I have reason. It looks to me as though you threw away all caution at the sight of a pretty face. If she were in the condition you describe you could have turned off into the trees and kept out of sight."

"She was in the condition I described and nobody with a drop of human blood in his veins could have left her in it; or failed to help her, if he could."

"I don't think he'll believe you."

"What else can he believe? I've even checked on the bottle. Lovely bottle of Rhenish it was!" His face hardened. "I shan't give him time for doubts, Daan. I shan't walk in and say, 'So sorry, Mynheer, I had the slight misfortune to finish off your victim.' I shall tell him straight out that he's a damned filthy swine and that I don't think I can do business with him any more."

"Yes," said Doctor Hootman thoughtfully and with approval, "that does lend a ring of conviction. And it will set him thinking. That's the line to take."

"It's not a line. It's how I feel. I shall have a hard job to keep my hands off him."

Doctor Hootman looked with mild interest at the harsh-lined face, now scoured with angry disgust.

"I shouldn't have thought that Psyche's plight . . ." he began.

"Damn it all, I'm not thinking of Psyche—though that was bad enough. It's the girl. Of all the vile things to do, to fetch out that poor innocent child and marry her off to . . . I'm tough-bellied, but when she said she was *married* I did feel bloody sick."

One of Doctor Hootman's eyebrows moved a little.

"You needn't concern yourself about *that*, Charles. They live quite separately. And theirs is really rather a touching relationship. She plays with him as though he were about four

years old and just a little backward, or as though he were a
dog."

As he spoke, something deeply buried, most intricately coiled
at the very roots of his mind, moved, cold and sluggish, a snake
stirring from its winter sleep.

"She seems to have made quite an impression on you,
Charles. Was she equally taken with you?"

"She probably wouldn't recognise me again if she saw me.
Poor girl, she was half out of her mind with distress and terror.
She'd got an idea that he might put *her* in his cage. She said
she thought of that every time she went—but she'd gone, just
the same. That's pluck, if you like. Every day, in cold blood,
not the way we work. And getting nothing out of it either."
Some memory moved; the planes of his face shifted, the look
of troubled disgust gave way to a half-rueful smile.

"She was grateful," he said. "What's her name?"

"Julia."

"Julia," he tried it over; he liked it; it suited her. He caught
Doctor Hootman's eye, and broke into a self-derisive laugh.

"We can't all be like you, you old eunuch! It's a hell of a
long time since I *saw* a white woman, much less talked to one."

"The brown ones are well spoken of."

"They're all right; but they do so stink of that nutmeg
cheese." He turned his attention to more immediate matters.

"Get hold of Mynheer, Daan, as soon as he lands, and tell
him a man—you can say a rough-looking character if you like
—came to see him and you shut him in the library. Then, from
your lair you can listen to the explosion."

"I'd like to know what excuse you'll give for being here today—unbidden by him."

"Stern business—and it happens to be true. London seems
to have tapped another source and the price dropped by two
shillings a pound. So he probably will burst, and I'll have killed
the goose that laid the golden egg. For once I don't care. There's
always the nutmeg. Your gleanings are in the same place, I
take it. Good. I think this time we really must make an effort

to get some to America. It's amazing, isn't it, how they don't grow. You and I alone have shipped out enough to start a forest, and we're not the only ones. And the demand goes on."

"We should be grateful for that. Now, as regards the patrols."

"I'd clean forgotten."

"You are not yourself this afternoon. The seventeenth; the twenty-third; the first of next month. But the Lonthoir run, on the fifteenth, is full moon. So have a care then."

"Thank you, Daan," Charles said warmly. "It's due to you we've eluded them so long I do verily believe. He's a mean swine about that too. He has all the information, and every one of his own little jobs is pin-pointed, timed to a second, but never another word or hint that a poor struggling chap could take advantage of. I'd be interested to know who supplies his information."

"I don't think anybody does," said Doctor Hootman, rising and brushing, with scrupulous care, every bit of clinging leaf from his dark clothes. "A patrol officer, in his cups, one evening dropped a hint about general principles of routine, varied by tide and the moon; and after that, clever fellow, he could work it out for himself. On the first of the lunar month, as regularly as it comes round, he sits down and makes his little chart; at which I look next time I pass. Well, I'll go ahead; wait ten minutes and then follow. I'll be on the look-out. I hope your luck holds."

"Thanks. And Daan . . ."

"Yes?"

"Keep an eye on . . . Julia."

"I can promise to do that. I also admire courage. I have my human side, you know."

He walked, unhurried and ponderous, through the grove, where the twilight was thickening and all the island scents were intensified, as though the earth had let out a deep breath of relief as the sun went down. As he walked he snapped his fingers coaxingly at the snake which had just moved in his mind. Come out, little snake, let me inspect you and see whether you are what I wish, what I hope you might be. Are you just a harmless little grass snake, or a deadly viper?

He could remember every word, every inflexion of voice, used on the evening of Julia's arrival when Mynheer had said, "Listen . . ." and then unfolded his audacious, incredible scheme. Every word had been a blow to his own plans and hopes. But now, after what had happened this afternoon, it was just possible, just-barely-possible, that Julia might be a weapon snatched from Mynheer's hand and fitted to his own.

Doctor Hootman was neither religiously nor mystically inclined. Ignoring Providence and Destiny he was therefore forced to bend a superstitious knee in the worship of another controller of human lives, the great goddess Coincidence. Coincidence was responsible for the fact that the ship on which he had sailed as doctor-surgeon and spy for the owners, should sink in the Banda straits and that he should be without a job, awaiting a passage at the very moment when Mynheer Vosmar was searching for new medical attention for Pieter. Again it was Coincidence which had ordained his meeting with Charles Youngman; they had, literally, walked into one another in the dark, got to talking, chanced to make one another laugh, and so founded a partnership which had been very profitable. So far, so good. Had Coincidence now stretched out her long arm and simply by throwing a man and a girl together offered him the ghost of a chance of defeating Mynheer's scheme and prospering his own?

Pondering these things, not with optimism but with a calm determination to make the most of every opportunity, Doctor Hootman plodded back to his place of imprisonment, while Charles lay in the dusk on the scented leaves and thought of Julia and how she had kissed him.

He kept coming back to that. His mind was like a dog tied to a stake with a good length of rope. It ran this way and that. He thought of Daan's unlimed nutmegs and of all the people who were anxious to buy one, just one that was fertile, that might grow into a tree which would make a crack in the solid stone front of the Dutch monopoly. He thought of the patrol boats making their futile, regular prowls on the look-out for smugglers. He thought of his fellow outlaws, the disillusioned, dispossessed, risking their lives for ten guilders, living in squalor and daily danger, but gallantly and cheerfully. He thought of Mynheer, and how presently his eyes would redden and bulge and how the froth would gather at the corners of his mouth. He thought of Psyche, once a woman, now dead, like a dog, on the dunghill. And he thought of a long avenue of elms, noisy with rooks, that led to what had been a gracious house, tawny-pink in the English sunshine, now a heap of blackened rubble.

But always his thoughts came back to Julia, to the memory of that sweetly innocent and yet passionate kiss and the way it had stirred him.

Ten minutes. So many of his jobs called for perfect timing that he could gauge a given period to a few seconds without the aid of a timepiece. He rose, brushed himself down.

He might never see her again. There was no room in his life for sentiment. He told himself that he was overdue for a whiff of nutmeg cheese.

CHAPTER VIII

When Mynheer returned, with his guests, from Banda, she was bathed and reclad, and the dress she had been wearing that afternoon had been washed and hung at the back of the closet. Outwardly she looked calm enough, but the marrow of her bones still thrummed with a hidden vibration; and she decided to stay in her room until Pluto rang the miniature silver tong-tong as a sign that dinner was on the table. However, after a few minutes Mynheer himself came and tapped on her door.

"My dear, could you come and entertain my guests for a short time? Daan has just informed me that I am wanted. I know what it is—a business that won't take more than five minutes, but it seems rude to leave these gentlemen alone."

She went with him to the verandah, where the two gentlemen sat in the cane chairs with drinks before them. Mynheer made the introductions and slipped away.

Now was the moment for applying one of Mevrouw Helmers' little rules of behaviour: "Always remember that gentlemen like to talk about themselves and their business. Open with a question or a remark which invites them to do so, and then sit and listen, pretending to understand, but now and again asking a question, so that they can explain to you. They like explaining, too."

It was a sound rule. The gentlemen talked, the sun went down in all its blossoming glory; the gentlemen refilled their glasses, and talked again. Mynheer's five minutes stretched out to thirty, and Julia, with her guilty knowledge of what was being said, and experienced, somewhere else in the house, grew so uneasy that it was difficult for her to stay still.

At last, however, Mynheer stepped onto the verandah, and from within the house came the sound of the tong-tong. He apologised for the delay.

"Really, a most trivial bit of business that anyone could have dealt with," he said. "One day I shall get an agent. . . ."

She could see that, during his absence, he had been intensely, violently angry. His always prominent eyes were bulged out and the whites of them very red, and the hand which he laid on her arm as he made his apology had the same tremor as was shuddering through her own bones. His manner towards her, however, was unchanged and her heart went out in gratitude to the man who had rescued her.

The meal was lengthy, the conversation, however often brought back to general topics, constantly drifting away again towards business. She wanted to escape and knew that, in their hearts, the men would be glad when she went. The shadows of Doctor Hootman and Pieter passed across the screen, and were duly commented upon and she was thinking that now, in a moment, she might rise and go, when the man beside her, abandoning a spirited attack upon some new rule of the Company, turned to her and said, "I expect, like most ladies, you spend a good deal of time making pretty things with your needle, Mevrouw."

Needle! Embroidery! My bag!

Caught off guard her hand went to her mouth; she could feel her face change.

"Mynheer . . . that has reminded me of a promise I made and failed to keep." She turned to the head of the table. "I promised Marie that I would begin, at once, to make her something. . . ." The vagueness and the confusion would be attributed to the something being connected with a baby, unborn and therefore unmentionable; when she had gone Mynheer would tell the others and they would laugh!

"You haven't lost much time, my dear," said Mynheer indulgently.

My bag! she thought. Now I must go . . . in the dark . . . to that dreadful, dreadful place, alone. Or, worse still, perhaps Mynheer has been already—that would account for the delay. Perhaps his smooth manner was assumed because there were guests. . . .

The trembling within—though when she looked down at her hands they *looked* steady—had now reached the paralytic stage, and though she wanted to jump up and rush out in search of the bag she felt unable to move.

Pluto, moving soundless as a shadow, paused by his master's chair, spoke in a low voice. Mynheer nodded,

"My dear, Pieter would like to see you for a moment."

A new, and rather telling touch to the masquerade, she thought.

"I'll go at once," she said, and willed her legs to support her as far as the door. Mynheer smiled at her with approval. He couldn't know; nobody could be so consummate an actor.

In the cloister she stood still for a moment, leaning her hot face against one of the cool stone pillars, steadying herself against its solidity. She was glad that this latest ruse gave her a chance of speaking alone to Doctor Hootman; he would know whether Mynheer had rushed straight to the scene of tragedy; he might even know whether he had believed the invented story or not. And he could, certainly, tell her something about the man who had helped her.

"Ah, Mevrouw," said Doctor Hootman, opening the door of Pieter's room. "I trust that this last little proof of a happy connubial relationship was well-received."

It seemed to her that there was a marked, though subtle, change in his manner towards her; the words, with their hint of derision, seemed to place her on Doctor Hootman's side of some invisible boundary line. She wondered whether she dared ask him to go out and retrieve her bag. It was, she knew, a good deal to ask. Before she could find the courage, or the words to make the request he had turned from her and gone to one of the cupboards in which Pieter's clay and beads and paints were all tidily arrayed. When he turned back he had the brocade bag in his hands.

She said, "Oh," in a fading voice and groped her way to a chair, tears of sheer relief filling her eyes and rushing saltily into the back of her throat.

"I did consider putting it on your favourite seat in the garden," Doctor Hootman said. "Then I thought you might remember it and be worried."

She swallowed painfully.

"I did remember it, just now, at the table. I nearly died. . . ."

"That must have been a bad moment," said Doctor Hootman sympathetically. "All is well now."

He sat down on a chair on the other side of the table and looked at her. There was something new in his regard; it was —she searched for a word—it was speculative.

"You're a brave woman," he said. It was a statement made without intent to praise, without admiration, without surprise. It was like his expression, speculative.

"Oh no. All along I've been terrified."

"Indeed? I wondered whether you realised what a risk you were taking: whether perhaps Mynheer's paternal, indulgent manner had led you to think that you could do what you liked."

"Far from it," she said, with a little shudder. "This afternoon I was half out of my wits. So much so that I didn't even ask the name of the man who helped me."

"I gathered that you were somewhat distressed."

He did not volunteer the name.

"Was Mynheer very angry?"

"He was so angry," said Doctor Hootman with ghoulish relish, "that he almost fell into a fit. By your charitable—and if I may say so, somewhat sentimental—action, Mevrouw, you have compelled two very stubborn men to break two of their own most inflexible rules. The man who helped you by taking the blame for Psyche's mishap has what we might call a business connection with Mynheer; he never comes without an appointment, and on those occasions he is invisible to me. You understand. He and I, on less frequent occasions, meet, less formally perhaps, and then he is invisible to Mynheer. Today, in order to tell his tale he did an unprecedented thing, presented himself without an appointment. And when he had told his tale Mynheer, in his turn, did an unprecedented thing. He sent for me. So there we were, all three together," he nodded towards the library and something that was not quite a smile lightened his heavy face. "Very funny, really. It took all my skill and resource to have Mynheer ready to meet his guests in time. I don't suppose he has been so enraged since the day of Pieter's accident."

"You knew about Psyche?"

"I know a number of things. I have learned not to interfere."

"So have I."

"I wonder," he said. "In this case, I must admit your temerity astonished me—if you knew what you risked. But then, I know very little about women. They look frail, but I suppose they can be resolute where their sentiments are concerned."

He made the statement, but it had a questioning sound.

"I don't think it was sentiment. It was a kind of self-defence. I used to wake in the night and think about her. It made me so miserable, I had to do *something*. I know it wasn't much, but it probably comforted me more than it did her."

Doctor Hootman's expression changed, took on something of astonishment, something of—yes—respect!

After a moment he said, "Mevrouw, that does as much credit to your head as to your heart. Many people are kind, as you say, from self-defence, but those who realise their motive are very few, and those who would admit it still fewer. Yes . . . now and again justice is done. You deserved your miracle this afternoon."

"It was a miracle—that he happened to be there and was willing to take the blame. Doctor Hootman, what is his name?"

"To me he is known as Charles. Whether that is his name or not I don't know."

"I was so confused and upset . . . but afterwards, thinking about it . . . his voice . . . he isn't Dutch, is he?"

"Oh no. He is English. The situation is very complicated and very changeable. Some years ago the English Royalists were welcome in the Islands, you know. Cromwell was the enemy of the Dutch, therefore his enemies were regarded as friends. Then, when Cromwell gained the upper hand he demanded a few small islands as compensation for the so-called massacre of Amboyna, and naturally all the settlers there were not Royalist, and not welcome neighbours. There is a tendency, now, to lump them all together and to dislike them all. So each time Charles sets foot in Rua he takes a risk. When he comes to see me he takes another, a risk within a risk. I trust you to remember that, Mevrouw. I hold the secret of the truth about Psyche's death and you hold the secret of Charles' connection with me."

"I shouldn't dream of mentioning him to anyone," she said warmly. "After the way he helped me! I'd sooner die."

A girlish extravagance of phrase? Possibly. Doctor Hootman's hand went to his chin, finger and thumb moved in a rhythmical stroking.

"His behaviour this afternoon was quite out of character, I must say."

"In what way, Doctor Hootman?"

"I should have thought him capable of passing by on the other side—of, if expedient, stepping *over*—any number of weeping women in the pursuit of his unlawful occasions. The life he and his little group lead is not conducive to impulsive acts of chivalry."

He said the words with deliberate provocation.

"I thought you were supposed to be his friend. He spoke well of *you!*"

"I intended no criticism, Mevrouw. I was merely commenting upon the surprising contradictions of which man is capable."

"I don't think that even there you are right. When something happens and people have to act quickly, without time to think, then they show their true characters. I thought about that when I was trying not to be frightened about going to that place. You can't become brave all in a moment; and you can't become kind all in a moment either. I think Charles helped me this afternoon because he is kind, and brave."

"You may be right, Mevrouw."

He wondered whether to leave it there. But an opportunity of this kind might never come again.

"All the same," he went on, "you mustn't underestimate

the force of emotion. You, for example, say that you were frightened, yet you acted with courage because something in Psyche's plight appealed to you. I think much the same thing could be said about Charles' behaviour. Something about you must have made a strong appeal to him. He asked me your name, and was very anxious to know whether Mynheer treated you kindly—a subject upon which I was able to reassure him."

She said nothing to that, but the expression on her face told him that the words had not been wasted. After a moment he asked, in the voice which suited the change of subject,

"Well, the whole affair ended fortunately. In future, Mevrouw, you should be careful about allowing your will to come into conflict with Mynheer's."

"It never will again," she said, with some firmness.

"Can one be sure?" One of his eyebrows lifted.

"Reasonably sure. It's unlikely that I should find another Psyche, and short of that . . . Even then I think I might think twice about it."

"I suggest that you leave now, Mevrouw. The two fat fellows believe you to be with Pieter, but Mynheer knows otherwise and he might wonder what you and I have so suddenly discovered to talk about." He rose as he spoke, lifted the embroidery bag and handed it to her.

The blood had spattered it too, and the brownish-black spots stood out starkly against the pale pink shining stuff. She took it gingerly, with a resurge of horror and disgust. She would throw it away at once. Then she remembered that he had handled it, had contrived to return it to her. Immediately it became the most precious of all her possessions. She would clean it as well as she could; and if—as she feared was the case with her dress—some stains remained, stubborn and immovable, she would regard them as reminders, not of the evil thing, but of the kindness and comfort with which they were equally associated. They would be her link with the man she might never see again.

"It may never happen," said Doctor Hootman, moving towards the door, "but if it ever should . . . If Mynheer were away for instance, or some other circumstance made it quite safe to do so, I would try to arrange that Charles could see for himself that you were well and happy. That is if that should be agreeable to you."

"Oh, yes, indeed it would. Thank you Doctor Hootman. Thank you, too, very much for all you have done today."

"It was a pleasure, Mevrouw. Good night."

He fastened the door and went back to his chair; he did not take up his book. Busily and intently he wove and twisted and knotted the filaments of his thoughts, a gigantic spider, spinning a gigantic web.

Julia went to bed but it was a long time before she slept. Whether she lay with eyes open or closed, there passed before them, in a series of little pictures, all the events of the day. They came and went, their choice beyond her control. It was useless to turn shuddering from the memory of Psyche, drenched in her blood, and to think—I'll remember Charles instead. Then no picture came; just a few disconnected fragments which added up to nothing, had no life or meaning. An old shirt with a torn frill: a pair of very blue eyes, the white lines running out against the darkly tanned skin: brow and cheeks scoured by harsh living: a mouth firm against her own. But just before she fell asleep every other memory of the day receded and she saw him whole and clear, just as he had stood at the opening of the path and waved his hand. Once again her heart, her whole being moved out towards him.

Somewhere, in the very heart of the night, she began to dream. She was in the cage, chained and naked, just as Psyche had been. She knew why she was there; she had offended Mynheer and that was her punishment. She was not, however, unduly distressed because Doctor Hootman had promised to help her and she had only to wait for his coming. Then he came, but not alone. Mynheer and Pieter were with him. Mynheer carried his silver-knobbed cane and Pieter had a piece of knitting which was ravelling out as he walked. They came and stood by the bars and looked at her, and then they began to laugh. They all laughed in the same way, mockingly. She realised that she had been fooled. She had no friend. She would stay here, shamed and tortured until she died.

She woke, moaning and shuddering, with the sweat of cold terror crawling over her skin. Even when she was fully awake and sensible the evil aura of the dream remained, as a foul taste will linger in the mouth.

But it was only a dream. It was the natural and inevitable result of the day's excitement. She was in no danger. Charles had seen to that. She thought of him, at first with gratitude, and then, all at once, with longing. Now the things of which Frieda had whispered, things which so long had lain indigestible, a source of discomfort, became assimilated, became part of her being. Now she understood. With just the one, the chosen person, that would be possible . . . wonderful . . . right.

She lay quite still, stunned by the revelation, and her girlhood slipped away. She could think now with a rueful, tolerant amusement of her immature idea of love, two porcelain figures against a background of flowers! What nonsense.

Her thoughts shifted. She recalled, with a new, bitter understanding, some of the pitying things Mynheer had said to her about herself. "A married woman without a husband, with no hope of children." She recalled also Charles' words, "married to that idiot boy."

She realised, for the first time, the full extent to which she had been defrauded.

CHAPTER IX

Suddenly all Mynheer's talk concerned a young kinsman of his, Nicolas Vanderplasse, who was coming to spend three months at Rua.

"A long-standing, vague arrangement," he said, "which couldn't have fallen out more happily. If he'd come last year he would have found Rua intolerably dull, and I should have found the effort to entertain him quite exhausting." Nothing betrayed the fact that he was giving Fate credit for a timeliness which was of his own contriving.

He went on to explain that amongst planters of standing in the Islands there was a system of exchange not unlike that which had existed in mediaeval times when a boy would go and learn his knightly duties in another man's hall.

"Whether the young scamps really learn more than they would at home is debatable, but it does them good to get away; some of these planters are born and die in the same spot without moving more than twenty miles either way. The custom does contribute in some small measure to the dissemination of new ideas, and of course in some cases it helps to mitigate the danger of inbreeding. With Nicolas the wife-hunting does not apply, he has been betrothed from childhood to the daughter of a man who was Governor of Amboyna, a suitable match in many ways but in one regrettable; all the women of that family are plain and dull, a horrible combination. I am sure he will envy Pieter very much."

"Does he know about Pieter?"

"He knows what I have chosen the world should know. You, my dear and Doctor Hootman are the only ones I have ever taken into my confidence. Of course, on so prolonged a visit, and with a kinsman, things will be a little difficult, but we must do our best. It can't be helped. You, I am sure, will support me to the best of your ability."

"Of course. You see, Mynheer, the truth makes me look very silly."

He pondered that for a moment, sucking in his cheeks so that his eyes seemed more than ever disproportionately large. Then he said, and the simple words went to the heart of the matter with a frightening shrewdness,

"But the truth is known only to us three. Does Doctor Hootman's awareness of the situation embarrass you?"

She knew that it did not; it never had done. Even Marie's reference to Mucky Karl had been only an awkward blow to be parried. It was Charles, saying, "You don't mean to tell me that you're married to that idiot boy?" which had shown her the truth; and Mynheer's words came perilously near to asking, "Who else knows?"

She braced herself, looked him in the eye and said,

"I sometimes think about the servants."

"The slaves. My poor child. I never realised. I should have explained. Pieter has his own staff; a Hindu widow who counts herself fortunate to be alive at all; she does the menial work, and an Ethiopian whom I went to some pains—and was lucky —to acquire; he takes charge during the hours when Daan is free. He is, in point of fact, dumb. The Ethiopians have an amiable custom of making the punishment fit the crime, the hand which steals is cut off, and so forth. Echo, as I named him when he came into my employ, when he could speak told a lie, apparently. My dear, don't look at me like that, it was not my doing. I merely report a fact. So you see, you need have no thoughts about the slaves' thoughts! As for the outer world, they gossip and they speculate, but so long as we work together they can *know* nothing, and in the end we shall utterly confound them!"

It was not the first time that he had made such a reference to the future, and whenever he did so she had imagined that he was stubbornly clinging to the hope of some improvement in Pieter's condition; that had always seemed pitiable and now, in the light of what Charles had called Pieter, "idiot boy," it seemed doubly so. Her feeling must have shown in her face, for he said,

"I know now that he will never recover. I hoped. I told myself that the brain was delicate, out of reach of balm and plaster, that it must heal of its own accord, take its own time. I expected a change when he was twenty-one. There was no change; I have now resigned myself to the likelihood that there never will be. But . . . life must go on. And I am fortunate," his voice brightened, "in having such staunch support in Doctor Hootman. Sometimes, before he came, the burden did seem unbearable. And now I have *you*."

Thinking that he was counting her as an ally in the task of concealment, the pretence that Pieter was merely disfigured and misanthropic, she said,

"I shall do what I can to help."

"I believe that." He came towards her and put his hands on her shoulders. She could feel the dry heat of them through the stuff of her dress. His manner changed, so did his expression.

"I think God sent you. I did Him a small wrong, and in return He thrust me into torment that makes Hell look like a summer garden. He took all I had; a cruel usury. Night after night I've wrestled with Him like Jacob of old, demanding not mercy, but justice. And now for the first time, I see a little hope, a gleam of promise." He seemed to be overcome with emotion, strangled by it, his eyes popped and his whole face quivered. Dropping his hands, he turned and went quickly away.

Mynheer had last seen Nicolas when he was fourteen, six years ago, but he could have picked him out from a score of young men of the same age, identically clothed; he was so very much a Vosmar, with such a close resemblance to himself as a young man; even his eyes, grey and set well forward now, would be protuberant in years to come. He had the kind of good looks that come of youth, of perfect health and cheerfulness, and at the moment of meeting everything about him was touched by a not unpleasing shyness.

As Mynheer greeted his young kinsman, his heart contracted with a sickening spasm of pain. Just so should Pieter have been. Oh, what pride, what measureless pride would he have taken in a son like this.

The greeting he extended was cheerful, however, and as soon as they were seated in the prahau, he began to talk about the Pieter who did not exist; partly because there was a curious situation to be explained, and partly because he derived an obscure comfort from describing the mythical figure. It afforded him the same relief as a cover drawn over a dead face; the truth lay there, but it no longer stared up stark and bare.

"I think," Mynheer began, "that I must prepare you as regards Pieter. I suppose you've heard something from your parents."

Nicolas, who had heard a good deal of speculation and comment, said tactfully,

"We all knew that he had had an accident and that it had made him very . . . shy."

"Shy is an understatement. His passion for retirement has reached the point of mania now. I know he is greatly to be pitied, but he makes things very difficult. He has his own apartments, from which he never emerges, except sometimes for an evening walk. Even his meals he insists upon taking alone. Well, not entirely alone; he has a great friend, a Doctor Hootman. They are inseparable companions."

Nicolas mumbled that it was all a great pity.

"A great pity. And I, a few months back, made a most regrettable mistake. I encouraged, I *urged* him to get married."

"Oh." Nicolas' voice held surprise. None of the stories current in the Java branch of the family, stories fabricated from guesswork and embroidered with suspicion, had ever hinted of "poor Cousin Pieter" being a suitable subject for matrimony.

"You never told us," he said.

"No. I meant to write, but to tell you the truth, I was so disappointed by the way things turned out that I lacked the heart to spread the news. She's such a sweet girl, pretty, charming, willing to overlook . . . a really dear girl. And I had such high hopes. I really thought she would cure him; I thought that for her sake he would exert himself, face things. I thought the mere fact that a sweet pretty girl didn't shrink from him would give him confidence. She never did; from the first moment her manner has been perfect. I can't speak too highly of her. It may seem a strange thing for a father to say, but by his treatment of her Pieter has somewhat alienated my sympathy. That is Rua, over there."

The boy stared ahead eagerly.

"I've heard so much about it, from Mother. She used to spend a good deal of time here as a child, didn't she?"

"Yes, she and my father were cousins—he was much older, of course. There was a great affection between them. I've heard him say how sorry he was that she married in Java. Let me see now, you are betrothed, are you not?"

"I'm to be married almost as soon as I get back."

"Indeed. How time flies. And it's one of the Hoogenbeet girls, isn't it. Greta or Christine?"

"Fancy your remembering their names."

"My memory is pretty good. I never knew the girls, they were very small when their father retired; but I knew Mevrouw Hoogenbeet! That probably accounts for my remembering; one didn't forget anything Mevrouw Hoogenbeet told one! My word no. She was a most terrifying woman." He laughed, irreverently, almost boyishly. "Dear me, yes, it was once my misfortune to be in Amboyna when the Governor gave a ball, and there being nobody of much importance handy, I had to lead out Mevrouw. I know I'm no giant, but honestly, she seemed to me to be about seven feet tall."

Nicolas' shyness dropped away. The Java family held Uncle

Simon in grudging respect; he was very, very rich; he was very, very proud; he was more than a little eccentric; he was hard to please; critical, arrogant, a very difficult character indeed. Nicolas, weighed down with orders to be on his best behaviour, had embarked with some trepidation. And now, suddenly he found himself telling Uncle Simon of a secret fear that he had never mentioned even to his favourite brother.

"Everything I hear about Mevrouw Hoogenbeet fills me with alarm," he said. "I'm so terrified that Greta will be like her."

"She can't be as tall; rest assured of *that*."

"How can you know?"

"Because Mynheer Hoogenbeet was much shorter than his wife, and my observation tells me that girls are almost always shorter than their fathers, just as boys are almost always taller than their mothers."

"Is that so?" asked Nicolas, much interested.

"It seems to me a natural law, to keep the human race from breeding giants and dwarfs. Most men marry women slightly less tall than themselves—they lack Mynheer Hoogenbeet's courage, you see! Then the boys overtop their mother, the girls stop short of their father and a rough kind of average is maintained."

"Well, thank you, Uncle Simon. That's the first word of hope or comfort anybody has ever offered me. All I've heard was about Mevrouw Hoogenbeet's size and strong-mindedness and economical housekeeping."

"She was virtuous too!" said Mynheer drily. "You know, I often think these early bethrothals, glove marriages and marriages by proxy are a regrettable necessity. Take my poor Julia, who surely deserves, if ever a girl did, to be happily married. It may be quite revolutionary of me but I am inclined to think that there should be some slight element of choice in a matter which, after all, is going to be an important factor in two people's lives. I don't say the whole decision should rest with the young—if you'll pardon my saying so, few of them have sufficient judgement or experience to make such a momentous decision; but they should be allowed to meet first, to talk together, find out if they are agreeable to one another."

"That's exactly what I think," said Nicolas eagerly. "You not only thought so, you acted on what you thought and believed, didn't you, Uncle Simon?"

It was a mistake.

Mynheer's face went stiff and cold.

"You know my story? Yes, I acted. But of course that kind of . . . Never mind. I can tell you this, though, Nicolas. I've no doubt that when your female relatives discuss my affairs they say: Serves him right! But if I had the choice to make again I would act exactly as I did then, even if I knew what would result. Two years is a short time. A week is even shorter. But a week with a woman you really love is worth a lifetime of the other thing. That's not something I should say to you, perhaps. Look, you can see the house now, the long low white building."

Again Nicolas stared out, but the conversation was, for him, too intimately interesting to be lightly abandoned. It was the first time in his life that he had taken part in that kind of talk; in his home accepted customs were not criticised and, despite his twenty years and imminent marriage, he was treated like a child.

"The thing is," he said tentatively, "that the system seems to work. I mean, for most people. Most marriages seem fairly happy, don't they?" It was a thought from which he had derived a little comfort when he visualised himself as a married man.

"That," said Mynheer, "is the most damning indictment. Fairly happy. Who wants to be fairly happy? Scale the peaks of ecstasy, yes! Even if, afterwards, you're thrown down, like Lucifer. Taste the golden apple once, even if it turns to wormwood in your mouth. How much better than the dull jog-trot of 'fairly happy.'"

This was heady talk.

"Oh, I do agree. But some of us are doomed to jog-trot. Take me, for example. To tell you the truth I'm *not* looking forward to my marriage. But there it is, all arranged. And I have never seen any woman for whom it would be worth while to defy the rules and upset my father and . . . and everything. Perhaps that kind of, well, romance only happens to a few people."

"Perhaps. I think it also offers itself to many others who refuse it out of cowardice or a silly regard for what you call 'the rules.' I'm inclined to look behind the rules and ask myself who made them, and why. 'Thou shalt not covet thy neighbour's wife,' for example. Why, in God's name, if she's covetable? That one, I'm sure was slipped in by some very unattractive fellow who had a *supremely* covetable wife."

The son of the very strict, Reformed Dutch family experienced a slight sense of shock which made him jerk out,

"But Uncle Simon, that was one of the Commandments that God gave to Moses."

"Was it?" Mynheer's voice was elaborately casual. "I rather suspect that many of those edicts suffered some change during the process of being carved in stone. A lengthy business, you know. I for one, would hesitate to order my life on what may have been a slip of the chisel."

After a second's blinking astonishment Nicolas threw back his head and laughed. Something innate, inherent in his Vosmar blood, long subjected to the Vanderplasse stream, leaped up to embrace its own.

"Uncle Simon," he said, "you're not a bit what I expected. Oh, I think I'm going to enjoy my stay in Rua. Mother often said it was like nowhere else on earth."

"I don't know about that. I do most sincerely hope that you will be happy. I shall do my best to make you so. I hope you'll be company for Julia and that you will, as far as possible, ignore Pieter; that, believe me is the kindest thing you can do. And now, here we are. Welcome to Rua."

CHAPTER X

Nicolas Vanderplasse was twenty years old, a perfectly normal, healthy young man who had been rather strictly brought up, and who had his full share of the sensuality which is so often found in sons of puritanical fathers. He had made his first visit to a brothel when he was seventeen, staggered by his own daring, knowing it to be sordid and mercenary, and overcome by a paralysing sense of guilt. Nevertheless, he had returned. At the same time, as though to restore the balance, he had developed, and for rather more than two years maintained, a slavish, mooningly-romantic relationship with a married woman, who, at the age of twenty-five, was as much his senior as she was junior to her fifty-year-old husband. It had been an affair of soft glances, sweet speeches, a snatched kiss here and a hand-clasp there, of dreams without any hope of fulfilment. It had died a natural and quite painless death with the beginning of her first pregnancy.

Like most other young men of his age and in his situation, he would then have begun to look forward to marriage as an answer to the demands of both sides of his nature, and to dream of the wife about whom he could feel both romantic and passionate, but here was a handicap, peculiar to him. The ghost of Mevrouw Hoogenbeet still stalked the Islands. Fifteen years had passed since Mynheer Hoogenbeet's retirement from the governorship of Amboyna, but the memories and stories of her size, her parsimony, her tirades and her bullying persisted. Was it possible that Greta, daughter of such a woman, could be lovable? Nicolas doubted it and had begun to look upon his marriage as a life sentence.

However, he had still some months of freedom and he intended to make the most of them. Setting out for his visit to Rua he had made up his mind to sample—along with anything else that offered—the pleasures of the compound, the "Brown Satin" as men called it. This was a thing which decent men, men of sensibility, avoided on their own plantations, or even on those in their vicinity, since it was not altogether agreeable to see recognisable family features emerging from some small brown face.

He had forgotten this intention, and almost everything else, within a week, having fallen in love for the first time. Here was the very girl of whom—but for the shadow of Mevrouw Hoogenbeet—he would have been dreaming; lovely to look at, with grace and charm, delightful to talk to, a girl to adore, and one who could, at the same time, by a glance or the brush of her sleeve wake unimaginable hungers.

The setting, too, might have been specially designed to be the background of a love affair. Nicolas had been born and bred in the Islands; the colours and the scents were not new to him as they were to Julia. But now all the world was made new. The wealth of flowers, loading the air with fragrance, the brooding green of the trees, the sunsets, the water creaming on the pale beach, the silver and ebony of the moonlit night, all offered themselves to eyes hitherto blind. The very doves, mourning in the nutmeg trees, ceased to be greedy marauders, the planters' enemies, and became the disembodied voice of enchantment.

And there was in Rua also, unconsciously yet immediately assimilated, a sense of moral freedom, almost of laxity. Here nobody watched, nobody criticised. "You two young people must amuse one another," Uncle Simon had said as soon as he had introduced them, and after that he seemed to show no more interest or curiosity in their comings and goings than he did in the flight of the birds. His only concern was that they should be happy. At home, industry was, in its own right, a virtue, so great a virtue in fact that even the appearance of it was sought after, those who were not actually busy affecting to be so. Uncle Simon's attitude was the reverse.

"I go out when the tong-tong rings, and I see everything started. If you care to come with me that is as good a time as any to see how things work. After that, on a properly organised plantation, the business should proceed smoothly. I look in here and there at various times of course, where and when I'm least expected; and I invariably check on the stores myself. But you don't have to turn out every morning, Nicolas. Young people can sleep on, and they should. They should also be grateful that they can. I wake at dawn now, wherever I am, and once awake I must be stirring."

Most mornings Nicolas managed to wake and accompany his uncle on the rounds; and during those hours together the insidious process of undermining the home standards would go on. Uncle Simon laughed at things which would deeply have shocked Nicolas' father, and mocked at things regarded with reverence at home; and although Nicolas would often be disconcerted by the levity and the mockery, almost always, immediately afterwards he would think, "But he's right," or "I often felt that way myself."

One of the most startling, and pleasing, of Uncle Simon's attitudes was that which he adopted towards youth. At home youth was something slightly deplorable. "You'll know better when you're older"; "You're too young to understand"; "You're just a silly boy"; "Remember you are addressing your elders." In Rua youth was given its due. "It's the best time, my boy, make no mistake about that. Whatever the years bring they take away the capacity for enjoyment"; "It's one of life's ironies that by the time a man can afford the best wine he has lost his palate"; "Half the rules are made by old men to prevent young ones doing things that they themselves can no longer do."

Once he spoke, in terms of age, about Julia, who had just left them in order to make her morning visit to Pieter.

"I hate myself sometimes," Uncle Simon said. "I should

have persuaded him to marry an older woman. Thirty would have been the perfect age. How can a girl like that care what an interesting book he is reading? That is his main topic, you know; books! Life at one remove. She's at an age when life should be *lived*, not read about, talked about. Pieter, poor boy, never had any youth, he has to accept a substitute, but she . . . It's like seeing a bud flung out on the dust-heap with a bunch of dead flowers."

None of these speeches was momentous in itself, but each made its small contribution; and when the time for plain speaking came the atmosphere had been established.

It began with a morning walk. Julia had by this time become aware of Nicolas' infatuation and was trying to acquire the art of avoiding sentimental scenes without injuring his feelings. She had learned that it was advisable to have a definite destination when they took a walk, and, if possible, some impersonal topic for conversation.

"This morning I'm going to show you some trees which even your uncle doesn't know the names of, and see if you can tell me," she said.

"I doubt if I can. They must be rare if he couldn't name them. What are they like?"

"Red."

"There are dozens of red trees. And, of course, there are different names in different places for the same tree. At home we had a tree with a red trumpet-shaped flower, which we, and everybody else around us called Cardinal's Hat, but my Macassar cousins, when they came to stay, called it Bee Bloom. We had one of those is-isn't-is-isn't arguments about it and I got a walloping for not being polite to guests."

"These are quite a walk away, we mustn't dawdle."

"I never knew anyone who liked to walk so fast as you do, Julia. And you've been here such a short time, you should feel the heat. But I can't somehow imagine you getting hot and red in the face. Your face always looks as though it were made of ivory or alabaster or something like that."

They came at last to where the trees stood, all in a group together. Their tops were thickly massed with flowers of a deep, rich red colour which made a pleasant contrast with the feathery evergreen of the nutmegs and of the lofty Canariums which overtopped and shaded the groves.

"There, aren't they pretty? Why, Nicolas, what is the matter?"

He was staring at the trees with an expression of astonishment and profound dismay.

"They're . . . they're *cloves!*" he said in a voice of disbelief.

"Well, is that so astonishing?"

"Julia dear! There isn't supposed to be a clove tree in all the Islands, except in Amboyna. My God, if the Company knew! Uncle Simon must be *crazy!*"

"He doesn't know what they are. I asked him when I first saw them and he said, Oh, just a native tree."

"That's quite impossible. He's lived here all his life and they used to be quite common. Then the Company decided to concentrate the clove-growing in Amboyna, and every tree elsewhere had to be cut down. My father had to get rid of his, I've heard him speak of it. You can't go against the Company these days, you know." He looked at the pretty, sweet-scented trees and shook his head in a puzzled way. "Where does he sell them?" He answered his own question. "He *can't* sell them. So why on earth does he take such a risk? And waste the space? It beats me."

"I think it's quite likely that they've always stood there, and he thought they were pretty, so he kept them."

"Ye-es; with him that is just possible. Rua is his kingdom, isn't it? My mother always says he acts as though he were Royalty. Which makes it all the harder for him—Pieter, I mean."

"In what way?" asked Julia carefully.

"Staying at home, not showing off, not cutting a dash as the heir apparent. Uncle Simon cut no end of a dash when he was

young, or so I've heard, and no doubt he'd have liked his son
to be the same."

"I think it more likely that he thinks his heir is his heir and
therefore permitted to behave just as he chooses."

"That's a shrewd remark. That's one thing I do like about
you, Julia. Most girls as pretty as you—not that there are many
—never say anything worth listening to."

"Will you mention the clove trees?"

"You bet I shall. I shall warn him, too. Rua may be a kingdom, but the Company rules an Empire, and even Uncle Simon
is only one of its satraps."

"It's *what?*"

"It comes out of the Bible. Somebody, probably Nebuchad-
nezzar, had princes and satraps. I was brought up on the Bible.
Weren't you?"

"Not really . . . which is rather strange, though I never, I
must admit, thought about it until now. I spent quite a long
time in what was called, officially, 'The Christian and Benevolent Refuge for Orphans,' otherwise the Klopstock Home. It
wasn't very Christian, or very Benevolent, but it was completely Klopstock. To be quite honest, we didn't all have cloaks,
but for the daily walk that didn't matter because some of us
always had to stay in to finish work, or for a punishment or
something. But for Sunday church if we had all gone there
weren't enough. I think that must have been the reason . . .
we never did go."

"You don't realise how lucky you were. At home the sermons
last two hours. I can remember several that lasted even longer."

The innocuous, unprovocative comparison of their upbring-
ing and experiences lasted all the way back to the house.

Doctor Hootman always left the table promptly after dinner
and Julia soon followed him, leaving the gentlemen to their
wine. On this evening, as soon as they were alone, Nicolas said,

"Uncle Simon, you *do* know a clove tree when you see one?"

"I should hope so. I'm not blind or in my dotage."

"Then you know you have quite a number here, in Rua?"

"Of course. I know every tree on Rua. Why?"

"Why? Because if the Company ever found out they'd . . . they'd . . ."

"Fine me. A sum of money, large by their standards, negligible by mine, which I should not pay without protest, my boy."

Nicolas' eyes widened and bulged in a way which foreshadowed how like his kinsman he would be in later years.

"*Not* without protest," he repeated. "To whom could you make a protest in a case like this?"

Mynheer did not answer immediately; he offered the wine and then refilled his own glass.

"The Company," he said mildly, "is very large, and like most overgrown things is not constitutionally very sound. Also, like all large things it offers a wide target of vulnerability. In Holland there are many—in very high places—who view with grave concern this insistence upon monopolies and the overriding of civil rights. Only the other evening the Governor of Banda, here at this table, said that it was only when he dined out that he took precedence of the Company's Agent: he described himself as a mere figurehead, rapidly becoming a figure of fun. By what right does the Company—that conclave of merchants and stockholders—dictate to me what I should grow on my own ground? Those clove trees have always grown there, and as far as is humanly possible I have preserved this estate as I received it . . . as I hope to pass it on. Is that a crime? They could never prove that I had sold a clove. No man can do the patently impossible. I should have quite a case, Nicolas, which, properly handled, might easily do the Company more damage than they could do me. And I would see that it was properly handled."

Nicolas looked at Mynheer with admiration; he had heard, for as long as he could remember, complaints about the Company's growing autocratism, but he had never before heard words of open defiance. He was, however, except where women were concerned, of a realistic turn of mind.

"That's all very well," he said. "Meantime they could refuse to ship your nutmegs, and then where would you be?"

"Here, I trust. And losing no sleep, I assure you. I grow nutmegs because nutmegs have always been grown on Rua; but I do not, thank God, depend upon the nutmeg for my daily bread, or other small comforts."

Nicolas had always known that the Rua branch of the family was far wealthier than his own, but to talk of being independent of nutmegs hinted at riches of a fabulous kind; in the Islands everybody, everything, depended upon that small, brown, shrivelled object. But not, apparently, Uncle Simon. . . .

He said, in that special voice which people reserve for talk of money in large quantities,

"It must be nice to be so rich."

"It is nice to be independent—and in these days that demands money. It was not always so; the first Vosmar to own Rua had no money at all; he was independent by virtue of his strong body and indomitable mind. But those days are over." He paused, as though paying past history the tribute of a moment's silence. Then he said, "Yes, I am rich. I inherited a fortune, and by careful manipulation I have made another. Far more money than poor Pieter, with his simple tastes, will ever know how to spend." He sighed, and with an air of abandoning the subject, lifted his wine glass and sipped at it, daintily.

"You're the eldest of, which is it, I always forget, four, aren't you, Nicolas?"

"Out of date, Uncle Simon. There's baby Benjamin."

"Of course. That's three boys. And two girls to be provided with dowries. You won't—to begin with, anyway—have too much to do with, will you?"

"I should think not."

"Well," Mynheer said, "I've taken a liking to you; you are my kin, and as I said just now I have more than Pieter would know what to do with. Mark you, everything I inherited goes to him, it couldn't be otherwise. But of the money I made myself I propose to leave you a share, or give it to you in my lifetime if you prefer; I think one needs money more in youth than in age. This isn't a sudden decision, my boy. Long before you came I had meditated it, and decided that if you turned out to be a real Vosmar, as you promised to as a boy, and if I took a fancy to you, I'd do something substantial for you. And I will."

This was the realisation of a family hope which had peeped slyly out from behind the arrangement of the long visit. For some time references to Rua had abounded with little unfinished sentences concerning the one, rather unsatisfactory son, probably in delicate health, certainly taking no part in running the estate, and the chance which awaited Nicolas if he ingratiated himself with his relative. Now here it was. And all he could find to say was,

"It's wonderfully good of you, Uncle Simon. I don't know how to thank you."

"Then don't. I don't want thanks. It will please me to think that you can enjoy some slight independence. Will you take brandy?"

"No, thank you," said Nicolas with a slight self-righteousness.

"Do. To keep me company. I have something else to discuss with you. To my mind a much more serious matter."

"Oh. What is it?"

Mynheer knew the value of silence. Without speaking he poured brandy into two glasses, pushed his chair back from the table, crossed his legs and carefully removed a tiny thread which clung to the knee of his pale grey breeches.

"It concerns Julia. . . ." he said, and noted, with satisfaction, a slight deepening of colour in the smooth pink and white boyish face. "You're in love with her, aren't you?"

Put like that it sounded like an accusation; and coming so soon after the talk about money hinted at a bargain, an attempt to buy him off. Aware of this, yet unwilling to deny the first genuine love of his life, Nicolas played for time,

"What makes you say that?"

"If there is one thing that annoys me," said Mynheer testily, "it is to have a question answered by another. I asked you, are you in love with Julia?"

Julia was Pieter's wife and Uncle Simon was Pieter's father; and, however lightly and irreverently he might speak about one's neighbour's covetable wife, it would be a very different thing when it concerned the family. And a love affair with Julia, however delightful, could only last for three months. The money would last forever.

"I find her extremely attractive," he said, "but I do assure you, I've never touched her or said a word that couldn't have been overheard."

"That still doesn't answer my question."

"Very well, then, I am," said Nicolas sulkily. "How could I not be? I know she's Pieter's wife, but that is difficult to bear in mind, the way things are! But I swear——"

"Never mind that. For the rest, you have said it exactly. It is difficult to bear in mind that she is Pieter's wife. I'm not in his confidence, or in hers to that extent, but I'll tell you this. I'd wager my last guilder the girl's a virgin still. And I tell you this, also, and I say it as sincerely as I ever said anything in my life: If Julia could have one romantic, successful love affair, nobody would be more delighted than I!"

Now thoroughly taken aback and scarlet to the edge of his hair, Nicolas could only gulp out,

"Why?"

"I have many reasons. First of all, I'm sorry for the girl. Think of her position; married to a man who, just because his face isn't acceptable, won't offer what is. My second reason is more selfish. I don't know how well you understand women, I flatter myself that I do. All women need an emotional anchor. If you consider that a moment you'll perceive its truth. Some women live on mere memories, some take to religion, some lavish their affections on pet monkeys or dogs. They have to have something; and what they don't get in one place they look for in another. Unless my poor Julia is given, very soon, some emotional and imaginative ballast I shall have trouble. She'll take a lover and there'll be scandal to deal with. One really satisfactory love affair would give her something to remember, dwell on, be sentimental about, for the rest of her life. I know that is true, Nicolas. I remember three old Vosmar aunts—the Macassar side, before your time; all unmarried, two miserable, sour, spiteful, horrible old women, the third quite content and happy; the man she was betrothed to had been drowned at sea, but she had her memories. I think of her very often. I would like Julia to have a memory, at least."

It all sounded very sad and romantic, and very far away from the brisk, cool-hearted, hard-headed household in which he had been reared.

"I'm very fond of Julia. I'm very sorry for her. But I doubt . . . I mean, there are her feelings to be considered, too."

"By your own account you have never tested them," Mynheer reminded him. "It would hardly be maidenly for her to show her feelings, would it? She's very young, quite untouched. . . ." He contrived somehow to give the last word an unmistakable lasciviousness. Spurred by it Nicolas dared to say,

"And suppose we did . . . and suppose she had a baby."

"I hadn't thought of that. My thoughts always ended with Julia. Well, do you know, I think that would be even better than an empty memory. A child can entirely fill a woman's life. And she'll never get one out of Pieter at this rate. I don't think that that would be a tragedy at all. But that *is* carrying speculation rather far, don't you think." He smiled, and then said in a voice which struck exactly the right, seemingly irresponsible note, "Dear me, I'm afraid this has become a most unorthodox conversation. Quite reprehensible. How shocked and alarmed your dear parents would be! And really I only want everybody to be *happy*. Youth passes, and life passes and I've learned that it is what one misses that one regrets."

CHAPTER XI

Until Nicolas allowed his feelings for her to become obvious Julia had enjoyed his company very much. She was a little shy with him at first, for he was something entirely new, the first young man with whom she had been brought into contact; but as soon as he found his Uncle Simon so very different from the formidable person of family legend, his own diffidence disappeared and his naturally good spirits rose, so that it was impossible to be shy with him for long.

In the beginning the only jarring note in their gay companionship was his deep and persistent curiosity concerning his cousin Pieter. He had hardly believed what he had been told on arrival—that it was unlikely that he would see his relative; but as the days went on and Pieter remained invisible he became understandably inquisitive. It was not a subject to discuss with Uncle Simon, so he turned to Julia.

"Exactly in what way is he disfigured, Julia?"

Once again she gave the ready-made reply about the disfigurement being exaggerated.

"How much exaggerated? Is he awful to look at?"

"Not in the least." She could say that with truth now; she had become so accustomed to Pieter's appearance that she could hardly remember the shock it had been when he first turned his head.

"You can bear to look at him?"

"Of course. Don't I visit him every day?"

"Now you know, that is an odd thing to say. Visit. Wives don't visit their husbands."

She coloured with self-annoyance.

"We spend some time together. Is that better? He has pursuits that I can't share and he has Doctor Hootman for company."

"There's a curious character if you like!"

"In what way?" She turned to a discussion of Doctor Hootman with relief.

"Secretive," Nicolas said, after a little pause during which he sought for the right word. "As though, behind that dull, solid look all kinds of things were going on. I've often glanced at him suddenly and seen him staring at me, measuring me up. Then he'll look quickly away."

"I think he's shy, too. He used to look at me like that when I first came. He's quite nice, really."

"But what a way to live! Pieter presumably has a reason for his behaviour; but you'd think anybody else would go crazy. I should."

"Doctor Hootman probably enjoys a quiet life."

She was astonished to find how easily evasive and deceptive sentences would slip out. She would come from Pieter's room and find Nicolas waiting for her.

"And how is Pieter this morning?"

"Very well, thank you."

"What's he doing?"

"He was painting when I left him." A grain of truth there; Pieter enjoyed applying blobs and strokes of colour to his queer-shaped bits of pottery. And it was almost true to say, when she had left him busy stringing his beads, "He was doing some sort of sums." He *was* adding one to one. And if he were cutting up paper with his blunt-nosed scissors it could be called "paper-work." Nicolas was given to believe that Pieter, though a recluse, led a full and busy life.

But things changed. Nicolas began looking at her differently, long-resting, yearning looks. He began saying things which she found embarrassing, made attempts to take her hand. And his attitude towards Pieter changed too, became derogatory and spiteful.

One day, when she had parried a question, he looked at her closely and said,

"Poor Julia; you can't really bear to talk about him, can you?"

"I am talking about him now; or so I imagined," she said a trifle sharply.

"Without telling me anything."

"There's nothing to tell. And if you were Pieter, would you wish your wife to discuss you with someone else."

"If I were Pieter," said Nicolas, ceasing to walk and speaking with a dreamy intensity. "If I were Pieter I shouldn't care what I looked like. If I were ugly enough to frighten the English, if my head grew out of the middle of my chest—" (that was, actually, how he visualised his cousin, a hunch-back) "I shouldn't act like that. If I were lucky enough to be married to you, Julia, I should go round saying, 'Don't look at *me*, look at my beautiful wife! Look what I've *got!*'"

In the cool, prim voice which she used more and more often nowadays, she said,

"It's impossible to say how you would feel, or act, in another person's place."

"I know one thing. I'd give my right arm to change places with him!"

She thought of the marred red face, the ape-like stance, the heavy-hanging hands; of the whole empty, futile life. She spoke vehemently.

"Nicolas, don't say that. You don't know what you're saying!"

"Why shouldn't I say it? I would change places, not just with him, with the humblest, poorest little clerk, if I could be married to you."

He spoke sincerely, and was looking at her with admiring, passionate, almost worshipping eyes; and except for embarrassment she had no feeling at all. He was young and handsome, very likeable, and falling in love with her, and it meant nothing.

"Pieter had no right to get married at all," Nicolas went on. "He hasn't the slightest idea how to treat a wife."

"I don't know why you should say that. He's very fond of me. And very kind to me."

"Kind!" He repudiated the word with scorn. "Decent men are fond of their dogs and kind to their slaves. He doesn't love you."

"How do you know?"

"If he did he wouldn't let you be here, with me, now. He'd be as jealous of me as I am of him."

"He doesn't know the kind of thing you're beginning to say to me, Nicolas. And I wish you wouldn't. It just makes me uncomfortable and doesn't do any good. I am married, and very soon you will be yourself."

"Must you remind me of that?" he asked roughly. "When I was riding my hobby-horse and Greta was in her cradle our parents put their heads together and struck a bargain. Was that anything to do with me? Did anybody give one thought to *my* feelings? And the same with you. Somebody shoved a glove on your hand and somebody else said a few words. And they dare to call that a marriage! Then we see somebody else and we know, in our hearts . . . in our very bones . . ."

All unwittingly he was describing what had happened to her; that unlooked-for, uninvited recognition of the one, the only possible person. On that day, when Charles had kissed her and she had thrown her arms around him and kissed him, if he had said, "Come with me," she knew she would have gone, anywhere, to the world's end, and never even remembered that she was married.

Was it possible that Nicolas felt like that about her?

"It's like everything else," she said, "there has to be some sort of order, some sort of rule. Otherwise it would all be such a muddle. If you tried to go by *feelings* . . . You see, they so seldom fit. Everybody seems to be in love with somebody who isn't in love with them."

He supposed this to be her way of intimating that she was

not in love with him. But what did she know about it? He remembered the way in which Uncle Simon had said, "untouched." By comparison he felt infinitely experienced.

"Oh no," he said, "sometimes two people are in love with one another. And then everything is wonderful."

She looked at him, and for a moment tried to imagine Charles standing there in his place, saying such things to her, gazing at her in that way. It was to imagine the impossible. Not Charles' style at all, some instinctive knowledge informed her. But this was no time to think of that. Once again she must deal with this situation without hurting Nicolas' feelings.

"I've never known a case like that," she said with an assumed lightness. "Those I've read about always came to a bad end." As soon as the words were spoken they had a ring of doom. "Suppose," she said, "just *suppose* that I fell in love with you; think how miserable we should be when the time came to part."

"But we should have had something, Julia. We'd have known what happiness was. We'd have something to remember."

Ah, but *I* have that, already; a very small, shadowy thing, but I have it and nothing else must be allowed to cut across, to come between me and what I remember.

It occurred to her suddenly that what she had said a little earlier might be entirely true—everybody was in love with somebody who wasn't in love with them. That might be why Charles had so firmly loosened her clutching hands. . . . Well, all the more honour to him. She must profit by that example.

"I don't love you, Nicolas. I like you very much, but that is all."

He was sufficiently infatuated to tell himself that he liked her all the better because she was not "easy"; because she was, he thought, loyal to Pieter and her disastrous marriage. He was too young to hear in the words "I like you" the fatal denial of all hope. In fact, with no great difficulty, he was able to read into them a properly maidenly, entrancingly shy, promise of a warmer emotion.

So the languorous spice-scented days went on, and passed through the fields of the sunset into warm spice-scented nights full of stars. And presently Nicolas' stay in Rua had reached the half-way mark.

CHAPTER XII

There came a day when Mynheer announced that he would be absent for a night.

"I'm going to the Governor's very dull, gentlemen-only dinner party," he said. "And as I have some business to do in Banda tomorrow morning, I shall stay there and return about midday. I daresay you two will make shift to entertain yourselves. Oh, and Nicolas, I've opened a bottle of what, if it lives up to the shipper's promise, should be a rather special wine. Try it at dinner, will you, and give me your opinion."

In the late afternoon, dressed in his best and followed by a slave bearing a large bouquet of Rua flowers for Mevrouw Van de Lijn, whose efforts to make a garden within the walls of the Fort had proved unavailing, Mynheer stepped into his prahau and was rowed swiftly away.

Julia spent the afternoon with Pieter. Ever since she had allowed her tongue to slip and say "visit," she had prolonged the time she spent with him, and occasionally had refused to keep Nicolas company on the pretence that she had promised to do something with Pieter. Part of this pretence was a keeping faith with Mynheer, part of it was habit, and part was the result of the feeling of shame which she had felt when Charles had remarked upon her marriage; she was now anxious to hide the truth for her own sake.

This afternoon Pieter was busily and happily and messily

making clay pots. They were all lop-sided and flawed, but she admired them profusely and when she left he presented her with the largest of them.

The candles were lighted, and she had changed her dress and Juno was putting the last touches to her hair when there was a knock on the door between her sitting-room and the cloister. Juno put down the brush and went to the door, and Julia heard, with surprise, Doctor Hootman's voice. "Tell Mevrouw that Mynheer Pieter wants her for a few minutes." She called,

"I heard. I'll come at once."

Most likely, she thought, he wanted to give her another pot. Amenable and easily handled as he generally was, he had cantankerous moods now and then. At such times, unless given way to he would scream with rage and throw himself to the floor. Doctor Hootman would hasten to give way. "Indulging his whims, however fantastic, does him less harm than throwing himself about like that," he had once said. So if Pieter had forgotten that he had just presented her with a pot and was determined to give her another, Doctor Hootman would protest up to a point and then, with a shrug, say "Very well," and send for her.

She crossed the library and tapped upon the door of Pieter's room. Doctor Hootman opened it and said,

"Come in, Mevrouw."

Charles stood by the table.

She said, "Oh!" in the awed, rapt voice of someone confronted by a heavenly vision. And then she just stood and stared, and Charles stared back at her.

She had never, really, expected to see him again. The memory of him had been something laid away, sealed over, having no connection with ordinary everyday living. Now there he stood, living, breathing, real, just by the table where, a little while ago, she had been helping Pieter with his pots. There were no words. She could only look and look. . . .

Charles was dumb too. Unlike her he had not cherished his memories: whenever they hovered he had beaten them off.

He'd met, by accident, a girl whose looks and personality and situation combined to make an appeal to him, but he was a realist and he had faced his feelings realistically. There was no room in his life for love of any kind, certainly not for a mooning, hopeless love such as this might be if he let himself go. Nobody but a crass fool would give a second thought to a girl met once, a girl who was married. In common with others of his background and generation he was familiar with the song contained in Ford's "Music of Sundry Kinds":

> There is a Lady, sweet and kind,
> Was never face so pleased my mind;
> I did but see her passing by,
> And yet I love her till I die.

That sort of thing belonged to the poets; if it had ever been part of ordinary life it had been part of a life which had begun to die when the King raised his standard at Nottingham and had breathed its last at the Battle of Naseby. Aged sixteen, his father's sword heavy in his hand, a borrowed horse between his knees, he had been present by the death-bed. The old golden age was gone and gone forever, with its love, and its Ladies, its songs, romance and chivalry. Elmhurst was a fire-blackened ruin, and he was an exile, lucky to have got away alive. There is a Lady—think that, think of those eyes and the way her hair grows in a little point on her forehead, and of that sweet curve of the lip, and think of the sheer pluck—and *then* where are you? There are deprivations and yearnings enough, without contriving more for yourself. Fool! A pretty little Dutch girl, with a kind heart. You did your best for her. Forget it. Here a job, there a job, everywhere a pretty little guilder; an unlimed nutmeg, an unsupervised clove, a close brush with the patrol boat, one more brick towards rebuilding Elmhurst and to hell with everything else!

Daan had said, "Come up to the house, Charles. Mynheer is away for the night. We'll make free with his brandy."

And then he had said, "I promised Mevrouw that if ever it

could be managed I would arrange that you met. She feels that
she never thanked you properly."

"I don't want her thanks."

But he did want to see her. Just to prove . . . what? That
she was merely a pretty little Dutch girl; not the dream-
provocative, memory-troubling Lady who had passed by and
waked a love that would never sleep again.

So Daan had sent for her. And here she was.

Into the silence, so loud with unspoken things, Doctor Hootman said, "I must begin getting my charge to bed." He went
into the bedroom, closing the door gently behind him.

"I thought, since I was here, I'd like to see how you were,"
Charles said awkwardly. "You're thinner than I remembered."

So he had remembered.

"You look just the same." Just the same, even to the torn frill
of the shirt that had once been fine.

"You haven't been getting into any more trouble?"

"Oh no. And thank you for bringing back my bag. I was in
such a state. I didn't think of it. And I didn't even ask your
name."

"You know it now?"

"Oh yes. Charles." There was something special about it,
and about using it to him, for the first time.

"And you're Julia. I asked. So every now and then I can say
to myself, I hope everything is going right with Julia, or, I wonder what Julia is doing this fine morning."

What an utterly asinine thing to say! Sounds as though . . .

"I've thought of you, too. Every single day. And I never even
hoped I'd see you again. I don't even know where you live."

"I live on a little island called Ay. There are about a dozen
of us. In a hut. We live like pigs."

"Which way does it lie, your island?"

He took a mental bearing and jerked his head.

"Oh. One of my windows looks that way. I shall be able to
look out . . . and think . . ."

"Of me, in my hut? If it's in the morning you can think of me lighting the fire. I most imprudently let it be known that I have a talent for lighting fires, and so I was saddled with that job."

"I often had it, in the Klopstock Home; it was one of the unpopular ones."

None of these words meant anything at all. It was their eyes that were doing the real talking.

"Doctor Hootman told me that you are English," she began afresh.

"That's right; but I've lived in the Islands for a long time now."

"I think I'm English too." To establish a bond even so impersonal as a shared nationality was delightful and exciting.

"What do you mean, *think*? Don't you know?"

"Not for certain. It was in Ireland that I was found, but I could say a piece in English. Uncle Johannes told me what it meant in Dutch; and it said I was English. He believed I was."

"Who was Uncle Johannes?"

"The man who found me. He was a sea captain. He knew a little of several languages."

"Say me your English piece."

"In English? I don't know whether I remember it. It's so long ago. And even then he said I said it like a parrot. But I'll try."

Slowly, dredging up each word from the depths of her memory she repeated the simple identification which Maire had taken such pains to teach her.

"Ashley," he repeated as she came to the end. "That's English enough. In Ireland you say. When?"

"I was eight then—when Uncle Johannes found me. And I shall be seventeen in June."

"How long were you with Maire?"

"Oh, all my life I should think. I can't remember anything before. She said she taught me to walk and to talk."

"You were a baby then in '49. Cromwell in Drogheda.

That'd be about right. I think you could claim to be English. We're a long way from home, Julia."

"Perhaps that is why . . ."

"Why what?"

She floundered a little. "Well, that day . . . I was all confused, half out of my mind, but later on, when I thought about it, it was just as though we weren't really strangers. As though I had recognised you."

And it had been so with him. Miscall, deny it how you would, you recognised the Lady who just passed by . . . that was why the one glance was enough.

"So the Dutchman brought you out of Ireland. What then?"

"He was drowned. His wife didn't like me, so she sent me to an orphanage and I ended up in the Company's Daughters' Home. And then I came here."

He said abruptly, "They don't often live to be old." The jerk of his head showed where his thoughts had jumped; and as though it had been a signal, there came from behind the closed door a low grumbling sound, like distant thunder, Pieter's indistinct flannelly voice raised in complaining protest. "Things might work out right for you, yet. I'd like to think so." He brushed his hand across his face with a gesture of helpless confusion oddly at variance with his general demeanour. "I've worried about you, a bit; though God knows I've worries enough of my own and I can't do anything for you."

"I'm all right," she said quickly. "You mustn't worry about me." But it was sweet to think that he had. "What worries have you?"

He laughed. "All concerned with mental arithmetic and similar sordid things. I'm all right too. You and I have survived the break-up of a civilisation, Julia. We should reckon ourselves lucky to be alive."

The noise in Pieter's room was now loud and continuous. The words, "Julie. Want Julie," emerged quite clearly, and were followed by a bellowing roar, a purely animal sound of rage and distress. There were several heavy but soft-sounding thuds, one of which made the door shudder. They could hear Doctor Hootman's voice, firm and soothing, too low-pitched to be distinguishable above the noise.

"He knows I'm here," Julia said.

As she spoke the door opened a few inches, was sharply slammed. The bellowing cries rose to a crescendo, and then the door opened fully and Doctor Hootman and Pieter, locked in a Laocoön embrace, came hurtling into the room.

Though physically overborne Doctor Hootman was still in charge of the situation, and still calm.

"Take him, Mevrouw; distract his attention," he said, and released his hold on Pieter who plunged straight at her, quiet now except for gulping sobs of rage. He burrowed his head into her shoulder and clutched at her, saying, "Julie, Julie," over and over again between the sobs.

Doctor Hootman placed himself squarely in front of Charles.

"You must go. One word would be enough! I couldn't let the noise continue. We have a guest in the house." The calm of his voice was just touched with anguish as he spoke the last words.

Julia hugged Pieter to her, keeping his face hidden in her shoulder. Charles, hustled by Doctor Hootman, went to the door, and there turned. Over the large, nuzzling head thatched with the dry-looking hair, she smiled, and because they must not speak she put into the smile all the unspoken things. That was what Charles carried away with him, the memory of Julia, sweet and lovely and brave, smiling at him as she soothed the poor boy.

Just before the door closed he raised his hand; and it was not in salute to a pretty little Dutch girl. . . .

Doctor Hootman turned back into the room and said with genuine regret, "Mevrouw, I am *sorry!* I simply dared not risk the disturbance." Pursing his lips he looked at Pieter, who had stopped crying and was stroking Julia's sleeve. "I've never known him so violent; or else I'm out of condition. Come along now, Pieter. You've seen Julie and Julie has seen you being very naughty. Very naughty indeed!"

"Naughty," Pieter admonished himself heartily. "Naughty indeed!" But he did not assume the scolded-dog aspect ordinarily educed by the use of the word. On the contrary he seemed pleased with himself.

"Seen Julie," he added.

Doctor Hootman's heavy eyebrows knotted in a little frown.

"Some sort of animal instinct at work there."

He might have been speaking to himself, and Julia almost allowed herself to assume that he was, for to speak it was necessary to drag her mind away from its dream.

"What do you mean?"

Doctor Hootman looked at her, hesitated, and said,

"That he knew you were here. We shall have to be a little more firm, I think. Come along, Pieter. Time for bed."

"Time for bed. Good morning, Julie," said Pieter and allowed himself to be led away. At the bedroom door Doctor Hootman turned.

"I think, if you will excuse me, Mevrouw, I shall dine here. With Pieter, of course." He added the last words with the now familiar, derisive grimace with which he always marked any additional act of subterfuge.

She wanted to be alone, to relive, to remember, but she could hardly leave Nicolas to dine alone. She must wait. Tonight though, his yearning looks and sentimental words were more than usually irksome. They encroached; they also, in her present mood, provoked a tiresome form of pity. She could believe now that Charles was not without feeling for her and to come direct from the meeting which had inculcated that belief and be beset by Nicolas' pleading glances made her feel like somebody newly rich, his wealth not even yet counted, immediately accosted by a beggar.

"This is an occasion," he said, as they sat down to the table. "We've never dined alone together before; we never may again.

Oh Julia! When I think of Pieter who could have that pleasure every night of his life . . ."

Pluto's entry gave her an excuse to frown so that that sentence died on the air.

Nicolas tried again, and again, until her short, and finally impatient, replies gave him the key to her mood. He realised that he was becoming slavish and he had heard or read somewhere that with women slavish tactics were seldom successful. He must be gay and charming.

The wine helped. After two glasses of it his spirits and his colour rose, his wits and his eyes brightened.

"Uncle Simon was dead right about this wine, Julia. It is special. Let me . . ." he leaned forward and filled her glass. "I suspect that my father—himself a schnapps drinker—warned Uncle Simon that I was a wine-bibber as well as an idle scamp. So in his presence I always feel self-conscious if I have a second glass. Though I don't think he'd mind. It's odd, don't you think, how some parents seem to enjoy decrying their children —you'd think they'd be ashamed. I must say that—quite apart from other reasons—I'm not looking forward to my return to the family roof. For one thing my father will expect me to have acquired, in three months, all the secrets of Uncle Simon's success in business. And not one have I ferreted out. Careless, unobservant rapscallion that I am."

Encourage him to continue with this easy kind of chatter.

"Tell me about Java, and your home and everything," she said. He filled his glass again and with willingness launched into a description of his home and family. He could, when he wished, talk very entertainingly, and he did so now, with just enough exaggeration to be amusing.

"My mother," he said, "is one of those women who can see danger in *everything*, and can prove her case with a hair-raising tale. She must have known, intimately, the victims of more fatalities than anyone else in the world. For instance, if she saw you, sipping that wine, sitting on that solid chair, she would certainly say, 'My dear, do be careful; I once knew a woman who choked to death, drinking a glass of wine. And my sister's second cousin by marriage once sat on a chair, just as you are doing, and it broke under her. The fall injured her so that she never walked again. So do be careful.' She honestly would."

Of his father he said, with a slight decline of amiability,

"He was named Jacob, which was unfortunate because it gave him the notion that he is one of the Bible patriarchs. I very narrowly escaped being called Reuben. My mother had to beg, on her knees, for Nicolas. She saw danger in Reuben as the name for her first-born, you see."

"What danger?"

"Dear me, you are ignorant, Julia. Reuben was the eldest of twelve!"

"I see," she said, laughing.

"Benjamin she did accept, with good cheer, when my youngest brother was born."

He chatted in this fashion, refilling and emptying his glass. Then he said,

"Now I feel like making some music. I can play too. But only when I'm happy. Let's go and brave Pieter in his den and ask if I may play his clavichord."

"Oh no!" she said. She heard the real horror in her voice and knew it to be disproportionate to the occasion. "He always retires early. If we disturbed him he would never forgive us."

"That's just it. He should *be* disturbed," said Nicolas, with the intransigence of the near-intoxicated. "I'd ask nicely. I'd say, 'Cousin Pieter, I haven't come to stare at your scars or lick your sores. I just want to play your clavichord.' Who knows, it might be the turning point in his whole life; the opening wedge, as it were."

"He'd be very upset, and very angry. He'd blame me. Please Nicolas, don't even think of it."

"The idea is abandoned. Nobody could resist you when you speak so earnestly and look so seductive."

"If you really want to play, there is a clavichord in my sitting-room."

"You never play."

"I can't. But your uncle, when he furnished the room, provided everything that any kind of woman could possibly require. Therefore I have a clavichord."

"I've never seen your room. Come along, I will make you such sweet music as will melt even your stony heart."

"You won't, you know," she kept her voice light and casual. "If you have that in mind, Nicolas, I warn you, you'll be wasting your time."

Too late she realised that it had been stupid to invite him to her room. Done without thinking, to divert his attention from Pieter, it might easily be misunderstood.

He stumbled a little as they went along the cloister and the memory of the drunken sailor revived in her mind. She would have been wiser to let him go blundering along to Pieter's apartments; Doctor Hootman could have dealt with him.

At the door of her room she wondered whether to say, Now, if you come in, you must promise to behave. But that had a kind of implication, of coyness, which might precipitate the very thing she wished to avoid. A brisk matter-of-factness was probably the best defence.

She opened the clavichord and placed the candles near it, reserving one for herself on the far side of the room.

"There you are," she said to Nicolas, who was idly wandering about the room, looking at the furnishings. "I shall sit here and go on with my work while you play."

He surprised her by playing, even in his slightly tipsy state, remarkably well. The music he made was nothing like Doctor Hootman's wild sombre cry of discontent; he played light, graceful little tunes. They were all love songs and after a few minutes he hit on the idea of turning and announcing each title in a half-teasing way, laughing at her over his shoulder.

"Now this one is called 'You Are My Chosen.' Oh, how I wish I could sing. I'll teach you the words, Julia, then you can sing them. 'You are my chosen, the one that I love' . . . that's the first line. Say it after me."

"I can't sing at all."

"Have you no talent—apart from the talent for making people love you?"

"You're here to play my clavichord, not to catechise me!"

She went on stitching and he turned back to the instrument. Presently he said, "I play well, don't I? Better than Pieter, don't you think?"

"Differently."

"How very miserly! Julia, sometimes I think you must be in love with him, and he so surly he won't even speak to his own cousin. What is it? Pity? Would you be kinder to me if I wore my scars on my face instead of on my heart?"

It was asked flirtatiously rather than seriously and she replied in the same manner.

"No. I couldn't be kinder to you. I'm already so kind that I find it a strain."

He began to play again, passed from one tune to another and reached, at last, one different from the rest. No longer light and gay. A sweet, haunting melancholy tune that seemed to hold all the sadness of goodbyes spoken forever.

It had its effect on Julia, who ceased stitching and folded her hands on the embroidery bag with its eloquent stains. *His* hands had touched it, and in holding it she made some kind of contact. Her mind, her heart, went winging out, over the sea to Ay.

The music, and the wine he had drunk, took effect on Nicolas. Slavish adoration, pretty speeches, yearning looks, brought no return. A man should be masterful, ruthless, possessive. Youth went over and life passed by, and a man on his way to a life sentence was justified in snatching at a flower to take with him—even if it grew in another man's garden.

With his fingers still drawing sorrowful sweetness from the keys, he turned his head, and saw upon Julia's face a look which he had never seen before, unguarded, dreaming, desirous.

He left the clavichord and crossed the room in a single swoop-
ing motion, gathered her into his arms, and saying, "You do
love me, you do, you do," set his mouth to hers.

The fact that he was kissing her in the way that she would
have liked to kiss Charles, in the way she longed to be kissed
by him, added to her sense of outrage.

She turned her head, and freed her mouth, and put both
hands against him, thrusting him away.

"I don't! You forget yourself. Leave go of me!"

He was beyond control now. The touch of flesh on flesh,
even the way she struggled, fired him; and the weeks of meek
adoration had to be paid for as well as the threatening years
of a loveless marriage. He put his hand to the back of her head
and forced her face round; he fumbled at the lace on her breast.

Drunken sailor, drunken Nicolas. All one.

With a wrench that seemed to break her neck she got her
mouth free again and screamed. Useless. She knew that even
as the single shrill sound rang out. Doctor Hootman was at the
other end of the house; the slaves even farther away and heedful
only of the bells.

Yet immediately somebody tapped on the door, not loudly,
but with insistence. Nicolas heard it too and his clutch loosened. She gave another push and he stood up. She ran her hands
over her hair, drew in a breath and managed to call, "Come in."

The door opened, rather slowly, as though stiff on its hinges
and there was Doctor Hootman, looking mild and vague,
blinking like an owl against the light.

"I had to come," he said, with a note of apology in his voice.
"I heard music. . . . Music from a hand far more skilled than
mine . . . or Pieter's. Yours, Mynheer?"

"I was playing." He sounded sulky and curt.

"Most beautifully," said Doctor Hootman. He lifted his big,
heavily-haired hands and rubbed his eyes.

"Coming in from the dark, so many candles all together,
quite blinding," he said.

He might pretend not to see anything; but the sound of the scream still hung on the air.

"I spoilt it," Julia said in a voice so high-pitched and unsteady that it, as well as the scream, needed explanation. "I put my hand into my bag and a needle ran into my finger. Just for a second I thought a snake had crept in."

"That could very easily happen, Mevrouw. I've seen your bag lying in the garden." He turned to Nicolas who had recovered some show of composure. "Mynheer Vanderplasse, I had no idea that you were such a musician. Would you mind if I stayed and listened for a while, if Mevrouw would give me permission, of course? One becomes, as you will understand, weary of the same old tunes. All yours were fresh to me."

"Do stay. Sit down, Doctor Hootman."

Nicolas said, "I only know a few tunes. I've played them all and to repeat them would bore me."

Doctor Hootman, who had almost taken a chair, stood, uncertain, hesitant.

"Perhaps you would like to try *my* clavichord," Julia said. "Your old tunes might sound differently."

"Mevrouw, to do that would be to invite the inevitable, and I am sure, invidious comparison."

There was a moment's bristling silence. Then Nicolas said, rudely,

"Not from me. I'm going to bed. Good night, Julia."

The door slammed behind him and before the sound of it had died away Doctor Hootman was at the clavichord.

"I must play, Mevrouw," he said. "To a young man as angry as that one another comparison might suggest itself, old and ugly as I am. However, flown with wine as he is, he will soon sleep."

He played on for about five minutes, then ended a tune abruptly and stood up.

Julia said at once, "Doctor Hootman, thank you! How did you happen to be near enough?"

"I often take a little stroll after dark." He sat down on a chair near the table where the candle stood.

"I'll assume that my intervention was welcome," he said. "So we need not talk about that. Mevrouw, not long ago you told me that you would never again allow your will to come into conflict with Mynheer's."

Why should he say that, *now?*

"Yes, I did. And I meant it. Doctor Hootman, are you implying that what you interrupted . . . ? I assure you that that was entirely against my will. You must know that. You heard me call out."

"Mevrouw, please! Of course I understood that. Otherwise should I have dreamed of interfering?" He paused, looked at her gravely, then looked down and pulled at the fingers of his left hand with the thumb and first finger of his right so that his knuckles cracked. "I think the time has come," he said at last, looking up again. "Mevrouw, you must forgive me if I speak plainly. I'm no good at trimming things up, and I don't think it is a subject which can be broached delicately. I can only tell you the facts. What almost happened here this evening, and would have done, but for me, may have been against your will, but would have been in direct accordance with Mynheer's."

"What?" It occurred to her that Doctor Hootman had also—in Mynheer's absence—made free with the bottle. "Do you *know* what you are saying?"

"I am telling you that if you are truly compliant with Mynheer's will you will take that pretty nincompoop as a lover and pray that next year there will be a fine new branch on the Vosmar family tree."

She stared at him as though he had struck her in the face or used some word of extreme obscenity. Then cold common sense pushed its way through stunned incredulity and recognised the truth. It was true; everything, from Mynheer's talk on the way home after her visit to Marie to his absence this evening, all fitted in.

"I told you it was plain speaking," Doctor Hootman said. The blood had rushed into her face and he courteously refrained from looking at her for a moment.

"He spoke to you of this?" she asked in a low, shamed voice.

"On the night of your arrival. Mevrouw, you must not mind my knowing; rather be glad." His voice changed and took on an easier, more conversational tone. "I had, of course, quite understood the purpose of his elaborate deception, family pride was at the back of that; a wife seemed to me to be an unnecessary complication and risk. I said something to that effect and then he told me the plan he had been cherishing all those years. When that young man was a mere child this visit was proposed and Pieter's marriage was timed to dovetail in with it—a few months to spare so that his wife might have time to become fretful and discontented and begin to ask what life held for her. Have you never noticed how often Mynheer has said things calculated to make you sorry for yourself?"

She nodded.

"You see? Nothing overlooked, nothing left to chance. It is the careful work of many years which you have in your power to crown with success or doom to failure. The young man's mother was a Vosmar. I have no doubt that Mynheer includes in his plan a prolonged tour of the Islands, proudly and assiduously pointing out that the Vosmar family features have been reproduced once again."

"Don't," she said. "You make it all sound so horrible—just like animals."

"It is. That is what we are, not being Vosmars. Another Holy Family, and you know where that has ended?"

She nodded again.

"Not a pleasant plan, but in its way masterly."

"Is it? It seems to depend so much on chance. Nicolas might have hated the sight of me."

"Every man has his price, Mevrouw; and Mynheer is very rich. Not, I hasten to add that that has been necessary in this case but it was an eventuality for which Mynheer was well-prepared."

There was a silence. Then she said,

"I don't think I could do it. It goes against something . . ." she pressed her clasped hands to her breast. "It's so sickeningly cold-blooded. No, I couldn't."

Doctor Hootman seemed to settle more firmly and comfortably into his chair; he crossed one leg over the other and linked his hands around his knee.

"Then, Mevrouw, we must consider. I think that we should first look at the gravity of the situation. An heir Mynheer must have, and he will go to any lengths to get what he needs. He never fully believed that Pieter's accident was responsible, so he dared not marry again. Imagine having to conceal the existence of two idiots, invent a secret life for them both—that would have taxed even Mynheer's ingenuity. So you see what a normal child means to him, not an heir only, but a perfect vindication of all these years of make-believe. Opposition isn't going to be easy, or safe."

The fright showed in her eyes.

"It's always best to face a thing squarely. It is hardly likely that Mynheer, having come so far, will let one girl stand in his way. The world is full of girls."

"He'd kill me."

"Not with my consent. I am," he raised and shrugged one heavy shoulder deprecatingly, "of no particular importance, but —I play my part. The fact that Pieter has outlived so many of his kind is my doing, and at least half the façade Mynheer has raised is my work. I should use my influence to see that you got away with your life."

It seemed an outlandish promise to be made, here in this quiet, luxurious room.

"Before we go into that, look a little more closely into Mynheer's proposal. It is not without attractions, you know. You could be mother to the Heir of All the Vosmars, a Queen Mother in fact; pampered, revered. Mynheer would not be niggardly in his manifestations of gratitude. Many women would not, in the circumstances, mind acting as brood mare."

"That's what I said," she exclaimed sharply. "Like animals. Horrible!"

"Well, you may change your mind. If you stick to that, you will be dispensed with, and replaced. Poor Pieter Vosmar, in addition to his other afflictions, will suffer sudden bereavement, but, being the resilient character that he is, he will soon find another wife."

Even at that moment something in his tone jarred.

"Don't," she said, "none of this is his fault!" But this was not the time to think about Pieter. "Where should *I* be—if not dead?"

"That is where I should come in. I am in Mynheer's confidence; and I should be watchful. Up to this point he has been content to let things develop naturally. On his return he will begin to exert pressure. The day will soon come when he will say, will you or won't you? If you persist in your refusal he will begin to plan your removal, but I shall forestall him. My plan is already made."

"Already. What is it?"

"Remember, Mevrouw, this which is new to you has been known to me for several months. I have had time to think. When danger threatens—and make no mistake about it, it will be deadly danger—I shall get you away, safely. It will appear as though, too hard pushed, you drowned yourself."

No dream had ever seemed more fantastic.

"Where should I go?"

He looked her full in the face and said,

"To Ay."

Yes, she knew; he could see that. He went on smoothly,

"I have friends there into whose keeping I could safely commend you."

"Charles lives in Ay."

"That is so. He told you? He seems to have become very

communicative all of a sudden. Well, don't you think that you would be safe there? In Ay, with Charles?"

She almost laughed. The impulse to laughter was there but she was afraid that if she yielded to it she would cry as well and become hysterical. Nevertheless the idea of disappearing, pretending to be drowned, and then popping up safe and sound in the one spot in the world where she longed to be, pushed fantasy past the place where it could be taken seriously.

"Really, Doctor Hootman, that sounds so much like the ending of a fairy-tale that it makes me wonder whether any of the rest of it is true."

There came across his face that same look as when she had explained her reason for taking food to Psyche.

"Look," he said, leaning slightly forward, "isn't all the evidence in favour of Mynheer's plan being cold fact? Think carefully. What would have happened tonight had I not been ready, waiting?"

"Yes," she said, "that could be true."

"Isn't it also a fact that being a man accustomed to his own way he will be dangerous if thwarted?"

"Yes."

"I can't actually *prove* that I would not like to see you murdered; but can you take that for granted?"

"Yes. Yes, of course."

"Very well then; that brings us to the point. What could I do except get you out of Rua? And where else could I send you? What is so fantastic, so much like a fairy-tale about that?"

"It would be such a happy ending," she said, simply. The hot colour rushed into her face again.

"Mevrouw, after all our trials, don't you think we deserve a happy ending?"

Something peculiar happened to her mind; she could only see herself saying "Let me do that," and lighting the fire for Charles. "Let me do that," and lighting the fire. "Let me do that," and lighting the fire. Over and over again, like a clock which had stuck and went on striking the same hour.

Doctor Hootman uncrossed his legs, and shifted in his chair.

"You'll have a day or two to think it over, I expect. Your best plan, for the moment, is to appear to encourage the young man when you are in company and discourage him when you are alone. You have your full share of feminine guile and inventiveness, I think." He looked at the work-bag. "Remember that you can count on my support if it is needed; but don't, too hastily, decide to oppose Mynheer. Life in Ay would not be luxurious. There is a good deal to be said for being a brood mare. I wish you good night, Mevrouw."

The cloister lay sharply black and white in the moonlight. As he walked its length, moving from light to shadow, Doctor Hootman linked his hands and lifted and lowered them in a gesture very much like that of a man giving himself a congratulatory hand-shake.

Julia had known nights of uneasy, broken sleep, of sudden jolting wakenings and bad dreams before, but that night, for the first time in her life she did not sleep at all.

CHAPTER XIII

"You look unlike yourself, my dear," said Mynheer. "Is anything the matter?"

He watched for the betraying blush, the evasive glance, and was disappointed.

"I have a headache. I was lying down when you called me," Julia said.

It was midday when he returned and he had come straight into the house calling her name. The thought of facing him sickened her, but she must do so sooner or later, so she had come out of her room and found him in the hall, with a large parcel, wrapped in white linen, lying at his feet.

"I'm very sorry," he said in his kindest voice. "How long have you had it?" It wasn't credible that after all his careful staging a headache should have intervened. . . .

"It came on in the night."

"Well, I've brought you a present which I hope will cheer you, even if it won't cure a headache. Look."

He whisked away the linen and revealed some folded softness, a shimmer of blue and silver which, lifted and shaken out by his nimble hands, revealed itself as a sarong of silk and a little jacket of gauzy stuff.

"It'll be cool to wear, and I'm sure you'll find it very becoming."

He expected, and awaited, some exclamations of admiration and of gratitude. She forced herself to say,

"Thank you, Mynheer. It is very pretty," but the words came out listlessly.

Tainted, sinister, like every bit of kindness he had ever shown her. Decking out the brood mare!

"Your head *is* bothering you, poor girl. I'm sorry I disturbed you. Go and lie down again and tell Juno to rub your head for you. They have great cunning in their fingers and can often shift a pain."

As she turned to walk slowly away, he asked,

"Where is Nicolas?"

"I couldn't say, Mynheer. I have not seen him this morning."

"Never mind. I shall find him. I expect he is seeing to things for me. I hope your headache will soon vanish."

He went off briskly towards the plantation. When she reached her own doorway, instead of entering the room she turned, and, leaning her arms on the cloister wall, put her aching head in her hands, and stared out into the garden. Mynheer was just about to enter the rose pergola.

From that distance he looked very small; and perhaps for that reason she made another effort to think well of him. There was something admirable in the way he had faced what must, to a man of his disposition, have been an intolerable situation.

If I'd been different, she thought, his scheme, fantastic as it is, might have succeeded. Many women would not have found the bargain unduly one-sided. She thought of the hard-eyed woman in the tavern, who, for some trivial sum, was eager to sell herself to a drunken sailor. The rewards here were very large, and Nicolas was young, attractive. Many women . . . but then I'm not any other woman, I'm myself. I am as I am, I can only be myself, be guided by what I feel and know is right for *me*.

Mynheer met Nicolas on the path and, greeting him, observed that he also looked unlike himself. His eyes were bloodshot, the colour less smoothly spread in his young face, and his eyes *were* evasive.

They exchanged a few remarks about the morning's work.

"You seem to have taken my place most satisfactorily," Mynheer said. "No need for me to go any further. It's getting hot, too. Let us go and sit on the verandah and drink some well-cooled wine."

"Not for me, thank you," said Nicolas with a grimace. "I drank too much last night."

"Indeed? For you I prescribe lime-juice then. Does *your* head ache? Julia's does. What did you get up to last evening? A Bacchanalian orgy, eh?"

"I drank too much and I . . . Uncle Simon, I think I'd better go home. If you don't mind, I'd like to go to Banda, today, and wait there for a ship. After what happened last night I don't think I can face Julia again."

"Good gracious me!" said Mynheer, putting his hand on Nicolas' shoulder. "Was it so bad? What happened? Or is it too dreadful to tell?"

"I got drunk. Not very drunk . . . in fact I didn't think . . . but that was a very subtle wine, or something. Anyhow, I lost my head and threw myself on Julia and . . . well, you can guess what happened."

The patchy pink in his face was engulfed in hot scarlet.

"That's just what I can't do. Nor can I see, in anything you have told me so far, why you should see it necessary to leave Rua. Did she . . . rebuff you?"

"Rebuff! She acted as though I were trying to rape her."

"Which was, of course, far from your intention?"

Nicolas shot his favourite relative a look of utter loathing, and said nothing.

"So she rebuffed you. Well, she wouldn't be a woman if she didn't do that at least three times! Surely you realise that."

"Once is enough for me. Thank you!" said Nicolas between his teeth.

"Dear me. You are in a bad way. You're beginning to make me suspect that your feelings are seriously involved—to be taking the thing so much to heart. But I should be sorry if you cut short your visit—for my own sake, and for other reasons. Your father would look for some explanation."

"I could tell him the truth," said Nicolas, who was in a self-destructive mood.

"He'd be delighted to hear *that*," said Mynheer drily. And the boy's sense of reality held up to him the vision of his father's face, the thin humourless lips, the hard, strict stare. No; if he went home he would have to give an invented, an acceptable reason.

"I wouldn't do that," said Mynheer, giving the shoulder under his hand an affectionate little squeeze. "No harm has been done; you must make allowance for maidenly modesty and coquettishness, clumsily displayed. Poor Julia; I'll warrant that at this very minute she is trying some new dress or some new way of doing her hair in order to charm you."

"Or Pieter," Nicolas said.

Mynheer's hand fell away. "Did you say Pieter?" he had asked before the long-established censor within had had time to say—Careful, now, careful!

"I think you've been wrong about them all along," said Nicolas, with some slight satisfaction at being thus able to shift a little of the blame. "I've been thinking things over this morning and I've come to the conclusion that she's in love with Pieter—which makes my behaviour the more beastly. . . . And ridiculous," he added.

"Well, of course," said Mynheer, now completely on his guard again, "that would be most desirable. I should have said that no woman who wasn't blind and deaf and equipped with the hide of a rhinoceros could possibly love anyone who had treated her as Pieter has treated Julia. But of course there are women who like to be ill-used." His voice was thoughtful. After a pause he said, "Perhaps I've been a little blind myself. I've seen no sign. What makes you think so?"

"Nothing that I could put into words, really. Partly the cheerful way she goes off to spend time with him; and she won't talk about him. I admit I was . . . I mean I *am* . . . curious about him. You never . . ." He broke off and began again. "To you, I suppose it all seems ordinary, you're used to it. But imagine if you went to stay in Java, or Macassar, and there was a member of the family whom you never saw, wouldn't *you* be curious?"

"I most certainly should," Mynheer agreed. "So Julia won't talk about him. That could be evidence on the other side."

"No. What she does say is all in his favour—I realise that now. The fact is, what with one thing and another, I've made a complete fool of myself."

"And I concerned myself unduly, or prematurely, about her happiness. I wonder. I don't usually make mistakes of that sort —and I see them together, you know."

"I saw her face last night. I was playing for her . . . it was her look, as much as anything that was my undoing. She's in love with somebody, and it certainly isn't me."

Mynheer thrust his hand under Nicolas' arm.

"I'm to blame then, I misled you."

"I should have lost my heart—without any help from you,

238 SCENT OF CLOVES

Uncle Simon," the boy said, in an easier way; merely talking about it soothed some of the sting. "But had I known, I'd have kept better rein on myself. As it is, you do see why I can't stay here."

"I don't see that at all; but if you feel like that I have an alternative suggestion. I was in conversation with an acquaintance of mine, Gerard Barnevelt of Lonthoir, at dinner yesterday. I spoke of you and he extended an invitation for you to visit him. I think that would be a valuable experience, now that you are in this vicinity. I flatter myself that I run Rua with moderate efficiency, but my methods are my own; there are others, and perhaps you should see something of them."

"I should like to do so," said Nicolas. "When could I go?"

"Not today, I'm afraid. It could probably be arranged for the day after tomorrow, if I sent a message at once."

"That leaves me where I was as regards Julia."

"Do you carry a seal, Nicolas?"

"Yes . . . why?"

"Valuable?"

"It's silver."

Mynheer dived into his pocket and brought out his chain of keys from which his own seal swung. It was made of gold, inset with a large emerald upon which a bold V had been deeply cut.

"I'll wager this, against yours," he said, "that her manner, when you meet, will be charming. You see, I'm still not convinced. However, we shall see. . . ."

Under the soothing stroking, the gently prodding movements of Juno's firm fingers, the headache eased, and finally she slept, waking when the swift twilight had invaded the room and it was almost dinner-time. Instantly the memory of the information that Doctor Hootman had given her, and of the pattern of behaviour he had told her to follow, settled, like a heavy yoke, upon her spirit.

Pale cheeks could be tinted, but even when that was done

there was something wrong about her looks. Mynheer's eyes were sharp; and Nicolas' she dreaded to meet. She thought that perhaps if she wore the native dress it would divert attention from her face and account for her different look.

It was a wise choice, for the awkward moment of meeting was all taken up by exclamations of admiration, skilfully guided by Mynheer into a discourse about native weaving; how was it possible that human eyes, human fingers, could have worked, so successfully, on material so fine as the gauze of the little jacket; the threads were finer than the finest human hair; and wasn't it remarkable that primitive people, completely untutored, should have such perfect sense of design? The native Bandanese iron-work, for example, was said to be extraordinary.

"Of course it may be that the word primitive is here misleading. The arts of the so-called primitive people, in this part of the world at least, may be *remembered* things, the last echo of a vanished civilisation. They say that all these islands are, or rather were, the tips of mountain ranges of some submerged continent. Lost Atlantis, perhaps; who knows? Arts would survive a cataclysm of that kind because they depend upon the individual who could hand on what he knew to some likely youngster . . . just as, in a shipwreck, one might save a pair of shoes while a whole valuable cargo went to the bottom."

With this kind of conversation, impersonal, speculative, yet well within his listeners' range, he enlivened the meal; and Julia, catching Nicolas' sheepish, immediately-eager, smile, smiled back. All seemed as before.

Presently Mynheer, leaping chamois-wise from one subject to another, mentioned Nicolas' imminent visit to Lonthoir.

"And how we shall miss you, my boy," he said.

"When do you leave?" Julia asked Nicolas. He glanced at Mynheer, and he answered for him.

"I have despatched the message. I suggested the day after tomorrow, unless that is particularly inconvenient for Mevrouw Barnevelt."

Across the table Julia's eyes met Doctor Hootman's. They

were inscrutable and almost immediately he looked down at
the food piled on his plate.

It occurred to her that all he had said to her on the previous
evening might have been the product of his imagination. It
was a strange life that he led; hours and hours on end, locked
away there with nothing but an idiot for company, emerging
for an hour at dinner-time and then going back to his books.
It was possible that he invented things to amuse himself and
had reached the point where he no longer could distinguish the
real from the fancied. And no wonder, when, in Rua, the two
were so intricately entangled. Mynheer was now saying, for
instance,

"Daan—if Pieter hasn't retired when you go back, ask him
to wait up, will you? A proposition was put to me this morning
upon which I should like his opinion."

"I'll go now, and see if I can catch him," said Doctor Hootman, and rose and hurried away.

A few minutes later Mynheer rose.

"This business with Pieter won't take more than fifteen minutes," he said. "If you two would like to go into the salon and
set up two chess boards, I'll take you on both at the same time.
You'll find a second set in one of the cabinets, Julia."

Walking along the cloister Nicolas said, "Julia, I want to
apologise for my behaviour last evening. To say that I was not
sober, I know is no excuse, but I hope you'll take it into account."

"Let's not speak about it, or think about it any more," she
said.

"Will you forgive me?"

"I have."

They entered the salon and she went to the cabinet where
the chess-men she and Mynheer used as a rule were kept.

"Set these up," she said. "I'll find the others."

He stood there, holding the lacquered box in his hands.

"I wasn't just being drunk and . . . lascivious, you know," he said in a rather miserable voice. "I do love you, Julia."

There was something touching about him this evening, in this shamed and subdued mood, and with the first brightness of his good looks blurred he looked younger instead of older, as he should have done. She looked at him without speaking for a moment.

"I'm sorry Nicolas. I wish I loved you. I really do. But I don't. And there's nothing I can do about it."

For the first time he seemed to accept this.

"I wish to God I'd never come to Rua," he said. "Never set eyes on you."

There was hope for him then, if he felt like that, she thought, turning away to search the cabinet for the second set of chessmen. I've only seen Charles twice; I may never see him again, I have nothing to hope for; but I wouldn't *not* have known him for anything in the world.

But perhaps there lay one of the differences between women and men.

She found what she was looking for, and crossed to one of the tables and began to set out the game. Nicolas still stood holding the box she had handed him and staring at her gloomily.

"Uncle Simon's story was the only bit of family lore I ever found in the least interesting," he said at last. "Little did I think that mine was going to be the same—only more hopeless."

"What was his story?" Julia asked, hoping to divert him.

"He fell in love with a nun."

"With a nun?"

"On his way to Holland for his wedding with a girl to whom he had been betrothed for years." A tinge of that pleasure which comes from having a dramatic story to tell, crept into his voice.

"What happened?" Julia asked.

Nicolas moved then, sat down by the other table, and began, slowly, to set out the pieces between sentences.

"They wanted him to be married in Holland: his father and grandfather had been travellers in their day and his father thought he should see something of the world. The woman was on the same ship; she was Portuguese, going back to Lisbon from Goa. Older than he was; and she'd been a nun for years; and was so well-connected that she was practically royal. But this is where the case was different," there was accusation now in his voice, "she did love him."

In his youth, before his eyes bulged and his colour faded and his flesh shrivelled Mynheer must have been good-looking, very much like Nicolas, and there would be that charm of manner, the glib tongue, the flashing intelligence. Yes, easy to imagine.

"What happened?" she asked again.

"She got off the ship at Lisbon; he went on to Holland and talked himself out of his betrothal. That was more serious then even than it would be nowadays. They made a great fuss and demanded compensation for all the chances the girl had missed through being promised to him. Then he came home and tackled his family."

What, he wondered, was Uncle Simon's father like? Stern and strict, like his own? Tolerant, understanding, unconventional, like Uncle Simon? Still, it must have been a scene. Imagine any young man, expected home with his wife, walking in and saying, "I didn't get married. I've fallen in love with a nun."

"So he set to work," he went on. "It took him five years. Letters to everybody concerned, the various families, and the Head of the Order, and to the Pope himself—and all of them taking seven months each way. And more compensation to be paid. But he got his way in the end."

"You mean he married her?"

"Yes. She was Pieter's mother. And within two years she

was dead. My mother always says that that, and Pieter's accident, came as a judgement."

Mynheer believed that too. She remembered what he had said about having a feud with God; and about God being just, after all, and sending her to Rua. Suddenly that linked with what Doctor Hootman had said last night. Her momentary doubt of his sanity vanished.

Her hands went limp, fell onto the board, knocking over several pieces. Against what had she pitted herself, what defied, what foiled?

"It's quite a story, isn't it? And Uncle Simon told me himself that it was all well worth it. Two years with the woman of your choice, he said, was worth a lifetime of the other thing."

His manner changed suddenly; he stiffened in his chair, gripping its arms with white-knuckled hands.

"And that's made up my mind for *me*," he said in a harsh voice with something of hysteria in it. "I shall not marry Greta Hoogenbeet. Nothing, nobody, can make me. She can marry my brother and I shan't marry at all. It's too much to ask that when you're in love with one person you should be forced to go through the actions with somebody else!"

Just the way I feel, she thought, but I should protest, dissuade him, he'll ruin his life. It's no good his trying to copy Mynheer, he isn't made the same way, made of the same stuff. . . .

Before she could speak Mynheer himself came into the room, saying cheerily,

"Well now, are you both ready? Ladies first, so I'll start with you, Julia. My *dear!* How many times have I told you? What can you be thinking of?"

CHAPTER XIV

Two days later Nicolas departed for Lonthoir, and dinner that evening was a quiet meal. Mynheer spoke little and was distrait of manner. When Doctor Hootman, with his usual perfunctory, "If you will excuse me . . ." began to push back his chair, he said, brusquely,

"Sit down, Daan. I have something to discuss with you, and we might as well do it over a glass of brandy. I'll join you later, my dear."

Julia left, and Mynheer sat silent, his elbow on the table, his clenched fist pushed against his cheek, silent for so long that even Doctor Hootman's equanimity cracked a little.

"Help yourself," Mynheer said at last, indicating the brandy. "You'll probably need support when you hear what I have to say."

He'd heard—one of them had spoken about the interference that evening. Doctor Hootman braced himself.

"Well," Mynheer said heavily, "I have to confess myself defeated. It—just—wouldn't—work. After all those years of scheming and waiting and planning. A crushing blow, Daan. A mortal blow to hope."

"They always seemed to get on very well together."

"Dogs play prettily—when the bitch is not in heat!" said Mynheer coarsely. "And in this case that was the trouble. He was head-over-ears, poor boy. . . ." He brooded for a moment, then said, in a brisker tone. "Well, that's over and done with, and there's the future to be faced. How old are you, Daan?"

"Forty this year," his voice betrayed surprise.

"I wish you were younger. Still, you'll outlive me. I'm fifty-five and the years are beginning to tell. As you know . . . I'm not the man I was."

"If you could take things more calmly," said Doctor Hootman in a smooth, false voice.

"I might as well tell you to take things less calmly. We take things as we must. However, that's by the way. I've made new arrangements; they involve a radical change in your position, Daan; one that I think, I hope, will be welcome."

"What change?"

"When I die, I shall leave all I have to Pieter, who cannot even write his name, who cannot, must not, be seen by any-one from outside. Did you ever ask yourself what would happen if my plans came to nothing?"

"I never carried my speculations so far. Keeping Pieter amused and occupied, lending colour to the story . . . that has sufficed to exercise my wits."

"It all works in. You are recognised as his friend, his resident doctor, the one man whose company he tolerates, but it would hardly do, after my death, for you *suddenly* to emerge as his man of affairs. That role you must begin to fill *now*. I propose, from this evening, to stage a very gradual retirement. Then, when the change comes it will seem no change at all; people will be accustomed to doing business with you. I shall begin taking you about with me, introducing you and getting you familiar with the routine of running the plantation."

The bulging glass eyes looked—and looked in vain—for any sign of emotion on the heavy-jowled face.

"Well," cried Mynheer at last in a more sprightly voice than he had yet used this evening, "talk of taking things calmly! I tell you that in everything except name you are to be my heir and you sit there looking as though I had offered you a cup of tea!"

"I'm stunned," said Doctor Hootman. It was largely true. He was astonished beyond measure, not only by Mynheer's latest plan, but by the way he had taken the failure of his former one. At this very table, on the evening of Julia's arrival,

Mynheer had confessed how long that plan had been in his
mind, how deeply, how entirely, he counted upon its success.
Now, with hardly a whimper, he had abandoned it and was
off on another tack. Why? The world—as he himself had said
to Julia—was full of girls. Was Mynheer breaking up? Not very
old yet; but his life had been full of hidden stresses; did he
feel, as some men did, the beginning of failure within him?
Did that reconcile him the more easily to failure without? Or
was there, somewhere, carefully concealed, a trap in this new
arrangement? Mynheer had a devious mind.

But I think I am a match for him, thought Doctor Hootman.

"Stunned," he repeated.

"Well, you've always had my confidence, and stood by me;
and I shall feel that Rua—and my poor boy—are in safe hands.
I shall begin to initiate you into the business tomorrow and
then, in ten days' time, I think I shall ask you to undertake a
journey for me—to Macassar."

Instantly it was all plain. Ha! said Doctor Hootman to Doctor Hootman as the light broke. *He wants me out of the way!*
He does know of my intervention the other evening; probably
he knows more; the girl may have betrayed something. I probably made a false step in speaking so freely to her, but it was
necessary. Now, with me on my way to Macassar and Nicolas
back from Lonthoir, anything may happen.

"Macassar," he said thoughtfully. "That's a long way. I
don't think . . . It's Pieter I'm considering now. How will he
manage?"

"Pieter must be weaned, as it were. You can't perform the
duties of nurse *and* agent, Daan, that is evident. Echo can look
after him."

"Echo is useless," said Doctor Hootman quite angrily. "He
was dying of apathy, in Echo's charge, when I first came here."

"There's the girl now, don't forget. She is, I think, genuinely
devoted. She'll keep him amused."

"Yes, there is that." Doctor Hootman's voice was doubtful.
His mind raced forward, weighing, assessing. "Pieter is, so to

speak, my life work. . . . It isn't so easy just to hand over." He
took a gulp of his brandy. "I can spare time to learn the business, I should indeed like to do that. I waste a good deal of
my evenings, just reading. I could go to Banda with you, or for
you if you wished. But to be away so long, the first time I leave
him . . . that does need thinking over."

Now, if the voyage to Macassar is just a ruse to get me away,
he'll insist, Doctor Hootman thought: and if his suggestion is
sincere he will compromise.

"Yes," Mynheer agreed. "Anyhow, one of us must go. The
'Queen of the East' sails from Banda to Java in about ten days'
time, and she will call at Macassar. I bespoke a passage on her
this morning before leaving Banda. Whichever one of us sails
in her will be sure of congenial company—Nicolas will also be
aboard."

"Nicolas!!!" The single word, uttered in complete amaze-
ment seemed to ring out and vibrate in the silence. "But his
time isn't up."

"No. But he's of no use to me now. I don't want him back
here, making sheep's eyes and sighing. Also, between you and
me the young ass began talking of breaking off his betrothal.
The sooner he's back under his father's thumb the better. I
shall arrange that whichever one of us sails for Macassar can
take along what gear he left."

"I see," said Doctor Hootman.

There was no trick then; no double dealing. It was an honest,
straight-forward arrangement. Nicolas aboard the "Queen of
the East" and no other Vosmar nearer than Macassar. Safe.
Better than safe. Promoted, elevated . . . everything handed to
him on a platter. Was it possible? Could he believe?

"Of course," Mynheer went on, "if your devotion to duty—
and I'd be the last to deny that it is admirable and does you
great credit—is going to confine you here, this new scheme of
mine can't work. If, in the future you are going to act for Pieter,
you must begin to act for me, now; and not boggle about a

journey that will involve a few weeks' absence. Anyway, think it over, Daan. If you decide not to go, I shall; and if I go to Macassar I shall go on, to Java."

"To Java. Why?"

"Because if you don't go to Macassar I shall understand that you can't leave Pieter and therefore can't become what I want you to become. I shall consequently be compelled to make a different arrangement. I shall bring back a Vanderplasse boy. I'd prefer to have Nicolas, but he is the heir, they'd hardly spare him, and there is this complication of his lost heart to consider. There is, however, a brother, barely a year younger. I admit that that idea has certain attractions. Have done with all this pretence; tell the truth and adopt the boy legally. That might be best."

Doctor Hootman took a gulp at his brandy, and then, under cover of the table, wiped his sweating palms.

"I didn't say I *couldn't* go; I was just wondering how. . . . If Nicolas isn't coming back here it alters the situation. Alters it considerably. I thought that he was, and I could imagine Pieter in a screaming tantrum, me not here to control him, Nicolas in the house, all ears. After eight years, you know, one thinks of these things, almost without thinking. Without a guest in the house—which also means that Mevrouw would be free to give a little more time to Pieter—yes, I think I might go." Then, like a gambler risking all his winnings on one final throw, he added, "Of course to adopt a young Vanderplasse would be a solution, and as you say easier; but I do beg you, before you do *that*, give me time to get well away; I'm thick-hided, but I don't think I could face the talk and the scandal that would result from the divulging of the truth."

Mynheer did not wince; he had faced that thought himself.

"That is the drawback," he agreed. "Then I take it that what I propose is agreeable to you? I add that I think you have earned everything you'll get, Daan." He lifted his glass and said, "I drink to your happy future."

Mynheer came tripping into the salon and took his place at the chess table.

"I'm sorry to have kept you waiting so long. I've been persuading Doctor Hootman to take a little holiday, and an uphill task I found it. He is so conscientious."

Her whole inside seemed to fall away. It was true then. And somehow he knew that Doctor Hootman had promised to help her, so he was sending him away.

"Don't look so concerned, my dear. Is it that the thought of assuming more responsibility for Pieter distresses you? It really need not. Echo is perfectly competent. And Daan does *need* a holiday. He should have gone as soon as the rains stopped—but then Nicolas' visit was imminent. I confess that when we have a guest Daan *is* as indispensable as he likes to imagine himself at all times."

He had looked down at the chess-men, moving, with pernickety little nudges, one or two which were not in the exact centre of their square. Unobserved she could moisten lips gone suddenly dry.

"What about . . . when Nicolas . . . comes back?" she asked.

"He isn't coming back. He's decided to curtail his visit and join the 'Queen of the East' at Lonthoir. I thought you knew. So it looks as though you and I, my dear, will have to entertain one another. Now . . . my turn to be white, I think!"

So it was all over. That was, if it had ever existed. Her mind and spirit, having performed so many mental and emotional somersaults, relaxed and gave way to exhaustion. The will-of-the-wisp delight which had danced at the final point of Doctor Hootman's scheme—that in the last event he would find some way of sending her to Charles for protection—flickered away into darkness. And even that, at this moment, seemed not to matter much. She had never really believed it, anyway.

Now the future stretched ahead, serene, if dull. Making pots with Pieter; playing chess with Mynheer. She remembered the moment when she had felt that to be oneself was to fulfil one's destiny. My destiny—pots with Pieter; chess with Mynheer.

He beat her with more than his usual ease, and leaning back said, "Don't be discouraged; remember I was playing this game before you were born."

"I don't concentrate hard enough."

"No. And concentration is the secret. That and a certain flexibility. . . ."

He looked at the board as he spoke but it was not of a mere chess game that he was thinking.

CHAPTER XV

There followed some peaceful, ordinary days, during which, except at the dinner-table, she saw little of either Mynheer or Doctor Hootman. The latter's holiday was, Julia was given to understand, to combine a business errand, and in preparation for this the two men spent many hours in the library with books and papers spread before them.

They also went to the plantation together in the mornings and late afternoons, and the change in Doctor Hootman's way of life had a rapidly visible effect on his appearance and demeanour. He looked healthier and his manner was cheerful, almost buoyant.

Echo and Julia took over the duties which Doctor Hootman had relinquished. It was the first time that Julia had been in close contact with the huge, dumb Ethiopian, and her original feeling of pity for him gradually gave way to one of exasperation. He knew the value of his disability and traded on it. He performed, with clockwork regularity and precision, all his actual duties, but he took no interest and never pretended to. It was a machine attending a machine.

With Doctor Hootman in charge Julia had never entered the room and found Pieter idle, but now, very often, though the materials with which he busied himself were laid out on the table, she would find him sitting empty-handed, with Echo on the other side of the table, his arms folded, his eyes fixed on the wall, his thoughts who could tell where?

Doctor Hootman was to leave on a Thursday, in the morning. The "Queen of the East" sailed from Banda in the afternoon. The library that morning was deserted, the books and papers put away. In Pieter's room Echo sat with arms folded as usual, but Pieter was busily and happily employed applying some ready-mixed red paint in blobs and strokes to the sides of his collection of clay pots. Julia noticed that he, like the so-called primitive people, had a definite sense of design although his fingers were so clumsy that the pattern was laid on irregularly. Still it was there.

He rose, overturning the paint pot, and seized her hand.

"Julie. Good morning. Look. Pretty."

"Very pretty."

Doctor Hootman came to the door that led into Pieter's bedroom; he carried a shirt in his hand.

"Good morning, Mevrouw," he said affably. "I wanted to see you. I'm packing. Would you mind coming into Pieter's bedroom?"

He saw the spilt paint and strode to the table.

"Clear that up!" he said furiously. "Don't just *sit* and stare, you black fool."

"I'll come and paint with you in a moment," Julia said to Pieter. "Do one for me now. A pot for Julie. A pretty one."

"Pretty for Julie," he said, plunging the brush into what paint remained.

Doctor Hootman's room lay beyond Pieter's and through the open doorway she could see his bed, with a little open valise on it, and some clothes thrown about. Doctor Hootman stood by the door that led into the enclosed garden.

"Mevrouw, I have a favour to ask of you. You and you alone can enable me to go away with any peace of mind."

"I'd do anything to contribute to that, Doctor Hootman. What do you want me to do?"

"Look after Pieter," he said with a peculiar urgency. "Echo is useless, worse than useless; he has a most undermining effect. It's visible already. Pieter holds out something and says 'Look' and he won't even move his eyes; and to anyone like Pieter that is discouraging. It's as though he hit him."

"Oh, I will. I meant to anyway. I shall spend almost all my time with him."

"Thank you," he said, with some feeling. "It matters to me. Very much." His gaze slid away to the garden. "There was something else I wanted to say to you. It makes me feel rather foolish. About the other evening . . . The way things have turned out, I expect you think I was exaggerating, or inventing?"

She hesitated for a moment and then said, "Well, I did wonder."

"It was true enough, so far as it went. But I misjudged Mynheer." He stared into the garden. "Yes . . . an error of judgement. Anyway, you have nothing to worry about now, I think. And—perhaps this sounds a little like exacting usury— you will remember that when you looked like being in an awkward situation, I did promise my support, for what it was worth. So, if you find *him* a strain, as I know you must, well, bear it for my sake, will you, please?"

"Of course. I don't think you need worry. Echo can do all the dull jobs and I promise I'll keep him amused."

"You think I am overanxious. Perhaps I am. But you see, I've devoted myself, for eight long years to keeping a spark of something . . ."

He broke off as Pieter came blundering into the bedroom, carrying a pot to which the paint had been so hastily and liberally applied that it was running off again and dropping like gouts of blood to the floor.

"Pretty. For Julie," he said, holding it out.

"You see? No control. No interest. Pieter, dirty! Dirty! Let it dry. It must dry. Dirty Julie's dress. Dirty Julie's hands. Back on the table. On the table. To dry."

Slowly Pieter turned and ambled away.

"That is another thing, Mevrouw. He will obey if you say a thing firmly enough and often enough. It's like a weak sagging bell pull, the first jerk won't ring, but if you keep on, and hard enough, you get some response. Oh, and *another* thing . . . I don't think this will happen, I hope not anyway, but if he should on any account fall into a tantrum, don't let him throw himself about; and don't let Echo handle him roughly. Send for Mynheer." He brushed his hand over his forehead. "Really," he said, "I don't think I should have agreed to this. I should have refused."

"I think all this anxiety is really a sign that you need a holiday."

"I need a holiday. But there are many things I need more. I hope you can manage."

"I'm sure I can," she said.

That evening she and Mynheer dined alone for the first time. He remarked upon it, saying flatteringly that he preferred her company to all others' and having said that proceeded to talk as entertainingly as he had ever done at any party. Listening to him, fascinated, and now and again provoked to laughter, she took another step towards adulthood in the realisation that it was possible to derive pleasure from the company of someone of whom one disapproved. And from that she passed to the admission that it was impossible not to admire his tough resilient spirit. If indeed he had planned as Doctor Hootman had said, the outcome must have been a shattering, a crushing, disappointment; but of that there was no sign. There he sat,

neat, sprightly, composed, gaily juggling with words as light
and iridescent as bubbles.

He ended a story concerning a native Bandanese named Shal
Ahmi, who had successfully fooled everyone in the Islands a
few years earlier, and succeeded in organising the only really
successful slave revolt that had ever taken place; and then said,

"Now tell me what you have been doing all day."

She had devoted her time to Pieter and somehow he, to
whom hours and minutes were all one, timepieces without
meaning, days and months nameless, had sensed—she thought
—that he had been the centre of extra attention. When she had
left him he had clung to her and had lifted her hand and kissed
it again and again, wet, slobbering kisses like a dog's, just saved
from being distasteful by virtue of the otherwise inexpressible
feeling which lay behind them.

"I do see," she said, when she had given a brief account of
their activities that day, "that for purposes of concealment,
Echo is perfect; but I don't suppose Pieter can understand that
he *can't* talk to him, and Echo doesn't try, by look or gesture,
to make up for his dumbness. There's something flat and dead
in the room when they're together. You can feel it when you
go in, and it settles down again behind you as you leave."

"Yes; it is a pity. But anyone who could talk to Pieter, could
talk about him. Menials, I mean. And he must have an at-
tendant."

After a moment's silence, he went on,

"You have become genuinely fond of my poor boy, have
you not?"

"Oh yes. He has some endearing ways, like a child, or a . . ."

"Or what?"

Her face reddened. "I was about to say a dog. But not in
any derogatory sense. I'm very fond of dogs. I always wanted
one."

"My *dear* Julia! How many times have I told you to ask for
anything, anything at all that you wanted? Then you sit there

calmly and tell me you have always wanted a dog. Why did you never ask?"

"I don't know. Well, for one thing I didn't know whether people did have dogs in the Islands."

"Of course they do. And even if they did not, in Rua we have what we want. What kind of dog would you like?"

"One of those small, long-eared spaniels," she said promptly. "Mevrouw Helmers, at the Home, had one, so tiny she could carry it in her sleeve. They were very fashionable because King Charles kept them when he lived at Breda; people called them King Charles' spaniels. Mevrouw Helmers', though it was so small, was as brave as a lion. Once a drunken tinker came and was abusive because we had no work for him; Mevrouw Helmers said, 'See him off, Spider,' and that little dog did. I did admire it."

"You shall have one, as soon as possible. I don't know whether I can find one in Banda, but I will try. What a pity you didn't mention it sooner. Daan could have added it to his list of commissions. What shall you call it."

"Charles."

"Oh. Yes, yes, of course. You know, Julia, your choice is very revealing."

Did he mean her choice of dog, or her choice of name? What did he know? How did he know?

Colouring again and avoiding his eye, she asked,

"In what way, Mynheer?"

"Women," said Mynheer in his smooth, conversational way, "can be divided into many different categories, plain or pretty; witty or dull; but the deepest division is between the maternal and the courtesan types; and what they *like* is the surest sign. The maternal type likes things small, the courtesan type has a preference for large things. You, my dear Julia, are an outstanding example of the maternal type. The afflicted boy, the little dog, they make an appeal to you." He smiled at her, then looked away. Twirling his glass slowly between his fingers he added in a most casual manner, "But to poor Nicolas, hand-

some, healthy and head over ears in love with you, you could
be, and were, quite cruel."

Her heart, which had begun to leap and thud when she had
wondered if the word "Charles" had betrayed her, and then
steadied down, began to flutter again. So it wasn't all over. It
had, at least, to be talked about.

"I tried not to be, Mynheer. I didn't want him to fall in love
with me. When he said he had, I discouraged him as gently
as possible."

"Why?"

"Because, although I liked him, I didn't love him. And I
bore in mind that I am married."

"Yes," said Mynheer, his voice grown heavy. "You are married. And your husband, as a token of his esteem and affection,
can give you a lop-sided clay pot. Is that enough?"

"It . . . has to be, Mynheer."

"From Pieter, yes. I will say this, Julia, sincerely and from
my heart, your acceptance of an intolerable situation has, from
the beginning, filled me with admiration. I told you once that
you would find me not ungrateful. Were you blind to what I
offered you?"

It was one of those dangerous questions to which either yes
or no was an answer which gave recognition to what lay behind
the question. She parried it feebly.

"I don't think I understand you. Everything you have given
me I have accepted, gratefully."

"I didn't say given; I said offered. I'm not heartless, Julia.
I was obliged to find Pieter a wife. All these years I have presented a picture of him to the world, disfigured, misanthropic,
but *normal*; and normal men, especially when they are heirs
to great estates, have wives. I deliberately chose a Company's
Daughter because I felt that a girl who had known some pri-
vation in her youth would more easily find some compensation
in the comforts and small luxuries which I could offer; but I
knew, very well, that in the end they would be inadequate.
Man does not live by bread alone. I brought Nicolas here de-

liberately, knowing that he would fall in love with you, as any young man would. I hoped that you would fall in love with him and accept, from him, all that Pieter could not give you—the pleasure of love, the joy of motherhood. Don't be embarrassed by this plain speaking; I am old enough in years to be your father, in experience, infinitely older. I am being frank with you, be as frank with me. Dear Julia, why did you refuse?"

"Mynheer, one cannot be in love to order."

He made a little gesture of dismissal with his hand.

"Tell me this then. On the day when you arrived in Banda, if Nicolas had met you, if he had been your husband—what then?"

"I often thought of that. In that case he would have been my husband. It would have been my duty to love him, or to behave as though I did."

He gave her a long, hard look.

"So you did at least consider it?"

"Yes. Nicolas was always very charming to me. He said he loved me. I thought about it. Any woman would have done."

Mynheer put out one of his slender, well-kept hands and laid it over hers.

"My dear," he said earnestly, "think again. You have behaved impeccably, your loyalty and restraint have been beyond all praise; but facts must be faced. In Pieter you have no husband; from him you will have no child. You are young now; you do not realise the measure of your loss, but it *is* a loss, and in the years to come, when it may be too late, your awareness of it will grow, every day. This situation, which I freely admit is of my making, cannot be altered, but it can be mitigated. This would not be just an ordinary, sordid little adultery—if that is a suitable word to use—not just a passing love affair. Nicolas is deeply, genuinely in love with you. He has given proof of that; he has dared to write to his father saying that he will not honour his betrothal. That surprises you?"

"No. He spoke of it and I tried to dissuade him. I was appalled by the thought of his angering his family and spoiling his whole future on account of a passing fancy."

"It is not," said Mynheer, "a passing fancy. I can assure you of that. And Nicolas' future can be safely left to me. His father has other sons. . . . Nicolas could remain here. In everything but name you could be husband and wife. Of what account, Julia, is a bit of ceremony, when set beside a real, overwhelming passion?"

None, she thought; knowing that if things had worked out as Doctor Hootman had foretold, she would have gone to Charles without hesitation, abandoning her marriage as lightly as she would have discarded a torn handkerchief. But this was different.

She could see Mynheer waiting for an answer. She said slowly,

"Mynheer, I hope that what you call an overwhelming passion will prove to be mere boyish infatuation. But in any case, the sincerity of Nicolas' feelings does not affect mine."

He withdrew his hand. Now he is angry, she thought, and braced herself.

"Well," he said, folding his hands together, "you're honest and sincere. That gives us something to go on. Will you, just for a moment, look at it from another point of view. Mine." She saw him change colour, his yellow-grey complexion turned greyer and all the lines in his face seemed to deepen and darken. When he spoke it was with difficulty, in strong contrast to his usual glib facility with words.

"This family," he said, "is old, honourable. We've been here a long time, but that is no more than a moment in our history. In the Netherlands, under the Spanish Inquisition, a Simon Vosmar died for his faith . . . at the stake, with the agony pear in his mouth. His son, Pieter, escaped with his life and nothing else. With his two bare hands he set to work to restore the family. He laid the foundation of all that you see here. He named his son Simon, and *he* named his Pieter. A long, unbroken line. Today you have been painting pots with Pieter

Vosmar, the last of that line. I am to blame. I invited the curse and it fell. Doctor Hootman wonders, you may have wondered yourself, why I never married again. Anyone stricken as I have been does not invite a second blow." He unfolded his hands and took hold of the edge of the table, leaning forward. "Julia, you are my only hope; you alone can redeem us." He paused and swallowed twice, painfully, audibly. "Give me another Simon Vosmar, give me a bud to graft onto this barren stock. Let me once hold your child in my arms and cry Nunc . . ."

He broke off; a frightening change took place in his face. The bulging glassy eyes swivelled upwards, exposing the red-streaked whites; little blobs of foam formed at the corners of his mouth. Apparently conscious of them, he snatched up his table napkin and pressed it to his lips, saying through the muffle of the linen, "Nothing . . . trifling indisposition . . . leave me . . . go!"

She had jumped up and stood indecisive. She could remember Mevrouw Helmers saying in her bright airy way, "And then you *may* have fits to deal with. The symptoms are . . ."

The symptoms she had listed so blithely bore a horrid similarity to what was happening to Mynheer. His whole body arched and strained as though it were in the grip of two maniac hands twisting against one another. His teeth clamped down in a rigor which held the table napkin firm after his hands had fallen away to clench on empty air.

And then, just as suddenly as it had set in, it was over. His eyes rolled back into position, his teeth loosened and the table napkin fell to his knee. He gave a great sigh, his whole body relaxed and the perspiration broke out over his face and head so profusely that, as she watched, his curled silver hair went lank and the colour of lead.

But he was indomitable. With a shaking hand he lifted the napkin and mopped at his face and neck.

"This is nothing. Don't be frightened." He breathed as though he had been running, and the sweat continued to pour off him.

"Can I do . . . or get you anything?"

"Glass of water, please."

She poured it and would have held it for him, but he insisted upon taking the glass himself. When he had drained it he said, more steadily,

"I'm sorry, Julia. It happens if I let my . . . emotions get the upper hand. Nothing to worry about." He managed a ghastly smile. "You see how much it means to me. Think about it. Think about it."

Terrified of provoking a further attack she said,

"Yes, I will. I'll think about it."

CHAPTER XVI

They did not meet again until dinner-time of the next evening. Mynheer appeared to be fully re-covered and was in a genial mood. Julia, after another night spent in agonised indecision, had the worst headache of her life, so violent that she was incapable of thought and some-times barely conscious. Amusing Pieter during the afternoon had taxed her fortitude to its limit and she longed to creep away to her room and lie down in the dark; but to do so would look like evasion and merely postpone the evil moment.

Mynheer, and the table between them, and the room around them, kept being blurred out, as though whorls of fog were being blown about. Just as on the previous evening he chatted, courteously, entertainingly; sometimes she did not hear what he said, when she did, she made some kind of answer. The sight and smell of the food sickened her and the two or three mouthfuls she forced herself to take were as tasteless as straw.

Mynheer was oblivious, or affected to be oblivious, to her state; and at last Pluto, moving noiselessly as a shadow, placed the fruit bowls and the decanters on the table and withdrew. This is the moment, she thought. It was like being on the gallows, with the noose round her neck and the cart under her feet about to pull away. But there was still time . . . she could say yes. . . . All night and all day the arguments had gone on, chasing one another round the inside of her dizzy skull and here she was, still uncertain. . . .

"You slept badly?" Mynheer's voice was kind and solicitous.

"I didn't sleep at all."

"Poor Julia. Try a little brandy."

"It would make me s . . . ill."

"It wouldn't, you know. Believe me, it is the best restorative. Try just a sip, to please me."

He poured some into a glass and handed it to her. She lifted it. The scent of it had started its evocative business before the liquid tilted to her lips. She set the glass down. She was not conscious that it was brandy which Charles had given her that day on the path, or that it was this brandy, poured by Mynheer, which had, by its mere scent, called him so vividly to mind. She only knew that now, all at once, she was certain.

"I have thought," she said, so firmly that she was surprised by the sound of her voice. "I tried to look at it from your point of view, Mynheer. But I know that even if I said I would, in the end I shouldn't, so it's best to say so."

There was a long silence. The grey whorls of fog blurred everything. Out of the fog, from a great distance away, Mynheer said, kindly, sincerely,

"Don't distress yourself, Julia. I'm very much disappointed. But the decision was yours to make, after all. It's the end of my hopes, but not the end of the world."

Such calm acceptance, the last thing she had expected, broke down all her defences. She put her head in her hands and began to cry. Mynheer rose and came round the table, put an arm around her shoulders and with his other hand stroked her hair.

"I've been inconsiderate," he said. "I asked too much of you. Poor Julia, poor little girl."

His kindness filled her with a sense of guilt.

"I would have done it, if I could. I tried," she gulped out.

"I know. I know. Now don't think any more about it. Come along to bed and have Juno rub your head until you fall asleep. Please, Julia, the thought that I have upset you so much distresses me more than I can say."

He helped her to the door of her room, snapped out an order to Juno, bade her good night and went away.

She lay in the bed, soothed by the movements of Juno's firm brown hands, feeling as though she were recovering from a long and serious illness. The whole episode was closed now. She had made the right decision and Mynheer was not even angry. Her peaceful thoughts merged into sleep.

She began to dream again. This time it was a happy dream. It was a bright beautiful morning, with a little breeze blowing from the glittering sea. She was wearing a new dress, white sprigged with green, and she was playing with Pieter, not in his private garden but near the rose pergola at the back of the house. Doctor Hootman came walking under the clusters of flowers and said, "Pieter, fetch Julia one of your pots." Immediately, with that disregard for time and place which is the prerogative of dreams, they were all standing in Pieter's room, and Pieter was holding out towards her the same pot, dripping with red paint, which he had attempted to give her on Thursday morning. She saw that it was not red paint at all, but blood.

"It's blood! I can't take it," she said.

"Of course it's blood. What did I tell you?" said Doctor Hootman.

She woke, with his words ringing in her ears.

It was dark in the room. Juno had put out the candles and stolen away. A feeling of cold sharp terror laid hold of her, so that her flesh pimpled and her hair crawled on her scalp. Fool that she'd been, to be so easily deceived, to think for one moment that Mynheer would accept, in a few weak words, the defeat of a plan so vital. Paralysed with fear she lay and remembered everything that Doctor Hootman had said—that Mynheer would not let one girl stand in his way, with the world full of girls. Dispensed with, and replaced.

Somehow, in some uncanny way, Mynheer had known that Doctor Hootman was her friend, so he had been sent away. She was alone here, and helpless. His very restraint this evening now had a sinister implication; he was no more *angry* than one is with a pen which will not write—throw it down, choose another.

Cold sweat crawled over her. Even at this moment Mynheer might be coming near, intent upon smothering her as she slept.

But, unrecognised, unacknowledged, there ran in her veins the blood of the man, who, with his drawbridge jammed and his enemy approaching, had said, "We'll not be taken like rats in a trap. We'll do some damage before we die," and had ridden out, with half a dozen mounted men behind him in one last desperate charge.

I can't, she thought, just lie here, waiting. She forced her clammy quivering fingers to make a light, and then, carrying the candle, went into the sitting-room, whose door led to the cloister. It was closed, as usual, but not locked, though there was a key. She turned it, and then, after several minutes' struggle, dragged up a small heavy chest. As she tugged at it she thought, And I won't be poisoned either; I shall eat and drink only in the evening, at the table where he is, and only of what he is sharing.

Almost at once, with this resolution made and the chest looking oddly out of place by the door, she had another change of feeling. All this is mad, she thought. Between Mynheer and Doctor Hootman I've been driven out of my mind.

The night's thoughts and actions seemed crazier than ever in the morning, with the sun spilling great golden patches on the floor and Juno bringing in the silver tray with the clouded

beaker of cold fruit juice, the pretty painted tea-pot, the flowered cup. Nevertheless she made an excuse to send the woman
away, and when she had gone, emptied the beaker and most of
the tea down the sluice which took the water when she bathed.
She did it with regret and some sour amusement. It seemed
a silly waste, but . . .

When she was dressed she went along to Pieter's room,
where Echo was keeping watch but doing nothing more.

"What would you like to do this morning, Pieter?"

"Beads," he said positively. He had a large number of them,
big solid beads of many colours, bored with holes large enough
to be threaded, without a needle, on lengths of lightly waxed
string. He knew the names of the colours and showed a certain
artistry in the combinations he chose. He never strung them
haphazardly, but with great care, naming each colour as he
threaded the bead. "White one . . . now red . . . green one."

As usual, all he made was for her. "Pretty for Julie." When
he thought a string was long enough she snipped the thread,
tied the ends together, and slipped the necklace over her head.
When, towards the middle of the morning, Mynheer came in,
she was wearing a necklace of red-white-and-green, one of red-
and-green and one of red-and-white. Pieter was breathing hard
over a fourth, a green-and-white one.

Looking at Mynheer cautiously she saw that he did not look
well; his face was grey; and he, ordinarily so light and nimble
in his movements, this morning walked slowly, leaning on his
silver-knobbed cane. But he spoke with cheerful kindness,

"Good morning, my dear. I trust you slept well. Hullo,
Pieter; you're busy."

"Pretty for Julie," said Pieter, breathing hard.

"Very pretty." Mynheer turned to Echo. "You can go and
get your dinner while I'm here. I'll send for you when I want
you."

He came near the table and just touched Julia's beads with
the tip of his finger.

"He does choose colours well," he said. "There's *something* there, isn't there? And he *is* affectionate. Dog-like, as you said, my dear."

There was something rather pitiable in the way in which Mynheer was trying to find something in Pieter's favour. The phrase, "resigned at last" came into Julia's mind. And her heart smote her because of her night thoughts.

Mynheer sat down, and, after watching Pieter's fumbling yet persistent efforts for a moment, said, "Oh, Julia, do something for me, will you? On the top shelf in the library there are some black books, numbered. I want number three. The steps are in position, you won't have to search. I don't feel like climbing this morning."

"You don't look very well," she said, rising.

"Oh, I'm all *right*. Growing a little old, I suppose."

"White one . . . now green," said Pieter.

She went into the library and climbed the steps. The books were there, to her, even at the top of the steps, only just within reach. She found number three, and was balancing with it, swaying a little under its weight, and prepared to descend when she heard Pieter scream. The noise was nothing like that which he had made on the evening of Charles' visit, nothing like any sound she had ever heard him make; it was a shrill cry of sheer animal pain and terror. It came again, and again, and then, in the same piercing voice he called, "Julie! Julie!"

She threw down the book, scrambled from the steps and ran across the library, hearing as she did so another sound, the thwack, thwack of somebody beating a carpet. She pushed the heavy inner door and stood on its threshold for a second, immobilised by horror and disbelief.

Pieter cowered in his chair, trying to protect his head with his hands, from one of which still dangled the string of green and white beads. Mynheer stood over him, raining down blows with the cane, seeming to aim at his son's head but not heeding where the cane fell.

She was across the floor, and had Mynheer's arm in both her

hands, bearing down on it with all her force and weight, in the time it took her to think that he had gone mad. Nothing else could account for the insensate fury of the unprovoked attack, nor for the superhuman strength in that seemingly frail and brittle arm. It was as strong as steel, and when it lowered she knew that it did so in answer to Mynheer's will, not to her frantic efforts. Still, it did lower.

Pieter, who had screamed each time the cane struck him, broke into a dismal whimper.

"That's just a start," said Mynheer a trifle breathlessly. "If I must, I'll beat him to death. Stand over there and watch."

"Mynheer," she said, as steadily as she could force herself to speak, "you're not well. You don't know what you're doing."

"Don't talk to me as though I were an idiot too! I know what I'm doing. You don't like to see your dog hurt, do you? Stand back there then, before I hit him again."

She took a pace backward. As she did so, Pieter, still holding his hands over his head, crouched low, scuttled across to her and pushed his face into her skirt. Red weals were coming up where the cane had hit him, and one of his ears was bleeding.

She put both hands on his shoulders and said, "It's all right, Pieter."

"Now you can listen to me," said Mynheer. "So far I've given him a flick or two with this light cane, but as God is in Heaven, I swear I'll beat him until he is dead unless you give me your word to do what I want you to. Without you he's of no use to me, the slobbering idiot. I've only kept him alive all these years because to have a grandson a man must have a son. I hate him. I always have. I've never looked at his ugly face without wanting to smash it in, beat it to pulp. And now I will—and you will watch if I have to tie you in a chair!"

Against her knees Pieter burrowed, whimpering. She looked down at him, and then into Mynheer's bulging eyes.

"You know I'd bear you twenty grandchildren rather than see Pieter hurt," she said.

But Pieter had been hurt; and she had been tricked. Anger

as well as acknowledgement of defeat moved in her; and a desire to hurt him.

"I only hope," she said clearly, "that the Vosmar madness won't come out in Nicolas' child."

"You dare say that to me!" said Mynheer. He stepped forward, raised his hand and slapped her face, twice, on one cheek with the palm, on the other with the back of his hand. He had to reach over Pieter to do it, but the blows were heavy enough to jar her whole body and sharp enough to bring the stinging tears to her eyes.

Moving back he said, "I have you now. What I've suffered from your airs and graces, you little bitch from the gutter!"

He glared at her with pure hatred, and she glared back at him through the water standing in her eyes. The marks of his fingers stood out, bright scarlet on her ashy face.

Between them Pieter lumbered to his feet, lowering his arms and loosening his fingers so that the string of beads fell rattling to the floor. He turned himself about.

"Bad!" he said. "Bad. Hit Julie."

He began to shamble forward, his head lowered, his heavy hands swinging.

"Keep away from me," cried Mynheer, stepping back and raising his cane. But Pieter kept on.

Just too late Julie called, "Pieter. No!" Mynheer had lashed out, hitting Pieter across the face, and Pieter gave a great bellow of rage which drowned her voice. Bellowing, he put his hands around Mynheer's throat and began to shake him. Mynheer's dainty little feet chattered on the floor and then slipped. His fall brought Pieter down too, but the puffy, limp-looking hands did not loose their hold.

Julia ran forward and took Pieter by the collar, crying, "Pieter. No. No. Pieter, stop."

It was trying to restrain, trying to talk to, a gorilla.

"Bad! Bad! Hurt Julie! Bad! Bad! Bad!" said Pieter, at each word lifting Mynheer a little way from the floor and then smashing him down again.

She let go the collar, ran to the bell pull and tore at it, and then ran shouting to the door. Tearing it open she found herself face to face with Doctor Hootman. Except that he wore a hat, had a two-day growth of beard on his chin and carried his little valise he might just have been returning from one of his casual strolls.

"They're killing each other," she screamed at him and jumped aside so that he could rush past her. He did rush, and by the time she had turned herself and followed him back into the room he had his arms hooked into Pieter's elbows and had dragged him clear. He said, and the mildness of his voice, the word he chose, brought a sob-giggle of hysteria to Julia's throat.

"Naughty Pieter! Naughty! Naughty!"

Pieter gave himself meekly into the hands of accustomed authority.

"Bad. Hurt Julie," he said once more. And then, with bright recognition, "Good morning, Doctor Daan." He put his hand to his bleeding ear, looked at his fingers and said in a tone of rebuke, "Dirty. Dirty."

Doctor Hootman was on his knees by the broken thing that lay on the floor. He opened Mynheer's frilled shirt, laid a delicately explorative hand on his breast, held it there for a minute and withdrew it.

"Nothing can be done about *that*," he said, getting to his feet, "except be thankful that it didn't go the other way about. . . . Mevrouw, sit down," he caught her as she swayed, "put your head on your knees." She felt his hand on the nape of her neck, bearing down. She heard him say, "Pieter, go in the garden. Garden. Get some flowers. Go and get some flowers for Julia."

Over her bowed head their voices went on.

"Bad," Pieter said again and again. "Hurt Julie."

"Julia will be all right. Not hurt. All right. Go and get her some flowers."

"Dirty! Dirty!"

"I'll clean you. Soon. Flowers first, Pieter."

"Pretty for Julie."

"Yes, pretty for Julie." Doctor Hootman's voice never lost its patient insistence, but she heard him give a sigh of relief as Pieter went lunging away.

"Mevrouw, are you feeling better? Stay as you are. I think I have some brandy here." He removed his hand from her neck. She heard him moving about. Then he said,

"Here, drink this."

She lifted her head and said helplessly, "I can't," and began to cry.

"That's right. Have a good cry. You'll feel better afterwards."

He set the brandy within reach of her and went over to what lay on the floor. He stooped, and took from Mynheer's pocket the chain of keys; held them cupped in his hand for a moment, and then took out his own, a mere two or three held together by a thin leather strap, worn and greasy from much handling.

Mopping at her streaming eyes and still sobbing Julia watched him weighing the two lots of keys against one another; his face wore a look of immense gratification. With a sudden movement he opened one of the drawers in the table, the drawer in which he kept a few of his personal belongings, and tossed the leather-held keys into it. The others he slipped into his pocket. Then he came over to her and asked kindly,

"Better now?"

She nodded. As soon as she thought her voice was to be trusted she said,

"I thought you had gone to Macassar." The words were followed by a great sob.

"So did I," said Doctor Hootman drily. "So did he! But Nicolas was supposed to board the ship at Lonthoir. When there was no sign of him I disembarked. I realised that I . . . that we had been outwitted. Well, he'll never trick anyone again."

"Oh don't!"

"It must have been very distressing for you. Try not to take
it to heart. It is much the best thing that could happen. Oh
dear! How quick it can be about some things," he said, as
Pieter, clutching a few crushed flowers, came blundering in.
He laid them in Julia's lap and when she did not instantly acknowledge them said on a questioning note,

"Thank you?"

"Thank you very much indeed, Pieter."

"I must bestir myself," Doctor Hootman said. "There's a
great deal to do. Do you feel able to get to your room, Mevrouw?
Then go and lie down. There's nothing to worry about now.
Nothing at all. Just leave everything to me."

She stood up. Her legs felt too long and very hollow. Like
someone very old, or very sick, she handed herself across the
room, from the table to a chair, and to another chair, to the
edge of the open door. She had to pass the place where the
dead man lay and though she meant not to look that way some
kind of fascination made her, at the last moment, turn her
head.

Doctor Hootman was spreading his handkerchief over the
dead face.

CHAPTER XVII

At the head of the table Mynheer's
chair was empty.

Otherwise everything was as usual. There was no sign of the
confusion and break with habit associated with the sudden
death of the master of the house. The silver tong-tong had announced the meal punctually, and Pluto, with his expression-
less, trained-house-slave face, brought in the dishes. It was dif-

ficult to realise that Mynheer was not merely dining in Banda.

There was, however, one slight difference. Tonight Julia wore the dress in which she had arrived; the plain, dull, serviceable garment with which every Company's Daughter was supplied, and which, with the gayer wedding dress, comprised all the wardrobe considered necessary. And tonight she wore no jewels.

"Good evening, Mevrouw," said Doctor Hootman, taking his accustomed place to the left of the vacant chair. "I trust that you feel rested and restored."

"Yes, I do, thank you," she said. He had been, she thought, wonderfully considerate. She had gone to her room and had sat there, sick and shivering, for half an hour, cold despite the midday heat, unable to do anything except go over, and over again, the terrible events of the morning. Then Doctor Hootman had come along, with a glass in his hand, saying that he imagined she would welcome a sedative. She had taken it and slept all through the afternoon. When she woke everything that had happened in the morning seemed to have run backward in time; she could remember every shocking detail, but the sharpest edge of emotion was dulled. That, and the apparent ordinariness of everything, gave her a feeling of complete unreality.

"If you are agreeable," said Doctor Hootman, "we will wait upon ourselves. There are several things to be settled and not much time. Very well, Pluto, you may go." As the door closed he said, "It is remarkable, though not, perhaps, surprising, that the tragedy has been accepted with such calm. Rua has always run as though by machinery, and like a machine it goes on."

She remembered, but with that same sense of it being long ago, and drained of horror, Mynheer's attack upon Pieter.

"It would be hypocrisy for me to pretend to any grief," she said.

"Exactly. No doubt everybody feels the same—to some degree. Of course, if Pieter were capable of occupying that chair, some show of mourning would be expedient. For myself, I feel that the man was a fiend and that the world is well rid of him."

"How *is* Pieter? I should have gone along to see him, but I slept so long, I had only just time to dress."

"He is somewhat shaken. Not by the thought of what he did—he seems to have forgotten that. But he cried when I dressed the wound on his ear and showed signs of very considerable disturbance. Of course, nobody has ever struck him before in his life. I have once or twice been obliged to use force to control him, but I have never hit him, even with my hand. I am astonished that his father should have done so. What happened, Mevrouw? Can you bear to tell me?"

She told him, and even in the telling it was a tale of long ago. Doctor Hootman listened attentively, but without ceasing to ply his knife and fork; he nodded now and again and once or twice looked at her sharply.

At the end she said, "I don't know why, but it all seems to have happened much longer ago than this morning."

"You have slept. And your mind is putting up its own defence. All in all, you have had a very trying time. If I could I would spare you all exertion now and say leave everything to me. In a sense, certainly, you can leave everything to me, but there are things which I am forced to discuss with you because I need your help. With the funeral."

"You know best about such things."

"Ah, but this is no ordinary funeral!" He looked from his now empty plate to her untouched one. "Mevrouw, you have eaten nothing!"

"I'm not hungry. I don't think I shall ever be hungry again."

"Try, at least," he said. "Try some fruit. Drink some wine. I know you have suffered a severe shock, but you need your strength now. One more effort and you need never make another as long as you live. That one effort must be made, or we are both undone."

"In what way, Doctor Hootman?"

Before answering he rose and carried his plate to the side-

table, then removed hers and set a clean plate and two bowls
of fruit before her.

"We face," he said, coming back to his place with a fresh
plateful, "a problem quite unique, or so I should imagine. You
are aware, Mevrouw, of the picture of Pieter which Mynheer
always presented to the world. We can't, at this point, expose
its falsity. That would be fatal."

"I used to wonder," she said, "what would happen when
Mynheer died, but today I haven't even thought about it. I
haven't had time."

"I have," said Doctor Hootman drily. "I've had eight endless years. Mevrouw, try at least to drink a little wine while I
acquaint you with the results of my long thinking. . . . We
must, at all costs, conceal the fact that Pieter is not, in the
legal sense, competent. If we do not I can foresee danger from
two quarters. First, the family. Both branches, in Java and
Macassar, are well-to-do, but Mynheer was, by an incalculable
margin, richer. Once let the secret of Pieter's condition leak
out and down they will swoop, like vultures. You realise what
that would mean?"

"They would want Rua," she suggested.

"They would take Rua. Before we knew where we were,
another pop-eyed Vosmar would have the plantation, and his
wife would rule the house. You, Mevrouw, would be reduced
to the status of unpaid companion. It isn't only at formal
dinner parties, you know, that wives take precedence by their
husbands' rank. The family would always speak of 'poor
Pieter' and you would be poor Pieter's wife. We know the
Vosmar attitude towards the defenceless."

He filled his mouth, chewed vigorously and swallowed, washing the mouthful down with a great gulp of wine. His lips left
a greasy mark on the glass, and, with a little inward shudder
she looked away.

"So much for the family," he said. "The other threat comes
from the Company. Land tenure in the Islands is largely de-
pendent upon the Company's good will. Rua is undeniably

Vosmar property, but how long would they allow it to remain
in the possession of an idiot? The Company, remember, is
all-powerful, far above mere law. And there is a land famine.
I am positive that on the slightest excuse, or no excuse at all,
someone would whisper 'maladministration.' You and Pieter
—strictly for your own good, of course, would then become
wards of the Company. I trust I am making myself clear,
Mevrouw."

"Very clear, Doctor Hootman."

"Good. So here we are, back at the problem of the funeral.
Mynheer was a prominent man; many people will come to see
him laid with his fathers in the family burial place; the Governor and the Company's Agent will be among them."

He shovelled more food into his mouth, chewed, drank, swallowed and hastened on.

"I cannot help but feel that any man, however sensitive as
to his appearance, however retiring, would feel it incumbent
upon him to attend the funeral of his own father. After all,
we have proved—God knows with what effort—that he can
stand up and walk." He shot a glance at the screened window.
"Is it feasible that he should absent himself from the graveside? All our efforts have not prevented suspicions of a mental
rather than a physical affliction getting about and unless
Pieter Vosmar puts in an appearance at eleven o'clock on Monday morning, those suspicions are going to be confirmed—with
the results that I have indicated. You see our quandary?"

"Yes," she said. But it was his quandary; she could understand but not share it.

"Well; does any solution occur to you?"

With idle unconcern she fingered the idea of making some
disguise for Pieter. A hat pulled low, a collar turned up. Useless! The way he stood, the way he walked, betrayed his state
as clearly as his face did. And people would approach him,
making the proffering of condolence an excuse to satisfy their
long-standing curiosity.

"I can see no way out of it," she said.

Doctor Hootman spooned up the last mouthful, pushed his chair from the table and leaned back.

"Fortunately for us both, I can. We must provide a substitute. Someone who knows what Pieter is and whom we can trust. Now . . . Does the name occur to you?"

"Not . . . You don't mean Charles?"

"I do indeed! Who else?"

This was the end of being remote from it all; now she was entirely involved.

"He wouldn't do it," she said.

"Show him a guilder and he would do anything," said Doctor Hootman incautiously. He realised immediately that he had struck a wrong note and hastened to cover it. "He has every reason to be mercenary. He lost everything in the Civil War, and though the actual land has been restored, the house is a ruin. His mother and brother live like peasants; the brother actually works in the fields. Charles, like those with him, lives in daily danger for the sake of money, and in the hope of one day returning home. For *him*, at least, that day is much nearer than he dreams—if *we* play our cards with skill and care . . . and courage."

Now, she knew, she must think for herself.

"Tell me exactly what you propose to do."

"Well, first, as regards the funeral. I suggest that when the mourners have assembled, you and Charles come, at the last moment, and stand inside the burial ground, near enough to be associated with the ceremony, but far enough away to avoid close inspection. That would be in keeping with what is known of Pieter's character. No one there will be familiar with Charles, or with Pieter; why should they suspect anything? I can disfigure him, probably with a scar, convincing enough at a distance. And, of course, it is a funeral; a handkerchief held to the face would be allowable."

The last words enabled her to recognise the nature of her objection. It all sounded sly and shady, out of keeping with everything that she remembered, or had imagined about the

man she loved. A false scar, a false face of grief . . . Not
Charles! Yet, after all, she had only seen him twice; Doctor
Hootman, presumably, knew him much more intimately, and
believed he would do anything for a guilder.

I *don't* believe it, she thought stubbornly.

"All other considerations apart," said Doctor Hootman, "I
am sure that Charles, no more than I, would wish to see you at
the mercy of the family or of the Company. Once the funeral
is safely over it is all smooth sailing. We shall have established
that, apart from his aversion to contact with people, a harmless
eccentricity, there is nothing wrong with him. From the privacy of his room he will conduct his business, through *me*. I
have amused myself by perfecting a style of handwriting and a
signature—most impressive—quite unlike my own. And, by a
supreme irony, Mynheer, before sending me out on a goose
chase, carried his attempt to deceive me to the point of initiat-
ing me into such of his affairs as had hitherto been kept from
me. I assure you I can run Rua, even to the Company's satisfaction."

Smooth, feasible, cunning. Why object? Somebody must
run Rua; Pieter could not, so why shouldn't Doctor Hootman?
All she minded, at this moment, was the thought of that
macabre bit of masquerade by the graveside when respect, and
that kind of love which without respect must die, perhaps
would die.

"I'm sure you could," she said. "But it does mean keeping
up all that burden of pretence. Mynheer's family pride was
involved; we haven't that excuse. Do you think that perhaps
we overrate the threat from the family and the Company? I
am Pieter's legal wife and I am in my right mind. You understand the business. Couldn't we come into the open, admit
what Pieter is and act for him?"

Doctor Hootman did not answer immediately. His hand
went to his chin. His jowls had darkened.

"The drawback to that, Mevrouw, is that it leaves us just
where we are. You the wife of an idiot, and me the hired man.

Frankly I visualised a rather more attractive future for us both."

"Whether we pretend or not that is what we are; I'm Pieter's wife, you're his agent."

"Ah . . . but let us look a little farther into the future. I will now allow myself the use of a sentimental expression. Poor Pieter. Poor Pieter's kind seldom live long; it is rare, I believe, for one such to come of age. Eight years ago, when I took charge of him, he was moribund, dying, very slowly and easily, of apathy and boredom. He sat in a chair, Mevrouw, with his hands on his knees, staring at the wall; Echo sat opposite, staring at nothing. Twice a day they walked, for fifteen minutes, round and round the little garden. Pieter was dying and Mynheer dared not call in Doctor van Nagel, who lived in Banda Neira and who might talk. I happened to be handy. I saw at once that the situation had possibilities, vague, I admit, but my own circumstances at that time were such that even the frailest hope was something to be exploited. *I set myself to keep him alive.* And I succeeded. Every one of those trivial little activities has been a peg, holding Pieter Vosmar and life together. Oh, I know," his voice took on, suddenly, the complete sincerity of irritability, "it's nothing to boast of; in itself nothing to show for eight years' work, but he is *alive.* He has lived to finish his basket, to make a clay pot, to thread another bead, to hear me play the clavichord. You understand me? *Deprived of his activities he will die within three months.*"

Her mouth had gone dry; it was difficult to speak with the necessary casualness.

"And you will so deprive him?"

"Immediately after the funeral."

Once, long ago, she had told Mynheer that she thought he was cruel; she was wiser now.

"And then what happens?"

"Then, Mevrouw, we come into our own. That sane, non-existent Pieter Vosmar will have made his will—as any child-less man would upon coming into his inheritance. To you he

will have left the bulk of his fortune; to me, his close, indeed
his only, friend, he will have left his estate, Rua."

"I see," she said.

There was so much to see. Not only the future. The past
was all at once brilliantly illuminated. Now she saw why Doctor Hootman had been on guard that evening, why he had,
with a promise of support and help to escape, encouraged her
not to fall in with Mynheer's plan. An heir to Rua had no
place in his schemes. And his schemes were as far-fetched,
and as cold-blooded, as Mynheer's.

Once more, just when she had thought that the worst was
over, she found herself facing something worse still.

Doctor Hootman seemed to mistake the reason for her long
silence. He said, defensively, almost placatingly,

"You must not grudge me my share, Mevrouw. Remember
what my life has been these eight years. Every day, all day,
shut away with an idiot for company; using words of one syl-
lable and using them over and over again before they roused
a glimmer of understanding. It has often seemed to me to be a
miracle that I retained my own sanity. My God! When I look
back . . . the drudgery, the uncertainty, the sheer humiliation.
If ever a man earned anything, I have earned Rua."

She said hastily, "Oh, I agree. I don't grudge it. I don't
want it myself, is that what you were thinking? After all that
has happened here, I should like to go away and never see the
place again."

"And that is exactly what you can do, Mevrouw. Very soon.
You will be rich and free, and still young. I have imagined, in
my sentimental way, that there is a mutual attraction between
you and Charles. If that develops you can go back to England
with him and use some of your wealth to rebuild his house.
If it does not—well, you are a very attractive woman, and you
will be rich; you will also enjoy what you have earned. I use
that word advisedly; you also have had your trials."

The one essential was that he should continue to believe her
to be co-operative.

"Oh, we've earned it," she said with a pretended heartiness. "But . . ." She hesitated and managed a rueful smile. "You'll think this very sentimental of me, I'm afraid. Without knowing what he did this morning, Pieter saved me from a dreadful situation, and that makes me feel that I don't want anything that depends on his being dead. There must be some other way."

Quite amiably Doctor Hootman said, "I am open to suggestion, Mevrouw. Bear in mind, though, that while you appear to be willing to forego your reward, I am not."

"Suppose," she began, tentatively, "that I took him away. You could just as easily pretend that a sane Pieter Vosmar existed without the real one locked in that room, couldn't you?"

"Rather more easily; but I think you underestimate the difficulty of the removal. It involves—to say the least—a passage on a ship. Remember, dark stories, which have shown a strong tendency to survive despite lack of substantiation, are already rife in Banda, hinting that Pieter Vosmar is not quite as he should be. If one day Mevrouw Vosmar boards a ship, dragging behind her thirteen stone of plain idiocy, wouldn't that give rise to comment? Inquiry?"

"I suppose it would. I'm not a very good planner, am I? Then couldn't we just wait?" Without being aware of it she lifted her head and spoke in a firmer manner. "I can't just stand by and watch him made miserable and hurried out of life."

"I've done my waiting. Eight years of it. At any moment during that time Pieter might have died. Where should I have been then? Another three months of waiting for the end will be all that I can bear!" His voice changed, became soothing. "He won't suffer, you know; he'll just die, gently and gradually, as very old people do. For his kind he *is* old. And you need not stand by and watch, Mevrouw. You need never see him again. Nor need you feel any sense of guilt. You have made your protest and your earnest but quite futile effort to suggest

an alternative plan. You may comfort yourself with the thought
that neither you nor anyone else can stop me now."

Any further hint of opposition, or even of half-hearted agreement would now be fatal. Once again she was in conflict with
a ruthless and determined man, with nothing but her wits for
weapon.

"If you can assure me that he won't suffer . . ."

"I can do that. He won't even know what he lacks. All these
years he has been kept alive by what you might call artificial
means. I have supplied the stimulus, now I shall remove it.
That is all."

Like saying that a person kept alive by breathing; put a pillow over his face, remove the stimulus and that is all.

"When do you expect Charles?" she asked.

"Tomorrow. I sent him the usual signal and he should come
at the usual time. He will be expecting to see Mynheer on
business. I think he will be pleasantly surprised."

"I've so often wondered about that business."

"There's no harm in your knowing," Doctor Hootman said
pleasantly. "In defiance of all rules Mynheer continued to grow
cloves, and of course the ordinary channels of disposal were
closed to him. Charles was his outlet. Dear me, that reminds
me! Those trees must come down. Tomorrow. They're at some
distance from the burial ground and well out of sight, but somebody might go wandering, somebody with really keen, experienced scent might even smell them. I am deeply obliged to
you, Mevrouw, for bringing them to my mind. How easily one
overlooks even vital things." He brought his glance to bear on
her with an intensity that seemed to have actual physical
weight and said, more slowly, "Amazing as it may sound, I
had forgotten the cloves. I thought that Charles would act for
me on Monday partly from desire for money, partly for your
sake, partly even to oblige me: I had overlooked, until this
moment, the most powerful motive of all, the need to save his
own skin. On Monday morning Rua wouldn't be a very healthy
spot for an English clove-smuggler unless he *was* in disguise

would it?" The facial change which was not quite a smile became visible again.

So that was it. And she did not for a moment believe that the thought had just occurred to him. He'd withheld it, produced it at the last minute, a fine, flourishing, clinching move. She wondered if her face had changed, if the leap of her heart into her throat had been seen and noted.

"I've thought of another thing too," she said. "Wouldn't it look better, more natural, more in order, if Nicolas were at the funeral?"

"Admirable! Actually I had thought of that. I sent for him this morning. He should be back by tomorrow evening. His presence is necessary; it will, as you say, make everything seem in order. I regret it, though. I think his morbid curiosity concerning Pieter constitutes our one real danger. A faked scar across the width of the burial ground is one thing, face to face quite another. Pieter will just have to refuse to see him, promise to do so and then postpone the meeting, write him a letter, send him a message, anything. We must deal with that as it comes. After all, Mevrouw, neither you nor I are novices in the art of deception. We shall manage."

"Of course," she said. She knew now what she must manage. Tomorrow she must meet Charles as soon as he set foot on Rua, warn him and send him straight away again. Then she must see Nicolas and tell him everything; that would save Pieter.

Now at last she lifted her glass and said,

"Success to the plan, Doctor Hootman."

"Success to our plan, Mevrouw."

Was he deceived? Did he believe them to be one and the same? How could she tell?

Another bad night; and this time, in the heart of it something new; this time side by side with the old confusion and fear and feeling of weakness and despair there came a real and very urgent temptation. Why not give in? The situation had

changed. To have given in to Mynheer would have meant going against her own feelings and against her deepest instincts;
to give in to Doctor Hootman would be in exact accordance
with them. Why not do what she wanted? Why should she
bother whether a hopeless idiot lived another year or so of useless life? Who had ever bothered about her? She remembered
Aunt Geertruida's treachery; the miserable years in the Klopstock Home; the superficially kindly but fundamentally ruthless system which had shipped her out to Banda. Exploited,
she thought, exploited all the way along.

She reverted to the ethic of the Klopstock Home, to the person she had been there before Katje came. The world was a
hard, heartless place and only the hard and the heartless could
hope to survive in it.

Then the other arguments began. She hadn't survived in
Cloonmagh by virtue of hardihood or heartlessness, but because of kindness and pity. Johannes had saved her from starva-
tion; Charles had saved her from Mynheer's wrath; Pieter,
pitiably acquiescent when he was attacked, had risen up in her
defence. . . .

Tomorrow, somehow, she must outwit Doctor Hootman.

CHAPTER XVIII

Fifty years later, when she was an old
woman, one of the trees in the long avenue from which Elmhurst took its name was found to be unsafe and had to be taken
down. On that clear cold day in the English winter she walked,
leaning on the arm of one of her grandsons, to see the end of
the venerable tree. The sound of the axes striking home took

her straight back, across half a century, across half a world, to that Sunday in Rua.

"It might have been yesterday," she said suddenly.

"What might?"

"The day when your grandfather asked me to marry him," she said. And the boy who had never been farther afield than Canterbury, saw in his mind's eye a piece of English lawn, shaded—since this was in foreign parts—by palm trees, and in the shade a pair of china figures, all pink and white and blue and bearing no resemblance to his grandparents, placidly plighting their troth and sealing it with a chaste kiss.

That Sunday in Rua had not been like that at all.

In the morning she had gone to see Pieter. His face and neck were marked with long narrow blue-black bruises and his ear was swollen to twice its normal size. He was pleased to see her, took her hand and rubbed his head against her shoulder, but something had gone out of him.

"I'm so glad you felt able to come," said Doctor Hootman briskly. "I have so much to do and I didn't want to leave him with Echo. He's not himself today, not himself at all." He gave Pieter a glance of worried exasperation. "Off his food, most unusual. Try to amuse him, Mevrouw."

"Of course," she said.

"I've decided that when those trees are down, the flowers and the foliage must be buried, not burned. The scent would probably hang about till tomorrow; so I must get trenches dug. But I'll relieve you as soon as I can." He hurried away.

She asked the routine question, "Well, Pieter, what shall we do today?" and for the first time he was unresponsive.

"Cut some paper for me," she suggested. That was a favourite occupation, but this morning, though she rustled the paper invitingly and placed the scissors in his hand he showed no interest. At last, with a small inward shudder she suggested threading beads.

"No! No!" He spoke loudly and vehemently.

It was wrong to say that he had no memory, no feelings. Deep inside he was probably just like everybody else; the real Pieter was locked away inside this defective mind and clumsy body as a man might be clamped into a suit of armour.

"No," she agreed. "No beads today. We'll go in the garden. Garden. Ball. Shall we play ball?"

He rose and took her hand, but instead of tugging her towards the door, he went towards the clavichord.

"But I can't . . ." Then she thought, oh what does it matter? I can make some sort of sound.

She sat down and Pieter crouched beside her on the floor, resting his head against her thigh. She touched the keys gently, experimentally, making no attempt to link one with the other.

"Yes," he said in a satisfied voice and sighed with content.

From far off she could hear the regular, rhythmical blows of the axes on the clove trees and soon she found herself striking the notes to the same rhythm. Presently Pieter put up his hand and took her wrist and lifted her arm and draped it about his neck as though it were a scarf. With her left hand she continued to touch the keys until, looking down at him she saw that he had fallen asleep. On his poor face the innocent, defenceless look, shared by all sleepers, even the most guileful, even by Doctor Hootman, was very marked, and instinctively she tensed the arm which lay about his thick red neck. So far as was in her power, she would protect him.

Charles must be warned, Nicolas must be taken into confidence. Her heart began to race and shudder as she thought about time, and opportunity, and risk. . . .

To escape from the house in the afternoon had been relatively easy when one was eluding Mynheer, whose habits were regular; Doctor Hootman must be watched. He returned to the house at midday, but the axes worked on through the heat. She dared not go out until he had gone again; he might wish to see her; he might even be watching her movements. The latter possibility became almost a certainty as the afternoon wore on.

She had taken a chair into the now-shaded cloister, from which she had a clear view of the path he would take on his way back to the plantation. The warm air was heavy with the scent of crushed cloves which were being thrown into shallow trenches, covered with soil and stamped down. The lovely, forbidden trees were, by a few hours, preceding their owner to the grave.

At last she saw what she had been waiting for, the heavy sombre figure making its way across the garden and through the rose pergola where every rose lay flat and open-hearted in the heat. She forced herself to wait a little and then set off in a state of nervousness which made her expect to find Doctor Hootman lurking around every corner, in every shadow.

This afternoon she must take the path which ran past Psyche's cage. It was the way Charles had come on that fateful afternoon and she hoped to meet him there again today.

There was still something sinister about the path; even now the doves seemed to avoid it. The axes had ceased to sound as Julia crossed the garden and now the afternoon had an ominous silence. She hurried past the cage, not looking that way, and was then on the spot where she had stood, sick and shaking, and heard the footsteps. If only she could hear them now!

Once around the curve she was on new ground. The path narrowed and began to slope upwards; when at last she came to the edge of the grove and could see the sea it lay between twenty and thirty feet below, at the foot of a sheer cliff thickly clothed with ferns, with pink azaleas and the far-flung, twining wreaths of the island honeysuckle, brilliant yellow and scarlet, and so heavily scented that here the crushed clove odour was no longer detectable.

At this point the sea had taken a bite out of the island, making a little cove, a perfect place for surreptitious landing, shielded on either side from observation.

All this Julia noticed, but she failed to see, or, seeing failed to realise as significant, that today the little cove was awash with the incoming tide. The narrow strip of beach at the cliff's foot was already under water; presently the sea would reach

the level where the lowest ferns grew. It would be hours before
any boat could beach there.

Ignorant of this she went to the cliff's edge and stared out
into the shimmering blue distance. She willed Charles to come,
and to come quickly, with an urgency which left her as ex-
hausted as a fierce physical effort would have done. Nothing
stirred on the silken skin of the sea.

The watched pot, she thought, reverting to Anna's idiom,
never boils. Look away, walk this way, that way along the cliff
top, counting the steps. Stare down at the flowers and count
five hundred, a thousand, two thousand, three, and then look
up and see the dark speck on the blue. . . .

Always the sea was empty. In the west, on the other side of
the island, the sun began its rapid slide down the sky. The
slanting light turned to liquid gold on the face of the water
and for a few minutes it was impossible to stare at it, even
with squinted eyes. Now, now, while she was blinded, he
would come. Turn away, look into the thickening green gloom
of the nutmeg grove and then look back and see. . . .

But when she faced the sea again the only change was that
the brazen-gold had softened and was streaked with rose, with
amethyst, with daffodil, colours which, even as she watched
began to blur and merge into grey.

Soon it would be dark. Before dark she must be back in the
house. Up to the moment when she told Nicolas everything
she must retain Doctor Hootman's confidence, otherwise he
would find some way to keep them apart. Though she had
failed to meet and warn Charles, she might, even yet, save
Pieter. And to do that she must get back to the house.

She had run a long way before the comforting thought struck
her that perhaps Charles did not intend to come to Rua. Perhaps Doctor Hootman's message had miscarried. Perhaps he
had some other business on hand. Perhaps in some secret,
underground way he had heard of Mynheer's death and so
seen, in the "usual" signal, warning of danger. In that case

everything would be simple and easy; just take Nicolas along to Pieter's room and it would be done.

When she reached the pergola she adopted the sauntering gait of one who had, in the lessening heat, merely taken a stroll, and it was as well that she did so, for Doctor Hootman was standing on the steps that led up to the cloister and he was scanning the garden even as he placed a hand on the arm of Nicolas, who had evidently just arrived. Two of the house-slaves were carrying his little travelling trunk towards the door of his room. Both men saw her and came towards her, but Nicolas, by breaking into a run, reached her first and put his arm around her in a brotherly, comforting gesture. He began to say, "Poor Julia, it must have been awful for you . . ." and by interrupting him she had just time to say,

"I must see you, alone. There's so much to tell," before Doctor Hootman joined them.

"Mevrouw," he said, "I have looked for you everywhere. Pieter is being most difficult about tomorrow. You must talk to him."

His voice was heavy with hidden meaning and she understood that Charles had come.

Nicolas, taking the words at their face value said, tightening his arm,

"You can leave that to me, Julia. Ever since I heard the awful news I've been thinking about Pieter. He'll have to drop all his nonsense now, and I think I should be the one to tell him so."

"It may come to that," said Doctor Hootman, "but I feel that Mevrouw should try her persuasions first. I left him thinking things over." That sentence too was dark with implication. "Perhaps it would be as well to leave him for a little while and refresh ourselves. Mevrouw has eaten nothing all day, you, Mynheer, have been travelling, and even I . . ." He spread his hands.

"You must have been very busy," Nicolas said.

They went into the room with the Chinese cabinets; the

room where Julia had played chess with Mynheer and been told that concentration was the secret. If only she could concentrate now! The news that Charles had come, after all, and was here in the house, altered things; and something in Doctor Hootman's manner of conveying that news had warned her that he did not wholly trust her.

A cloth had been spread on one of the tables and set out upon it were the dishes always served in the Islands on casual occasions, small cakes, fruit, fresh and preserved, highly spiced and pickled vegetables and pieces of meat and fish capable of being picked up in the fingers and popped into the mouth. There was also a bottle of wine, which Doctor Hootman, with a nice show of courtesy, left for Nicolas to handle, while he set about the food.

There began, and lasted for about ten minutes, what, in retrospect, Julia thought was perhaps the most fantastic little scene of all. Nicolas was young enough to find any death disconcerting and sudden death particularly so. He had been geniunely fond of his Uncle Simon and for the whole of his stay in Rua he had been a witness to a most affectionate relationship between him and Julia, a kindly one between him and Doctor Hootman. He took it for granted that they shared his grief over the death, his dismay at its suddenness and everything he said had the effect of making Mynheer seem an ordinary man, to be, like other men, sincerely mourned.

"It was so appallingly sudden," he said. "He was in good health when I left."

"Not quite so good as it seemed, Mynheer. He was very sensitive on the subject, but he had had one or two minor attacks in the last few months. He was aware of his state; that was one reason why he was beginning to delegate more and more responsibility to me. I was about to travel to Macassar on business for him, was I not, Mevrouw?"

"Yes. Oh yes," Julia said.

"Was it a stroke?" Nicolas asked.

"Of a kind. A seizure. There's this to be thankful for, he didn't suffer at all."

"I still can't believe that I shall never see him again. He was quite unlike anybody else, wasn't he? So amusing, and understanding, and kind."

As he said these words he looked at Julia as though asking her to agree and confirm. He had not shaved that day and the faint golden downiness on cheek and chin made him look very young. She forced herself to say,

"Yes, he could be very kind."

Their eyes met, and in his she saw, behind the distress something else move, sharp and active. He was remembering her words upon meeting.

"You do look poorly, Julia," he said. "Let me take you to your room."

"Mevrouw *must* see Pieter first," said Doctor Hootman.

"Why can't I do that for her?"

"For the simple reason that being confronted by a stranger —which is, with all respect, what you are to him—would merely upset and anger him and leave him less open to reason. Mevrouw has far more chance of success. In fact if Mevrouw cannot persuade him to make an appearance tomorrow I don't know who can!"

"Now I'll tell you something," said Nicolas more brightly. "The Barnevelts, with whom I have been staying, asked me a lot of questions about Pieter. They could hardly believe that I had stayed here for weeks and never set eyes on him. When they realised that I wasn't lying and knew no more than they did they told me some of the stories that are going round about him. They weren't pleasant, I assure you. And if Pieter shirks his own father's funeral . . . well!"

"I know, I know," said Doctor Hootman, worriedly. "He must be persuaded."

"That kind of rumour does no good—with the Company I mean," said Nicolas. "In Java we had a neighbour who had so many bouts of fever that his memory was affected. They kicked him out, tactfully of course. They said there was a danger that he might ship out unlimed nuts or something."

"Had he no wife?" asked Doctor Hootman without looking at Julia.

"Oh yes, and a son, but only a child. They couldn't run a plantation."

"You see, Mevrouw, it is essential that these ridiculous rumours are quenched tomorrow."

"I still think I should talk to him," Nicolas said. "I'd contrive to act in such a way as to convince him that he hasn't all that much wrong with him."

"That," said Doctor Hootman, "would be extremely easy. When you see him, you'll be surprised to find how little is wrong with him. Don't you agree, Mevrouw?"

"I always said so," she said dully.

Suddenly she could bear it no longer. "Let's go and get it over with." She stood up.

"I shall take a little walk," Nicolas said. "I'm still cramped from the boat. Then I'll come back here and hear how you succeeded. And if he's still stubborn I shall have a good straight talk with him." The ghost of the old spite was in his voice. "I think you all pay too much attention to his fancies and foibles."

"Perhaps," Doctor Hootman said easily. "But you see . . . to those who *know* him, Pieter is very lovable."

And that, also, was for her ear alone.

"When did Charles arrive?" she asked, as they went along the cloister.

"A few minutes before you came back from your walk. Had you been in the house you would have had the opportunity for a little private talk."

Was that said ironically? Did he know why she was not in the house? A swift glance at his face gave her no clue.

"Is Charles against the plan?"

"As I said, Mevrouw, I left him thinking it over. His immediate response was unco-operative. But I admit I had done no more than outline the situation when that boy arrived."

They halted by the library door and Doctor Hootman took out Mynheer's bunch of keys.

"Now I have to lock *this* door," he said, with an almost humorous look. "It becomes more and more like Bluebeard's castle."

The door opened and Charles, who had been lolling in a chair, jumped up. For the third time they stood face to face.

He held out his hand and she put hers in it; he put his other over hers so that her cold, unsteady hand was folded between his two firm, warm ones. They looked at one another without speaking for a moment. He looked unconcerned, at ease, quite oblivious to the fact that he was in any danger. She tried, through her dumb hand, her dumb eyes, to convey some hint of the real situation, but he did not understand. He increased the pressure of his hands and said, in a voice warm with sympathy,

"Poor little girl, you have been through it. But it's all over now. Come and sit down."

"Yes," said Doctor Hootman, turning from his relocking of the door. "Sit down, Mevrouw, and let us get this thing settled; there will be time for everything else afterwards. All the time in the world. Well, Charles; have you thought it over?"

"I have," Charles said. He sat down in a chair beside her and, linking his hands, dangled them between his knees.

"I'm sorry to be disobliging, Daan. There isn't much I wouldn't do for a guilder, but I must draw the line at hiring out as a mummer."

"Now look here . . ." Doctor Hootman said, his jowls beginning to darken. Charles cut in,

"What's more, you should thank God that this wasn't something you could rush into on your own. The old chap's death gave you a jolt, Daan, and you've gone a bit off course."

"Morally, you mean?" asked Doctor Hootman with a look of the blankest astonishment.

"Morals be damned!—I ask your pardon, Julia—Practically, man, practically. You've thought up a scheme that nobody with a grain of sense left in his head would entertain for a moment."

"I refute that," said Doctor Hootman who had recovered his composure. "My plan is, above all, eminently practical."

"How much do you know about this?" Charles asked, turning to Julia.

"A good deal more than you do, my friend," Doctor Hootman answered for her. "We were interrupted, you know."

"Then you can see that it's crazy, can't you?"

She weighted her words with every hint of warning that an innocent-seeming speech could carry:

"Doctor Hootman has thought about this plan for years, Charles. He thinks it feasible, and he's very . . . very set on it."

"A slight understatement, but good enough. And you call it crazy. Why?"

"It's crazy because you couldn't carry it through. You've lived here, Daan, how long? Eight years. And you watched old Simon fool everybody; so you think you could do it too. You might—only don't count on me, but you could find another dummy—just muddle through the funeral. Afterwards you'd come a cropper. Say what you like about Simon Vosmar, he had a sort of power. People were scared of him. They didn't press his guard too close, even with questions. You ask yourself, how many men could have carried off such a thing for so long? Also, remember he *owned* the place. Nobody came here except by direct invitation. You wouldn't have that authority. Before you knew where you were somebody would up and say, 'Who the devil is this Doctor Hootman to stand between me and the man I want to do business with?' Or, 'I'm going to see Pieter Vosmar; if he doesn't want to see me he can order me off himself.' Can't you see that?"

She remembered suddenly a bull-baiting which she had seen, for five horrified minutes, in Amsterdam; lured there, all unknowing, by her young skater friends. Here was the dog, tail awag, eyes shining, begging the bull not to make a mistake!

"The thing wouldn't hold together for three months," Charles said.

"It has no need to. Three months is all I need. And low as you rate me, compared with Mynheer, I *think* I could make shift to hold the busybodies at bay for so long. Of course, my dear Charles, our conversation was cut short. We never looked beyond the funeral, did we? Grief, the press of business inseparable from sudden demise, would surely protect Pieter Vosmar from intrusion for three months. And after that there would be nothing to hide."

"He'd still be here, plain idiot."

Perhaps when he knew what Doctor Hootman planned for Pieter he would realise what kind of man he was and be on guard. That thought made her say, quickly,

"But Pieter wouldn't be here, Charles. Doctor Hootman thinks that if Pieter is deprived of all his little occupations and interests he won't live very long."

The silence seemed to stretch itself out to give every one in the room a chance to contemplate the future in terms of Pieter dead. Doctor Hootman spoke first.

"Mere chivalry compels me to point out, Charles, that over this detail Mevrouw did register a protest. But I managed to convince her that his—I assure you, painless—death would benefit us both. You see, the mythical, sane Pieter Vosmar is going to make his will. Mevrouw will get his money and I shall have Rua."

This time the silence was longer. She forgot even Charles' danger as she waited. This was the touchstone. What you were mattered, in the last extreme, more than what happened to you.

Charles got up, very slowly and deliberately, and took a position, just in front of, and facing her, with his back to Doctor Hootman.

"Julia," he said, "this isn't the time or the place to say such things,"—and he did look as much embarrassed as a man forced to take a bath in public might do. "I do love you, very dearly. Ever since that first day I've thought of you day and night, but I wouldn't have said so except that I don't want you to think . . . God knows I wish you were free, but not this way! It'd make it all so easy, but every time I looked at you, I'd see myself blubbing into a handkerchief by the grave of a man I disliked, or that poor fool pining for his toys. It'd ruin everything. If I say no to this, Julia, don't go thinking . . ."

His voice trailed away because, screened for a moment from Doctor Hootman's view, she was screwing her face into grimaces of warning and conspiracy.

"It is so many years since I saw a play," said Doctor Hootman, "that if time permitted I should enjoy this touching scene. As it is . . . Charles, will you oblige me by leaving the irrelevancies and saying whether or not you are prepared to help me tomorrow."

With one last, puzzled look at Julia, Charles turned about, and threw himself into his chair.

"With the mummery, no. I thought I had made that clear. I'd be the last to deny, Daan, that you've earned whatever you can walk away with; you've probably earned Rua, but you can't walk away with that, so pick something easier, and I'll help you. Collar the cash box or a sackful of silver plate, or a whole load of unlimed nuts."

"That's the English all over," said Doctor Hootman. "Noble sentiments, dignified behaviour and mercenary motives. You're looking ahead to the time when Mevrouw may inherit everything."

Offensive as the speech was Julia welcomed it; surely *now* Charles would see that Doctor Hootman was not his friend and would realise the truth of the situation.

He said, quite unruffled, "You're wrong there, and I can prove it. Call the nephew or whatever he is in, and hand over to him and Julia can come away with me tonight, just as she is." He swung round to Julia and said, "I'm taking a lot for granted, but I'd look after you. Married or not makes no difference, I'm yours for life."

"For God's sake," said Doctor Hootman, "will you stop talking sentimental rubbish! I've told you what I propose to do. I need Mevrouw. Will you get into your thick English skull that nobody, nothing, is going to turn me from my purpose. Now, for the last time, are you going to help me?"

"No. Get that into your thick Dutch skull." He said it without rancour.

"Then I must think of an alternative," said Doctor Hootman, quite calmly.

"This time think of something that won't take you straight to a rope's end at Banda Fort."

Yes, it was possible to love a man and yet think him a fool. She longed to say—It's you who'll end in Banda Fort if you don't agree!

Doctor Hootman's hand had gone to his chin.

"Work this into your meditations, Daan: murder is murder whatever the means. If you want to be rid of the poor fool, I'll take him too. You can play your game of invisible man whether you've got a lunatic locked up there or not, can't you?"

"And I should feel secure, shouldn't I, with the heir and his wife roaming about in Ay! Let's have no more inane suggestions. I am in process of realising how immensely stupid I have been." He dropped his hand and leaned forward as though they were two children to whom he—an adult—was telling a fairy story which had just reached the exciting climax.

"I have, I think, the perfect solution. I've known all along that it would be a little difficult to convert your rugged good looks into something that would account for Pieter Vosmar's behaviour. I could have done it, but it would not have been easy. This is. Pieter Vosmar shunned the sight of men because, poor fellow, he had coloured blood! It *will* crop up you know, even in the third generation; most people accept it. But a Vosmar wouldn't. It won't be beneath Mercury's dignity to stand by the grave tomorrow; and the beauty of it is that the closer he is inspected the more obvious will be his reason for hiding. Charles, I owe you a deep debt of gratitude."

"You've lost all touch with reality, shut away with an idiot and your own thoughts for company. You can dream of these schemes; you can't carry them out. Who's this Mercury?"

"A slave. Quite three-quarters white."

"And you seriously consider a scheme that depends on him? Wake up, Daan! What about the other slaves?"

"No other slave will be at the graveside. Mynheer would as soon have had his cows at his funeral."

"All right. Think for a moment of how you're putting yourself into this Mercury's hands."

Oh stop it! Stop arguing with him. Stop treating him like a dear old friend slightly demented. Think about yourself.

She dared not speak. It was just possible that having found a satisfactory substitute Doctor Hootman would let Charles go; and once he was gone, provided she had not committed herself, she might get a chance to talk to Nicolas.

"I put myself in nobody's hands," said Doctor Hootman. "Not in yours, which, like Pilate, you have so carefully washed; nor in Mevrouw's, so dainty and gentle. I know her; she'd ruin everything for the sake of an idiot who can't tell Sunday from Monday!" There was venom in his voice. "Luckily she is also sentimental about *you*. So tomorrow she will lean, very lovingly, and convincingly, on Mercury's arm; because you, my English, clove-smuggling friend, will be here, pledge of her good behaviour! Even the tide served me, you see. If you had landed in the usual place she'd have met you with words of warning on her lips."

So now it was all out.

"That is quite true," she said quickly. "I am against your plan—because of Pieter. But I promise, I give you my word, if you let Charles go I'll do anything you tell me to, tomorrow and afterwards."

Charles reached out and took her hand.

"Thank you," he said. "But you can't bargain with a crazy man. All right, Daan, what now?"

Doctor Hootman stood up, took the keys from his right-hand pocket and transferred them with a tantalising little toss into his left hand. His right hand he put into his pocket again, and kept it there.

"What now? Why, now you can continue your love scene while I find Mercury and get him dressed and ready to meet his kinsman." Still facing them he edged sideways and backwards towards the door.

There was now in the room, in the whole situation, an air of unreality and of falsity which had not been there before even when they had been talking at cross purposes. She, at least, knew where it originated—in Charles' behaviour. Why didn't he *do* something? Just to sit there, without even a protest, holding her hand and looking at it as if it were the most wonderful thing in the world . . . all wrong, somehow.

She decided to try something on her own. More than once during the last few minutes she had been aware of a sound of movement in Pieter's room. If she mentioned it now, and Doctor Hootman went to investigate, as he most surely would, he would cross the room; Charles could shoot out his legs and trip him, make a grab for the keys, do something. She twisted her hand and dug her nails into Charles' palm, hintfully, and said,

"Doctor Hootman, I can hear Pieter moving about."

He laughed outright, a hearty, delighted laugh.

"Dear Mevrouw! Who once found a snake in a work-bag? No wonder you love her, Charles! She's wonderful. I could almost love her myself."

"But it is true. I can hear him."

"His movements have ceased to concern me," said Doctor Hootman. He gave his attention to putting the key into the door with his left hand and without turning.

Then Charles jumped.

It was like the leap of a panther, swift and sudden and silent. One second he was lolling, holding her hand and the next he had Doctor Hootman by the linen throat-band and was grappling for the keys. The older man was so much taken by surprise—Julia thought—that he did not even remove his right hand from his pocket. All he did was to put the keys behind him, a curiously childish, futile gesture. When Charles reached for them and began to twist his wrist, maintaining at the same time his grip on the neck-band, Doctor Hootman said in a choking voice, "You're throttling me. All right, have them!" And he flung the keys to the floor. It was all over in a half a minute, an oddly spiritless and unvicious little struggle.

Without letting go of the linen, Charles half stooped and reached for the keys. Then Doctor Hootman's right hand came out of the pocket, its fingers clenched round the barrel of a short pistol. As Julia screamed he brought it down, with deliberately measured force, on the back of Charles' skull, just behind the ear. Charles' body gave a convulsive jerk and went limp. As his hand loosened and his arm lowered Doctor Hootman caught it, breaking his fall and letting him down, quite gently, to the floor.

She ran forward crying, "You've killed him."

"Nonsense," said Doctor Hootman cheerfully. "One does not kill a hostage. A mere rabbit punch which will keep him quiet for half an hour. I've hit many men like that before sawing off a limb. A ship's doctor must be his own surgeon, you know. You'll find brandy in that cupboard, but don't give it to him while he is unconscious; many people have been choked that way."

He unlocked the door and as she knelt by Charles she heard the key turn on the other side and the sound of his footsteps going along the cloister.

Despite the reassuring words and the logic behind them she was frightened when she looked at Charles' face. His eyelids were only three-parts closed and looked stiff and wooden. All the bones in his skull seemed to have become prominent, pressing in white patches against the sun-tanned skin on brow and nose and cheek. But he was breathing, shallowly and a little noisily, and his heart was beating.

The wound was nothing; a thin sluggish trickle of blood ran from it and beaded slowly at the edge of his hair, and even that stopped as, under her eyes, the swelling began. The bump grew visibly and with incredible rapidity. She took comfort, remembering Mevrouw Helmers' theory that the more an accident or illness manifested itself the less dangerous it was. From that her mind moved on to the methods of restoring people to consciousness. Hartshorn was best, but she had none. Burnt feathers were good, but the cushions at Rua were stuffed with raw cotton. Quills? Yes, on the desk, a jar of swan feathers, dyed yellow to suit Mynheer's whim.

Patiently she held them, one by one, to the candle flame and passed the resulting stinking, black, blistering mass to and fro under the white-boned nose. Nothing happened. Doctor Hootman knew his business. Presently she gave up and, sitting down on the floor, took Charles' head in her lap. Conscious or unconscious, she thought drearily, made no difference. They were trapped now. Doctor Hootman might make crazy schemes but he was sane enough to know that they both knew too much. How it would all end she couldn't even guess, but it would be badly, like all the lovers in the stories.

Except for the sound of Charles' breathing the room was very quiet. Now and again a night bird cried raucously in the groves, now and again an insect would throw itself against the window screen; otherwise it was so quiet that she could hear the sea slapping gently at the jetty and whispering on the beach.

And then she could hear something else; Pieter was still moving about. Ordinarily he slept heavily from his early bedtime until dawn, but he had been unlike himself all day; he had slept during the morning. . . .

She had seen Doctor Hootman toss his own keys into the table drawer.

Pieter knew one object from another; if he wanted his scissors it was useless to offer him his knitting.

Pieter was obedient and anxious to please.

It was so frail a chance that she was almost reluctant to recognise it; but it was a chance. She laid Charles' head on the floor, rose to her feet and went to the door of Pieter's room, tapped on it lightly and called his name.

Absolute silence answered her. She had expected him to come blundering to the door and then, perhaps, to become enraged at not being able to reach her. But he had a kind of rudimentary conscience, he was probably standing stock-still, stricken with guilt.

She tried again. "Pieter, it's Julie."

No sound. Was it her imagination which attributed a strained, listening quality to the silence? Or had the sound of movement itself been imagined?

"Pieter, I want to come in. Want to see Pieter. The door is locked."

No reply. No movement. Only that feeling that she was not speaking to emptiness, the feeling of someone there, listening, almost holding his breath.

"Doctor Daan's drawer, Pieter. The key. Look for the key in Doctor Daan's drawer. Get the key, Pieter. Let Julie in."

It was like trying to thread a fine needle with coarse thread while wearing three pairs of gloves on your hands. The effort to impose her will, to make him understand and act, was so great that she seemed to be in the dark, all the light of her consciousness poured out, streaming away towards him. Sweat broke out on her forehead and under her eyes and rolled down her face like tears. His mind was so limited, a key might be outside his range of recognition; the key might not even be there; Pieter himself might not be there. Oh Gǫd! Our only chance. . . . This door once open and I could run through, into Pieter's little garden and over the wall, I could find Nicolas. . . .

Doctor Hootman's drawer always screeched a little when it

was opened and that sound now, harsh in the silence, turned her faint. Her hands tingled and pricked as though touched by nettles. He *was* there. He did understand.

She knew that to her racking impatience every second seemed like an hour and she restrained herself from asking— Have you found it? A question would only distract and confuse him.

"It's the long key, Pieter. Long key."

All was quiet again. She could imagine him standing there, perhaps even with the keys in his hand, blankly wondering what next to do.

It was almost impossible to speak calmly.

"The long key, Pieter. In this door. Push it in."

He could thread a bead on a string, he could unlock a door. But he had to be told things over and over. She went on telling him, agonised because she could not hear him come towards the door. The sound of the key, pushed, with the minimum of fumbling, into the lock sent the tingling prickle all over her. She thought—Of course he came quietly, he is barefoot.

She tried to speak encouragingly to him, but she lacked the breath. She could only implore him, turn it, Pieter, turn it, wordlessly, with the very pounding of her blood.

The lock clicked. She put her hand on the latch and for half a second it resisted her, as though he were trying it from the other side. Then it moved and the door opened.

But it wasn't Pieter who stood there with bits of leaf and twig in his hair, his face and shirt-front smeared with green from the mossy boughs.

It was Nicolas.

CHAPTER XIX

Now she knew full, perfect happiness. People said that the times when you were happy went by unrecognised, that only afterwards, when you looked back, when the joy had gone over, you said nostalgically—I was happy then. That wasn't true; she was happy, and she knew she was happy and revelled in it.

One shining happy day slid into another, there were no nights. There were no anxieties, no responsibilities. Even the effort to speak was not demanded of her.

It was a blue and white April day in Cloonmagh; the clouds raced across the sky and their shadows raced over the shining sands. All the air was full of the fresh clean scent of the sea, softened and sweetened by the fragrance of some unseen gillyflowers. She ran on the beach and the sand squeezed between her bare toes. Maire was there, not the sad, emaciated Maire of the later days, but the earlier, just-remembered Maire, full of hope and strange old tales. Maire spoke of another bright shining day in the future, when the proper people would be back in Arghama and they would go there together and Maire would say, "You see she knows her manners." They were lucky and gathered a good basketful of cockles and took them home and cooked them and ate them with crusty, fresh-baked bread. Delicious. She ate greedily and Maire rebuked her, "Eat dainty, darling, as a lady should."

Then it was summer. She wore a pretty cool dress and her loosened hair brushed against her neck. She walked along the sun-filled streets with Uncle Johannes, on the way to the docks to visit the "Sea Maid." He was talking about his next voyage, which was to be to Africa, and he promised that if, before he sailed, he could get Aunt Geertruida to give consent, he would bring her back a little monkey for a pet. They paused by a tavern on the corner and he said, "Are you thirsty, sweetheart? I am." Inside it was cool and smelt pleasantly musty. She drank something deliciously flavoured with lemons.

It was no season, one of the warmth-laden, spice-filled island days. She sat on her favourite seat, overlooking the bank of flowers, all pink and purple against the sapphire sea. Charles sat on the ground beside her, his face peaceful. He lifted her arm and put it around his neck. He said, "I love you very dearly." There was still no need for her to speak. She tightened her arm around his neck and bent down and laid her face against his hair. They understood everything.

She was in her own room, playing the clavichord better than she had ever heard anyone play. Wonderful music. Because of it she did not hear the door open, and Psyche and Katje were there beside her before she was aware of them. But she was not startled; they looked so well, and so happy. She held out her hands to them, and Katje said, "We came to tell you that we're in the place where everything is being made up to us." She wanted to say, So am I; isn't it wonderful? But there was no need. They knew.

Even her beloved little green bird was there in its cage. It stood on the window-sill of her bedroom between two pots of scarlet geraniums. Pieter came and looked at it and said, "Pretty. Pretty for Julie." His coming struck the first jarring note. Unlike the others he did not look well, or happy. And he was idle. There were all his things laid out on the table behind him and he was doing nothing. She knew that she must make an effort to rouse him. To him she must speak. It was more of an effort than anything she had ever done, worse than lifting the heaviest washtub in the Klopstock Home.

"Pieter, cut some paper. Cut some paper for Julia." She held out the blunt-nosed scissors, snapping their blades invitingly.

From somewhere immeasurably far away someone said,

"Pieter is quite all right. There's no need to worry about him."

And she knew that that was true. Nicolas would look after everything.

She was free to go back to the happy places, the loved happy people.

The wind began to rise in Cloonmagh. It came from the east, a leaping shouting wind. It whipped the sea in the little bay so that the grey-green, smooth, carved-marble waves were edged with lace and mountain high. One, higher than the rest, reared up, held itself suspended, translucent. It would drown her. She must run, run, run! Too late. She was caught, lifted, tossed about, limp and light as a strand of seaweed. Drowning; drowned. No, washed up and left by the receding wave, in her own bed.

It was evening and the candles were lighted. Two faces were looking down at her. One was a woman's, pale and fat and plain between the edge of a little linen cap and the collar of a print dress. I don't know you! The other was a man's, thin, sharp-featured, with a bright, bird-like eye. I don't know you either.

The man said, "There. I told you there was no reason for alarm. Merely a matter of time and good nursing."

That's because I opened my eyes. What a mistake! But I shan't speak. If I don't speak I can go back, and back, and back. I shan't speak. I shall close my eyes, give myself to the wave's sweep and swing and be carried far away.

The voices pursued her for a little while; one said something about a natural, healing sleep and being much better tomorrow; the other, female, rather lugubrious, said something about a daughter. A sleep, a daughter . . . but they are not my people, this is not my place, I shall go away again.

The happiness however was not to be recaptured.

She heard Nicolas' voice and the woman's. Now she must

wake properly; she must speak to Nicolas. There was so much she didn't know, and must know.

She opened her eyes; there was Nicolas, looking anxious, and the woman. She was familiar after all; Mevrouw Van de Lijn, the Governor's wife, would look like that, with her face bare of paint and powder, and out of her party dress. What was she doing here?

Nicolas was now on his knees by the bed. "Julia. Do you know me?" He spoke as though a sound might break something.

"Nicolas . . ." There he had stood, in the doorway, and she had known that he had climbed the wall of the little private garden and must have come through Pieter's room, and knew everything. That was where reality had broken off; she had thought—He knows, it will be all right now, and then she had gone down into the dark.

"Everything's all right, Julia," he said in that same muted, careful voice.

"Charles?"

"Perfectly well and all right. I promise you. Nothing in all the world to worry about. You just lie still and get better."

"Pieter?"

"He's all right. I'm taking care of him. I'm taking care of everything"

"You know about it all?"

"Everything."

Mevrouw Van de Lijn came to the other side of the bed, lifted her a little and held a glass to her lips. Milk, creamy and very cold. Lovely.

She wanted to know more about Charles; but her mind was active now; mustn't talk about Charles in front of the Governor's wife.

"Everything is all right? Everybody safe?"

"Safe as houses. You go back to sleep again, Julia."

She heard Mevrouw's voice. "I wonder who Charles is?"

"A cousin she was fond of, back in Amsterdam," said Nico-

las. Good Nicolas, taking care of everything: knowing just
what to say.

Next time she woke everything was quite different. It was
morning, she knew by the way the sun came in from the window on the cloister side. She was alone in the room and as soon
as she woke misery assailed her like a savage animal that had
lain in ambush for a long time, awaiting this moment. Her
mind was perfectly clear, she remembered everything; she remembered Nicolas saying that everything was all right—but
how could she believe that? All the dread possibilities of the
situation she had abandoned when she fell down by the door,
now came thronging back; how could Nicolas have dealt with
everything, with two senseless people flat on the floor and Doctor Hootman coming back, pistol in hand? How could she have
allowed herself to be so easily lulled by a few soothing words?

In addition to everything else there was something badly
wrong with her head. It felt cold, and when she turned it on
the pillow it felt light and strange. Hesitantly she raised her
hand and touched her head. She had no hair, no hair at all.
The whole of her head was covered with sharp bristles. No
man ever had hair so short. Who on earth had cut her hair,
and why? Did they cut madwomen's hair, or criminals'? Had
she been mad? Did they think she was somehow incriminated
with Doctor Hootman's wicked plan? Was it perhaps one of
the duties of a Governor's wife to act as guard to the mad, or
the wicked? And what had really happened to Charles? What
were they hiding?

She began to cry and instantly the door of her bathroom
opened and out rushed Mevrouw Van de Lijn, clad in her petticoat, her face and arms beaded with drops of water and a
towel in her hand.

"My dear, my dear," she cried, hurrying to the bed. "What
is the matter? You mustn't upset yourself—the very worst
thing. You're better, everything is all right. It's over now, all
over. There, there, just be calm."

"I don't *know* anything. I don't even know what day it is. I don't know what happened. Why are you here? And my hair. Who cut my hair?"

"I did. You have been ill you know. The doctor advised it."

"Doctor Hootman?"

"Oh no, no. Doctor van Nagel, from Banda. You see we had to put wet cloths on your head to cool your brain, and the hair was in the way. You mustn't fret about that. It'll grow again. I can say that for certain. My own little girl had to have hers cut, and do you know, it grew again in the loveliest curls you ever saw, though it had been straight as a poker."

"Why are you here, Mevrouw?"

"I've been looking after you, my dear. I came for the funeral and I heard you were ill, so I stayed and took care of you."

"That was very kind." But is it true?

"Oh, I was glad to do it. I welcome anything that takes my mind off my worries and helps to pass the time till I hear. My daughter—I don't expect you remember . . ."

"I do. Yes, indeed. She was to have a baby and you must wait seven months."

"You *are* better. Fancy your remembering that." Mevrouw began to dry herself vigorously.

"You came for the funeral, Mevrouw. Was it yesterday?"

"No, my dear. On Monday. Today is Friday. You have been ill, you know. Four whole days. We were very worried; but Doctor van Nagel assured us there was no need. He said you must have been living under a great strain ever since you came to Banda, and that this was Nature's way of giving you a rest. You do feel better?"

"I feel quite well. Mevrouw, what happened at the funeral?"

Mevrouw Van de Lijn had turned to the chair where her print dress, freshly laundered and smooth from the iron, lay. She began to put it on, and spoke in a rather absent-minded way.

"What happened, dear? Well, Mynheer Vosmar was buried, and then young Mynheer Vanderplasse brought my husband

and the Agent into the house and disclosed to them what Mynheer Vosmar had hidden all those years. It was a great shock to everybody, of course, a great shock."

Nothing about an Englishman, a clove-smuggler, being brought to justice.

Mevrouw, busy with the buttons of her bodice, turned around.

"Some people are inclined to be critical of Mynheer Vosmar's behaviour, but do you know, I understand. If such a thing had happened to my little girl I might have acted the same way, if I had been able to." She looked at Julia and it was evident that her maternal feelings suffered some cleavage, mother-hen against mother-hen. "All the same, it was very wrong and heartless of him to bring you here and involve you. You must have had a horrible time. Thank God, I *know* the man my daughter married. If I didn't I should have gone mad by now, to think that such things were possible."

"I want to see Nicolas," Julia said.

"He always looks in at about this time, when he comes back from the plantation for breakfast. How fortunate it was that he was here, all ready to take charge of everything. I wonder if poor Mynheer Vosmar knew that his days were numbered and took that precaution." She had finished her dressing, and came to the bed; expertly she lifted Julia and pulled the pillows around to support her. "I'm a handy nurse," she said. "I've had lots of practice. My daughter was never very robust; that is one reason why I am so concerned about her at this time." Punching the last pillow into position, she said, "I think I hear Mynheer Vanderplasse now."

She rustled away. Julia heard from the sitting-room a few sibilant words—much better, almost herself, talk too much, nothing to upset. What did that mean?

Nicolas came tip-toeing into the room.

In some way for which there was no accounting in physical terms he had aged. The thick shining fair hair, the fresh complexion, the clear, slightly prominent grey eyes, were all just as they had been; but the stamp of authority and responsibility—yes, and of a calf-love outgrown—were on him now, aging him by ten years. One day, and not so far ahead, he would be the very image of Mynheer.

He said, "Hullo, Julia. You really are feeling better? I'm so glad. You look almost like yourself."

"I look hideous," she said, "but never mind that. I have so many things to ask you." She dropped her voice. "Is Mevrouw Van de Lijn out there?"

"No, she tactfully decided to drink her tea on the verandah."

"Nicolas, what happened? First of all, what happened to Charles?"

"He went back to Ay. I had to hustle him off. I couldn't keep him here, with half Banda coming to the funeral, could I? But he was fit to go and I know got back safely."

"How do you know that?"

"We arranged a signal. I realised that that would be the first thing you would ask. And he, naturally, wanted to know about you. So we arranged to use the old signals, but with different meanings. There's a tall tree on Ay and another on the tip of Rua; through glasses they're visible, and with flags of different colours—that's how it's done."

"And he got back safely, and nobody knows about him?"

"That is so."

She rested back more easily against the pillows.

"Now tell me all the rest. How did it happen? Where is Doctor Hootman?"

"You don't need to worry about him, Julia."

"I'm not worrying. I just want to know. There's a great gap in my mind. I must fill it in. That door opened and there you stood, and I saw you and I thought, he knows, now I can give up! That's the last thing I can remember. Now, Nicolas, please, go on from there."

The look, half-smile, half-grimace, with which people acknowledge a comic element in a situation not fundamentally amusing, came into Nicolas' face.

"Well, there I was, with the two of you flat on the floor. I knew nothing—and I'd just seen Pieter, I wasn't feeling too steady myself. You remember, the moment we met, you said you had something to tell me, and I gathered, from the way you stopped talking that you didn't want Hootman to hear. Then you went off and I got to thinking . . . all that mystery you know, and things the Barnevelts had said. I thought I'd see for myself. So I climbed the wall. . . . Julia, I am profoundly sorry for the way I used to talk to you about Pieter. It must have added to what you had to bear. And I'm sorry for the rest of my behaviour too. Of course, as soon as I understood . . ."

"Go on, finish the story."

"I stood there, not knowing why you had been locked in, or who the man was, or anything. I knew where Uncle Simon kept his brandy, so I got it, and went from one to the other of you in a dotty sort of way, like a hen with two chicks, a hen with its head off at that. It made no difference to you, but it brought him round. He's . . . he's a good fellow, Julia. He got himself up and pulled himself together and said to me, 'You're the cousin or something, aren't you?' and in no time at all he'd explained everything, what Hootman was up to, and why, and why you were scared, everything." He broke off and looked at the pale, sunken face on the pillow, with its violet-lidded eyes and the naked look the lack of hair gave it. "Mevrouw Van de Lijn said I shouldn't talk too much, Julia. Everything is all right, be sure of that. I'll tell you all the rest another time."

"Go on, go on," Julia said. "I want to hear it all now. It's like starting a story and having the book snatched away. I can't bear it. If you don't want to upset me you'll tell me everything, just as it happened."

"Charles said that Hootman was slightly crazy and had a pistol and would be dangerous. So we made a plan to disarm him. When we heard him coming, Charles, whom he expected to see, sat in a chair and held his head and I got behind the door. He came in, very cock-a-hoop, and said that Mercury was delighted to oblige and was having the time of his life going through Uncle Simon's wardrobe. As he turned to lock the door I pounced out and took his pistol away. And that was the end of that."

"But not the end of the story. Go on."

Nicolas' lips curled with distaste.

"He went to pieces. He dropped into a chair, put his head in his hands and he . . . cried. Being so big, that somehow made it worse; he went to jelly. I tried to be sorry for him, but I couldn't. Charles was. I will say for the English they do love their enemies once they're disarmed! He got him some brandy and said, 'Bear up man. It's the end of that little gallop but it couldn't have lasted anyway.' I tried to be generous too and said he could stay on and look after Pieter; whereupon he cried the harder."

Little boys in the streets of Amsterdam had a game which they played whenever they could cajole a butcher to give them a pig's bladder. They blew it up and kicked it about until the toe-iron on somebody's clog, worn thin and sharp, pierced it. Then the air would seep out with a long-drawn hiss and that was the end of the game. She could visualise Doctor Hootman, similarly punctured, similarly collapsed.

"So then?"

"Then Charles lost his patience and got up and gave him a shake, and said, 'You're a doctor, do something for her!' Her being you. He said you'd come round in time. So Charles and I carried you here and Juno put you to bed. Then we had a sound good supper; we talked about the signals and he went off."

"Do you know a signal asking him to come here?"

"Of course. I'll run it up whenever you like, Julia."

"That's very kind."

"*Just,*" he corrected her. "I remember that it would have been much to his advantage to play Hootman's game. And to yours."

She raised herself a little higher on the pillows.

"Now tell me about Pieter."

"There's nothing to tell. He's there. That's all."

"Is he *doing* anything?"

"What is there for the poor thing to do?"

"Who is with him?"

"That great dumb Negro."

"Where is Doctor Hootman?"

"You don't have to worry about him, Julia."

"Is he dead?"

"Yes."

"Did he kill himself? I can see by your face. That doesn't upset me. He's better dead. He'd lived all those years on hope. When that was gone, what had he to live for?"

"I offered to keep him on here," Nicolas said, not understanding. "And Charles offered to take him to Ay. He said they were all rogues and vagabonds there, and that a doctor would be very welcome. Hootman said he'd do that, and went to get his things. He had a pair to the pistol we'd taken from him, and he shot himself. There, now you know everything."

And it had done her no harm; she looked better, restored and lively.

"Thank you very much, Nicolas. Now you go and have your breakfast. I want mine. Could you come back in about an hour?"

"Of course. As soon as you feel well enough we must have a serious talk. But for the present I just want you to understand Julia, that although I'm looking after things for you, I don't wish, in any way, to usurp your authority." His voice had taken on a faintly pompous tone.

She said, "I'm very grateful to you for looking after things." And now it seemed quite safe and quite ordinary to say, "Dear Nicolas."

When he returned she was in the sitting-room, wearing a wrap and propped up in one of the long chairs with a leg rest brought in from the verandah. On one side of her stood the

clavichord, open, and on the other a solid table, cleared of all
its small ornaments. The rugs had been rolled up and everything fragile put away. It reminded him of a room prepared
for the spring-cleaning upon which his mother, a good house-
wife, insisted even in this land where no spring came.

Julia cut short his protests at finding her out of bed, his questions about the altered room.

"I want you to fetch Pieter here to me. I'm too wobbly to
walk, and I don't much fancy that room any more, but he can
come here and I can amuse him. The change of scene in itself
will do him good and there's no reason now to keep him locked
away. Bring all his stuff, Echo knows where to find everything."

"Honestly Julia, I think you're making an unnecessary exertion. He doesn't know one room from another. And if he has
stuff to do why doesn't he do it. I've never seen him do anything except sit."

"That's just it. Unless he's roused he'll sit there till he dies.
His toys are his link with life—but there has to be somebody
taking an interest. I understand all about it. Doctor Hootman
has kept him alive for eight years."

"And now you're going to keep him alive?"

"To the last moment. Charles said it. When we come together we don't want to be haunted by thoughts of Pieter."

After what seemed a long time she heard their footsteps,
Pieter's clumsy and shuffling, Nicolas' sharp and precise. Then
they were in the doorway, Nicolas holding Pieter by the arm.

Nicolas, who had not known him until this week, probably
thought he had always looked like this, but Julia was appalled
by the change in him. He looked twenty years older, there
were even some white hairs amongst the dull dusty brown ones;
he had shrunk, and all his clothes were too big for him. Like a
parasitic plant which has no roots of its own, severed from its
host, he had begun to dwindle and droop and die.

His dull, uncomprehending, earthen stare wandered about
the strange room. Nicolas' face took on a what-did-I-tell-you?

It-is-hopeless-look, and he withdrew his arm, glad to be free of the contact. Behind them Echo loomed up in his Ethiopian darkness, his arms piled with the bead boxes, the clay, the cane, the string.

Julia said, "Pieter. Good morning, Pieter. Come to Julie."

His dull stare swung round, focussed and brightened.

"Julie," he cried, "Julie!" It was the voice of the lost one who has been found.

He lumbered over towards her and then, just short of her out-stretched hand stopped short, lowering his head and looking at her suspiciously out of the corners of his eyes. Something wrong. Something different. On top of all the things that had been wrong and different lately.

"It's Julie," she said, in a steady, reassuring voice.

"Julie! Yes! Yes! Julie."

He gave his pathetic, wide-open smile and came forward. When he was near enough he lifted one of his limp red hands, slowly, awkwardly as though it weighed very heavy. Tentatively, experimentally he laid it on her head. Then he said, with delight,

"Pretty! Pretty for Julie!"

CHAPTER XX

Once again she was standing at the top of the little cliff and looking out over the sea, waiting for Charles. The green grove which the doves avoided lay silent behind her; the ferns and the azaleas and honeysuckle poured a cascade of colour and fragrance from the place where she stood to the level where the water lapped at high tide. Today the wave-rounded rocks and the narrow band of beach at their

base lay exposed. Today Charles would have no difficulty in
landing.

Inevitably she remembered that Sunday afternoon when she
had waited here, racked by anxiety and impatience, with every
heart-beat marking danger's approach, every moment making
disaster more sure. Now she was safe, and Charles was coming
and the whole golden future lay ahead. After all the tumult,
life had smoothed out into a calm, in which she could once
more feel a natural, if somewhat absurd, concern for her appearance. As she waited, her hand went to her head again; ap-
praising the improvement which twenty-two days had brought
about.

For it was only twenty-two days since she had first touched
her head and cried, "My hair!" Very often in that short space
of time she had reflected upon the irony of Doctor Hootman's
fate; by so narrow a margin had he missed attaining his heart's
desire. She had said to Nicolas,

"He'd waited and worked for eight years. If he'd been content to wait a little longer and not talked to me of slow murder,
I should have fallen in with his schemes, and he would have
everything he wanted."

That was true; it had taken so short a time for Pieter to
relinquish his hold on life. From that morning when she had
roused herself to rouse him it had been painfully clear that,
cherished or neglected, entertained or not, he was dying.
Watching the end approach she had clung fiercely to the remark which Charles had made so casually regarding the place
where everything was made up to people who had suffered in
this world; those words, and their echo from her dream of
Katje and Psyche, were her support during the days when
Pieter, ignoring all her efforts to interest him, sat for hour after
hour with his head resting against her shoulder, and cried so
bitterly when parted from her for however short a space that
in the end she had been compelled to sit by him, even after
he had been put to bed, and to hold his hand until he fell asleep.

Now and again, during the day, his desire to please her

would wake for a moment, and he would take up some piece of handwork that she offered, stare at it with lacklustre eyes, turn it over and lay it down again; he showed a similar lack of interest in his food and ate only in response to her coaxing. He grew older and more shrunken every day, and in the end he died, as do the very old, in his sleep. On the morning when he failed to waken Julia stood by the bed and looked at his face through her tears. It wore the peaceful dignity of death and had changed in a strange way, had been wiped clear of the stain of his mental infirmity. It was as though, Julia thought, the idiot face had been a mask which the Dark Angel's hand had lifted and lain aside. Once again she remembered Charles' words. If they held any truth Pieter must now be very happy, for there was so much to be made up to him. And in any case he was now beyond trouble; beyond help, too. She could turn to the living of her own life.

During all these days which lay like a breathing space between two phases Nicolas had been immensely and—once he had overcome his first aversion to Pieter—imaginatively helpful. He had spent many hours in Banda, consulting with the Governor, the Agent and Mynheer's attorney. On these interviews he would report to Julia in the evenings after Pieter had fallen asleep. With regard to the management of the plantation Doctor Hootman had been an accurate prophet. The Governor had said tactfully that it would of course be *preferable* for some male member of the Vosmar family to take it over and administer it on Pieter's behalf; the Agent said bluntly that it was *necessary*. Nicolas, seizing the opportunity of escaping forever from his father's dominance, told Julia that he was willing to remain in Rua, paying a rent and also an annual instalment towards its purchase.

"But it's yours, Nicolas. If, as you say, it will belong to me, I give it to you gladly, as a token of the gratitude I feel."

In these conversations they never, though death was so inevitable-seeming, used the word. Always they said, "When it happens . . ."

"When it happens," Nicolas said, "Charles will have to be consulted."

"Charles," said Julia, with perfect assurance, "will feel as I do. We don't want Rua. All we want is enough money to go back to England, rebuild the house and get started again."

"Well, there's enough to do that twenty times over. But we must hear what Charles has to say."

He spoke of Charles often; indeed it was he who was generally responsible for introducing his name into their conversations. He seemed to have a nervous compulsion to mention him, to keep him in mind. On that Sunday evening the shock of discovering the truth about Pieter, his remorse concerning the things he had said about him, the discovery of the connection between Charles and Julia and then his anxiety at her prolonged unconsciousness had all combined to shatter his infatuation. With comparative ease he could take up his new role, brotherly, managing, comforting. But as the days went on, every now and then he would find himself on the verge of relapse, and then, he had proved, the best, the only, thing to do was to mention Charles by name and learn once more, by the way Julia's eyes lighted and her whole face softened and glowed, the truth of what Charles had said in his hasty summing up of the situation, "She couldn't appeal to you while I was here, she was afraid for me. You see, we're in love with one another." With a wisdom and self-knowledge more often associated with age than youth, Nicolas realised that if he could firmly face and accept the truth he would spare his own feelings. He trained himself to think kindly of Charles and to regard Julia as already betrothed.

One day, shortly before Pieter's death, Nicolas returned from Banda wearing an air of achievement and self-approval. As he and Julia sat down to dinner he said,

"Now Julia, I think I really have done something for you. Something *tangible*."

"Saving us all from Doctor Hootman was tangible," she said.

"That was an accident. This is something I did deliberately, something I fixed. And I think that when it happens you will be grateful."

"I'm grateful now. I always shall be. What is the new thing?"

He could not resist the temptation to heighten the drama of his achievement by a few preliminaries.

"First you tell me what you plan to do—when it happens."

Without thinking she put her hand to her head where the bristles were growing out and softening as they lengthened and just beginning to curl again at the ends.

"Well," she said, slowly, savouring the words, "the very first thing I shall do will be to ask you to run up that signal and ask Charles to come here. Then we can talk and make plans."

"What would you plan?"

"To go to England of course. You knew that, Nicolas."

"Did you ever ask yourself *how?*"

Her anticipatory thoughts had never carried her so far; always they had stopped short at Charles' coming, at the joy of meeting him openly and at leisure.

"No," she said. "I never did. I shall leave all that to him."

"Well, it wouldn't be easy. When he and his kind came out to the Islands the Dutch were not unfriendly to the King's party, at least. They came from Holland, in Dutch ships. It's different now, you know. English ships are not allowed in the Dutch ports, and English people wouldn't be welcome in Dutch ships."

Her face whitened and her eyes darkened, but she said calmly,

"Then I shall go to Ay, and live there until things change again."

"Ah," he said, happily, "as it happens that won't be necessary. That is what I have arranged today. I was talking to the Governor and I mentioned Charles. I didn't tell him everything, there was no need, but I did explain that Charles had helped to prevent a great wrong, maybe a serious crime. And I asked whether, in return, he could be given a safe-conduct. So, my dear, when it happens, you and Charles can embark

openly at Banda and be set down at Lisbon. From there you
can easily get an English ship."

"That's wonderful," she said. "Wonderful. Oh I do thank
you, Nicolas. Only you would have thought of it, only you
could have done it."

"I wanted to do something real for you, Julia. So that if you
remember me at all you'll remember me kindly."

That was true; but in the action there had also been a touch
of the Vosmar taste for pulling strings, for twisting established
authority to serve a private purpose. That taste was, in Nicolas,
as yet vestigial and largely unconscious, but his persuasion of
the Governor, his bold admission that an Englishman had
been on Rua, held within it a shadowy forecast of the time far
ahead when Mynheer Nicolas Vosmar of Rua, so stubborn, so
intransigent, was to be a thorn in the side of successive Governors and Agents, and the spearhead of the planters' revolt
against the growing autocracy of the Company. At the moment
the pleasing sense of power, the awareness of having acted
magnanimously in having attained a favour for the man whom
he still, at odd moments, regarded as his rival, helped on the
process of overcoming jealousy.

Julia laid away the good news at the back of her mind, to
await, like so many other things, the moment when it could
be shared with Charles. She went on devoting herself to
Pieter, refusing to look forward very much, patiently sharing
the timelessness of his last days.

And now it was all over; and here she was, waiting for
Charles again. When he came it would not be as a furtive ven-
turer upon enemy soil; there would be no hiding, no hurrying
away, this time. Now she could look forward; and as the little
dark blur which was his boat broke the shimmering blue sur-
face of the sea and grew momentarily larger, more distinct,
more real, she allowed her thoughts to run ahead to the time
when Rua and all that had happened there would be only a
part of a long memory. They would go on, together, bound by

the love which they had found lying at the heart of danger and evil as a precious stone lies in its matrix. She could imagine their lives, so full and busy, their minds so richly occupied, that the day would come when it would take some homely dish, flavoured and scented with cloves, to wake memories and set them looking at one another, wondering at the sharpness of the reminder.